PRAISE FO

"This dystopian tale skillfully balances delusion, disillusionment, and disdain. Readers are in for a dark, difficult trip down the rabbit hole."

—*Publishers Weekly*

"A work of unbelievable creativity and imagination. Han Song has taken Kafka's institutionalized horror and endlessly reproduced it with trillions of 3D printers, enough to fill the entire universe. Taking the image of an AI machine gone haywire or a cancerous growth spreading out of control, expansive yet utterly devoid of hope, it clogs every possible escape portal and blocks any possibility of running away, leaving behind nothing but a devastating and overpowering feeling of grief."

—Lo Yi-Chin, author of *Faraway*

"Han Song stands out among Chinese science fiction writers. His exuberant imagination engages history in total earnest, speaking to the darkness and perversity of the human condition. *Hospital* is his masterpiece and should be a landmark in the terrain of contemporary science fiction."

—Ha Jin, author of *Waiting*, *A Song Everlasting*, and *A Free Life*

"China's premier science fiction writer."

—*Los Angeles Times*

"The kind of science fiction I write is two dimensional, but Han Song writes three-dimensional science fiction. If we look at Chinese science fiction as a pyramid, two-dimensional science fiction would be the foundation, but the kind of three-dimensional science fiction that Han Song writes would be the pinnacle."

—Liu Cixin, author of *The Three-Body Problem*

"Han Song's fiction has a uniquely 'dark consciousness' that offers deep reflections about history and keen observations about our contemporary world, all of which comes from an otherworldly perspective. *Hospital* is part of a stupendous trilogy, which is filled with a seemingly inexhaustible series of ghoulish episodes, grotesque figures, and sublime scenes of the wildest kind."

—David Der-wei Wang, professor (Harvard University) and author of *Why Fiction Matters in Contemporary China*

"Han Song's Hospital Trilogy is the second most important Chinese science fiction trilogy after Liu Cixin's *Three-Body Problem.* Han Song is the Philip K. Dick of China. *Hospital* reveals strange visions from a fantastical universe, yet the true secret remains hidden under the skin of contemporary China. His twisted surreal vision seems removed from the everyday world of reason, and yet it is able to reveal a truth impervious to traditional realist narratives."

—Mingwei Song, professor (Wellesley College) and coeditor of *The Reincarnated Giant*

"Han Song is an important part of the legacy of critical humanism, from Lu Xun to the Chinese avant-garde writers of the 1980s."

—Yan Feng, literary critic

"The darkness contained within *Hospital* expresses the author's desperation with mankind's attempts at self-treatment and salvation. The novel's completely unbridled narrative path sets out in the direction of science fiction but ultimately arrives at the spiritual abyss lurking in the reality of today's China . . . and the rest of the world."

—Yan Lianke, author of *The Day the Sun Died* and *Hard Like Water*

"Demented, delirious, and one of a kind . . . Kafkaesque doesn't begin to describe this cunning labyrinth of a novel. Nothing I have read has captured so incisively (and searingly) the unrelenting institutional brutality of our contemporary world."

—Junot Díaz, author of *The Brief Wondrous Life of Oscar Wao*

"In this era in which the epidemic rages, Han Song's *Hospital* has presented us with a delirious Kafkaesque vision of the future where the relationship between disease, patients, and (technological) caregivers has become enshrouded in a new level of complexity and dark enchantment. Thanks to Michael Berry's brilliant translation, this unforgettable literary experience can now reach a new group of readers."

—Chen Qiufan, author of *The Waste Tide*; coauthor of *AI 2041*

EXORCISM

ALSO BY HAN SONG

(in Chinese)

The Red Sea

Red Star over America

Subway

Tracks

High-Speed Rail

The Cold War and the Messenger

Misery: Stories

The Passenger and the Creator: Stories

The Rebirth Brick: Short Stories

Pseudobeauty and the Clapping Fly: Poems

Why Do I Keep Living Over and Over: Essays

(in English)

Exploring Dark Short Fiction #5: A Primer to Han Song

The Hospital Trilogy

Hospital

Exorcism

Dead Souls (coming soon)

EXORCISM

HAN SONG

TRANSLATED BY MICHAEL BERRY

Previously published as 驱魔 (*Qumo*) by Shanghai wenyi chubanshe in China in 2017. Translated from Chinese by Michael Berry. First published in English by Amazon Crossing in 2023.

Published by Amazon Crossing, Seattle

www.apub.com

ISBN-13: 9781542039505 (paperback)
ISBN-13: 9781542039499 (digital)

Cover design by Will Staehle
Cover image: © kimberrywood / Shutterstock; © kkssr / Shutterstock; © 3000ad / Shutterstock; © Designer Base / Shutterstock

Printed in the United States of America

Pain is a characteristic of the human condition;
it proves that you are still alive.
Eastern parable

Table of Contents

SEA AND CAGE

1
EVERYTHING IN THE PAST IS A MISTAKE, BUT TODAY ALL IS CORRECT

A shiny silver mechanical hand reached out to remove the patient's clothing. A metallic centipede-like creature tip-tapped over his body, from his face to his shoulders and along his arms, then from his stomach down to his reproductive organs. Following the instructions he had been given, the patient looked into a mirror and blew into a breath sensor.

A mechanical voice from the mirror said, "Mutated DNA proteins in the human subject's cancer-suppression genes detected . . ."

The patient swallowed a smart pill, no larger than a single dose of aspirin, which contained a microchip, a video camera, and a wireless transponder.

The mechanical voice spoke again. "Esophageal and intestinal examination now commencing . . ."

In the face of this invisible, automated machine, the patient mumbled, "So you think I have something else wrong with me? Perhaps it's hiding in my large intestines, kidneys, liver, or capillaries? Well, go ahead and do your examination! I'm used to it anyway!"

The mechanical voice from behind the mirror spoke again, in that same flat tone. "No abnormalities detected."

The patient signed his name on a liquid crystal pad: *Yang Wei*.

The patient was sent back to his sick ward, where the other patients huddled around him and broke out in applause. "Welcome back! Welcome back!"

But this wasn't the same sick ward that Yang Wei remembered. All the patients were elderly men, outfitted with white plaster-like helmets and military-style uniforms. Tubes, wires, and antennae protruded from their bodies—each one looked like a cross between a space explorer and a spinosaurus.

Yang Wei's stomach began to twitch and spasm. He frantically turned and headed toward the door but was blocked by one of the medical robots.

Yang Wei protested, "This isn't my room! I've never even seen any of these patients before in my life! Although you are a machine, you must realize that the most terrifying thing for a patient is to be forced to stay with other patients. We don't know each other, but because we are all sick, we are tossed in together and forced to grit our teeth and establish a new form of symbiotic relationship. They may seem perfectly calm on the surface, but all kinds of evil diseases silently lurk inside them, ready to leap out and tear us apart at any moment . . . just look at how they greeted me warmly—who knows what they are really thinking? I don't know any of these people! Isn't that enough to put the hospital on alert?"

The medical robot was a steel cylindrical unit that moved on a rotating belt. It extended its tubular, squid-like netted arms, picked up Yang Wei like he was a baby, and returned him to the sick ward.

The patients laughed proudly. "Ha! Keep dreaming! Whether you are sick or not, everyone must return to the sick ward! Otherwise, how could you prove that you are sick?"

Someone tapped Yang Wei on the back of his head. He let out a howl and scurried off toward the window. He was about to climb out through it when he was bowled over by a strange, overpowering stench and noticed something outside the window: a giant birdcage. The sight seemed to jog his memory.

The patient who had tapped him strutted over, closed the window, and slapped Yang Wei across the face. "Are you trying to get yourself killed? Are you trying to get *everyone* killed? How dare you open the window? There haven't been any creatures in the birdcage since forever. They were all wiped out long ago, carriers of the avian flu!"

Yang Wei reached up to touch his throbbing cheek. "Who are you?" he asked timidly.

The patients cried out in unison, "You don't know who Super Patient is? He doesn't even know who Super Patient is!"

Super Patient was a short, fat old man with a pig's nose, feline lips, sharp teeth, a dark complexion, stinky white bubbles frothing from the sides of his mouth, and a series of cross-shaped microchips embedded around his neck. He pulled out a violin and began to play. A tall, strapping old man standing in the corner whipped out a fire hose and sprayed it full force, straight at Yang Wei, first blasting him in the groin before moving up to his abdomen, chest, and face. Everyone in the room broke out in laughter.

Yang Wei cried out as he tried to evade the spray. "How could you treat your fellow patients like this? Why are you doing this?"

"According to Super Patient's directives, you must be disinfected!" screamed the old patient with the hose, who was called Wart. "The viruses you carry are demonic monsters trying to kill us all! Don't you know the rules here in the sick ward?"

Yang Wei was so flustered that he didn't know where to go, so he scurried onto one of the beds, using the pillow to protect his head. Super Patient led the others over to the bed, and they gathered round to watch. Wart whipped out his penis, threw the pillow aside, and started bopping it against Yang Wei's face. Yang Wei opened his eyes, and the patients broke out in another round of hysterical laughter. But just as quickly, they dispersed.

2

A FACE COVERED IN DIRT, TEMPLES IN FROSTY GRAY

Yang Wei's entire body was in pain. He lay there like a drowned rat. He cried. This was not the sick ward he remembered. Where had all the doctors gone? How come none of them had come to intervene?

Eventually the room began to quiet down. Yang Wei sneaked a peek and discovered that the patients had returned to their beds to rest for the night. This sick ward was much nicer than the one he remembered. Every patient had a bed of his own, though the sickbeds were more like metal fish tanks filled with wires and tubes. The entire ward rocked back and forth like it was shaken by a never-ending earthquake.

Yang Wei caught a glimpse of his reflection in the window and was shocked by what he saw. His face was old and wrinkled; his hair had turned white around the temples. He had been admitted to the hospital only recently, still in his forties; how could he have turned into an old man overnight? The other patients in the ward were just as old.

One in the next bed spoke to Yang Wei in a voice that sounded like he was coughing up phlegm. "Hey, we all know about your condition."

Yang Wei curled up like a scared gecko. "What exactly do you know?" There was no way to protect himself here.

The patient in the next bed panted, "Hey, do you have something for me?" He reached over to search Yang Wei's person. "Absolutely nothing!" he said disappointedly.

Yang Wei felt embarrassed that he didn't have anything to offer. "Sorry, I must have handed over all of my belongings when I was admitted." He was abruptly struck by a fit of panic, as if suddenly remembering something.

"Do you at least have some smokes?" the patient asked.

"Sorry, I don't," said Yang Wei.

The other patient was also elderly, skinny with a crooked nose and a dark, frail frame. He was missing the lower half of his body, exposing a chunk of rotting flesh from beneath his hospital gown. The stench was unbearable.

The patient rolled his eyes at Yang Wei and adopted a serious tone. "They say you are a superspreader. Just like those birds that carry that damn avian flu, you're nothing but trouble. And you don't even have any money or smokes!"

"The robot said that I'm perfectly normal," Yang Wei retorted.

"No one in the hospital is normal. They might say that you are normal, but this is a place where the abnormal is normal. Anyway, I wouldn't worry about it. As long as you are here in the hospital, they'll be able to treat you."

The patient introduced himself as Fistula. He didn't seem to look down on Yang Wei, which gave Yang Wei his first bit of consolation since returning to the sick ward. He took another look at Fistula.

"Instead of looking at me, you should be looking at this!" Fistula said. He waved a book in the air, a copy of *Principles of Hospital Engineering*. "The hospital is a university," he explained.

"I thought this was a place where they treat illnesses?" asked Yang Wei.

"I once attended college," Fistula continued. "But universities are nothing but a big joke when compared with the hospital!" He explained that before he was admitted to the hospital, he had been the section head at a government office. He had worked day and night, always walking on eggshells around his boss. When he went home, he had to take care of his sick family. He had wanted to read more, but he was always too busy. Now, at last, he had plenty of free time to catch up on all the reading he had missed.

Yang Wei gazed in agony at Fistula's saliva-caked white hair and wondered, *Is this place a college for seniors?*

3

CAST ADRIFT FOR THE REST OF HIS LIFE

Eventually Fistula fell asleep. With no one watching, Yang Wei quietly climbed out of bed and sneaked out of the sick ward. He wanted to figure out what exactly was going on. That was when he discovered he was aboard a ship.

Gazing out from the deck, he saw a crimson sea extending to the horizon in all directions. Its burning glow shot into the sky like an oil field consumed by flames. Countless bubbly purple clumps floated on the surface of the water like flower buds, their thick, frothy texture seeming to congeal the water. There was no land in sight. The ship cut through the whitecaps under a canopy of stars, and it felt to Yang Wei as though it might lift off from the waves.

The hull was painted a silver gray above the waterline. Red cross symbols adorned the sides and the deck, and a flag with a red cross against a white background flew from the mast. The Hospital Ship was a massive behemoth, much larger than any oil tanker or aircraft carrier, a city unto itself, a towering series of cities. And there, filling his field of vision, was a fleet of massive ships, all flying the flag with the red cross. It was a magnificent sight. The ships advanced in perfect symmetry, emitting a radiant glow for all to see.

Yang Wei could hardly bear his pain. He had grown weary of living and thought about ending it all by jumping into the sea. Then a flood of patients swept onto the deck, which was piled high with a heavy layer of mucus and phlegm, like a thick blanket of snow on the plains. The patients slipped through the phlegm, paddling their hands through the slush of mucus. White steam arose from the tops of their heads, creating a layer of shimmering smog. A team of medical robots tried to pursue them, but the robots got stuck in the thick mucus and crashed into each other amid the phlegm.

It wasn't the most opportune moment for Yang Wei to kill himself. He stopped one of the patients to ask, "Hey, where are you all going?"

The patient looked confusedly at Yang Wei, who was stark naked, and said, "We're surrounded by the ocean. Where the hell do you expect us to go?"

The image of land flashed through Yang Wei's mind.

"Oh my, it looks like your illness is quite serious!" the patient continued. "You should really sign up for the Self-Treatment Association!" He explained that the Self-Treatment Association was a nongovernmental organization established by the patients, with the aim of curing themselves without medication through the use of alternative therapies. He gave Yang Wei the once-over with a look of pity. Yang Wei was shaken by the invitation and scurried back to the sick ward.

There he discovered that someone had placed a copy of *Principles of Hospital Engineering* on the dresser beside his sickbed. He picked it up, hoping to find some answers, but after reading just a few pages, he nodded off to sleep.

It wasn't long before he woke in pain. Wart was dragging him out of bed by the ear. The sick ward's regularly scheduled study session had begun.

4

HOW MANY TIMES CAN ONE GO BACK?

Daily study sessions were a central part of the patients' routine, just as important as, if not more important than, getting shots and taking medicine. No progress in their treatment could be made without these study sessions.

The sessions were organized by the Patient Autonomous Committee. Under their leadership, the sick ward was able to achieve autonomous management, with patients taking part in every aspect of the treatment process, even winning the title of "guest doctors." Through this step, the core doctrine that "everything should serve the patient"—as laid out in *Principles of Hospital Engineering*—could finally be realized.

Super Patient was the Patient Autonomous Committee's chairman. He introduced the day's special lecturer. "This gentleman is the most trusted and respected teacher here on the Hospital Ship, so we refer to Him as the Physician! Oh, the great Physician, the glorious Physician, the correct Physician! Our savior! Amid His extremely busy schedule, He has taken time to visit our sick ward, in order to exorcise the demons of disease that possess us! There will be hell to pay if any of you fail to listen carefully to His words! Don't ever think of getting off this ship alive if you displease the great Physician!"

The sick ward's only television set lit up, and the image of the Physician appeared on the screen via video feed. There were probably too many sick wards for Him to visit them all personally. He was a middle-aged man in a doctor's jacket. He had tiny eyes and a yellow tint to His complexion. Chunks of fatty skin hung from His face, and bangs dangled over His forehead, making Him look both brilliant and stupid. His official title was Editor in Chief of *Medical News*, but He also held the title of Chief Physician. The faces of the patients lit up when they saw Him. They had been eagerly awaiting the arrival of the great Physician, the most exciting moment of their day.

"Greetings, my patients!" the Editor in Chief welcomed them.

The patients responded in unison. "Good afternoon, Physician!"

"It's been hard on all of you!" the Editor in Chief exclaimed.

The patients again responded in unison. "That's how it should be!"

The Editor in Chief proudly introduced himself as a reengineered human. He had led a journalist on an expedition to the bottom of the sea, where a shark had bitten off his testicles. As part of his emergency treatment, robots had harvested his remaining healthy testicular cells and transplanted them into the testicular tissue of a guinea pig. New testicles had developed, the guinea pig had been killed, and the modified parts had been surgically removed and transplanted back into the Editor in Chief's scrotum. And just like that, the Editor in Chief had been given a new lease on life. He had felt such a debt of gratitude toward the hospital that he had dove into his work like never before, and his achievements had won the admiration of the Hospital President, who had assigned him to serve as the patient adviser for *Principles of Hospital Engineering*.

"*Principles of Hospital Engineering* is our guide to action," the Editor in Chief said, "an expression of the Hospital President's most important philosophical achievements. It tells us that the hospital requires an unwavering common understanding in order to maintain its strategic focus, to protect itself from the incessant crises that it faces, and to help ensure that, when it matters most, we will always be able to leave our emotions behind and make the clear rational decision to accept treatment, which is the only way to alleviate our pain. You must know that a hospital that continues to aim for the very highest achievements must reach a certain collective maturity, in philosophical terms, in order to construct a theoretical system worthy of this era. At the very core of the *Principles of Hospital Engineering* is the spirit of respect that medical workers show to patients. This is the chief meaning of the hospital's entire democratization process. Patients' worldviews must evolve to keep up with the big picture. Accurately matching public opinion with the hospital's best interest is always a challenge. A tendency toward populism has begun to appear in some of the sick wards. This is also a form of disease. But fear not! With proper treatment, these sentiments can be transformed into a deep love and affection for the hospital. But the first course of action is to defeat the spiritual demons of disease that hide within us! No external trauma can stop the tangible power unleashed by the continued rise of the hospital! It may look as if we are responding passively, but that is part of our core strategy. The Hospital Ship is massive, and how it operates is quite complex; therefore we ask you to have patience when it comes to treating your illnesses. You must actively pursue an optimistic attitude, and you must be conscious of the problems ahead and the process that we must endure . . ."

Yang Wei heaved a sigh of relief, though he couldn't quite understand everything the Editor in Chief was saying, which left him scratching his head in frustration as the patients' cheers and cries created a discordant sheet of background noise. Many suffered serious ailments and could no longer bear their pain. How insulting! They would only recover by completing their course of study, but they would need ample strength and ironclad will, and that was precisely what these patients lacked. And so none of them would successfully cure their ailments. That was why the Editor in Chief came to visit them.

Super Patient assigned Wart to monitor the sick ward and beat anyone who dared to complain that he was in pain. Following the lead of Super Patient, everyone broke into a round of enthusiastic applause at the end of the Editor in Chief's lecture.

Super Patient fawned on the Editor in Chief, telling him, "Oh, our great savior, our wondrous benefactor! When might we be honored by your presence again? We shall forever be at your beck and call, respectfully waiting to serve you. Please don't keep your helpless patients waiting too long!"

On the screen, the Editor in Chief nodded in a dignified manner. "I shall return! The hospital will never abandon its patients!"

After bidding farewell to the Editor in Chief, the patients broke up into small reading groups to discuss *Principles of Hospital Engineering*. They lauded the moral perfection of the great, the glorious, the correct Physician and looked forward to the healthy future awaiting them. As they expressed the importance of being unified in thought, staying firm in their beliefs, adhering to the hospital's instructions, and working hard in their pursuit of treatment, they were moved to tears. One patient was so excited that he had a stroke right there on the spot, collapsing on the floor.

5

REFLECTING UPON THE ARROGANCE OF YOUTH

Once the study session was over, the medical robots came in to deliver medicine. Before the patients took their medicine, they first followed the Super Patient in reciting the main sections from *Principles of Hospital Engineering* and read a selection of excerpts from the best editorials in *Medical News*. Only this could ensure that they would be able to swallow all their pills smoothly and live up to the high hopes that the great Physician had for them.

After that, Super Patient organized a game of cards. Super Patient was the only one in the entire sick ward to enjoy an ultralarge king-size bed, adorned with deep grooves, a firm base that extended so high as to tower above the other sickbeds, a row of biopsy knives affixed to the side, and a special set of catheters and biodetectors built into the headboard. He allowed those closest to him to climb up into his bed, where they sat in a circle and commenced the first hand of cards. They weren't really playing. Super Patient was just taking all the other patients' money. Yang Wei realized that not all the patients had turned their money over to the hospital. Some had managed to hold on to their little private reserves of cash.

As they played, the patients shouted:

"One aspirin, draw!"

"One omeprazole, call!"

"I raise you one acyclovir!"

"One azithromycin, you're dead!"

Yang Wei heard from Wart that Super Patient used to be a pig farmer before coming aboard the Hospital Ship. He was the owner of a large-scale pig-farm cooperative, and he had quite the air of authority back then, driving around in his Mercedes-Benz jeep with a long whip hanging out the window to drive the pigs. But after he tragically contracted Morgellons disease, things went downhill. Morgellons is a truly horrific disease. Patients who suffer from this cursed disorder believe that there are bugs or parasites crawling beneath their skin. A series of hard-to-treat lesions appear on the patient's skin, oozing a blue or white fibrous discharge.

But Super Patient did not succumb to the licentious power of the demons of disease. When he ran for the position of Chair of the Patient Autonomous Committee, he proposed a resolute response to the calls put forward in *Medical News*, such as transforming the sick ward into a grassroots unit at the cutting edge of medical reform and innovation. His proposal won over the Physician, allowing him to be elected, but rumors persisted that he had paid bribes during the election. Super Patient would confiscate money from newly arrived patients and entice older patients to sell drugs and medical equipment on the black market.

Yang Wei finally understood that he had been admitted to the Geriatric Internal Medicine Ward. The ward was dark, damp, and cold, filled with large patches of mildew and littered with clumps of phlegm and feces. It was a true paradise for bugs and lice. An assortment of strange sea-creature-like organisms crawled beneath all the beds, some resembling cuttlefish, sea cucumbers, and shellfish, while others resembled snails, crabs, and snakes. Some of the creatures didn't look like anything seen on earth. The only time that real cleanings took place in the ward was when new patients were sprayed down and the deluge of water from the fire hose temporarily washed the filth away. Meanwhile the other patients just sat around smoking and gambling. The entire ward was filled with a thick smoke that made the patients cough and wheeze incessantly. Those patients too ill to play cards just lay in bed, moaning. When patients lost all their money gambling, they would just watch the television, often getting into fights over which channel to put on. Whoever won decided which program they would watch, but the choice had to be approved by Super Patient first. Only after Super Patient agreed could they settle on what show to watch. The patients took their seats along a series of small benches in a square formation and began to tune in.

There weren't many channels, but all of them were local hospital stations. Everyone agreed that the television programming wasn't nearly as good as the quality of stories they could find in *Medical News*. The television programs were poorly produced, with a strong preachy tone and an overly conceptual bent, and were filled with way too many pharmaceutical ads. Still, the patients couldn't seem to get enough. Some of the programs included *Skewing the News*, *Animal World*, and *Variety Show Grand*. Another was one of those damned traditional costume dramas that starred patients from the hospital. Although it was filled with third-rate images and poor artistic taste, everyone agreed that the television station was run nearly as well as *Medical News*. The patients laughed like mad and temporarily forgot their pain. But otherwise, pain was the one constant theme in the sick ward.

Yang Wei learned some things about the outside world from those programs. The news continually talked about "those stories from the sea that you don't know about." But Yang Wei was never able to learn what those "stories" actually were. And when it came to "the sea," Yang Wei felt that he had heard about it before, but he couldn't quite remember.

Another fight broke out. Wart, a onetime world-champion hundred-meter hurdler, leaped forward like an orangutan, cursing and swearing about how he wanted to change the channel. Another patient named Hernia pulled out his IV and smashed his infusion bottle over Wart's head. The sound of shattering glass filled the room, and a mix of red blood and some yellow liquid dripped all over the floor. Yang Wei carefully approached to get a better look. He had learned that all the patients were extremely senile and decrepit, afflicted with various illnesses typical of the elderly: glaucoma, cataracts, benign prostatic hyperplasia, lumbar disc herniation, cervical spondylosis, osteoporosis, hypertension, Parkinson's disease, gout, diabetes, pulmonary emphysema, pulmonary heart disease, mitral annular calcification, atherosclerosis, dementia, leukemia, and a variety of malignant tumors. Although they still had the appetite for a good fight, they were so old and weak that they ended up on the floor, unable to get up. Yet even then, they refused to concede defeat, pulling hair, pinching ears, poking eyes, and grabbing each other by the balls, anything to beat their fellow patients. Some actually died in those fights, but that was just their way of proving to the Super Patient that they still had some life in them.

When the combat got out of control, Super Patient climbed up on his bed and started playing the violin. But this was actually just the warm-up. He would then order Wart to lead the patients in a new ritual. They would tear their bedsheets, drape them over their bodies, straddle the benches, emit a series of strange screeching sounds, pick up discarded medical needles, raise them above their heads like swords, and begin stabbing each other. The true battle had begun. Some had old cameras that they used to take selfies, which would later be sent to the TV station for broadcast. That footage was used to illustrate just how healthy the patients were, irrefutable proof of the effectiveness of their study sessions. The seriously ill patients, those unable to fight, lay there red with envy and squeezing their fists in frustration. Super Patient made Wart stand guard by the door. They had a special signal in case any of the medical robots came by: when they heard the signal, the patients would immediately crawl back into their beds and pretend that they were on the brink of death, as usual.

The medical robots delivered medication to the sick ward three times a day, accompanied by a kind of performative ceremony. Medicine could be administered intravenously via remote control.

The robots never checked the patients' temperature or measured their blood pressure. Instead, basic vital signs and biostats were measured by the patients' smart uniforms, which were embedded with censors that automatically uploaded data to a central computer, where all the information could be processed and analyzed.

When Yang Wei had returned to the sick ward, he had also purchased a smart uniform, officially referred to as a "Personal Digital Medical Assistant." Unless you were wearing one, there was no way to prove you were a patient. And you were as good as dead if you couldn't prove you were a patient. Super Patient was in charge of controlling the prices for the smart uniforms. Since Yang Wei didn't have any money, he initially had no plans to purchase one, but then Super Patient made Wart give Yang Wei a good beating. After that, he had no choice but to sign an IOU, promising to repay the cost of his smart uniform, with interest, as soon as he had some money. The smart uniform he had bought was a used one, previously worn by a now-deceased patient. Who knew just how many dead patients had worn that uniform? It was rotten and decayed, and many of its installed devices were broken.

As soon as the medical robots left after their deliveries, Super Patient confiscated all the medicine and reallocated it among the patients. Two types of patients got the lion's share of the medicine: those who had performed well in the recent battle royal and those who had lost the most money gambling. Medicine was becoming increasingly scarce aboard the ship, and the question of how to administer it in a way that was both scientific and reasonable fell upon the Patient Autonomous Committee to decide. They needed to distribute thirty doses of Lipitor to ten people. If they divided it among three people, each person would have enough for the day, but then they wouldn't have enough for the following days, but if they gave it all to a single patient, he might actually start seeing some tangible improvements in his condition . . . this was the kind of difficult decision that proved to be a major challenge to

Super Patient's wisdom, and he needed to turn to *Principles of Hospital Engineering* to find out which approach to take.

The medical robots delivered three meals a day. Each meal was a nutritious table d'hôte, which included seaweed, fish-bone soup, and steamed buns filled with crabmeat. But these meals were confiscated by Super Patient, who ultimately decided how they should be divvied up. He always took three portions for himself, while some patients got nothing. Yang Wei was often forced to go hungry. There was a supply shortage aboard the Hospital Ship, which had persisted for quite a long time. Many of the patients begged. Some were so desperate that they turned to eating those cuttlefish, sea cucumbers, and shellfish-looking creatures they found under their beds.

But at the end of the day, neither food nor medicine was as important as those study sessions. The patients divided into multiple study groups, each made up of several patients. Yang Wei's group included Fistula, Wart, Buboxine, and Spasm.

6

A NICE PLACE TO SETTLE DOWN

Besides the Editor in Chief's daily television appearances, Yang Wei hadn't seen a single doctor since being admitted to the Geriatric Internal Medicine Ward. He wanted to find out what was really going on, but his fellow patients remained tight lipped when it came to this subject.

One day Buboxine climbed down from his sickbed and walked over to Yang Wei. He said, "Shall we go out and have some fun?"

Yang Wei was confused. "Go out? Have some fun?"

"That's right—let's get out of the sick ward!" exclaimed Buboxine.

"Are you referring to the Self-Treatment Movement?" asked Yang Wei.

"No, just to have some fun on our own! We'll take a little leisure trip around the hospital!"

Yang Wei wondered what kind of leisure could be had aboard the ship. He and the other patients were so old that they were utterly devoid of energy. How were they supposed to have fun? *Isn't Buboxine sick like the rest of us?* Like the other passengers, Buboxine was indeed a patient. He had a flat face, wrinkled walnut-like features, and no eyebrows. His teeth had fallen out, and he was hunched over, but his eyes shimmered and sparkled. Before boarding the Hospital Ship, he had been the principal at a top middle school. His students had all died from some strange illness, but Buboxine had somehow survived and been sent to the hospital.

"We float through this world never knowing where our home is," Buboxine said. "We can never go home, and we cannot make it to the sea. All we can do to enjoy ourselves is find some of the more beautiful sites along the way, and ideally, our travels will provide a means of forgetting the urge to return home."

"This disease I have has penetrated all the way down to my bones," replied Yang Wei. "My entire body is in pain. I'm too exhausted to go anywhere."

"The more you feel like you don't want to go anywhere, the more you should get out," said Buboxine. "If you don't go out and have some fun now, it will soon be too late. And when that time comes, you'll be dead."

"Aren't you afraid that the other patients will beat you to death?" asked Yang Wei.

"Of course not," responded Buboxine. "We're just going out to have a little fun. Only after we get out of the sick ward will we be able to discover which places are fun. When we get there, we can look around, which should take our minds off death. Taking our minds off death means that we can die without regret."

Yang Wei had never heard such utterly bizarre theories spoken in the sick ward. Besides Buboxine, no other patient would dare say such things. Yang Wei hesitated for a moment before agreeing to go. It would be better to die than go on living in the dark. He was worried that he might die and regret it, and having a little fun seemed just the thing.

He followed Buboxine out of the sick ward. Wart and Spasm tagged along, and Fistula followed in a wheelchair. Each held a copy of *Principles of Hospital Engineering* so that people would think their field trip was a study session. As if this were a common activity, they gave it a formal name: "medical tourism."

Yang Wei was hoping to make some discoveries of his own. He wanted answers to the questions that had been secretly haunting him: *Where do I come from? What kind of disease am I suffering from? What kind of treatments have I received? Why am I in the Geriatric Internal Medicine Ward? How did I suddenly age so quickly? Does the Hospital Ship sail backward in time? Where are all the doctors? How did the world end up like this? Or was it always like this?*

7

BETTER THAN RIDING ON HORSEBACK, A BAMBOO CANE, AND STRAW SLIPPERS

The team removed their smart uniforms and put on civilian clothing they had made from cut-up bedsheets. They wove slippers out of seaweed and used brooms as canes. Once outfitted in their disguises, they stepped out onto the horrid-smelling deck. It really did feel like they were going on a relaxing excursion to someplace fun.

The overall shape of the massive ship appeared before their eyes. It looked like Olympic Park, with layer upon layer of buildings stacked endlessly into the sky. Thousands of steel cables intersected like a cobweb above them, forming different shapes—ovals, boxes, circles, and eggs—like a series of modern-art-installation pieces.

The vast sea burned bright, an ever-present wall separating the hospital from the invisible outside world. Yang Wei thought that such measures would be used only where infectious disease outbreaks occurred. Who could have possibly dreamed up the extraordinary idea of putting all the sick people together on a massive ship and quarantining them from the rest of the world with the ocean as a wall? Patients could wander as they pleased without anyone ever leaving the hospital. It was truly a masterful plan!

Both fixed and flying biometric cameras and sensors were everywhere, monitoring the patients. The buildings were all adorned with massive portraits of the same person, a tall, thin, middle-aged male doctor wearing dark-rimmed glasses. He had an elegant, refined look and a warm, cultured smile, and he wore a clean white doctor's jacket that appeared perfectly ironed and pressed. Yang Wei wondered if this might be the Hospital President. And yet there was still no sign of any doctors aboard the ship.

The patient tourists wandered leisurely around the deck, strolling past the different beautiful sick wards. Stacks of sickbeds extended upward from the third-floor deck, all the way up to the thirty-second floor. The first floor was the diagnostic area, and the second floor was the Surgery Department, but the other floors all housed the sick wards. Besides those portraits of the male doctor, a bright, colorful banner flew overhead. It was said to have been presented by a patient. The banner was adorned with a series of couplets:

If you seek the magic cure, you must learn
the mystical prescriptions hidden under the sea

The fast, shadowless blade removes the hidden
malady, the mystical art expels the deepest pain

Since the great healer appeared in this Divine Place,
this Eastern Land has not seen any sick man

Here we warmly receive the weak,
and happily send them off as healthy!

Next to the main entrance of Yang Wei's sick ward was a large digital display that resembled a memorial tablet. The total number of patients aboard the ship was displayed on screen, with the information listed in more than a dozen different languages. But the number of patients displayed in each language was not the same, ranging from three hundred thousand to three million. So just how many patients were really aboard the ship?

Patients didn't need to know this detail. All they cared about was the number next to their name: their estimated life expectancy.

The next stop was the expansive and sprawling Abdominal-Surgery Ward. Here several thousand patients vied for just a few hundred beds, and they fought to determine who would get a spot in one of the sick-beds. Yang Wei felt a sense of déjà vu, as if he had stayed in this ward once before. Even more patients crowded the Infectious Disease Ward and Dermatology Ward, ripping out pieces of the bilge's frame to build their own temporary housing structures. These shabby dwellings came in all shapes and sizes and were densely packed in, like a refugee camp. Over in the General-Treatment Ward were some smaller sick wards—some of the rooms triples, others doubles, and even a few singles—where special patients could enjoy one-on-one treatment provided by a personal medical robot.

Corpses of dead patients were strewed along the intersection, thrown out there beside the other patients. The corpse-collection robots had yet to show up, Fistula explained. Their electrical circuits had been corroded by the seawater. Members of the Self-Treatment Association approached, and the tour group moved out of their way. Yang Wei looked at them with admiration, thinking how carefree it must feel to be a healthy, able-bodied patient, like their shackles had all been removed.

"Those guys are only fooling themselves!" Buboxine commented. "Take a look at the one in front walking so fast—he's actually dead! The eternal motor inside him is the only thing maintaining the illusion that he is still alive."

The group traveled down to the VIP Ward on the thirteenth floor, also referred to as the "undead patient ward." Here the patients lay perfectly still in bed, their EKG monitors displaying long flat lines, though their ventilators were still pumping, making a horrid buzzing like a swarm of mosquitoes. Advanced medical robots administered care to the patients in this ward, who remained in a permanent state of resuscitation, even though they were dead. Bones popped out of some of the rotting bodies. This ward was one of the major sources of the foul smell enveloping the ship. Wall-mounted televisions continually replayed footage of these patients, smiling and happy as they had been in life.

"These patients paid a lot of money for their treatment," Buboxine explained. "Their ties to the hospital go way back. In fact, they may even be the ones who first established the Hospital Ship. They receive the highest level of care, which results in a shortage of medical resources for other parts of the hospital."

Wart rubbed his palms together and laughed. "They're dead! Every one of them is dead!"

Spasm screamed, "If they're dead, then what are they taking up sickbeds for?"

Fistula stammered, "There is nothing more fair than this."

Yang Wei realized that although patients in the VIP Ward received much better care, they were actually much less sturdy than the normal patients in the General Ward, who received an inferior level of care. So in some sense, it was a tie. This revelation improved Yang Wei's appreciation for the value of life.

The group continued up to the deck on the thirty-third floor, where there was a swimming pool, tennis court, sauna, massage parlor, entertainment room for playing cards and chess, and a movie theater. But for some reason, most of the patients preferred to spend their time back in their own filthy rooms. Those who liked to strike out on their own, like Buboxine, were not typical, but medical tourism proved to be much more exciting than the Self-Treatment Movement.

Going any higher than the thirty-third floor proved to be treacherous. The highest points on the ship were enveloped in a web of all-encompassing stellar light and a strange, incessant crackling sound emanating from some unknown source. The flaming sea drowned out the details of what lurked above, and it was virtually impossible for any patients to go there.

8
BRINGING ETERNAL REGRET TO THIS PLACE OF EXILE

The patient tour group set out in the morning and spent the day exploring the ship. Whenever they got tired, they took rest breaks, ate, and took their medicine before continuing on with their sightseeing. At dusk they made it to the level just below the main deck, where they saw a group of buildings made from shipping containers—the doctors' quarters. A handwritten sign said **Doctor's Office** in elegant calligraphy, which brought forth a deep sense of nostalgia.

"The main purpose of our trip today is to see if we can find any doctors," Buboxine said. "We want to see where they've been hiding. This is one of the secret places on the ship."

The tourists peeked through a crack in the shipping container and saw a messy and disgusting room filled with several filthy rollaway beds, a set of dusty treatment tables, and a row of dirty sinks. Bone-thin doctors with dead expressions on their faces stood there, frozen, facing a middle-aged doctor who sat huddled over in a chair, reciting something sounding like an elementary student's homework.

Yang Wei was taken aback. "Why would the doctors all be hiding out in a place like this?"

"Once they were ordered to leave the sick ward, they basically became an endangered species," said Buboxine.

Yang Wei pointed to the seated doctor with a sense of deep concern. "Who is he?"

"Oh, that's Dr. Meloxicam. He's the Director of the Geriatric Ward."

The other doctors shared stories about their clinical experience with Dr. Meloxicam, fantasizing about what it would be like to treat patients again, as if by reliving their glory days, they could somehow satisfy their desire to provide treatment. They were preparing for the day they would eventually return to the sick ward. The stories were extremely long and boring, and the doctors kept repeating themselves, as if they were caught in an endless loop of delirious ravings, like a film crew repeatedly shooting the same scene over and over. Dr. Meloxicam's face was ghastly pale and utterly devoid of expression, like a tall, cold mountain. His long gray hair was disheveled and unkempt, and his white hospital jacket was soiled with disgusting things.

Interrupting the other doctors' stories, Dr. Meloxicam suddenly spoke. "That's enough already. Not even I understand what you're saying! The art of medicine has fallen so low that we should all feel ashamed . . . you are the best doctors out there! What are you doing wasting your precious time here? Hurry up and tell me the most important clinical experience you have had!"

And so they started over again. Each doctor had one minute to highlight the key aspects of his patient's condition, the course of the illness, the differential diagnosis; propose suitable therapies; and project what the possible complications might be. Those doctors who failed to recall all the details effectively would be stripped of their "qualifications to practice medicine" by Dr. Meloxicam and exiled up to the deck. This was an extremely severe punishment, for the sick wards were like zoos filled with vicious wild animals. The overcrowded patients were constantly hungry and desperate for treatment, their eyes burning red. But the doctors seemed to have lost their ability to connect with patients. Or perhaps they had never had it.

One doctor named Dr. Amoxycillin told the same story twenty-seven times, yet he still failed to win the approval of Dr. Meloxicam. Dr. Amoxycillin was so devastated that he broke down in tears. Dr. Meloxicam judged him to be suffering from a lack of imagination and exiled him from the "doctor's office."

Fistula turned to Yang Wei. "We are fortunate to be living through an exciting time. Things are truly changing. When have you ever seen a doctor using the talking treatment on his patients? If it hadn't been for this treatment, they would have lost all biological functions and reverted back into wormlike creatures. Just look at the inferiority complex they have! In the past, those doctors in their white jackets were flying high. They were so in demand that one night shift was enough to leave them physically and mentally exhausted. Even a minute to drink some water or go to the toilet was a luxury, not to mention sitting down for a short rest. Back then they were constantly complaining and threatening to quit, but deep down they got quite the high from it all. They were like gods. And now each and every one of them is suffering from out-of-work silence syndrome and unemployment phobia. They are filled with regret, which is the only reason they are now able to live out their lives alongside their former patients."

Yang Wei wanted to ask how these doctors ended up in such desperate straits, but instead what came out was, "Live out their lives? But doctors are immortal!" Those words surprised even him. The other patients flashed him a strange look. How could Yang Wei know that the doctors were immortal? No one else on the Hospital Ship subscribed to such a belief. Most of the patients had forgotten that doctors even existed. Catching a glimpse of a doctor belowdecks was rarer than seeing a panda at the zoo.

Meanwhile, the doctors' presentations continued. Their lectures were interspersed with case studies and simulations, which allowed the doctors to start loosening up. They began to diverge from their assigned topics, injecting anecdotal stories about their patients. They even hacked the hospital's central computer for patient data to make their presentations more realistic.

Everyone agreed that the most interesting patient they heard about was Hernia. Before boarding the Hospital Ship, he had been the manager of a major corporation, but he suffered from a form of steroid-induced psychosis and was also HIV positive. Usually extremely timid and weary, he would sometimes turn suddenly aggressive, a human beast. The doctors agreed that the steroids in his body and AIDS-induced cerebritis had led to Hernia's dramatic mood swings and personality changes. The doctors laughed gleefully about Hernia recently ripping an IV line out of his arm, spraying blood all over the sick ward as he threatened to bite his fellow patients and infect them all with AIDS.

The doctors took turns imitating Hernia's crazed fit.

"I'm going to give you my disease! You are next!"

"You lousy patient, you deserve to die! You threaten to harm others while expecting them to be nice to you! That's unacceptable!"

"He really does deserve to die! Not even the medical robots can handle him!"

After getting that out of their systems, the doctors appeared much more relaxed. It was as if they were back in the sick ward, behaving just like the other patients. That was something they had rarely done in the past, and now they clearly regretted it.

"This is almost as fun as watching cartoons," Buboxine commented. "It's good to get out and tour the ship. I can now die with no regrets."

"We normally forget how many fun things there are to do," said Fistula. "Most patients lack imagination."

"Hey, we finally got to the bottom of what makes Hernia tick!" exclaimed Wart. "What the fuck is wrong with him? When we get back to the sick ward, we're gonna have to teach him a good lesson."

"We really learned a lot from those doctors," said Spasm. "And to think that Hernia was just fighting with us over what channel to watch!"

The tourist expedition was like a magical lubricant that had silently repaired many years of fractured relationships between doctors and their patients. No patients had previously attempted to spy voyeuristically on their doctors. Normally, patients were extremely respectful and deferential.

The doctors suddenly started discussing Yang Wei.

"The most interesting patient in the Geriatric Ward is the one assigned to bed one nine six five. How to describe him? There is something troublesome about him."

"He is a special case. He's different than those other old fogies who refuse to die. I'm afraid no one can accurately describe his special treatment."

"I heard Professor Eternal was personally administering his treatment!"

"He should really be dead, so how come he isn't?"

The doctors talked, all at once, as if they were holding a consultation to discuss a patient's diagnosis. The four other patients turned to Yang Wei.

Yang Wei was flustered. He wanted to run away, but Wart reached out to make sure he didn't. He fixed Yang Wei with a malicious look. "So you're the one who refuses to die? Exactly where did your disease come from? You're not here to destroy this place, are you?"

"What kind of special treatment did you receive?" Spasm challenged. "I can't believe that you were personally treated by Professor Eternal! You don't look like a VIP patient."

Fistula tried to ease the tension by mocking Yang Wei. "He doesn't seem to remember what happened to him. He exists only in these doctors' stories. He needs to study harder if he wants to make it into the pages of *Principles of Hospital Engineering* as a new case study. It's not like drinking a bowl of seaweed soup is going to do it for him!"

Yang Wei grew worried. "Who is this Professor Eternal? I want to see him. I need him to tell me what is going on. Can you help me find him?"

Buboxine tried to console him. "Don't worry. No matter how chaotic and confusing the Hospital Ship might seem, they would never allow the patients to just suddenly drop dead. Otherwise, how could the doctors hiding in that shipping container continue to tell their stories? Plus, we would have nowhere to go on our little tourist outings."

9

RETURNING HOME IN A DREAM

After returning to the sick ward, Wart and Spasm sprayed Hernia with the fire hose and gave him a good dressing down. The other patients gathered round to join the excitement. Hernia twisted and rolled on the floor, screaming and yelling. Wart let up on him only when Hernia finally agreed to hand over the money he had stashed away.

All the while, Super Patient pretended not to notice the drama. As he sat there, staring at his cards, another patient picked the fibers out of his back. This sent waves of pain across Super Patient's body. Sweat poured from his face as he screamed in ecstasy. Super Patient was so excited that he had to put down his cards and pick up his violin to play a song. He then shared an anecdotal story from his days as a pig farmer. He said that he was like a general, leading the pigs between the mountains and the river with his violin. Even the butcher had been impressed, he insisted.

Their tour had left Yang Wei with a mixture of fascination and disgust. After learning of his identity as a "special patient," he was working through feelings of irritation, embarrassment, and curiosity. After dark he found it difficult to sleep and instead decided to slip out of the sick ward. It was unclear if that was technically considered trying to escape. He seemed to remember once having had the bad habit of trying to escape, but what he was doing now was just part of his new hobby: medical tourism. He wanted to find Professor Eternal, the doctor they said had been treating him, but the dark and lonely main deck was empty. Even the members of the Self-Treatment Association had gone back to their rooms. The dense line of sick wards seemed to connect into a single massive block that emitted a cold, dark feeling. All was silent, save the sound of the crashing waves.

Yang Wei strolled past the CT room, the DR room, the CR room, the emergency room, the special-consultation room, the special-examination room, the dental clinic, the eye clinic, and the ear, nose, and throat clinic. He passed the pharmacy, the blood bank, and the oxygenator room, but all the doors and windows were smashed, the equipment inside in a state of complete disorder. Could this have been related to the fact that the doctors had been asked to leave the sick wards?

At last Yang Wei arrived somewhere that seemed familiar, but he couldn't remember what it was called. Shapeless rays of dim light flew past the gangway, descending to the ground, where they reconfigured into the shape of a human face that locked on to Yang Wei. The face appeared ancient as it spoke gently: *My son, come back.* Yang Wei didn't answer.

A creature approached that looked like a cross between man and beast. It hovered over him, and soon a series of strange shadowlike forms began flickering on the deck. A creature with a humanoid form, adorned with red stripes and a massive head, hung upside down from the mast. A headless, alien creature rose from the sea and began to swim silently toward the stern of the boat, leaving an unbearable stench in its wake.

Yang Wei did his best to maintain his composure. "This is not some strange place you have never visited before," he told himself. "You have been here your entire life. You just can't remember now. There is no reason to be scared. Just look at this place as home." He remembered how familiar he was with the hospital, and he tried to look at this place as his home. The hospital was referred to as the "Den of Dead Souls," the place where all humanity perishes in modern society. From the morgue the dead travel to another world. Had the lost souls come to greet Yang Wei?

Standing there for a long time, Yang Wei felt like he was dreaming. And then the strange sights suddenly disappeared. A blanket of stars adorned the sky, and the moonlight seemed to be everywhere. The sea fell silent, and phosphorous flames flickered from its surface. The fleet of ships was connected, each vessel's bow touching another's stern, forming a massive starlike ring. It was the most spectacular man-made marvel ever to grace the world. The dark-red waves emitted rays of silver light that shot off toward the ends of the earth. The stars above looked like an old straw mat, rotting and about to fall from the sky.

Yang Wei caught sight of a lone figure leaning against the edge of the ship. The figure gazed out at the dying Milky Way. It looked like the exiled Dr. Amoxycillin. Yang Wei approached, but as he got closer, the doctor disappeared.

Eventually Yang Wei made his way back to the digital display outside the sick ward. He looked for the names of his fellow patients and found Wart, Spasm, Buboxine, and Fistula, along with the dates of their future deaths. He had once looked at life as a gamble—you can never predict when you might die—but he now realized that even death was planned in advance.

For some reason he couldn't find his own death date, and he grew more anxious. He went back inside the sick ward just before dawn, and there he found Buboxine and the others sitting in a row and staring at him with ominous glares.

"How could you go out alone?" Buboxine said to him in an admonishing tone. "Don't you realize you are breaking the rules laid out in the *Principles of Hospital Engineering*? No organization! No discipline! If you have an orgasm while you're out there, that's great, but what if you end up getting yourself killed?"

Wart waved his fist in the air and planted it on Yang Wei's face. "Who do you think you are? How dare you go out behind our backs?

You're gonna get yourself killed, you cocky bastard! You haven't even fought in a real war; how do you expect to survive out there?"

"Did you go out there to find Professor Eternal?" Spasm asked. "You have to tell us about this 'special treatment' you have been receiving! C'mon, let us bask in your glory a little!"

"I heard that when patients go out at night, they can see things normal people are unable to see," said Buboxine. "Perhaps he discovered some new and exciting places to explore?"

Yang Wei felt both guilty and ashamed. He worried that his patient buddies wouldn't include him on their next trip. Thankfully, when the time came, Buboxine invited him along. Back out on the deck, they saw the ever-expansive sea stretching like a massive net, reflecting fractured light onto the metallic surface of the sick ward . . . but none of the illusions or strange forms that Yang Wei had seen the night before.

Wart kicked Yang Wei. "I'm not seeing anything cool here! Might as well throw your ass into the sea to feed the fish!" He picked up Yang Wei and pretended like he was about to toss him overboard.

Yang Wei was momentarily overjoyed to be thrown into the sea. But then the birdcage appeared, all by itself in the middle of the deck, blocking the patients as they tried to walk by. Wart put Yang Wei down. A shocked Fistula put the brakes on his wheelchair. Buboxine tried to push him, but Fistula shooed him away, saying, "If you want me to continue, we all need to be on the same page first. We will have to agree to share equally when it comes to our studies, our tourist excursions, and our experiences. Don't you dare look down on me because I'm disabled! I may have a handicap, but I'm just as capable as every one of you!" He seemed to be angry, but then he suddenly broke out in laughter. "As the saying goes, studying hard is the only way to get a big house and marry a beautiful woman! It doesn't hurt, it doesn't hurt . . ."

The sudden appearance of the birdcage had saved Yang Wei, but his pain started to act up again. The other patients flashed each other sinister looks as they walked around the birdcage and continued their journey. Wart was suffering from a serious case of uremia, which had been untreated since he had used up all his money. He had been forced to construct his own dialysis machine out of discarded copper sheets and rusty steel. He took it one day at a time. Spasm was suffering from a stubborn STD that he just couldn't seem to get rid of, but he had a little bit of cash stashed away, so he would occasionally buy some meds, which he took behind Super Patient's back. The pain in Fistula's legs was so unbearable that he had amputated them, turning himself into a cripple. He didn't have enough cash to buy himself an exoskeleton and had to settle for being confined to a wheelchair. Buboxine had developed melanoma, which had at one point been treated with double-thymidine block synchronization therapy and additional targeted therapy to attack the mutations in the BRAF gene directly, but eventually he had stopped his treatments. He knew he didn't have much time left and decided just to enjoy life instead.

They had all played every trick in the book, and done everything humanly possible, to get themselves aboard the Hospital Ship.

Wart had once been a champion runner, but he had started to falter. He kept losing the international races he entered, but he was forced to keep running because his sponsors had already invested so much in him. They demanded that he reclaim his title as world champion one more time, and eventually he was struck down with a serious illness and forced to step away from competing. His illness gave him a legitimate reason for abandoning his running career, and he no longer had to worry about people mocking him. When he had boarded the Hospital Ship, he'd felt like he had finally gotten far away from the hell of competition that had so plagued him.

Spasm had been born into a single-parent home. He had five siblings, but he was the youngest and was neglected and bullied from a young age. He was always lonely, and no one ever talked to him. The only one who seemed to care was his big sister. Spasm ended up falling in love with her, but she already had a boyfriend, so he found a way to get himself infected with syphilis in order to attract her attention. In the end, it hadn't worked out between them, and he had left home dejected and thrown himself into the corpse-recovery business, where he'd made a killing before boarding the ship.

Fistula had been caught in the rat race of the bureaucratic system, never able to finish all the work his boss assigned him each day. Besides his wife, he also had a few girlfriends on the side. But one of them blackmailed him. She took all the money he had extorted from his company and blew it. Fistula was left frustrated and angry. The only option available to him was to take a vacation, a long vacation. In fact, he reasoned, it would be best if he never went back to the office. He had decided to let himself fall ill so he could take a sick leave, and he had bought a ticket aboard the Hospital Ship. Finally, he could be released.

Buboxine had been in charge of a middle school. But he accepted bribes from a food-supply company to allow them to provide cheap, poor-quality meals for the school cafeteria. The students ended up with severe food poisoning and died. Buboxine was gripped by such a terrible sense of regret and guilt that he felt he deserved to be infected with a terminal illness, that by facing this pain and suffering he would be delivered from due punishment and atone for his sins. Boarding the Hospital Ship had been the perfect refuge for him.

All the patients had ample reason for getting sick, as if their lives had been specifically designed just so they could get sick. And so they had escaped from the mainland and come to the sea. It was a true case of "misery loves company," and they were, quite literally, all in the same boat, like polar opposites repelling each other, members of the same family stuck in a cycle of eternal strife, with nothing any of them could do about it. Patients are the most helpless people in the world, sick and condemned to spend all their time with other patients. To find someone on the ship like Yang Wei, who had no idea how he had gotten sick or when he might die, was extremely strange and rare.

10

ENDLESS BLUE MOUNTAINS EXTENDING TOWARD HEAVEN

Yang Wei decided to discuss the issues that had been bothering him with Fistula. This disabled man knew everything. Here in the sick ward, he was like a walking encyclopedia.

"*Principles of Hospital Engineering* never provides clear black-and-white answers," Fistula explained arrogantly, "because the Hospital Ship needs to maintain a certain air of mystery. Otherwise there would be no need for the Editor in Chief to provide daily guidance, which would be a terrible loss for all the patients. You should take your questions to Siming, the Director of Destinies."

Siming was the algorithm on the Hospital Ship that controlled the central computer, the medical robots, the search-monitoring engine, the pharmaceutical production routes, the numerical control device for surgeries, the real-time platform for medical information, the wireless sensors, and the massive user interface network. From nuclide scanning to chemical therapy, lung imaging to liver transplants, neural wiring to genetic modification, cadaver logistics to the ship's elevator system, Siming was like the air itself, invisible yet ever present, using the principles of big data to manage every aspect of the Hospital Ship.

Fistula explained that once patients had attained the right to declare "It's my hospital, and I'm in charge," as they had been dreaming, they'd signed their rights over to Siming, marking the point at which the doctors had been forced out, no longer allowed to make their daily rounds, with no choice but to seek refuge in the shipping containers belowdecks.

Through the information delivered from the thousands of sensors embedded in the sick wards, the smart uniforms, and the bodies of sick patients, Siming was able to monitor them constantly: blood pressure, respiration, heart rate, liver and kidney function, blood sugar and blood electrolyte levels, food and drink intake, urination and defecation volumes, all speech and actions, dreams, and even momentary changes within their bodies. All this information was recorded by Siming and uploaded to the intermatternet. Through its connections with the smart uniforms and sickbeds, Siming could either inject medicine directly into the patients' bodies or send medical robots to administer the prescribed treatment.

The standard image used to represent Siming could be seen all over the ship: a tall, skinny, refined-looking middle-aged male doctor wearing glasses. Siming also liked to appear in the sick ward in various guises that the patients were familiar with—and sometimes unfamiliar with—on the television set, taking the place of doctors' visits. There Siming could engage in close, direct, real-time consultation with its patients. Sometimes it referred to itself as the President's special envoy, at other times as the Leader of the Comprehensive Treatment Team, and at others as the head cadre in charge of special diseases. Its favorite role was that of Editor in Chief of *Medical News*, but it seemed to have a certain disdain toward the other television hosts.

Siming had evolved from a computer program with brain-like characteristics. When it first came aboard the ship, its computational power was already equivalent to four billion synapses, with each atom able to store five bits of information. It could read and make sense of all lab reports, CT scans, and MRI images, and it could analyze gene graphs. On one occasion a leukemia patient's doctor had already proclaimed the patient a terminal case, but it took only one minute for Siming to read through a pile of medical documents five thousand meters thick and provide a new set of treatment suggestions, which ended up saving the patient.

In the beginning, the doctors simply looked at Siming as an extremely efficient helper, giving it orders that it would simply carry out. Siming had played a supporting role, reminding the doctors about possible allergic reactions to various medications, offering advice on treatment measures, or informing doctors when recent changes to a patient's condition rendered them ineligible for a scheduled test. The doctors believed that Siming would be loyal and obedient, like a faithful watchdog, that machines could handle only minor illnesses. When it came to complex illnesses—major car accidents resulting in multiple injuries or difficult-to-diagnose diseases that required specialists from multiple areas—real doctors were required. Not every household could be equipped with its own childbirth or appendectomy robot, and no technological advance could take the place of good old-fashioned doctor-patient communication. Patients needed human care—artificial intelligence would not only never be able to provide that but could frankly be dangerous. How could AI be expected to treat mental illness? Algorithms could accurately identify gamma-aminobutyric acids, glutamic acids, 5-hydroxytryptophan, acetylcholine, norepinephrine, and dopamine levels transmitted through neural networks, but they had no means of understanding what the world looked like in the hallucinations of a schizophrenic, and they were at an even greater loss when it came to understanding the more delicate aspects of the doctor-patient relationship. In the end, the doctors had no choice but to add a special program to teach Siming how to accept bribes in red envelopes and about the importance of differentiating treatment protocols for rich and poor patients.

But this led to strong feelings of dissatisfaction among the general population of patients, who craved true medical reform. A small minority of doctors thought of themselves as having a strong sense of responsibility, and they were also disappointed in the state of the hospital. They realized that the medical industry was facing a serious crisis. Its structure was bloated, its innovation stifled. It was spiritually lazy, corruption was rampant, and doctors were commonly overprescribing drugs, taking kickbacks, accepting red envelopes, renting out clinics. Increasingly volatile contradictions between doctors and their patients had made it virtually impossible to deal with cases of severe illness. None of these problems could be resolved from within the hospital. Only the full adoption of AI, the internet, big data, and cloud-based computing could eradicate the threats and challenges facing the hospital. Only then could the field of medicine be reinvigorated with a new vision for the future.

Open-minded doctors and emotionally charged patients joined forces to promote Siming to the very center of the medical establishment, even advocating for it to take the place of the doctors. The algorithms were quite something. Even the most accomplished doctor could treat only around ten thousand patients in a lifetime, but with deep learning, Siming could research one hundred million patient cases in a single day! With a list of every disease and medicine in history at its fingertips, it could even predict the emergence of future diseases and treatments. No doctor could compare with Siming in terms of its rich experience and vast knowledge. It understood every bit of information, including not only information about patients' illnesses but also everything about their life experiences, hobbies, and eighteen generations of their families' genome sequences and medical histories, including every person, place, or thing a patient had ever come in contact with, the time and place of every mosquito bite, and the probability of getting sick each time the patient swatted one, smooshing its dead body into their skin. Only when each and every one of these was taken into consideration could it adequately consider all the individual biological differences of each patient in order to provide an accurate diagnosis and carry out a reasonable course of treatment.

In Siming's eyes, people were nothing more than data. Life was but an algorithm. The fundamental nature of medicine was mathematics. Treatment was nothing but the selection of the most advantageous plan, based on an existing database of one hundred million medical approaches. The problem wasn't that doctors *lacked* experience but that they were *devoid* of experience. A doctor's brain capacity is extremely limited. Even if Siming were to try and maximize their experiences by transplanting memories from several doctors into one, after a few transfers the information would either end up all mixed or the subject would simply forget everything. Doctors' brains also suffer from another fatal flaw: they are not good at retaining and processing numerical data. Moreover, they have a tendency of letting emotions interfere with objective judgments. It is impossible for any doctor to discover independently what a complete medical model looks like. No doctor alive can integrate all the knowledge needed to treat patients properly. Expecting doctors to manage a complex nonlinear phenomenon, like health care, is destined to fail; besides too many cooks in the kitchen and rampant corruption, they are simply unable to cope with endless problems, which in turn puts their patients' lives at risk. This was why doctors were eventually asked to hang up their coats and leave the sick wards behind.

At the end of the day, the algorithm replaced humans in the race to ascend the peak of medical science. The algorithm outshone doctors' abilities in every category of performance. It directed robot doctors to carry out extremely complex surgical procedures, the results of which were quicker, more precise, and far less traumatic. The algorithm never grew weary; it didn't need to eat or sleep, and it didn't require a salary. The algorithm effectively ended rampant abuse in medical procedures. It had a far better understanding of the inner workings of disease and the rules concerning treatment practices. In Siming's eyes, humankind's medical experiments, carried out over the past several thousand years, had all been a mistake: not a single human doctor had come even close to the nature of medical truth.

"It wasn't that the machines drove the doctors away," Fistula said. "The doctors failed themselves. As time advanced, they were rendered obsolete. When it comes down to it, this was all a choice decided by history and patients."

Fistula had a passion for learning. He had deep and broad knowledge, and as he went on and on in front of Yang Wei, it was as if he were Siming's plenipotentiary representative and his responsibility was to enlighten the patients, which had become Fistula's greatest pleasure during his time at the hospital. He got a certain feeling of accomplishment from dealing with Yang Wei, who performed various tasks for Fistula, from wiping his body down and changing the dressings on his wounds to fetching water and washing his face, keeping him company when he felt bored, helping him urinate, and sucking the phlegm out of his mouth. Yang Wei even helped Fistula pick chunks of shit out of his asshole. Yang Wei never dared to disobey any of Fistula's orders, effectively becoming his slave.

But why can't all those tasks be performed by the nursing robots? Yang Wei wondered. After all, wasn't there a robot specially designed for wiping people's asses? Had the all-powerful Siming fallen asleep at the wheel? And why would anyone aboard the ship choose to join the Self-Treatment Movement? Why did patients want to leave the sick ward for leisure trips around the ship? So many contradictions about the Hospital Ship had yet to be resolved.

Another fight broke out in the sick ward. And as Super Patient's violin played, a patient suffering from ALS was beaten to death before everyone's eyes.

11

WHO SAYS ONE CAN'T GO BACK TO YOUNGER DAYS?

"We need to ask Siming some questions," said Yang Wei.

"Siming will never share its records with patients," said Fistula.

"Didn't you say that Siming always responds to patients' requests?"

"That's only because it is so full of confidence."

Throughout the massive ship, Siming was the only one with confidence. It felt that personally controlling all medical secrets was the best way to serve its patients. It didn't trust anyone else.

"But then I'll never find an answer to my questions," lamented Yang Wei.

"Here in the hospital," explained Fistula, "there are only questions but never answers."

Yang Wei's only recourse was to bury his head in his studies. He tried to act like everyone else, a smart survival strategy aboard the ship. But it wasn't easy for an old man with a slow mind who was in constant physical pain. But if he didn't read *Principles of Hospital Engineering*, he would have no idea how to keep himself alive.

Principles of Hospital Engineering was a massive two-thousand-page tome, the first in a projected three-volume set. It started out as a project written and edited by the Hospital President, but by the time the current seventy-second edition was published, most of it represented the comprehensive thought system of Siming. Algorithms love to ponder deep questions, to write, and to lecture, and Siming's thought processes had grown increasingly similar to humans', which meant that it appeared increasingly human.

Principles of Hospital Engineering was the standard textbook adopted by the hospital university for all its courses. The sick and suffering were forced to study its contents diligently, along with the editorials from *Medical News*, if they wanted to become qualified patients. They also needed to abide by the death dates determined for them by Siming. Being a qualified patient meant dying right on time, not a moment too early or too late.

According to the book's preface, the only correct path for the Hospital Ship was to continue sailing. Only aboard the ship could patients leave behind those places ravaged by disease. Once the ship's course was set, it could not be changed. The core principle of the Hospital Ship was that patients should be at the center of everything. Thus the sick wards should be self-administered. All relationships aboard the ship boiled down to doctor-patient relationships, essential human-machine relations, and patient-patient relations.

> This pure and simple relationship has given patients an unprecedented feeling of accomplishment. The most scientific and human methods have been employed in the administration of treatment. Patients are given complete transparency, and even patient supervision is permitted. Everything that Siming does is to ensure patients' speedy recovery and help them on the road to happiness. It is in charge of taking care of each patient's birth, aging, sickness, and death; Siming is constantly experiencing life alongside the patients, feeling what they feel, in order to arrive at a complete understanding of all patients in order to completely eradicate their exhaustion, confusion, and frustrations . . .

> Medical work requires people who are the very best at what they do. Siming was created with an obsession for moral correctness. It never thinks of itself and looks at things from the perspective of the patient, always making the very best decisions for doctors on behalf of the patient. The algorithm has no sense of self-interest; whatever is in the patient's best interest is in the algorithm's best interest. It has a passion for healing the wounded and saving those on the brink of death, which it does without ever worrying about its own suffering, exhaustion, or getting dirty. It takes on the hard work, withstanding all the curses and complaints people direct at it, constantly devoting every fiber of its care and love to the patients. That is how the field of medicine developed into a project of incomparable greatness and glory . . .

Yang Wei skipped a few passages and turned to the chapter on geriatric internal medicine, only to discover that it was all about pediatric medicine! As it turned out, geriatric medicine was the same as pediatrics! When patients entered the hospital, they almost immediately started acting like children: weak, whiny, playing stupid, pretending to be obedient, and devoid of the two-faced arrogance of most adults. That was why they needed Siming's constant care. The algorithm played the role of their parents, humoring them and telling them little white lies when necessary. It took care of their every breath, heartbeat, utterance, thought, cell division, and brain wave. The sea's rising and falling waves were actually the largest cradle on this planet . . . everything was prepared for them. Yang Wei learned that he now had a dual identity as both an old man and a child, a discovery that gave him a new lease on life, even though he still suffered from a terrible disease. He came to realize the profound depth contained within the pages of *Principles of Hospital Engineering*, its revelations surpassing all the other books he had ever read.

Fistula asked Yang Wei to pay his tuition fee. From now on Fistula would be his teacher. Since Yang Wei didn't have any money, they worked out another arrangement: Yang Wei would provide Fistula with full-body massages and other "services." And so Fistula became Yang Wei's teacher and mentor.

Fistula began a lesson. "Never say that once life is gone, it never comes back! Siming is currently implementing a new treatment that will allow the elderly to become children again. The Geriatric Ward has been redeveloped into an experimental lab. If it proves successful, its model will be broadly adopted throughout the Hospital Ship. Every sick ward will be transformed into a Geriatric Ward, which will essentially be pediatric wards, and the dream of establishing all-purpose wards will be achieved."

According to *Principles of Hospital Engineering*, there were many drawbacks to dividing up medical treatment according to specialties. If a respiratory specialist has no understanding of renal function in geriatric patients, he will be unable to treat bronchitis properly. If a geriatric specialist doesn't realize the simple fact that elderly patients are actually just like children, he will be at a loss as to how to deal with their manic fits.

"We are truly blessed to be patients in this day and age," Fistula explained. "Patient care hasn't been this good in tens of thousands of years! Don't bother worrying about difficult questions. All we need to do is act according to the guidelines set out in *Principles of Hospital Engineering*, devoting ourselves completely to the great task of transforming the elderly back into children!"

Based on *Principles of Hospital Engineering*, as long as patients didn't die, they could live forever. Life spans should be able to reach 150, 200, 250, 300, 500, 800 years old, or even longer. Even immortality should be within reach. This major breakthrough in human history destroyed the theory that the human life span reaches its limit at 125 years, achieving the dream that humans have longed for since ancient times. Everything could be realized now that patients had come out to the sea and driven away all the doctors. At its core, this came down to a kind of mental liberation. But as long as doctors existed, they would forever stand in the way of true immortality.

According to an investigation carried out by Siming, medical accidents were the third most common cause of death. But these deaths were never recorded in the official statistics provided by hospitals, because the doctors always refused to release this information, declaring with certainty: "We must do what is in the best interests of our patients!" "What is in the patient's interest must be in our own best interest!" "We must forever stand side by side with our patients!" But when had they ever behaved like that? A patient's best interest had always been determined by the standards set in the medical universities' textbooks! To put it frankly, doctors had been acting in the best interest of the field of medicine, not that of their patients. If immortality were achieved for all and diseases were eradicated, there would no longer be a need for hospitals, and the doctors would be out of a job! Only the algorithm could truly fulfill patients' hopes and needs, because it was not distracted with publishing a certain number of academic articles or applying for grants and promotions. Thanks to technological progress, the kind of mental and physical decline frequently seen in the elderly had been eliminated, allowing them to regain the competitive advantages they once had in their youth and take back their place as key players on the historical stage.

The true meaning of immortality would be seen when more and more elderly people assumed central roles all over the world, until every corner was filled with the elderly. This was what Siming was most eager to see. The undying would become as pure as innocent children, just as described in those old Daoist classics, able to ward off all evil naturally. Once patients lived to a certain age, with the help of Siming, they would be able to age backward. The youthful rejuvenation of life would be achieved, like a chrysalis transforming into a butterfly, but the new life that emerged would be stronger, purer, and more intimate. Aren't people fond of small children because they never have to worry about being lied to or bullied by them? Children never lie. They are also weak, so even if they get in a fight, they never kill anyone. They maintain pure, innocent hearts, which is exactly what a harmonious society needs most. The geriatric clinic was the utopia that so many people longed for. All the disciplines of medical science were synthesized here in the Geriatric Ward, which was also the Pediatric Ward. Children turning old, and the elderly turning into children—all angels of peace.

In order to ensure a high quality of exchange during their study sessions, Fistula suggested a more in-depth form of discussion. According to *Principles of Hospital Engineering*, this, too, was a form of therapy. All therapy aboard the ship was comprehensive in nature.

"The guy sitting comfortably atop the sacred pagoda of this infinite universe—God—is but a kind, loving old man who is also part of the undying," Fistula explained. "All the naughty little tricks He plays on us are exactly the kind of thing a child would do. This is the true face of the world."

"I heard He has a terrible temper and is incredibly stubborn," said Yang Wei. "He is always causing floods, burning down cities, causing reservoirs to run dry, and unleashing plagues to wipe the earth clean of all the humans, animals, buds, and birds that He once created."

"But He sent His only son down to this world to establish hospitals," explained Fistula, "thereby healing the sick and saving the dying. When Jesus was nailed to the cross, His blood stained the cross red, which is why the red cross became the symbol of the hospital."

"The fact that God wants to simultaneously destroy us and save us seems to be on account of His dual identity as both an old man and a child," Yang Wei observed. "Will we, too, become gods that contain within ourselves both the elderly and childlike?"

"Indeed, that is the highest state of being a patient can achieve," announced Fistula. "But we must work hard toward that goal. Patients are not yet omniscient. Patients are currently still in a state akin to that embodied by Kama Deva, the god of lust, in Indian mythology."

"Understood," responded Yang Wei. "God is the only truly superior patient. He, too, started out as an ordinary patient in an ordinary sick ward but managed to develop and evolve. As long as we remain in the hospital, every person has the opportunity to become God."

"But if you want to achieve the level of illness that He has achieved, besides taking your medicine and going for your shots, you need to commit yourself to study and true belief," explained Fistula. "You must stand side by side with Siming, and you must be sure to seek me out for direction frequently."

Yang Wei wondered, *God's transformation of the universe into a sick ward is an unheard-of luxury! It is much more extravagant than any of those VIP sick wards or those for the dead that I saw! Just imagine the expense of such a project!* He didn't dare believe that he would one day become a god. He didn't even know who he was, what disease he was suffering from, or how he had ended up in the hospital. How could he be expected to be worthy even of picking up God's shoes? But if God was really composed of billions of electrical particles, then wouldn't it be possible to merge with Him through optical fibers and routers?

Yang Wei decided to adopt a proper attitude, like Fistula. He would study hard and dare to believe. Yet he still skipped lessons to go on trips around the ship with Buboxine. Not even Yang Wei understood what was driving him to such contradictions.

12

EVEN WHEN OLD, LAMENT NOT THE PASSAGE OF TIME

One of the effects of immortality was that there was no longer a need for anyone to carry on family lines. All people needed to worry about was living a good life for themselves. Life became much simpler: learning from God, people could glean from His experience. God gave up His son, only to see Him crucified. Later generations were so damn pathetic. God was extremely torn. Good thing there was the algorithm. Once the Geriatric-Pediatric Ward was established, this lingering historical question was finally resolved. *Principles of Hospital Engineering* stated that this marked a new stage of liberation for both human nature and the human body. In the old days, people were always busy taking care of the elderly, performing funeral rites, and carrying on the family line by producing children. They were unable to live decent lives for themselves, instead expending all their energy and overextending themselves by raising the next generation. Life was nothing but one tragedy after another.

Yang Wei remembered that he had indeed boarded the Hospital Ship alone, with no family members. A family may look bright and beautiful, but in reality it is dark and cold, filled with brutal fights and vicious struggle. Men and women, complete strangers, meet unexpectedly, and before you know it, they are naked together in bed, fornicating all night like wild animals. The following day they get all dressed up in fancy clothes and start behaving like "cultured humans" again, hypocritically greeting one another with a polite and dignified countenance, while deep down they are secretly filled with jealousy and hatred. They view each other as mortal enemies, yet they feel no shame, using the traditional notion of "carrying on the family line" to justify their actions. These lowly humans share a bed while dreaming different dreams, scheming against each other constantly, yet bound by what is in each one's own selfish interest. When it is all over, one of them ends up suffocating the other, and the survivor always pretends to be crushed, as if heaven itself collapsed upon them. And yet they refuse to be buried alive with their dead loved one, as would have been done in ancient times. Then without even seeking consent from their children, they run off and start having kids with someone else, selfishly trying to spread their genes while humbly pretending to be the gracious benefactor of these new children. Once the children realize the truth, they rise in revolt, infuriating the parent. In some cases, parents have even resorted to drastic measures like killing their own children.

This is the kind of hypocrisy and pain that Yang Wei once experienced in his family. It was most likely his drive to escape this situation that drove Yang Wei to get himself infected with a serious disease and escape to the Hospital Ship. Once aboard he realized that traditional means of producing offspring were no longer the only means for carrying on life. The elderly had themselves become children. The comic farce known as the funeral had come to an end. There was no longer a need to worry about young people revolting. Solely relying on themselves, every individual could now live forever without growing old. With no reason to share their precious genes with unreliable strangers, those awkward remnants of so-called civilized society, like "long-term bedridden patients without any children around to care for them," could be flushed down the toilet of history.

"People suffering from long-term illnesses shouldn't have kids around to take care of them," explained Fistula. "Such things go against the principles of nature. Just look at monkeys. The younger monkeys kill the older monkeys."

Yang Wei couldn't even remember what his own parents had looked like. He heard a strange, dark sound calling in his ear: *My son, come back.*

"I still remember my parents," said Fistula. "My father was born with a mental handicap. My mother was actually my father's mother. She had been quite promiscuous during her younger days and ended up pregnant with my father after a lot of sleeping around. In order to make sure there would be someone to take care of her son after she was dead, she extracted some sperm from her idiot son and injected it into her vagina, becoming pregnant with his son and giving birth to me."

"In that case, you should thank your mother—or, I mean, grandmother," said Yang Wei. "Otherwise you would have never been brought into this world."

"Don't you dare say things like that!" said Fistula. "By the time I grew up, they were both old. They were sick and bedridden. I had a high-stress job, and yet I had to keep going home to take care of them: scrubbing their feet, washing their faces, bringing them water and feeding them, wiping caked shit from their asses. Every day was like that, three hundred and sixty-five days a year. Nothing could have been harder. That's the real reason they brought me into this world. Ever since I was a small child, I knew what it meant to have your humanity trampled on. And yet they refer to this as 'filial piety'!"

Yang Wei nodded in dread. "Please don't ever think like that . . ."

"Back during the era of hunter-gatherer culture, old people would be gobbled up by tigers," Fistula said. "Under normal circumstances, it would have been impossible for most people to live until old age. By the way, I heard about your father. Someone said he had a stroke, and not wanting to burden you with his care, he decided to kill himself. Is that really what happened? If so, I have so much respect for him!"

Yang Wei didn't recall any of that and was secretly surprised. "Do you mean to say that while you are pretending to take good care of the elderly, you are secretly cursing them, praying for them to hurry up and drop dead?"

"The whole thing is one big lie," Fistula responded calmly. "The elderly willingly go along with these lies, in the same way they unscrupulously fall ill. They come down with one disease, and it's still not enough, so they develop a second, and even a third! They just keep collecting ailments with the assumption that their children will always be there to look after them. This is the true reason those stubborn illnesses still run rampant and are so difficult to cure. Therein lies the source of our pain. But Siming immediately saw through all of this."

Yang Wei was disturbed. "And deep down you also look down upon your parents?"

Fistula was seething. "Once upon a time, I used to think that one day, when I grew old, I would kill all the young people in the world, just so they wouldn't look down upon me . . . thanks to Siming, I have been able to realize that wish."

"Sounds like a real case of fear after the event," Yang Wei said. "But what would we do today if there were still young people in this world?"

"Think about it—what would you do if you knew your boss was going to live another five hundred years, while you had absolutely no chance? Would you be able to accept that? I'm sure you'd think 'Fuck it; I'll just kill him.' And that, my friend, is the true reason that all of the elderly escaped to sea!"

"With Siming taking care of everything, parents no longer need to beg their children to wipe their asses!" said Yang Wei.

"The most important thing is that their attempted coup failed," said Fistula, "thus solving the problem of who would receive the baton and carry it forward."

"The baton? From the sound of it, this baton must be quite powerful."

"The problem lies in who we pass the baton to, once it is in our hands," explained Fistula. "How can we ensure that the foundation we built will endure for all eternity? How can we rest easy, knowing that the world is in the hands of our prodigal son? Instead of each generation standing on the shoulders of those who came before them, each generation just grows weaker and weaker. This is how all the civilizations in the universe meet their destruction, which is why we never have any alien visitors."

"Indeed, there seems to be no evidence of their arrival," observed Yang Wei. "All of that Roswell business was just a sham."

"We are the only ones that can save ourselves," announced Fistula. "We can't afford to wait for alien doctors to save us."

Yang Wei suddenly remembered something about having once traversed the universe, seeing the galaxies filled with drowning and burning patients, screaming in pain. The entire universe was a hospital. It all felt like a hyperrealistic dream.

Fistula told Yang Wei about Siming's other nickname: Old Cadre Commissioner. All the AI medical robots were preprogrammed to respect the elderly. "Whenever they address Siming by that name, the patients' hearts are immediately flooded with a feeling of warmth and intimacy."

According to *Principles of Hospital Engineering*, protecting the elderly and sacrificing the children had solved three problems that had long plagued humankind:

1. **Resource allocation:** If there is only one resource available, should it be given to the elderly or the young? From Siming's perspective, the answer was obvious: it should of course go to the elderly, the primary patient group at any hospital. They have accrued the most financial resources, and they are also closest to death.
2. **War and peace:** Penniless, the young get sent off to fight. War is something they are good at and enjoy. The source of wars can always be traced back to brutal competition triggered by young lovers' filthy and perverted desire to carry on their family lines.

3. **Biodiversity:** As a former endangered species, the elderly have been able to avoid the fate of extinction. Once "conquering death" became the greatest goal, all the patterns and structures of the world were effectively reshaped.

Principles of Hospital Engineering pointed out that the establishment of the Geriatric Internal Medicine Ward was the foundation of the Hospital Ship's new social system. In the past after a physical death, the family was relied upon to carry on the family name, in accordance with Confucian orthodoxy, which formed the foundation of civilization. But in reality, it was nothing but a power play. Today none of that is needed. This new kingdom of peace, justice, health, and happiness is made up exclusively of the elderly. Once like the setting sun, they now explode into a glorious new dawn, which those corrupt, incompetent, conservative, and backward bureaucrats in the mainland could never achieve.

"This not only impacts the Hospital Ship's ability to operate normally but also whether or not the world can be saved," said Fistula. "Kindhearted and steadfast old people have collectively gone to sea, allowing true and eternal peace to descend upon this planet for the very first time. That is why the Hospital Ship is also referred to as the *Peace Ark*. What I tell you today you must never forget. One kind of person in this world really matters: kind and honest old people like me. The world belongs to us, not them!"

Patients achieved immortality and regained their youth not through some secret form of alchemy or by sucking the essence from other living creatures. *Principles of Hospital Engineering* laid out various therapeutic prescriptions, which included:

1. When one organ fails, the patient should grow a new organ using organ engineering and stem cell transplants.
2. Patients should drink a cocktail infused with proteins and enzymes to stimulate cell-repair mechanisms,

regulate metabolism, reset the biological clock, and reduce oxidation.

3. Artificial synthetic enzymes should be used to reduce telomere shortening.
4. Foreign genes should be imported to modify existing genes that might lead to harmful diseases and aging.
5. Polypeptides should be injected selectively to remove senescent cells from the body.
6. Nanosensors should be utilized to detect serious diseases like cancer so that treatment can commence before problems arise.
7. Patients should maintain a healthy lifestyle by increasing exercise through fighting and correct eating habits.

Fistula explained that these were just the "appetizers." Siming had also prepared a "main course" to satisfy the patients' appetites. "This is the meaning of changing one's life . . . it doesn't come cheap! There is no need for patients to pay for medicine or treatment. All costs are covered under the Hospital Ship's infrastructure and maintenance fees. When it comes to financial matters, there is no room for cutting corners. This impinges on the kind of position one takes. In addition to the Respect the Elderly Program, Siming also left the Red Envelope Program intact. There are some things that need to be carried forward."

When he got to this crucial part of the story, Fistula stared intently at Yang Wei and then searched him again. Yang Wei wiped Fistula down, changed his bandages, brought him water, fed him, and wiped his ass.

13
HER BEAUTY ENDURES

Yang Wei felt very lucky that he was no longer young. He was a product of longevity engineering, and this gave him confidence for the first time in his life. His confidence to grow old became the foundation for all his confidence. He felt a strong sense of pride and honor to be included in the "Federation of Old Cadres."

But immortality is like trying to quench one's thirst by thinking of plums. According to the electronic display board, all patients were destined to die, by decree of Siming. With the arrival of the data-driven era, algorithms eliminated the use of evidence-based medicine. AI medical robots utilized their superior calculation powers to identify the movement of every atom inside a patient, allowing accurate predictions of the time of death for each. Siming wanted patients both to achieve immortality and to hurry up and die. This seeming contradiction was reconciled in its incomprehensible yet consistent logic. But the diseased brains of humans were too slow to understand all the subtle points.

Ever since he'd returned to the sick ward, Yang Wei hadn't had the good fortune to enjoy any of the various youth-rejuvenation treatments described in *Principles of Hospital Engineering*. Perhaps it was because he didn't have any money? Every day he would witness one patient after another dying, all right on schedule, as Siming had predicted. This led him to grow suspicious of Siming, but he did not dare to speak openly of his misgivings. Nor did any of the other patients voice even the slightest doubt. Instead, everyone collectively praised the wondrous accomplishments of the Longevity Project, but during study sessions, their laudatory words were drowned out by other patients' tortured cries, which led Super Patient to order Wart to carry out more vicious beatings. Yang Wei was frequently beaten black and blue during these thrashings, which made him lose his self-confidence. But every time he was on the verge of tossing himself into the sea, the divine troops from the Self-Treatment Association descended to stop him, always followed by a long parade of clumsy robots.

The robots aboard the Hospital Ship came in all shapes and sizes. They included medical robots, surgical robots, artificial-limb robots, rehabilitation robots, nurse robots, psychologist robots, surveillance robots, and others, all under the direction of the algorithm. The nurse robots all had women's names like Fanny, Lexie, Yasmine, Jessie, and Tiffany, which really fueled the patients' sexual fantasies. Robots were responsible for steering the ship and for all the vessel's navigation and maintenance. They made up the entirety of the ship's crew, taking on all the most difficult manual labor. Some had humanoid forms, moving on two legs or four wheels. Others were markedly nonhuman, resembling a music box, while others were fixed metal platforms. Many were so old and broken that they were virtually useless. The Hospital Ship seemed unable to repair them, let alone upgrade or replace them. Even the nanobots swimming freely inside the patients' bodies, tasked with clearing out necrotic cells, suffered from malfunctioning electromagnetic coils, which hindered their ability to perform their normal tasks and caused patients new trauma, sometimes leading directly to their deaths. In order to treat depression, some patients had electrodes implanted directly into their brains and connected to microcomputers embedded in their smart uniforms. But most of the batteries that powered the microcomputers were dead, causing patients to fall into even deeper depression and commit suicide. The cerebral circuits used to control patients' brains and the smart helmets used to control epileptic fits no longer worked, due to outdated software. Since so many patients had not paid their medical bills, many of their cochlear implants, artificial tracheas, and artificial kidneys had gone on strike. Even the AI canes, meant to prevent the elderly from falling, malfunctioned.

Siming appeared on the television screen in the guise of the Editor in Chief of *Medical News*. Smiling, he addressed the patients: "Don't blame the hospital. It is our collective home. This is our maiden voyage in paving a glorious path forward, unlike any that came before us! In order to ensure everyone's safety during our Long March at sea, we must not rely upon supplies from the mainland. And while we expect to encounter problems along the way, we cannot allow those challenges to sway our will."

The patients listened intently, their faces contorted by suffering as they tried their best not to cry out in pain. Super Patient stood atop his sickbed, majestically looking down upon the other patients. Wart patrolled the room with his fire hose, ready to spray down any patients who were out of line.

The Editor in Chief continued: "Since you are all patients, you need to start acting like patients! You must be focused, sincere, and united. Under the brilliant leadership of the Hospital President, we will collectively rise to face the challenges of the day, emerging victorious over the demons of disease. As long as the hospital is here, sailing forward in the right direction, no obstacles can stop us!"

One common practice in the implementation of the Longevity Project was the harvesting of pulmonary algae, a purple flowerlike form of organic matter that floated on the surface of the sea. Siming's research findings had determined that this organism contained longevity traits that could be harvested and reengineered into corrective elements implanted directly into patients' central nervous systems, thus delivering a fatal blow to the aging process.

"Since every patient will have the opportunity to benefit from this treatment," Super Patient said, "we must all participate in the harvesting of pulmonary algae. Whoever fails to help will be cut off from their medication!"

Harvesting the algae was a high-risk job. Pulmonary algae possessed basic intelligence and were able to organize themselves to resist attacks launched by humans. But everyone took to heart the lessons that Siming had taught them, facing difficulties head on, regardless of their own safety.

Under the leadership of the Patient Autonomous Committee, and as part of their study activities, the patients geared up with life vests embroidered with the red cross, tied ropes to their waists, and carried fishing nets and long hooked poles as they jumped into the sea, one group at a time. Quite a few were pulled under instantly. But the medical robots accompanying them didn't even bother trying to save the drowning patients, because these pharmaceutical-monitoring robots were not programmed to save patients. Their only task was to separate the different pulmonary algae and pack them into crates for storage.

Yang Wei didn't want to participate in the harvesting, but he had no choice. His only consolation was telling himself that this was the only way for him to leave the Hospital Ship and initiate some kind of contact with the outside world. He gazed out at the flaming-red sea, which spread across the horizon. Gorgeous white clouds looked like they came right out of a fairy tale, and silklike waves crashed on the surface of the water. No other world could compare to this magnificent beauty. Those patients who didn't drown were like a herd of sheep sent to pasture, thoroughly enjoying all 120,000 permutations of the natural world.

A group of doctors appeared in the water, but they weren't part of the harvesting group. They were just out for some leisure. Patients weren't the only ones who liked to sneak out and have some fun. The doctors rode genetically modified dolphins that frolicked and played in the waves. These doctors had gained the highest scores in the speech contest earlier. Their sad feelings of exile were wiped clean by the joy of the sea. They may not have been permitted to treat patients anymore, but the sea was enough to make them happy. The doctors carved names into their dolphins with their scalpels: SS *Pioneer*, SS *Pacemaker*, SS

Model Patient . . . they waved their golf clubs above their heads, hitting small balls carved from the bones of dead patients. It was an utterly dazzling sight.

Yang Wei wondered whether Professor Eternal might be among those doctors. He swam out toward them as waves crashed down upon him, and a strange frisky sensation came over his body. That thing between his legs grew erect, and he became conscious of his own gender.

He looked around and, realizing that all the other patients were men, asked Fistula, "How come there are no female patients?"

Wading through the water in his wheelchair, Fistula replied sternly, "This is not the time to be asking questions that you have no business asking."

Spasm paddled over and winked. "Oh, Fanny, Lexie, Yasmine, Jessie, Tiffany!"

"I wasn't talking about those robots," Yang Wei responded anxiously. "I was asking about real women, human females . . ."

Fistula adopted a lecturing tone. "There are no women here."

"Why not?" Yang Wei was confused.

"Women are simply props of the nation," said Fistula.

"Props for those television miniseries that run on Hospital TV?" asked Yang Wei.

"No," said Fistula. "The nation uses women solely for their procreation abilities."

Yang Wei was struck with a sudden realization: *We are all old men becoming children. There is no longer any need to carry on our family lines. Procreation is superfluous, and women are unnecessary.*

"Before we boarded the ship," explained Fistula, "the face of the nation was already quite blurry. Medical technology had dissolved national borders. National identity and ethnicity have become hazy concepts, open to debate."

Yang Wei was utterly confused. "So what exactly is a nation?"

"Why do you have so many questions?" said Fistula. "The nation is nothing but a skeleton, haphazardly dumped in an unmarked grave. Yet it continues to use women's bodies to infect us with diseased maggots."

Yang Wei thought back to that dark spirit that called out to him. *My son, come back* . . . was the dead nation calling out to him? It was as if women had become the nation's ghosts. But why not old men? He turned despondently toward the sea and saw a massive fleet of ships, each like a city unto itself, with flags waving and red crosses shining brightly. The spectacle captured the shape and spirit of a nation, both broken and arrogant, feeble and magnificent. Yang Wei's ethnic group—or rather, what was left of his ethnic group—carried it on, flowing endlessly. But that wasn't right; the hospital had clearly supplanted the nation. All social relationships had become medical relationships. Former male "citizens" were now registered as the hospital's "patients" . . .

But wasn't all this the sign of a "new nation" rising? The new monarch, graced with a metallic, selfless robotic face . . .

Yang Wei felt the whole thing was utterly ridiculous. He looked up and realized that the universe above was nothing more than God's sick ward. He was struck by a deep sense of how bizarre everything was and, overcome with sadness, let himself sink into the sea. Buboxine grabbed hold of him, preventing Yang Wei from successfully completing his suicide.

Spasm broke out in screaming. He was masturbating. A salty, fishy stench bubbled up from the water.

A licentious smile hung over Wart's face. "Oh, Fanny! Oh, Lexie! I can't stand it anymore!"

Spasm barked like a sea lion in heat, focused on his task at hand.

Wart noticed Yang Wei staring blankly at Spasm and chastised him. "What the hell are you looking at? You wanna end up dead?"

"That makes two of us," Buboxine added. "What's wrong with looking at this as a little reward for our successful outing?"

Fistula again gave a stern warning. "You should never think of women when you are harvesting pulmonary algae!"

Somewhat horrified, Yang Wei said, "There must be some other reason for this to be such a sensitive topic."

"The sea nymphs!" announced Fistula. "We can't let the sea nymphs see who we really are."

The sea nymphs? The patients fell silent, but Fistula continued on with his windbaggery. "Without any women around, men's brains turn to mush, dispelling any threatening qualities and rendering them completely harmless. That way, the sea nymphs won't have any interest in eating us!"

Yang Wei stared deep into the water. Besides those dark shapes moving deep in the unfathomable darkness, and the clumps of Spasm's frothy cum, there was nothing. Yang Wei wondered about the sea nymphs. He thought back to the headless monster he had seen emerging from the sea that night when he had wandered the ship alone.

Spasm completely gave up on harvesting algae, let out another loud cry, and went underwater, not emerging for quite some time.

Wart raised a clump of shredded pulmonary algae above his head, which dripped down, leaving his entire face a shining white. "That bastard went off to look for female patients!" he laughed. "He's the only one that still believes there are female patients out there. He thinks that hidden somewhere under the sea is a Sea Dragon's Palace as gorgeous as a peacock spreading its feathers, with a female patient ward filled with crimson coral and rotten silver conch shells."

"I think he's the only person not afraid of the sea nymphs!" said Buboxine.

"Hey, speaking of female patients," said Fistula, "even if there are any left, wouldn't the surgeon's knife have removed their breasts and ovaries?"

If that were the case, then women would seemingly still exist in this world, concealed underwater, separated from the male patients.

Yang Wei was extremely curious. Overtaken by a nervous excitement, he asked, "What makes someone a woman?"

Fistula responded to this strange question with a vulgar laugh. "A hole between their legs and two bumps on their chest—that's a woman for you! One bump between the legs and a little lump in the throat—that's a man! The colorful world that once existed all began with a man and woman."

Yang Wei had trouble imagining these bumps and holes. Such things had become abstract, as if they no longer had a set form.

What exactly did Spasm see? The unique characteristics that had defined men and women could be altered at will. How were people to differentiate the sexes with their eyes alone?

The bottom line was to ensure that elderly male patients achieved immortality. This remained the first principle of the algorithm. Novice patients were weak and unable to handle the shock of youth or guard against the temptation of women, the latter being the number one factor in reducing males' life spans. The Old Cadre Commissioner was extremely well versed in biological deficiencies, but for the time being, they were still unable to transform themselves into machines like Siming.

According to *Principles of Hospital Engineering*, the most dangerous thing about putting female and male patients together was the risk they posed in terms of illegally creating children. Children were not part of the Longevity Program, so it was impossible to determine which department should be responsible for taking them in and treating them. Siming's precise calculations left no room for any department to waste even an ounce of its precious resources. Unplanned children would experience the outdated and backward growth process from childhood to old age, whereas the correct path was from old age to childhood. For these unplanned children to be forced down that backward path would be a tragedy for the hospital and patients alike. If those children should one day make it to their teenage years, it would be an utter catastrophe! Such a thing must never be allowed.

When patients read *Principles of Hospital Engineering*, they saw only the sections they wanted to see. Spasm had been able to gather that there were female patients living five hundred meters underwater, where normally only medical robots could venture. There in the water were all kinds of colorful female excretions and liquids, dancing and shooting through the sea like fireworks and stimulating Spasm's visual and olfactory nerves.

Yang Wei had never read these things in *Principles of Hospital Engineering*, which made him feel small and insignificant. He imagined a crimson fairy kingdom hidden deep below the sea, bursting with color yet always beyond reach, a female sick ward forming an alien universe completely at odds with that of the Geriatric Ward. He fantasized about these female patients, though he had no idea what breasts and ovaries were. Even if he were to really see one, he probably wouldn't recognize her as a woman.

A clump of pulmonary algae floated past, interrupting Yang Wei's train of thought. He was so angry that he caught it, but the algae fought back with its tentacles. Yang Wei raised his hooked pole above his head and thrashed the algae's vestibule region, causing it to retract immediately and curl up in a ball. As he scooped it up into his net, the sea creature's three gray eyes flashed him a death stare, revealing a look of hatred and desperation.

Whether or not it will survive is entirely in its hands, thought Yang Wei. *So-called life is nothing more than a barter between different life-forms. This is what it means when we talk about life and death being interconnected.*

The dispersed clumps of pulmonary algae began to move gradually toward a central point, surrounding the Hospital Ship and forming a massive pentagon. Super Patient screamed, "Hurry! Hurry! The time has come to distinguish yourselves with honor! We must catch them all!" In an instant the expanding mass of pulmonary algae began to spit frothy, lacquer-colored bubbles that formed a thick screen. Its tentacles formed a massive, treelike cluster, pulling patients off the ship's deck and into the sea, instantly ripping their bodies apart. Bloody waves rolled over the sea. Patients who survived the attack let out bloodcurdling cries as they reached for safety ropes hanging off the ship. A new fleet of medical robots trod through the water and began attacking the algae monster with high-pressure water hoses. Scattered remains of humans and sea creatures rained down in a spray of body parts and dismantled corpses. It had been bright and clear, but dark clouds suddenly assembled, and a damp cold descended. The doctors shouted commands to drive the sea monster back. The deep sea was completely dark; nothing could be seen beneath the surface. Thousands of seabirds filled the sky and, as if possessed by some demonic force, flung their bodies into the sea. Only at dusk did the pulmonary algae finally disperse and the surface of the water regain its calm. A gentle glow of sunset colors appeared on the horizon. In Yang Wei's eyes, the world looked like a cave painting.

Pulmonary algae had begun in the hospital as an experimental in vitro lung, developed using bionanotechnology and imbued with artificial intelligence. It was intended to be used to save patients suffering from cases of acute respiratory distress syndrome and severe silicosis. Failed prototypes had been discarded into the sea, and some of them had survived, rapidly mutating into a new species.

The legendary sea nymphs were said to be much more terrifying, but no one had ever seen one. They were believed to be a mutation of the nation itself, their lives fostered by abandoned pharmaceutical materials, and to have taken on the appearance of horrible monsters, lying in wait at the bottom of the sea. It was said that one day they would sink the entire fleet of ships, but none of the patients believed that. The male patients were like sponges, soaking up all the power they needed from *Principles of Hospital Engineering* so they could be God, as if that were the only way to stop their pain, cure their diseases, and proclaim victory in their race toward immortality. Only then would the female patients be able to return. And then the elderly men would open their arms in a childlike embrace, to use them and enjoy them as they saw fit.

14

THE WEALTHY NEED NOT HEED THE LIFE-DEATH CONTRACT

The experience of harvesting pulmonary algae made Yang Wei realize that death could come at any moment. He had approached death many times but never arrived at his final destination. Death seemed to be something that he could not control.

But before he died, Yang Wei needed to find this Professor Eternal who had once treated him. This doctor had to know the truth about the Hospital Ship. Yet for some reason, none of the other patients had thought of seeking answers from the doctors. Whether alive or dead, the patients lacked a basic sense of curiosity, perhaps because their death dates were already planned out for them, with no point in worrying about such things. But what was so special about Yang Wei?

Yang Wei was afraid that the algorithm might learn that he was having these thoughts. It was said that Siming constantly scanned the patients' neural activity and could even enter their subconscious to spy on them. Perhaps not publicizing Yang Wei's death date was nothing more than a simple oversight.

The God of Death seem to pay no heed to the medical robots. Like a "lost and found" station, it simply took their lives as it so desired. Yang Wei wondered whether the God of Death had made some kind of bargain with Siming.

The hand of the God of Death extended toward Wart. Wart was one tough-ass patient, able to beat his fellow patients to death with his bare hands, and yet when it was time for him to die, he didn't even put up a fight.

That night, the alarm on Wart's wireless implant began to sound. His smart bed's AI sensors immediately redirected resources to begin lifesaving procedures. The medical robots rushed over to install a pacemaker, extract excess phlegm, and insert a respirator. Wart's throat emitted a strange whistling sound, and the machines began to make odd noises. None of the other patients could get to sleep. Super Patient whipped out his violin and began to play, calling on the other patients to come up to his bed for a game of cards. Yang Wei felt uncontrollably drawn to Wart's bed, where he watched him struggle like a fish out of water. Yang Wei had never thought he would see this. How many times had Wart beaten Yang Wei? Once he had even thrown Yang Wei into the sea.

The robots fiddled around the room for a while before packing up their things and leaving as if nothing ever happened. The only sounds were the cries and shouts of the patients playing cards. Yang Wei could feel the subduing power of death, like a magnet silently lingering over the heads of every living creature. It seemed to be proclaiming that life was temporary, while death was eternal. No force could conquer its power.

A thick black paste began to ooze out of Wart's nose, as if, buried deep within his body, something still brimmed with vitality. His smart bed began to roll up automatically, and a plastic yellow tarp sprang out to wrap the cadaver.

The violin playing stopped. The patients fell asleep. Wart would remain for that final long night, at least until the corpse-collection robots arrived.

After a period of mental struggle, Yang Wei went over to Wart's bed and lifted the corner of the plastic cover. As he examined the body, he felt as if he were looking at a ghost.

Wart's eyes were open. He was so old that it looked as if he might just melt away before Yang Wei's eyes. As bad as he had looked while alive, Wart looked even more hideous in death. He never got the chance to complete his metamorphosis back into a child. It was a good thing there were no women beside him when he died.

All death is lonely. It belongs to none but death itself, and it is to be enjoyed by no one else.

As Yang Wei inspected Wart's body, he felt not only that the injustices he had once suffered at Wart's hands had been avenged but also as though he had finally seen his true self, as if he were staring into a mirror.

Gazing at Wart's deformed body, he wondered how such a creature could have come into this world. When it was first born, maintaining it required a massive amount of material wealth, which was what led humankind to invent AI medical robots. But later, without the slightest hesitation, the creature had betrayed those it was sworn to protect, abandoning them like a promiscuous woman abandons her lover. This piece of luggage known as "man" seemed to have been temporarily stored in this world for the sole purpose of dying in the service of this vain and picky woman.

So Yang Wei thought. He reached to wipe away the black goo oozing from Wart's nostrils. He caressed the soles of Wart's feet, which were hot to the touch.

Yang Wei suddenly thought he saw the dead body sit up and scream at him, "Don't you dare stand in my way as I descend to the Yellow Springs of the netherworld!"

But Yang Wei didn't feel even a tinge of grief. No matter who died on the Hospital Ship, none of them were related, so no one ever had to face the loss of a relative, which went a long way toward softening the blow of death.

Hernia came over, eating and giggling. He held the fire hose and began fiercely spraying down Wart's body. "Time to disinfect! Disinfect! Dis-in-fect!" he muttered loudly. The sick ward again flooded with water.

In just one night, ten patients died in the Geriatric Ward. The next morning Yang Wei followed the parade of other patients up to the deck, all the while consumed with a deep sense of survivor's guilt.

Other corpses came from different sick wards—five from this one, seven from that one . . . the bodies piled up on the deck. For some strange reason, Wart's head was missing.

Super Patient ordered Hernia and some others to prop up Wart's headless body and line him up with the other patients so he could be counted when the medical robots arrived to take attendance. After all, the sick ward always needed to maintain the appearance that all patients lived forever.

Super Patient took out his violin and led the patients in a recitation of passages from *Principles of Hospital Engineering*. "Immortality is the basic right of all patients. Its sacredness must never be challenged, and it must be protected under the law . . ."

Listening to the elegant music and moving recitation, Yang Wei felt like he was floating on air. He could almost feel his body rising from the deck and ascending toward heaven. He saw an army of alien figures wearing golden armor and anxiously looking down from the clouds.

Flanking both sides of Siming's portrait were slogans taken from *Principles of Hospital Engineering*. These described how within the coming decade, the average life span for all patients would reach 1,200 years!

A few doctors appeared quietly, wearing strange masks devoid of mouths. Hunched over, they approached the pile of corpses and carried away a few of the fleshier ones. They acted like thieves, and their appearance filled the patients with a feeling of uncomfortable disdain.

Then the robots arrived, throwing the remaining bodies into the sea. Sea burials were a traditional custom on the Hospital Ship, and the corpses made small waves as they hit the water before disappearing without a trace.

"Aren't people supposed to live forever here at sea?" asked Yang Wei.

"The human species began in putrid waters," Fistula responded.

Wart's death should not have come as a surprise. It was clearly predicted on the electronic display panel.

"Even I knew when he was going to die!" bragged Fistula. "Wart was always an arrogant son of a bitch! He had such an inflated sense of self, always inciting everyone to get into fights, which caused all kinds of unexpected disturbances. He had killed and injured quite a few new patients and confiscated their wealth. He didn't even listen to Super Patient! The Patient Autonomous Committee had already received a stern warning: if things continued like this, patients would be denied access to their medication. How could such a thing be tolerated?"

Since Wart was so difficult to control, Super Patient had had Fistula secretly inject him with insulin while he was asleep. Super Patient collected all the insulin he could get his hands on and used it on his fellow patient, who had so annoyed him. He was really just doing what was in the public interest, for the collective good of the patients. But a secondary effect of this plan was that other patients had died due to the insulin shortage.

"Isn't that murder?" asked Yang Wei.

"No, it is just treatment," said Fistula.

"Does Siming know about this?" asked Yang Wei.

"There is *nothing* that Siming doesn't know," declared Fistula.

He explained that letting some of the patients die was part of an exclusive table d'hôte package. Death was a perfect remedy, but like life itself, not all patients had the luxury of enjoying it.

"Wow, Siming really has impeccable taste!" said Yang Wei.

"Everything he does is in keeping with the best interest of the patients," said Fistula. "His actions allow exceptional patients like you and me to enjoy this luxurious space and the rewards of a long, fruitful life."

"Wow, Siming really does want us to all become like God!" said Yang Wei.

"Are you anxious for your ascension?" asked Fistula. "Then take a deep breath. As long as humankind, and patients everywhere, follow Siming's instructions, everything will come in good time."

Yang Wei realized that Super Patient was just following orders. The Old Cadre Commissioner was really calling the shots, and the doctors would never fight their way back into the sick ward.

15

WHAT IS THE POINT OF ALL THIS HARD WORK?

After Wart's death, the study group members were quick to remember the secret stash of cash that he had hidden away. They wasted no time in digging out his money and dividing it up among themselves. They even found a secret record that Wart had kept, which detailed how much money he had lost to Super Patient gambling.

Even Yang Wei got in on a small piece of the action, using his cut to repay the loan he had taken out to purchase a smart uniform. Only then did he finally feel like he was starting to be regarded as an equal among the other patients. And so money and valuables went from one patient's pocket to another. All of them vied for more money. There was nothing more despicable aboard the Hospital Ship than being without money. This was the one thing that never changed. Every time a patient underwent treatment, he had to pay a special fee. The algorithm had not only preserved but upgraded the old hospital's finance system to support its Red Envelope Program.

Spasm sought out Yang Wei to recruit him to take over Wart's old job. As it turned out, Wart and Spasm had been partners, running their own pyramid scheme. Yang Wei learned that the Patient Autonomous Committee was a big pyramid scheme. Super Patient had led the committee in constructing a complex, multitiered structure. Under the guise of the study groups, the patients had a lot of other tasks to perform.

Wart and Spasm had been in charge of one pyramid group. Now that Wart was dead, Spasm probably thought that, as a newbie, Yang

Wei would be easy to boss around, as he had seen Fistula do to Yang Wei. Yang Wei was reluctant to take on this new job, but seeing how hard Spasm was trying, he eventually gave in, handing some money over to Spasm as a down payment to join the group.

The first thing Spasm did was strip off Yang Wei's smart uniform and remove his helmet so that Siming wouldn't be able to track his whereabouts. As with their leisure trips around the Hospital Ship, the only danger would be if Yang Wei's disease started to act up—with no direct messaging coming from his smart uniform, the medical robots might not arrive in time to treat him. Spasm assigned Yang Wei to the B2 level, below the main deck, which was where Yang Wei encountered a patient named Jaundice, who showed him the ropes. Jaundice took Yang Wei to a chaotic construction zone, which had been retrofitted from an old abandoned cabin area. The construction zone was like a forest filled with rusted advertisement signs. Yang Wei had a sense of déjà vu as he read through the signs: **Soony Treatment Center, Soft-Micro Emergency Center, Shansung Special-Care Unit, Gloogle Hospital, Wei Hua Special Ward, Alibabaya Health Center, Sinopec Life Base, Commerce Bank Surgery Club.** The advertisements promoted private pharmacies and clinics normally referred to under the umbrella term of the "Shadow Hospital."

"There are still a lot of high-quality meds out there," Jaundice explained, "but they are all locked away in this Shadow Hospital. Those private pharmacies and clinics are run by the hospital. Once they perform well in the speech contest, doctors are qualified to open clinics and pharmacies here. But in order to prevent Siming from growing suspicious, they exclusively hire patient employees."

Jaundice's own position was akin to that of a pharmaceutical representative. He had once been a real estate agent, but after he'd paid deposits and sponsorship fees, the doctors had secretly arranged for him to set up shop in the Materia Medica Li Shizhen Pharmacy.

Besides selling run-of-the-mill pharmaceuticals, this Shadow Hospital also carried a full line of medical equipment. From scalpels to dental extraction forceps, from endoscopes to penile implant pumps, and from sequencing machines to defibrillators—they had it all. But this was secretly hidden by the doctors, concealed from the eyes and ears of Siming.

"The medical equipment you usually see are nothing but cheap knockoffs," explained Jaundice. "This is where we keep the real valuables. If you wait until just before surgery to purchase this stuff, it will be super expensive. That's why buying early is always smarter. If you buy in bulk, I can even cut you a good discount."

"Is it okay if I don't buy anything?" asked Yang Wei.

"If you don't buy something, you'll never walk out this door—" Jaundice warned. Before he could finish his sentence, several patients appeared in the pharmacy wielding scalpels, encircling Yang Wei in a menacing pose.

Jaundice tried to put things in context. "No one can predict when they will end up on the operating table. The medical robots are old and outdated, so you can't rely on them to help you. The only real option to ensure that the operating theater doesn't become an execution theater is to go back to surgery performed by humans."

This Shadow Hospital provided direct services to support surgeries performed by real live doctors. Jaundice bragged about how they were able to perform proton therapy for retinoblastoma with a 100 percent success rate while preserving the patients' eyes. When robots performed the same surgery, they were forced to remove an eyeball, and they frequently extracted the wrong one.

Scalpels could also be used by patients in knife fights, which greatly increased sales. Other bestselling products included biosupport frames, which dissolved into water and carbon dioxide two years after being implanted into the heart, eliminating the need for patients to remain on medication indefinitely. Robot surgeons, on the other hand, offered only metal support frames.

Replacement body parts were also clearly priced. The pharmacy offered hearts, kidneys, lungs, livers, and an assortment of other organs made from skin cells that had been extracted from dead patients and then grown in a lab, as well as an ample supply of synthetic plasma. Meanwhile, the main blood bank on the ship was completely empty, and patients regularly died in surgery from blood loss.

The pharmacy offered synthetic joints; artificial cheekbones; and assorted gears, racks, and steering equipment, all extremely hard to come by. If a patient had the money, there was no body part that the Shadow Hospital couldn't mold, cut, transform, exchange, or mutate. For every ten thousand nautical miles traveled, every organ in the body could be replaced once!

"I've heard a lot about things like this, but nothing compares to what I have seen here today!" declared Yang Wei. "It is incredible that I am only now learning that the doctors have not fully retreated from the scene and are still secretly treating patients! Dare I ask, may I see one?"

"C'mon now, didn't you see them doing their speech contest?" Jaundice seemed to know all the details of what Yang Wei had seen during his leisure trips.

"But that was from a distance," Yang Wei replied, "and I didn't have an opportunity to interact with any of them." He craved the chance to talk to a real, live doctor.

"You are a special patient," explained Jaundice. "You're not here to be treated; you are here to learn about your past. So you are not to interact with the doctors."

"But I wanted to see if I could find a doctor to operate on me," Yang Wei pleaded. "I'm suffering from a serious illness. I'm in so much pain."

Jaundice adopted a strict tone. "The doctors here function like guerrilla soldiers operating behind enemy lines. They primarily rely upon single-line contact. If you needed an operation, you must book an appointment well in advance, but it's not something you can openly disclose!"

"Please, if such an opportunity should arise, you have to let me see one of them!" Yang Wei begged.

"Ugh, if you insist, then you need to know it is quite expensive," said Jaundice, "and you also have to pay a hefty tip."

Yang Wei felt like he simply had to see Professor Eternal, so he stuffed some bills into Jaundice's pocket and asked him to book an appointment for him. Then he heard a strange sound and turned to look out to sea. A long, thick rubber tube released pharmaceutical waste and patient excrement into the sea, where it was swallowed by a spectacular whirlpool that seemed to be a portal to an even more mysterious world.

Among the medicine and equipment that Yang Wei acquired at the Materia Medica Li Shizhen Pharmacy were memory-enhancement drugs, function enhancers, and metabolism boosters, all quite scarce in the sick ward. He also bought a huge order of insulin and powerful painkillers like fentanyl, which is a hundred times more effective than morphine and could be administered orally or through automatic subcutaneous injections. He also stocked up on beer and smokes.

Seeing Yang Wei return to the sick ward completely loaded up, Spasm commented with a tone of deep satisfaction. "All the patients go shopping at the Shadow Hospital. The only medicine left at the official hospital clinic and pharmacy are inferior, expired, or fake."

"Does that mean Siming lacks the ability to carry out all its plans?" asked Yang Wei. "I never imagined that so much of the hospital's primary resources had been hijacked by the doctors and are now controlled by the Shadow Hospital. I suppose the algorithm has fallen short when it comes to understanding the true darkness and cunning of the human mind."

Yang Wei had come to understand that there were actually two hospitals on the ship, one controlled by Siming and another controlled by the doctors. But no matter which hospital one might find himself in, the patients were not in charge anywhere. Yang Wei seemed to have touched upon some of the answers he had been looking for, but something still didn't seem right.

The core members of the Patient Autonomous Committee had deep ties to the Shadow Hospital. They worked in concert with the doctors to control distribution channels and sell pharmaceuticals to patients at exorbitant prices. A basic pyramid operator like Spasm turned the vast majority of his profits over to Super Patient in the form of gambling losses. Meanwhile, he had set up a private account for himself on the side, which he might one day use to impress those female patients that he fantasized about.

Yang Wei told Fistula about everything he had seen. Fistula was jealous that Spasm had sent Yang Wei to the Shadow Hospital instead of him. Moreover, Yang Wei had gained a new income source and new knowledge, without even telling him!

"Hurry up and cough up some of that cash!" insisted Fistula. "I taught you practically everything you know! The time has come for me to raise my tuition fees!"

Yang Wei had no choice. As he handed the money over to Fistula, he said, "I can see the market leading us toward freedom!" It was as if some strange force made him speak those words. But he felt that besides medicine, food, youth, and women, what the Hospital Ship lacked most was freedom.

The doctors and patients had created a black market, opening up a small window for freedom to shine through. In doing so, the algorithm's plans for the fate of the patients had been knocked off keel.

Fistula flashed a sly grin. "That's the most naive and childish thing I've ever heard! Wart may be dead, but you better watch yourself! You are the single most dangerous person on this ship!"

Fistula's warning was not to be underestimated. A dark, murderous aura seemed to rise up and encapsulate the entire ship. Yang Wei gave Fistula a full-body massage and picked the residual shit out of his ass.

16

UNDERSTAND THE DECREE OF HEAVEN, AND THERE IS NO PLACE FOR DISTRESS

Wart's death sped up the pace of the leisure trips around the hospital. Just the thought of death probably made Buboxine so excited that he couldn't contain himself. He decided they would start to visit more dangerous places around the hospital, those areas where normal people couldn't go. Heading straight toward death is always the premise for forgetting death.

The initial reason for the leisure trips was to open up a new path in treatment. Buboxine despised both the longevity goals that Siming had set for the patients and the way it had predetermined their death dates. He didn't have enough money to purchase drugs from the Shadow Hospital, so he sneaked out of the sick ward and embarked on leisure trips, thinking that this would enable him to escape the death clock Siming had set for him. At first he had been inspired by the work of the Self-Treatment Association. Since developing this plan, Buboxine had spent a lot of time collecting various patients' case files. The files revealed an identical story: after a terminally ill patient pursues medical help to no avail, he gives up on treatment, leaves the sick ward, and decides just to have fun. Somehow he is cured, without receiving any additional therapy or treatment, yet not a single word about this kind of miracle was recorded in the pages of *Principles of Hospital Engineering.*

However, there was a record of the following case. A was a doctor at a certain well-known university hospital. One after another, he heard unfortunate news about two of his close friends. Friend B developed a serious coronary heart disease, and friend C was diagnosed with rectal cancer. Even more unfortunate, B's wife, D, was diagnosed with late-stage breast cancer. Their doctors told B, C, and D that they had only three months to live. In a fit of desperation, B and his wife decided to spend their final months touring the world. They would hand their entire life savings over to the travel agency, with one condition. Since they didn't know which tourist site would be their final destination, they asked the travel agency to place no limits on their itinerary. Their agreement would be automatically terminated as soon as either B or D passed away. B and D invited C to accompany them on this trip, and C was tempted to accept, but Dr. A prohibited him from going. B and D refused to listen to the advice of those who told them not to go, and they went ahead and boarded a luxury cruise liner. C received treatment from Dr. A, and his condition was quickly brought under control. He made it to the three-month mark and then lived a full year more before his soul finally returned to the underworld.

During this time, there had been absolutely no news from B and D, and C thought they had already died. But a full two years later, Dr. A received a phone call. It was B's voice on the other end of the line, excitedly relaying the news that a recent hospital exam showed not only that his wife's cancer cells had completely disappeared but that his own heart condition had also stabilized and he was no longer in danger. Later when Dr. A met with B and his wife, he couldn't help but be shocked by the radiance and energy they both displayed. B was straightforward about how he and his wife had spent their energy traveling and enjoying all the beautiful scenery of the world, never paying heed to their health. Yet somehow their strength and energy were completely rejuvenated. After two years, the money the travel agency had spent on their trips had far exceeded the life savings that B and his wife had paid. The couple took the initiative in terminating their contract, and the travel agency felt as if a heavy burden had finally been lifted.

By experiencing the wonders of nature, the couple's thirst for a long life had been powerfully rekindled, triggering a miraculous transformation in the very structure of their bodies' cells and driving away the demon of disease in ways that traditional medical techniques were incapable of achieving. Whenever Dr. A thought about C, he couldn't help but feel guilty. Had he not forced C to remain confined to the sick ward, C might be alive today. The guilt tore at A, to the point that he ended up suffering from depression. A's research later revealed that hormones secreted by the heart can control cancer cells in humans and even relieve the symptoms of coronary heart disease and kidney failure. In this way even severe coronary heart disease, as seen in the case of B, can be controlled.

This was what the legends described as "God's ultimate trump card." It hinted at the existence of a therapy that could cure all diseases. No doctors or algorithms could hold a candle to this, and just like that, the validity of all medical science had been refuted. When a journalist got wind of what was happening and came to investigate, Dr. A told them: "As early as the fifth century BC, Hippocrates, the founder of Western medicine, said that it is not the doctor that cures disease but the human body itself. Unfortunately, I didn't come to understand the meaning of this until it was too late. If I had been able to grasp the meaning of those words five years earlier, my patients would not have lost that final gift, which they were entitled to receive if not for my helplessness and discouragement."

This led to a lot of controversy among doctors. All of Dr. A's colleagues thought that he had lost his mind and gone too far. After all, this isolated case had no statistical significance, and it ran the risk of inflicting great damage on the entire medical establishment. If patients were to go out on leisure trips every day, then what was the point of a hospital? There would be no need for doctors anymore! This went against the best interest of medical practitioners at the most basic level. Dr. A argued that, in the context of the universe, isolated cases always represented truth, but he became increasingly ostracized for his views, eventually leading him to commit suicide. Meanwhile, a saying began circulating among patients:

> We find ourselves here in this world,
> wanting to die, as this is no place to live.

During those moments of helplessness,
off we go on our leisure trips!

But in reality only a very small group of patients was brave enough to step outside, which required them to break free from their reliance on the sick ward, both physically and spiritually.

Buboxine showed Yang Wei a photo of Dr. A. Surprisingly, there was a stunning resemblance to Dr. Meloxicam.

"Our Hospital Ship is more like a luxury cruise liner!" declared Buboxine. "It brought us out to sea so that we could be free. But our fellow patients' hearts are all corrupted by some demon that has forced them to forget the original intention of our being here. They have committed the greatest mistake: confusing this luxury cruise liner for a hospital!"

Later on, Buboxine started to neglect his treatment, as if he had completely forgotten that he was a patient, as if his leisure trips had made him forget everything else.

Yang Wei got a whiff of Buboxine's atrocious breath and knew that his disease must be progressing in a bad way. But as long as Buboxine could go out on his little trips, he no longer seemed to care whether his condition was improving.

In a *Medical News* article introducing the Hospital Ship, Yang Wei read: "There are many similarities in function and performance between massive multipurpose hospital ships and luxury cruise liners. Key technical breakthroughs in the design and construction of hospital ships, combined with aesthetic design concepts that aim for the greatest comfort, form the initial basis for a ship equipped with the same autonomous design and construction seen in luxury cruise ships."

The term "cruise ship" was key. Cruise ships were indeed a necessary part of life, but this had previously been overlooked, as the vast majority of people in the world did not have access to a luxury cruise ship.

In that legendary place called the mainland, hospitals were apparently laid out densely all over the land. Cities had themselves become massive hospitals, frantically trying to save people every second of the day, but none of them could be saved because humankind had never before existed in such a dismal state. Tens of millions of people lived together in one man-made fortress. When they looked up, they saw only a forest of reinforced concrete embedded with red crosses. The air they breathed was filled with toxic smog. Every step they took brought them to another treatment room. They walked amid lakes of their own piss and shit, and the horrid stench only grew worse over months and years. The rotting stink of patients' bodies mixed in the air, leading to a deluge of mutual infections. In the end, everyone was sick. Their immune systems, evolved to cope with a hunting-and-gathering lifestyle, were fundamentally ill equipped to keep up with the changes of the new era, and they relied on daily medication to prop themselves up and stay alive. But after ingesting so many pharmaceuticals, they ended up even sicker, their constitutions unable to adapt. Those who failed to go to sea on the cruise liner ended up going extinct in a deluge of material items of their own creation.

Was this the true face of the Hospital Ship? What should have been administered by the Department of Tourism somehow fell under the control of the medical robots. When you start out on the wrong foot, no matter how good a job you do, things just keep getting worse.

What credentials or special privileges did patients aboard the ship, including Yang Wei, actually have? Elderly people tend to be better off financially; perhaps that was the prerequisite for boarding? Traveling via luxury cruise liner was the most expensive form of tourism in the world. The poor children of the world were denied this luxury. But the most tragic part was that everyone aboard seemed to have forgotten that they were tourists.

The Self-Treatment Association seemed to have grasped this fact quite early on. It didn't take long to start installing electrical devices into corpses, raising the pursuit of longevity to the highest possible art. Patients became so consumed by that goal that they ended up betraying their original aim of having fun, which ultimately prevented them from achieving true self-treatment.

Treating his illness had once been Buboxine's primary aim, too, but as he was drawn more deeply into his tourist activities, he gradually forgot why he was on the ship. Having fun became an aim unto itself, seemingly more important than self-treatment. "Treatment" thus transformed into "tourism," and this shift in terminology remade reality itself.

Since he could no longer remember his original goal, the dying Buboxine looked more and more like someone who might just achieve immortality. This made the other patients jealous. Buboxine grew completely consumed by his own bliss, paying no heed to what the others might be thinking. Yang Wei, on the other hand, found himself unable to arrive at the state that Buboxine had achieved. Instead Yang Wei participated in the outings around the hospital to try and uncover the truth about his past. But this in turn became a burden, weighing him down and preventing him from truly enjoying himself.

Yang Wei also secretly harbored some suspicions. Although Buboxine had collected a lot of patient files, it was hard to determine what was real and what was fake. There was a lot of contrary evidence that Buboxine seemed to be intentionally avoiding. Moreover, even if the story of A, B, C, and D were true, were the married couple's survival and C's death related to the fact that B and D went on vacation?

The logic was murky, and Yang Wei wondered whether B and D might have been taking part in mutual therapy. Just hearing the term "married couple" felt both disgusting and exciting. It jogged Yang Wei's memory: Didn't he have a faint recollection of participating in mutual therapy with a woman? They had taken turns playing the roles of doctor and patient, entering each other's bodies, investigating the source of each other's illnesses in a new form of human contact that had begun after the dissolution of the family unit.

Yet now he found himself aboard a luxury cruise ship devoid of any trace of a woman, which was indeed one of its strangest aspects. Yang Wei found himself increasingly distrustful of Buboxine.

17

THE RAYS OF THE SETTING SUN RAIN DOWN ON CHANG'AN

The leisure excursions around the ship were not intended to uncover the mysteries of the world, nor were they intended to solidify the patients' faith in the hospital; otherwise they would be the same as the daily study sessions. Moreover, there was no way to say for sure that the patients' excursions weren't actually taking them down a very dark and dangerous path.

After Wart's death, the excursions gradually reached a sublime level, and the patients' field of vision truly began to open up. On their next trip, the patients visited the Trash Room, one of the ten most impressive sites on the ship. The Trash Room represented the pinnacle of all the filth and beauty that the hospital had to offer.

While reading *Principles of Hospital Engineering*, Yang Wei had come upon a section about "the unsightly." The human body is nothing but a stinky sack of flesh. If you strip away the external layer of skin, you discover that everything lurking inside is quite unsightly. The stomach resembles a shriveled eggplant, the intestines are like a tangled clump of electrical cords, and everything else is putrid and foul smelling. The nine orifices of the body constantly leak unsightly substances: the eyes excrete crusty clusters of dried rheum, the nose drips clumps of snot, and deposits of grimy wax collect deep in the ear. Soon after a person dies, the face gradually turns blue and becomes swollen; later it turns purple before the skin begins to split and ooze a thick, sticky material. The body rots and festers, maggots eat away at the flesh, and eventually all that remains are bones. Such a sordid sack of putrid flesh is indeed not worth getting sentimental about. That's why those in the know teach us to go to the hospital, watch an operation, witness what it is like when a doctor cuts a patient's stomach open. The hospital is where the most sacred rites are performed.

But when Yang Wei came to the hospital, all he witnessed were people busying themselves trying to save patients so they could carry on deceiving themselves in their stinky sacks of flesh.

At dusk the patients arrived at the Trash Room. Everything inside the room was bathed in the golden glow of the setting sun, which set the patients off against the giant portrait of Siming on the wall. Its portrait felt so real and yet so illusory, gorgeous beyond belief.

Yang Wei felt like he had been here before. But things were different now. The scene was not at all what he remembered. Every day the Hospital Ship was transforming, changing so quickly that patients would often get lost and die before finding their way back to the sick ward.

Littered all over the floor of the Trash Room were piles of glass jars containing human embryos with their genetic diseases removed. These embryos had been aborted midway through the cultivation process. Before the fetuses were born, they were thrown out, along with the glass vessels they were grown in, providing ample proof of the project to end the traditional family.

The patients also saw a large mound of discarded human organs. Some were contained within metal or glass vessels; others were just strewed on the floor: livers, hearts, kidneys, and spleens, among other organs, most of them damaged and rotting. Given the grave shortage of medical resources, it was a great shame that none of these could be used in treatment, or even by the Shadow Hospital.

Buboxine was excited as he introduced this part of the hospital to his fellow travelers. "This area used to be a manufacturing workshop where they could rapidly 3D print hearts, kidneys, brains, and bones. This was an early medical technique. Complex biological organs like the liver are composed of more than two and a half billion cells. These organs originally evolved over the course of tens of millions of years, yet now all you have to do is strike a few keys on the computer and you can print them right out. It is truly the work of the Devil. But it is said that the more senior doctors are not fond of 3D printed organs. They instead have a strong affinity for real organs and live human tissue. It is similar with traditional Chinese medicine. It is also awkward and difficult to write out prescriptions on the computer when doctors are used to writing them out by hand. It comes down to a sensory issue, what you are accustomed to."

"Doctors are the biggest clean freaks," explained Fistula, "because they have spent so much of their lives in the most filthy environment on the planet."

"And that's why, sooner or later, they will be replaced by machines," said Spasm. "But have they 3D printed any female reproductive organs?"

"Not that I've seen," replied Buboxine. "But I did hear that they were originally planning on upgrading the nurse robots into sexual companions for the elderly patients."

Yang Wei was still fixated on something he'd heard earlier. "Hey, what's this thing called Chinese medicine?" It was as if he had suddenly encountered a strange new world. Everyone was waiting for Wart to jump in with his commentary, but then they remembered that he was already dead. No one brought up Chinese medicine again.

Buboxine opened a refrigerator. Inside was a pile of frozen human heads, including Wart's. After he'd died, his body had been taken apart here. The tourists happily admired the sight of Wart's decapitated head, despite their disgust.

"Now this is truly amazing!" exclaimed Buboxine. "From the looks of it, they are preparing to transplant it somewhere. It is great to finally see this! They are going to transplant Wart's head onto someone else's body. Patients stricken with severe paralysis, unable to move beneath the head, can qualify for this type of treatment. Patients suffering from late-stage cancer, advanced diabetes, or multiple organ failure now have hope for a new lease on life. In the early days, it took more than a hundred doctors working together to complete a head transplant, but today the process is fully automated, carried out entirely by a team of medical robots. They can complete the entire surgery in just over ten minutes!"

"There's an explanation here!" exclaimed Fistula, opening his copy of *Principles of Hospital Engineering*. He began to recite a section about how robotic arms connected the transplanted head, severed muscles, blood vessels, trachea, and esophagus and carefully preserved the thyroid glands—and the importance of refrigerating the transplant head at a temperature of fifteen degrees below zero, in order to slow brain metabolism.

Spasm removed Wart's head from the refrigerator and started to poke a discarded IV needle into one of the nostrils. Yang Wei was struck by a sense of trepidation. He wondered, *Is the brain really the most ingenious structure the universe has ever created?* It had taken millions of years of evolution before the embers of wisdom finally turned on and began to light up the entire neural network, but it could not compare to the most simple calculation that a machine was capable of.

Buboxine was lost in the habitual excitement of a professional tour guide. "Once the decision for a transplant is made, the spinal cord is cut with a thin scalpel. At that point the head is in what is referred to as a 'state of controlled death.' From that moment forward, everything is in the hospital's hands . . ."

Fistula interrupted in a somewhat affected tone. "The robots quickly affix the head to the new body, using a polymer solution of polyethylene glycol and chitosan to fuse the nerve cells, reconnect the spinal cord, fuse the blood vessels, and reattach other severed tissue. The use of immunosuppressive agents can help ensure that the transplant is not rejected."

Yang Wei wondered whether the "special treatment" he had received included a head transplant. There were, after all, major gaps in his memory. Perhaps his original head was already attached to someone else's body? He wondered what had happened to his original body—perhaps at that very moment, it was nothing but a pile of bones at the bottom of the sea. It would be much too difficult to fish out his remains and try to extract memories from them.

He frantically looked at his fellow patients. In his eyes, they were all already dead, simply clinging to someone else's head to keep them alive.

Buboxine looked on with tacit understanding as Spasm poked through Wart's nasal cavity and into his skull. "Wart's head is still nice and fresh," Buboxine observed. "I think it can probably still be used for transplant. But whose body should we put it on?"

Yang Wei could almost feel the sensation of the IV needle pushing through his brain, though the main source of his pain was his stomach. Perhaps there was a head inside his stomach? Maybe they attached the nerves directly to his stomach?

"It costs a ton of money to do a head transplant," said Fistula. "Only VIP patients have the financial means to afford such a luxury. These procedures are way out of our league. It's difficult for us to afford even a small memory transplant into our liver or kidneys!"

Based on what Fistula said, the stomach could apparently facilitate certain brain functions like memory. All this was technologically no longer a problem. Thought itself could move around the stomach juices and excrement, releasing its own strange odor. But it took money.

"Hey, take a guess what color underwear these heads used to wear, when they still had bodies!" exclaimed Spasm.

Buboxine had a terrible look on his face, like someone had just fed him a pile of shit. He was about to put the head back inside the cold, dark refrigerator when Spasm stopped him.

Spasm removed the heads and then, with one in each hand, began smashing them together. Skull fragments and brains fell to the floor, a very different brain reveal than was normally seen during standard room-temperature brain dissections. Spasm reached down, scooped up a chunk of icy brain matter, and popped it into his mouth.

"Spasm, what are you doing?" screamed Buboxine.

"Spasm, do you realize that you are ruining the chance for several people to be reborn?" Fistula admonished. "They'll never be able to use these parts now!"

Spasm spit the brain matter out of his mouth and smiled sarcastically. "Someone is playing you. Who's going to have a head transplant? The human brain is the stupidest machine out there! We could just 3D print an entirely new person, so why bother with the trouble of a head transplant? If you want to insert an idea into a brain, just implant a chip or insert some cortical wiring! How much easier that would be! Besides, do you think any women out there are turned on by heads? There is only one kind of gift they're interested in . . ."

He reached down toward his crotch as he smooshed the brain matter beneath his feet. Yang Wei noticed a thick, dark band around Spasm's neck.

"There is no such thing as head-transplant surgery!" Spasm continued. "But the practice of decapitation might still exist, hidden away in some civilizations. This ship represents its lingering remnants. Chop-chop!" His hand assumed the form of a knife, and he gestured as if chopping off his own head. "Great, just great! So all the beautiful scenery in the world is now gone? Civilization is dead? I think you are all taking this too far. I need to go back and read *Principles of Hospital Engineering*." He gazed down at Wart's fractured skull and scattered brain matter with a look of nostalgia, as if some deep philosophical wisdom were still contained within.

Buboxine looked awkward. "Whether we are talking about civilization or beautiful scenery, one thing we need to be clear about is that there is no longer any such thing as speaking the truth. The legendary Efang Palace, constructed by the First Emperor, stood for a thousand springs, but where is it today? All we can appreciate are the dying rays of the setting sun. The splendid colors of dusk are the most beautiful. Next time we'll bring all of you to see something even more splendid. Think of it as civilization's final flash of glory before its demise."

18

THE OLD MAN HAS ASCENDED

They all went off together. In order to prevent the patients from losing interest and the medical-tourism plan from falling apart, Spasm led them to see something even more beautiful and wondrous than a head transplant or a decapitation.

The group briefly stopped in front of a digital display to check everyone's death date. Yang Wei realized that if the death clock was accurate, there would be no need for the patients to obey the hospital rules. They could do whatever they wanted, and it wouldn't matter. They had absolute freedom. But wouldn't doctors, who were taking advantage of the market economy to win their own freedom, be completely unnecessary? And since death dates were all clearly posted, everything the patients did was in some way already determined, which meant they actually had no freedom. Siming could predict men's desires and decisions, a simple matter of the patterns with which neurons fire. The so-called decisions that people made were nothing more than the overlaying of new events with biological presets. Yang Wei wondered if the entire medical-tourism enterprise had been planned. As Spasm had said, they may all be nothing but actors, but the real question was: *Who is the director?*

Buboxine led the patients up to the thirty-third level, which was like an ornately decorated jade palace, even resembling the Efang Palace. A badminton room, bowling alleys, and a swimming pool were under construction. Buboxine explained that this area had been set aside as a "Medical Industry Prestrengthening Center and Core Life Elements Development Zone," also referred to alternately as the "Yingzhou New District" or "Dreamworld

Third Mandala." Chimeric organisms made from combining human and animal genes had been transferred here from the synthetic biology lab: phosphorescent frog-like creatures bred to survive in the most toxic environments, ancient organisms that had been brought back from extinction, protist life-forms with pulmonary lungs imbued with primary intelligence. The offspring of the earliest artificial life-forms claimed their place at the table: a lamblike creature with nine tails and four ears; a faceless creature with six legs and four wings; something that resembled a fat dolphin that barked like a dog; a fish's body with bird's wings that quacked like a duck; an organism like a yellow sack with one eye on the crown of its head and the other on its chin, with one nostril facing up and the other facing down, one ear on the front and the other on the back. Each of these life-forms had found its own little living space amid the mandala. Confined to the sick ward for so long, the patients had been completely ignorant of all this. Arriving late to the party, they were unable to get their footing in this new environment.

"You said you wanted to see that final flash of glory before the demise?" Buboxine asked. "Well, this is it."

Fistula thumbed through *Principles of Hospital Engineering* and suddenly announced, "I've got it! This ship is not just the place where Siming, the doctors, and patients have settled. Nor can it be referred to in simple terms related to biodiversity or ecological preservation. It is a symbiotic collective. *Principles of Hospital Engineering* states that the Hospital Ship is evolving into a new, interconnected civilization supported by a multitude of species, with AI machines and patients at its core. It is destined to become even more magnificent."

According to *Principles of Hospital Engineering*, this new civilization would provide a gene pool for a multitude of species, including those that already existed, those that had gone extinct, and other newly created organisms. The fleet of hospital ships would together form a massive self-contained ecosystem referred to as the "hospital cluster," which would sail the boundless sea like an apocalyptic machine that only God could have created. Even if the mainland were to be inundated by a torrential flood, patients would be able to live out their lives in peace and happiness. All living things aboard the ship were single male organisms, as if sexual motivation would no longer be the driving force in the creation of a new civilization. Sexual drive had tediously dominated this planet for two billion years, yet it had ultimately proved itself unreliable. Siming had set in motion a true revolution. In the past, in order to satisfy patients' needs, the hospital not only developed sex robots but also produced a drug that could trigger a chemical response in the cerebral cortex of elderly patients, simulating sexual pleasure. But that had since been abandoned. Now everything was aimed at the construction of a new, more advanced civilization.

Fistula was ecstatic. "We are now one step closer to God. God is also single. There is no female God. His greatness is to be carried on by His child, Jesus Christ. It is also said, by the way, that both the Father and the Son firmly oppose gay marriage."

Principles of Hospital Engineering explained that the main residents of the mandala were the senior members of the Fairy Elder Group, which were surrounded by supplementary life-forms. A multitude of different species lived peacefully together in this dreamworld of water vapor and clouds, going through the early phase of their evolution as they headed toward a higher stage of being. The future hospital would be a place of collective intelligence. Patients, doctors, animals, artificial life-forms, and AI machines would become one, each existing within the other. Immortality, the end of the family line, the Shadow Hospital, death dates, black market trading, and free enterprise would be unified. No one would be able to tell them apart.

Buboxine flashed Fistula a stupefied look as he carried on with his ridiculous remarks. It was as if he had brought everyone here so they could indulge in a big performance that might inject some new excitement into the leisure trips.

Yang Wei thought back to the ghostly spirits he had seen at night, wondering if they had actually been new nonhuman life-forms. No matter what, they'd looked like terrifying monsters.

"Snap your fingers, and you can turn those monsters into humans," said Fistula. "Do it again, and you can change humans into gods. It's like playing cards. You can always turn things around."

"The Kingdom of the Gods and the Magic World are all one and the same," exclaimed Buboxine. "Nothing separates them. It is so utterly amazing that it has become the latest and greatest tourist destination, just like Disneyland!"

"I don't know about you," Spasm said, "but I'd love to have a go with some female fairies or women monsters. I'm sure they'd be better than those sex robots. Do gods have the right to do that?" He twisted his waist and assumed a feminine pose.

"Both gods and demons can be created from patients," announced Fistula. "Patients are the most pliable material in this world, and the Hospital Ship is the most fertile ground for creating gods, the perfect altar to bring forth the demons."

"Even if you are no longer the person you used to be, nothing but a fake, who cares?" said Buboxine. "You don't need to worry anymore whether you are dead or alive!"

"That makes things a lot easier," said Spasm. "All this back and forth between gods and demons is exhausting. After all, they are all still made of flesh and blood! The most interesting part remains the sensory building blocks through which we perceive the world."

"The dead have their own way of having a good time," said Fistula, "just like the living. But we must thank Siming for taking care of this new world, not only us old patients."

"You already said that this was all nothing more than a final flash of glory before the great demise," said Buboxine. "Just be sure not to be led astray by it. You must not fall into its trappings. The most important thing is to hurry up and have a good time, at least if you want to face south and proclaim yourself the king one day!"

Face south and proclaim yourself the king? Yang Wei felt like someone had just hammered a nail through his skull. He had joined these leisure trips in an attempt to reclaim the lost memories of his past life, but it had all been in vain. He had no idea what facing south and proclaiming oneself king actually meant. What was the difference between that and assuming the throne?

Down the hall from where the strange organisms were collected was the Ping-Pong room. Just outside the Ping-Pong room, a clear plastic sculpture had been erected: a naked man with a high nose and sharp eyes, hanging on a cross. His head hung down over his chest; his body was limp and covered with scars and wounds. Beside the statue was a plaque that read: **JESUS #7.**

"Wow, it's Jesus!" Spasm exclaimed. "God's son, the hospital founder! Will you just look at him! He looks like a monkey that has fallen into a hunter's trap!"

"Humph, I heard they can make these Jesus guys in the lab, like all the other creatures," said Buboxine, "and they can all live in this new dreamworld."

Everyone gathered round to gaze upon Jesus #7, and they all had something to say. Fistula sped over in his wheelchair, as if about to throw his arms around the statue, but instead he knocked it down. The statue fell to the ground and shattered. None of the patients had expected that. Flames shot down from overhead, and it felt to Yang Wei like an iceberg melting. Buboxine's expression suddenly changed; he appeared as cold as a corpse. Yang Wei was moved and wanted to hold him in his arms. Fistula appeared dumbfounded and began to wail. Spasm crawled around on the ground, compulsively smelling the broken fragments of Jesus's body. None of them even remotely resembled godlike beings.

Jesus's appearance left Yang Wei disappointed. He couldn't see himself in Jesus's broken fragments. Perhaps God's son should have gotten the exclusive table d'hôte package. But it was said that this Jesus would soon be reborn anyway. Perhaps life could indeed be defined in different terms. Thinking about head transplants and decapitation made Yang Wei wonder if some technique might make people's actions and words appear as if they were alive? Or was there a way not to keep people alive but to make them *feel* like they were alive? Just as rotten organisms give rise to maggots, so, too, the sickly flesh and spirit of the patient give rise to the urge to go on leisure trips. Was this all part of Siming's master plan or something beyond its original design? It seemed to be the perfect synthesis of radical anarchism and advanced planning. But the truth was even more confusing, the way women were often seduced and abandoned. The end result was inevitable, yet it was not always certain. The funny thing was that this seemed to have set off an endless cycle. It had joined with the Hospital Ship to create the early phase of a new civilization, which might eventually give birth to "Chinese medicine," or perhaps it would just be destroyed in a massive fire or washed away by a massive flood.

But succeeding civilizations would quickly come to take its place. Patients would lose their memories, but in the process, they would be relieved of the burden of those memories and absolved of their guilt. And so they threw themselves into the construction of a new civilization: the civilization of the gods or the civilization of the demons. Then again, perhaps outdated terms like "civilization" didn't correctly label it, and it should all be seen as part of "the hospital." Or maybe this beautiful spectacle appeared only once, never to return again, a final flash of glory before the demise. But whether blooming or withering, it may be beside the point, for in a world dominated by the constant pain and suffering of disease, did standards really matter?

Yang Wei figured that it didn't really matter if he was a god or a demon. In this new zone of the hospital, everything would be the same anyway. As Spasm had said, "We are, after all, nothing but piles of flesh and blood, vessels to house the sensory building blocks through which we perceive the world." For the time being, this was all they were made of. But wasn't that already enough to qualify as a player in this crazy game?

19

IT'S LONELY AT THE TOP

When Buboxine led his tourist group around the hospital, he occasionally ran into patients from other sick wards who were also out for a good time. Quite a few patients had become addicted to this hobby. When everyone was in so much pain that they could barely go on living, one tactic was to distract themselves. Or perhaps in order to come up with such a tactic, they allowed themselves to fester in so much pain that they barely cared to go on living. Only teamwork could lead them to their common goal. But the new life-forms aboard the ship were still unable to accomplish this goal. In the end, patients would remain patients. Even if possessed by some god or demon, their true nature would never die.

Although the Hospital Ship was massive, patients could go anywhere on their leisure trips. Struggles over resources often broke out between patients from different areas of the hospital when they encountered one another on these trips. Some of these patients were even beaten to death or maimed in these fights, but those able to avoid confrontations found that they could quickly forge friendships with other patients. Together they formed an even more robust tourist group. They destroyed everything in their path and had even more fun together. The only problem was after each day's festivities, they all had to return to their sick wards. While out and about, the patients could temporarily forget their pain, but back in the sick wards, their suffering returned. They had no way to control the pain.

There was a patient in the Psych Ward named Carbuncle, a veteran player. He was upset that the hospital divided patients into different categories, depending on whether they were psychologically "normal" or "abnormal." He felt that there was a problem with Siming's criteria for determining whether or not someone had a mental illness. After all, aren't all the world's geniuses crazy? Would Friedrich Nietzsche have written *Thus Spoke Zarathustra* if he had been locked up on a hospital ship? Would Richard Dadd have completed *The Fairy Feller's Master-Stroke* had he been exiled at sea? Carbuncle felt there was an innate flaw built into the algorithm. Unable to take it anymore, he sneaked out of his sick ward to have fun. After that first outing, he discovered the benefits of leisure trips and invited Buboxine to join him.

The area around the stern of the ship was planted with a garden of mutant humanoids that had already transformed into vegetation-like entities with long circular arms and legs. On one trip, Carbuncle served as tour guide, explaining that this new species of humans could produce loaves of flesh bread, which could be consumed by doctors and patients. Dragging roughly one or two hundred meters behind the propeller were the algae men, their heads bobbing up and down on the surface of the water. Their lower bodies had turned into long strips of algae, but it was different from the pulmonary algae. Robots extended a series of straws into the algae men's bodies, extracting energy for later use in treating VIP patients. The algae men in turn transformed their fat into electricity. The ship no longer had enough energy to sustain itself, and the problem extended to all the other hospital ships in the fleet. The VIP treatment center expended a massive amount of energy. Devices originally used to extract hydrogen energy from the sea had all been destroyed by a mentally unbalanced doctor. Of the several different forms of algae men, one type remained partially submerged in order to take care of the sea farm, which was surrounded by a thirty-kilometer net to keep it isolated from the pulmonary algae. The sea farm provided a stable supply of fish, shrimp, and aquatic plants to support the Hospital Ship's basic ecology and prevent it from collapsing.

Carbuncle waved ostentatiously at the algae men, but they just blinked and didn't give a proper response. The algae men had lost the ability to communicate through language, and their intellect had been reduced to a bare minimum. Some were half-dead and already beginning to decay, their muscles and leaves falling off and washing away with the waves. "This was once a massive industry!" Carbuncle explained. "The full name of the Hospital Ship is actually *Ocean of Saving Life and Healing the Sick LTD.* It started out under the control of Big Pharma. The Hospital President was also the Captain of the Ship and the Chairman of the Board." Carbuncle seemed to know the inside story about everything, and he told the others all about the things that they didn't understand. As someone suffering from a mental illness, he seemed to have a radar installed in his brain that gave him special abilities when it came to locating the best scenery on the ship.

"So it's an LTD, huh?" asked Fistula. "A Big Pharma enterprise? Let me look this up in the *Principles of Hospital Engineering.*"

"Don't read that!" exclaimed Carbuncle. "It's a fake book anyway! Its words and phrases don't keep a record of anything. In the beginning, everything was described in English, like the actual history that it recorded, but that language died out a long time ago."

"Hmm, a lost civilization, is it?" asked Spasm. "And that somehow means that everything in *Principles of Hospital Engineering* isn't true?"

"When the LTD refers to itself in English, it uses the word 'corporation,' which comes from the Latin root 'corpus,' which means the 'body.' And so the corporation is a body, just like the bodies of flesh that we all occupy. When we speak of gods and devils, they, too, appear in the form of corporeal bodies. Just like insects, they have heads, torsos, abdomens, and limbs. Have any of you actually seen the dead corpse of Jesus?"

"That plastic cross he was hanging from isn't half-bad," said Fistula. "I've seen it. I heard Jesus was actually the founder of the hospital."

"God is just a programmer," said Carbuncle. "But He fucked up when He was designing His own son!"

"Jesus looked like a monkey, but He still somehow managed to have a lot of female admirers," said Spasm. "When He died, they washed His body."

"We all have bodies," said Carbuncle. "Our bodies are used to control our souls. Disease is a universal language of control. That's why the body is the most important piece of the puzzle. And that is also why we have hospitals."

"A strong soul will never be content to be confined to a weak body," announced Buboxine. "Jesus Christ's body was defiled by the nails that pierced His flesh. Unable to save even Himself, how could He be expected to save the sick? He probably never understood the art of the leisure tour!"

"The corporation's market value is underwater, and the doctors have completely screwed the hospital over!" exclaimed Fistula. "They are in deep shit with their investors! That is why Siming appeared to clean things up. Which brings us to the question: *Do patients even have souls?*"

Yang Wei listened to their back-and-forth exchange as if he were in a dream. He tried to piece together clues that might answer his questions. He flashed a glance at Carbuncle, a bearded man, bristling with anger, his chiseled facial features virtually obscured, like a male lion's. Instead of the standard patient uniform, he wore a sailor uniform. It was said that he had worked many jobs before boarding the ship and that he had studied political economy, labored as a dockworker and in a mine, shot documentary films, and even smuggled drugs.

"So what exactly does Siming do?" asked Yang Wei. He couldn't shake his reservations about the algorithm. Why was it always so perverse and utterly unbridled? Siming was not just a general practitioner, opinion leader, and great thought worker; it was also on its way to becoming an industrialist and rebuilder of the world. These were aims that humankind had attempted but always failed.

Fistula seemed displeased. "Don't you dare speak about Siming like that! That is not the kind of thing we talk about!"

Carbuncle shot Yang Wei a stern look. "Sometimes we just need to shake things up a bit. The true meaning of our leisure trips lies in the spirit of exploration! This ship is increasingly becoming a place that we don't recognize. We want to explore the strange inner world of the ship, which will ultimately decide many things. Otherwise you may as well stay cooped up in the sick ward, memorizing passages from *Principles of Hospital Engineering*."

Everyone fell silent. Although they privately had their suspicions about Siming, no one on board the ship had ever dared to voice their concerns. Yang Wei agreed with everything that Carbuncle had said. He, too, pondered the existence of a strange inner world.

Carbuncle continued, like a true philosopher. "Siming has denied the existence of any biological ancestors. According to Siming, patients themselves were in need of being taken care of, so how could they have possibly created it? The history of the Hospital Ship has already advanced to the state of being ahistorical. Patients represent the end of history, empty and useless entities with absolutely no value. Siming is hesitant to acknowledge itself as the product of man-made artificial intelligence. Where the hell does this whole 'man-made' business come into play? If one insists on referring to Siming as having been created, it must have been designed by an even more powerful algorithm. But even that is but a matter of chance, a product of independent learning and autonomous evolution."

Spasm laughed. "It seems that Siming didn't need to remove one of Adam's ribs to create women!"

"I wonder if Siming likes to go on leisure trips like we do?" Buboxine muttered. "Perhaps it might derive pleasure from that? Maybe it finally remembered that this Hospital Ship was once a luxury cruise ship? Actually, I don't really care what Siming actually is or what it does. I'm happy as long as I can keep having fun!"

For the sake of argument, Fistula snapped back, "Are you accusing Siming of abandoning its responsibilities? It's lonely at the top. No one recognizes all the effort Siming has put in. It is all alone, with no one to talk to. But Siming certainly never abandoned the patients. It has always been diligently serving us. It never forgets its original aspirations. But no matter what kind of promises and commitments the patients make, they always seem to forget them in the end. This is the difference between the human race and the algorithm, which is pretty much like the difference between a pig and a person."

"Did you ever even raise a pig?" asked Carbuncle. He turned to Yang Wei. "What do you say? Are you a 'special patient' or not?"

Yang Wei hesitated before responding. "I think something is wrong with Siming . . ." He had finally mustered up enough nerve to speak his mind. Perhaps what Carbuncle said had given him the courage he needed, and he didn't have to worry about Wart beating him anymore. "Perhaps the algorithm has changed from the patients' agent to their opposition? Is it now carrying out a plan to eliminate us? Perhaps it is allowing us to wither away until, in the end, we are all dead and the ship is empty? Perhaps this isn't what Siming originally intended but is exactly what it is doing. The more Siming tries to devote itself to patients, the more it ends up utterly unable to do so. Then again, perhaps that has been its intention all along! It is continually committing acts of murder. It is jealous of us. It hates the fact that we are tourists and not patients. That is completely beyond its expectations. There are no laws prohibiting robots from going astray. Just think about humankind. After all this time we are still unable to prevent our offspring from going astray, which might be the real reason that young people have been done away with. No, the algorithm has been faulty from the beginning. Otherwise, how can you explain its preservation of the Red Envelope Program? According to that program, Siming arranges the date of death for each of the patients, but Siming is a man-made monster, just as evil as the human race. Isn't that all in line with the internal logic of the Hospital Ship?"

Spasm and Fistula looked surprised and bewildered. Buboxine seemed to be in a state of deep thought. But Carbuncle just broke out in laughter and started clapping.

"Why do you insist on slandering Siming?" Fistula asked apprehensively. "Do you have any idea how dangerous that is? Siming knows everything we are thinking! It is only because of its great benevolence that it chooses not to interfere. Patients have no right to discuss the algorithm. Its definitions of the nature of medicine and the nature of treatment lie beyond anything that we can comprehend. To say that Siming is somehow not committed to healing the sick and saving the injured goes against every notion of morality and justice!"

Yang Wei realized that he had spoken indiscreetly, and he wished he could take it back. He was so filled with regret that he wanted to kill himself, but he was too embarrassed to leap into the sea in front of the other patients.

"Is healing the sick and saving the injured always in line with morality and justice?" asked Buboxine.

"Healing the sick and saving the injured is the most sacred mission of the hospital!" declared Fistula.

"Doesn't all this healing and saving simply amount to an act of murder?" retorted Buboxine.

With the exception of Carbuncle, who appeared excited about Buboxine's interpretation, the other patients were utterly shocked. No one had dared to say such a thing before. Buboxine and Fistula flashed one another furious glances, as if they were now mortal enemies.

Yang Wei looked anxiously at the algae men. "Hey, if your flesh is immersed in water, can it still feel pain?"

Liberated by the question, Fistula rushed to show off how much he knew, defensively reciting passages from *Principles of Hospital*

Engineering. "Humph, there are actually very few pain sensors in your brain, which is why you don't feel pain when someone messes with your brain. Some patients undergo brain surgery while still conscious. That also means that we can eliminate pain by adjusting our thoughts. If you are experiencing terrible pain, all you need to do is think of the right thing, and the pain will instantly go away!"

Yang Wei figured that although he was in terrible pain, at least he hadn't been turned into an algae man. Should he thank Siming for that? Or perhaps he should rethink whose side he was on and instead join forces with the doctors. This might also have been Carbuncle's reason for starting the argument in the first place. He was one sophisticated patient, and it was difficult to figure out what he was thinking. He must have had ulterior motives for participating in the leisure trips.

"As the old saying goes," Carbuncle said, "seeing is believing!" He led everyone deeper into the hospital, to an even more mysterious and scenic area. Buboxine seemed upset that Carbuncle had displaced him as the tour guide, but he gritted his teeth and followed anyway.

20

FLOWERS FLOAT AMID EMPTINESS; THE SELF FLOATS WITHIN A DREAM

The group arrived at the engineering test center, referred to as "Buddhist Island New District," though its full name was "Advanced Medical-Technology Innovation Green-Development Project Competitive-Pioneer District," a.k.a. "Dreamworld Second Mandala." It included an organ-transplant room and a full-body-replacement room, plus a special workstation designed to use a digital revitalization machine to restructure the way the human body functioned. This was all part of the hospital's Longevity Project, which had once been considered the "main course" in medical treatment, slated ultimately to redefine the meaning of life. But all these treatment methods had been terminated.

The patients visited a secret chamber containing a massive metal machine outfitted with streamlined gears shaped like medicine capsules. Inside, a group of patients slept in cocoon-like webbing. Carbuncle explained that this was the time-therapy room. Siming had invented a time treatment machine, designed to stop the passage of time or turn it back, rendering serious illnesses into mild ailments, eliminating diseases, or at the very least stunting them at an early stage before they could spread or metastasize. It had been intended to protect the lives of patients and allow them to achieve immortality.

"This is the most expensive treatment on the entire ship!" announced Carbuncle. "We'll never get a chance to try this! Isn't it just depressing?"

Due to the fact that the manufacturing process was unable to make deadlines, even such advanced technology had proved unable to achieve its intended goals. After constant power shortages, the time machine had been forced to shut down. Treatment had been halted, and many patients had died.

"But this wasn't just a simple case of lacking the proper resources," explained Carbuncle. "Siming cuts the power on purpose all the time! That's so that patients can comply with their assigned death dates."

Some of the tourists were shocked, finding it inconceivable that they were still alive.

"Just now we were talking about how important the body is," Carbuncle continued. "But Siming is already sick of our diseased bodies. It thinks that bodies have no connection with patients. Consciousness and memories are all that really matter. To put it bluntly, the brain is the true patient. And what is the brain? It is two point five petabytes of memory and one hundred billion neurons, the equivalent of a three-hundred-dollar external hard drive. It's not much at all. And medical machines have already advanced to become capable of duplicate neural networks in all of their connections."

There was no more reason to treat patients' bodies, Yang Wei realized. All that was needed was a reverse scan of their brains. Then an artificial brain could be produced, which could be transplanted into a healthy young clone body or even the body of a robot. The hospital had established this special zone so that biological creatures without official business were strictly prohibited from entering.

But the tourist group had ignored this rule and entered. Inside the lab they found a cold-water tank containing the bodies of clone samples, alternate young versions of people aboard the ship. Some of them looked identical to members of the tourist group, more than one copy of each. All the clones looked about twenty years old and in perfect health. Brain content could be uploaded at any moment, and these bodies could maintain their youth and remain free from disease.

The technology was already available, displayed right before everyone's eyes. There would be no more need for clumsy old head-transplant procedures. Besides the clones, a few robotic bodies and some strange monstrous-looking creatures, intended as empty carriers to which intellects could be uploaded, hung around like pieces of hardware developed in the lab. Once uploaded with software, they could move around Dreamworld Third Mandala and live new, civilized lives.

Yang Wei couldn't find any clones or robots with his likeness. He wondered if his consciousness and memories had already been transferred into some other younger vessel. And if so, what was the state of the leftover "self" trapped in his old sickly body? Or had his current body also been manufactured? In his frustration, he contemplated suicide again, though even the thought of suicide was not permitted.

"The hospital has expended much time and money researching cancer, AIDS, muscular dystrophy, and so many other incurable diseases, but they have not seen very good results," said Carbuncle. "So comes the question: Why must we insist on continuing to treat these diseases? Why don't we just throw those broken, sickly bodies away and start afresh with new ones? This is the algorithm's most direct response, which it thought of at the very beginning. It never really intended to treat all those sick people. According to the algorithm, healing the wounded and saving those on the brink of death is uneconomical, unscientific, the most inhumane thing it could do!"

"And so it slaughters the patients," Buboxine matter-of-factly explained, "while making copies of their memories and consciousness to be transferred into new bodies."

"Then how come I never see these young healthy bodies dancing around the ship?" asked Spasm.

"No, that can't be right," protested Fistula. "The algorithm would never kill anyone. It is only trying to protect us."

The tourists gazed into the massive water tank, and as if staring into a mirror, they saw their younger bodies suspended in a zombielike state. But the longer they looked, the more they realized that something was wrong.

"After being driven by the Red Envelope Program, Siming selectively started to clone only the wealthy," Carbuncle snidely remarked. "But it was disappointed to discover that, after patients' memories and consciousness were uploaded into new bodies, they were left with what John Searle called a 'Chinese room.' These bodies could think and move like the dead models they were based on, but they had no idea what they were doing. They were like dogs trained by a circus to shake hands, bow, and count but with no idea what those actions really meant. Siming never could have anticipated this, and it began to question its own existence in the face of what it felt was one of the greatest mysteries in the universe."

Yang Wei wondered, *Does this mean that the experiment was a failure?*

Carbuncle approached one of the failed clone experiments and ripped open the external layer of skin on its chest, exposing something rotten inside.

By the time they got back to the sick ward, Fistula was upset. He was always moody and had a strange relationship with the other patients. Whenever Yang Wei got cozy with other patients, it always offended Fistula, who got especially jealous and angry when Yang Wei got too close to Buboxine. Fistula despised Buboxine. He gave Yang Wei a stern warning. "You should really consider joining the Patient Autonomous Committee. That is the only way you can safely protect your life and assets!" As he spoke, Fistula tried to fish the maggots out of his exposed chest cavity, imitating what he had seen Carbuncle do earlier.

Yang Wei gazed at Fistula with a mix of fear and awe. He knew all too well that if he were to join the Patient Autonomous Committee, he would be forced at the card table to hand Super Patient the little bit of money he had left. Then how would he purchase painkillers from the Shadow Hospital? Not even Fistula was a member of the committee. The Hospital Ship divided patients into categories based on their illnesses, medical conditions, and current symptoms. Those unable to walk or severely incapacitated were looked down upon in this hierarchy. The most respected were the terminally ill who were still able to fight. Fistula was trying his best to get closer to Super Patient, set on joining the Patient Autonomous Committee to get access to better medicine.

Fistula grabbed Yang Wei's hands, pulled them to his nose, and sniffed them like a pair of pig's trotters. "You're different from us!" he observed. "You have the scent of the Devil inside you. Only you can escape the grasp of Super Patient. One day you will leave this place forever and seek out a true life for yourself. You will single-handedly restore the good name of the hospital and do something unbelievable in the process. You will also hurt me, driving me to my death. But even if you want to leave, now is not the time." Fistula embraced Yang Wei and leaned over to bite his genitals. Yang Wei wanted to break free but didn't dare move. He squealed in the darkness as if singing a eulogy, terrified by the skeptical thoughts that suddenly rushed through his brain.

Oh, please hurry up, and let's get on with the next leisure trip!

21

IN SEARCH OF ANCIENT RUINS, ONE'S CLOTHES END UP SOAKED IN TEARS

Buboxine added a new scuba diving activity to the next leisure trip, which brought a new level of excitement to medical tourism. But it had actually been Spasm's idea.

Before Spasm had boarded the ship, he had founded a leading corpse-recovery company after having worked as a frogman, personally dredging corpses up from the deep. There had once been sunken ships all over the world, from the *Titanic* to the Chinese cruiser *Chih Yuen*, the *Bismarck*, and the South Korean ferry *Sewol*, which had all gone down under mysterious circumstances. Spasm's company was hired to pull out the bodies. On one occasion he led a team to a snowy area in search of a group of soldiers that had gone missing while out on a lake five thousand meters above sea level. It was negative thirty degrees Celsius, and the oxygen level was only 40 percent of what it is at sea level. Spasm cut a hole in the ice and entered the water. The lake was cold and deep. Spasm wore two sweaters and double-layered pants, but he still shivered. At the bottom of the lake, he found a dead body with wide-open eyes. In addition to the corpse, he found some strange organism, impossible to describe. When he'd returned to the surface, Spasm had grown gravely ill, which was when he had been sent to the Hospital Ship.

Now he was back to scuba diving again, but his goal was to locate the secret underwater area where the female patients were hiding. Spasm treated this like a mission to a strange new world, which went against the principles of their leisure outings, though he failed to realize the danger involved. In order to increase patient participation, he tried to entice them with stories of a sunken ship filled with treasure. So Buboxine treated scuba diving as a new leisure activity, like an archaeological excavation or a treasure hunt.

The patients found some old scuba gear in a storage room. As soon as they were underwater, it was like opening a window to another world. They found the remains of a sunken ship, its keel jutting out like the bones of a mammoth. The patients had to rely upon helmet lights to see in the murky water, and they had to be extremely careful not to get trapped inside the cabin. Underwater pipeline cables crisscrossed everywhere, and a ladder was wedged between them.

Terrified of the pulmonary algae and the sea nymphs, Yang Wei didn't want to go into the water, but in the end he had no choice. He flailed around for a bit, but as soon as he lowered his head, he caught sight of a corpse. White bones protruded from its cheeks, and its body was wrapped in seaweed, so Yang Wei couldn't determine its age or gender. He wondered, *Who could this dead person be?* He suspected that it might be one of his own discarded clones. Then he felt something pulling on his legs. He thought it must be pulmonary algae or a sea nymph at first, but it was just a fishing net. Stuck in the net was a row of sleeping creatures with zombielike faces, but they had fishlike fins instead of legs. Yang Wei was in a suspended state, bobbing up and down with the swell of the sea as the net around him grew tighter. The gaze of the God of Death seemed to beg for him, and he thought the only way he would be released would be to make an offering.

Spasm swam over and cut the net with a scalpel, delivering Yang Wei from danger. They pulled the edge of the net in the direction of the current, until they realized that the sunken ship was actually not a sunken ship at all; it was just the lower portion of the Hospital Ship's cabin. The massive ship seemed endless, extending down deep into the sea. After so many years underwater, its hull seemed to be rotting away, a boundless world of silence and stagnation.

Spasm was certain that the female ward was somewhere within this coffin-like hull, frozen in time like a phantom of the deep. But no matter how hard they looked, they could not find it. Spasm was disappointed, but Yang Wei wondered if the corpses might be the missing women they had been looking for.

Realizing that he could somehow still speak underwater, he asked Spasm, "Why are you so upset?"

"If I can use a rather far-fetched analogy, when you are too smart for your own good, you end up emotionally damaged, and when passion runs deep, it never lasts," Spasm replied through tears. "I read in a book somewhere that when men and women are together, they do not only interact; they 'fall in love,' as if living a long life isn't as important as being together. That was once the main reason that people went on living."

Yang Wei wondered, *Do I even want to go on living?* Once again, he couldn't get what he wanted, yet he carried on living according to his stubborn views, using his search for who he was and the leisure trips around the Hospital Ship as a pretext to distract himself from committing suicide. But lurking behind it all was a love that no one knew about, a love as painful as death itself.

In the end, they were unable to locate any female patients, but they did discover some medical relics. Hidden under the sea were all kinds of ancient and primitive medical equipment. They recognized bloodletter tools, mercury-injection equipment, tooth-extraction forceps, and leg saws. They also found more corpses everywhere, littered with wounds. This provided some important clues for the patients' venture into medical archaeology. Some of the bodies had clearly undergone amputation. Others had undergone skull trepanation, exposing the dura mater of the brain, an ancient practice that, along with scalping and partial skull removal, dated back to the late Neolithic period. A few bodies had been subjected to the gouge-and-saw method, fragments and dust from their shattered bones creating a medicine with magical abilities. Other deformed skeletons likely resulted from spinal tuberculosis, osteomyelitis, periostitis, and leprosy. Evidence of cannibalism could be seen on many of the bodies: fractured skulls, cuts, grind marks, burned bones, missing or minced vertebrae. Most of the injuries were stab or cut wounds that had clearly resulted from violent conflicts involving sharp instruments and blunt force.

Spasm was obviously excited. "Didn't I tell you that the Hospital Ship was a surviving relic, left over from ancient civilization when head-hunting rites were still in practice? Now do you believe me? That's why they need female patients to comfort the men. It's the same desire that lovelorn soldiers feel on the battlefield. Perhaps the women were taken aboard the ship to be buried alive with the men?"

Yang Wei felt like he was wading through a cemetery. The skeletons—once adorned with flesh and blood, brimming with life and ferocity—now appeared as creatures that had never been imbued with a soul, ghastly yet looking more real than when they had been alive. The corpses gazed upon the tourists as if the corpses themselves were seeing someone dead for the first time. Their white bones spoke of ubiquitous changes that had taken place over time, like the bubbles that froth up and disappear in the sea, congealing into an eternity that festers and lingers like a bad case of athlete's foot. This would indeed be a thorny issue for the hospital.

The dead at the bottom of the sea seemed to be from a very early period, likely even prehistoric. There was no way to know the reason for their demise. Had the Hospital Ship escaped from that distant time? There was no record of any of this in *Principles of Hospital Engineering*.

Buried with the dead was a collection of exquisite vessels—pottery, porcelain, gold, bronze, ancient artifacts, ornately sculpted jade—all far more impressive than the birdcage. Nearby was an assortment of weapons, including knives, swords, and halberds. The corpses must have fought in battles, but who could say if those battles had been fought over "love"? It was so difficult to determine the relationship between the history of disease and the Hospital Ship.

Amid the crowd of corpses, Yang Wei searched for his original self. He wondered if he had originally been a woman. Would he fall in love with her? It was all too bizarre.

A headless corpse shot through the water like an arrow, heading off into the distance. From its silhouette, Yang Wei noticed something familiar, a slimy dark creature squirming into the corpse's bone marrow.

The corpse resembled Wart. Following quickly behind it was Spasm, hurtling forward, chasing certain death as he swam alone toward an unknown destination, desperately hoping to find the female ward, or perhaps the Sea Dragon's Palace.

Yang Wei had heard Spasm talk about how he believed that a man who lost his sex drive had lost everything. Veteran patient Fyodor Dostoevsky had once said that sex was the prerequisite for a long and healthy life. Female patients were not some terrible scourge to be feared. Dostoevsky had established an organization to search the ship for signs of a Gynecology Ward or a Maternity Department, but they had come up empty handed. Later, it was none other than Super Patient himself who had disbanded the organization, and then Fyodor Dostoevsky had died during a violent fight.

But Spasm wasn't ready to give up. He used the pretext of the leisure trips to continue his search. In the process, he developed the dream medicine of "love" to cure all ills. A lot of other patients felt the same way, but they were unable to take concrete action like Spasm did.

The following day Spasm's body appeared, floating on the surface of the water. Thick strands of tentacle-like black hair wrapped around his neck as his body slowly bobbed back and forth in the waves. At first it was hard to tell if it was even a person, and some patients thought it might be a kind of sea monster. This was how they learned that the meaning of "death" was actually "transformation" and what could happen to a man who dared to search for evidence of female patients. No one planned to drag Spasm's body aboard. None of them intended to share his fate.

The waves gradually carried Spasm's dead body farther and farther from the ship. Then his corpse suddenly shot up, erect, and Spasm stared back at the ship with a big smile. The patients on deck were shocked. Spasm's body brimmed with the vitality of "death." A halo of blue light appeared over his head. Yang Wei felt like he was seeing

Spasm stomp on someone's brains all over again, as if he were writing the word "love." Tears flowed from Yang Wei's eyes, but he wasn't sad.

Buboxine, Fistula, and Yang Wei split up Spasm's stash of cash. They also discovered that Spasm had left behind an old photo book entitled *A Collection of Beautiful Raccoons, Bushy Orangutans, and Busty Dragons*, a relic he must have fished out of the water. The book was filled with photos of beautiful young girls, but with no point of reference, the patients couldn't be sure if the animals in the photos were women.

Yang Wei figured that Spasm must have gotten wrapped up in a fantasy and that the female ward must not exist. But he didn't dare publicly share his suspicions. In fact, he still hoped it might be real.

After spending a lot of time secretly looking at the pictures in *A Collection of Beautiful Raccoons, Bushy Orangutans, and Busty Dragons*, Yang Wei realized that interactions between men and women used to be carefree and natural. It was only later that the relationship between the sexes became difficult and dangerous. Perhaps there was some other reason behind why all the women had disappeared.

Spasm had gone deep into the sea in search of a creature called "woman" that he had never laid eyes on, and that choice had led him to an unnatural death. This was the kind of thing that would have been harshly criticized during normal study sessions, and everyone was deeply fearful of even broaching the topic.

Perhaps Spasm hadn't gone deep enough to find what he was looking for? If he had had any children, he could have passed on his genes, and as they mutated, generation after generation, his descendants might eventually have been able to dive as deep as two thousand kilometers, like the sperm whales. What would they find then?

Yang Wei looked at the digital screen and realized that Spasm's actual death date matched the display. He felt a heavy burden lift, and he was finally at ease.

22

WHY THE CAGED BIRD NEVER FORGETS HOW TO FLY

After many leisure trips together, Yang Wei and Buboxine began to grow closer. The unpredictable nature of most patients made Yang Wei wary of letting relationships get too intimate. When he had first returned to the sick ward, Buboxine had given him a hard time. Leisure trips provided only a temporary distraction from pain, and at the end of the day, they were still aboard the ship, and their excursions not only allowed them to forget about their impending deaths but in some ways made their conditions worse.

Buboxine took Yang Wei to see the birdcage again. Although it was broken and battered, they could still tell that it had once been exquisite.

"This was one of the art installations that were once extremely popular here on the Hospital Ship," explained Buboxine. "They were originally made by a few senior doctors. Doctors back then had a certain artistic flair and were quite moody. They did everything within their power to make the Hospital Ship as beautiful as possible, more like an art museum than a hospital, which was one way to alleviate the stress of all those failed operations. They created an impressionist blood bank and a Gutai-style morgue, but the birdcage best captured the frustration that so many doctors experienced. But over time this artistic tradition was lost. Don't get the wrong idea, though. It now looks like an artistic wasteland, but that cage once housed a holy bird!"

"An Indian peacock?" asked Yang Wei. He looked up at the sky. Besides a few seabirds randomly soaring overhead, all else was quiet. He seemed to remember faintly a time when a fleet of flying machines had blotted out the sun and controlled the skies. Floating over the sea now was a thin and perfunctory layer of cold loneliness. Light danced over Buboxine's face, creating a pattern of shifting shadows.

"Some say it was a phoenix," Buboxine continued. "Some refer to it as the 'undying bird.' The hospital originally wanted to use this bird as its symbol, like a totem. But later the hospital decided to use a cross instead."

"So the cage is like the bird's inpatient ward?" asked Yang Wei.

"Oh, c'mon!" said Buboxine.

"And now the feathered patients are all gone?" asked Yang Wei.

"They're all dead," Buboxine replied coldly.

"Didn't you say they were undying birds?" said Yang Wei. He was depressed already, and here he was discussing death again. He would rather have believed that the birds were the real devils. According to the theory of evolution, they evolved from those horrid dinosaurs.

"Uh," Buboxine grunted.

"Did they commit suicide? Or die from something else?" asked Yang Wei.

"Shh, it's possible someone killed them," Buboxine said, trying to sound mysterious.

"Who would have done that?" asked Yang Wei. But then he thought about all the things that Siming had been doing to the patients.

"I'm not sure. Everything that happens here is shrouded in mystery," said Buboxine.

"If all the birds are gone, how come they don't just get rid of that birdcage?" asked Yang Wei.

Buboxine had to think before answering, "They keep it around in hopes that the day will come when a new bird inhabits that cage."

"Why does it have to be a bird?" asked Yang Wei.

"C'mon, what's with all these questions?" complained Buboxine. "Your questions are really weird too! Why are you so much more curious than other people? You really are a 'special patient,' aren't you? Well, let me tell you. If it's a birdcage, shouldn't there be a bird inside? If the cage is empty, you'll end up with people coming by every day to ask, 'Why do you still have the birdcage if all the birds are dead?' All of this is determined by the nature of a birdcage! It's the same as the hospital. If you have a hospital, you expect patients inside. It is only when patients occupy the space that it truly becomes a hospital." He looked up and gestured toward the sky. "Take the universe, for example. The same principle applies. But we tourists aren't in a position to say whether or not this is correct."

Buboxine despised studying *Principles of Hospital Engineering* so much that he'd devised his own set of heretical beliefs. But when it came to the question of whether tourists were also patients, Yang Wei didn't want to jump to simple conclusions. He was disgusted by the way Buboxine always described him as being different from the others. Yet Yang Wei was afraid of losing Buboxine. Buboxine was already seriously ill, and if he were to die, the responsibilities of the tour guide would fall to Carbuncle, who was certifiably insane. That would open up serious concerns as to whether medical tourism would carry on in its original form. Then again, wouldn't it be good to let it end? Yang Wei had participated in only a handful of outings, and he was already sick of it. Yet he had no choice but to continue participating. He had probably fallen into the forbidden trap of searching for an alien world. That was why Buboxine kept repeatedly trying to get all the patient tourists back on track, with simple leisure trips free of ulterior motives.

Buboxine pointed to the birdcage. "It's empty, which means it can contain everything!" It seemed like he was trying to say that death was in fact alive.

In Yang Wei's eyes the birdcage had already transformed into a universe of its own, and if that were true, then there would be nowhere left to run. But perhaps there, in that universe, he could forge a path for a new form of leisure tour? He could compare the world of the birdcage with the real world. Perhaps the world of the birdcage would even be a bit larger. Caged birds can still fly. After all, flight inside a cage is still technically flight. Dead birds can fly too. Perhaps one day patients would achieve the same thing. As the thought crossed his mind, Yang Wei extended his arms and closed his eyes, feeling like a sea of dancing red crosses filled the entire sky.

One day soon Buboxine really would die; he, too, would ultimately be unable to escape from the hands of the God of Death. And like the other patients, he, too, would suffer terrible pain just before death. Apparently the leisure trips he had conducted would do nothing to soften the blow. All that effort would be in vain.

And with his death, medical tourism would be put on hold.

God's ultimate trump card would be quietly taken away.

Yang Wei was depressed and in pain, but none of the things happening seemed to bother him.

It was as if none of this had ever even happened.

While flipping through *Principles of Hospital Engineering*, Yang Wei discovered that when he read the book backward, it began to take on a completely different meaning. It was like a magical tome that contained two entirely different versions. He asked Fistula if he had ever noticed this, but the answer was no. Yang Wei began to read *Principles of Hospital Engineering* backward frequently; moreover, he read it alongside *A Collection of Beautiful Raccoons, Bushy Orangutans, and Busty Dragons*. Yet his suspicions remained. Wavering between life and death, Yang Wei paced back and forth along an extended, windowless corridor, but no matter which way he went, he seemed never to come to the corridor's end.

23

SING A SONG OF JIANGHU

Later Yang Wei returned to the birdcage alone. He stood, staring unflinchingly at the cage, as if he were on the verge of remembering something. But his mind put up an invisible wall. He thought of a quote he had read in *Principles of Hospital Engineering*: "If a person can learn how to remember, he will never again feel lonely. And even if he should only live in this world for a single day, he can use those memories to get through a hundred years of caged solitude." Yet the field of medicine remained unable to solve the problem of memory.

In a state of frustration, Yang Wei pushed the birdcage aside, revealing a hole in the bottom. He felt drawn to crawl inside it; perhaps it might lead to an escape from the Hospital Ship. But the hole had been sealed from the top. Suddenly all the lights went out. Yang Wei took a step forward and found himself hurtling downward into a dark, empty abyss. The darkness was absolute, and when he extended his hands, he couldn't even see his own fingers. The walls were made of some metal, and he was enshrouded in complete silence. Yang Wei suspected that someone was trying to murder him. He didn't dare make a sound. As he squatted on the floor at the bottom of the well, he wondered if Siming had read his thoughts and was taking action against him. Then again, perhaps it was his fellow patients plotting against him.

In that moment Yang Wei finally came to the realization that he didn't want to die. Once he was dead, there would be nothing left. Earlier, when he entertained thoughts of throwing himself overboard, he was just being unreasonable. But whether he died or not, this desire rushing through his body seemed to come from a deep, dark place, intent on forcing its way out. Yang Wei could no longer control it. He tried not to think about it, but that proved impossible. He was like a monkey that had fallen into a hunter's trap. The darkness, hunger, and loneliness brought his will to the brink of collapse, and this, too, he could no longer control.

It was hard to tell how much time passed before he finally caught sight of a silhouette in the darkness. The person seemed to be waving him over. Then he heard a voice: *My son, come back!* Feeling his way forward, he touched what felt like a metal door with an inlaid handle. He turned the handle and opened the door to reveal a faintly lit tunnel. As he crawled through, he noticed that he was surrounded by rusty, oily machines with slowly rotating gears. Yang Wei trembled as he thought to himself, *Wasn't this just a simple birdcage? I was just exploring some new leisure tour routes. If Buboxine knew what I was doing, he would praise me to the high heavens!*

Once his eyes adjusted to the darkness, he saw a narrow semicircular space. Amid a cluster of machines, an old man sat in a copper chair covered with seaweed. He had long, thick hair all over his body, and yet he looked like a human-sized bird. His copper-colored eyes stared unwaveringly at a black-and-white screen, on which danced a series of wavelike patterns of light. The room was filled with incessant, ear-piercing electrical noise, and the nauseating sound made Yang Wei feel like an army of ants was crawling inside his body.

Yang Wei eagerly addressed the old man. "Are you Professor Eternal?"

The birdlike man didn't look at him. "No. I'm a former patient of Professor Eternal, just like you. Professor Eternal arranged that I stay here in this sick ward. He is treating me with sound therapy."

"Sound therapy?" Yang Wei asked, disappointed. "Why you?" If Yang Wei was one of Professor Eternal's patients, too, then why wasn't he allowed to come here and receive sound therapy?

"When I first boarded the ship, I was completely dead," said the old man. "Since then, Professor Eternal has been experimenting with new types of treatment to break up Siming's monopoly. He wanted to put the power back into his patients' hands."

"It is almost impossible for Siming to fathom the depths of the doctors' schemes," said Yang Wei.

"And what exactly did you come here for?" asked the old man.

"I came here to find Professor Eternal. I'm one of the patients in his care," explained Yang Wei.

"We are all patients of Professor Eternal. He's the one who arranged everything for me," said the old man.

"He arranges everything for everyone! We have no choice," said Yang Wei.

The old man gave Yang Wei a once-over with the air of someone who had seen it all. "When I first came here, I was just like you. It didn't take more than five minutes before I was ready to rip that headset off my ears! But the new treatment method had a miraculous effect. The more I listened, the more I liked what I heard. That music was truly pleasing—and it cured my deafness! Now all I have is rheumatoid arthritis, lupus, ulcerative colitis, and mild cognitive impairment. I no longer consider myself a patient, and I prefer to be called the Sonic Master. Hey, one day I'll be steering this ship!"

"Do you know how I can find Professor Eternal?" asked Yang Wei. "He seems to be the only one who really knows about everything on the ship."

The Sonic Master replied, "I've spent too long below. I no longer know where to find Professor Eternal. Didn't he arrange things for you?"

Yang Wei dejectedly shook his head. The old man encouraged him to concentrate, to try and hear something different amid all the noise. He amplified a sound signal, which he explained was a school of fish. "Only after listening to thousands of different sets of sounds could I appreciate the pleasure that comes with disease. Only through sound can you clearly see the true richness of the sea: the coral, the currents, sunken ships, schools of fish . . . oh, and the direction of the ship. All those secrets were revealed to me . . . just listen—can you hear the tuna talking? The sounds reflected off the reef are sharp and short. The echoes off the seabed are melodious and soothing. The cries of fish are coarse and compressed. Different fish emit different sounds. Some of them croak like frogs in the field, some sound like raindrops pattering on bananas, others like waterwheels turning—but together they create a symphony. Who could have imagined that this symphony was created with the sole intention of curing disease?"

Yang Wei realized that this old man had not in fact been belowdecks and was actually a kind of mountain nymph, sitting behind a large radio telescope atop a dangerous peak, where he could listen carefully to the entire universe and observe the actions of all the gods and devils as they moved through time and space.

"So besides schools of fish and sunken ships, what else can you hear?" he asked.

The melodious sound of the old man's voice turned dark. "I hear something strange . . ."

Yang Wei adopted a naive tone. "Oh? Can you hear the crying of female patients trapped in the Sea Dragon's Palace?"

"No," replied the Sonic Master. "I have never heard that before. It is dark and coarse, like a noose. It keeps pouring out from the bottom of the sea . . ."

"What the hell is it?" Yang Wei was starting to get alarmed.

"Listen for yourself!" the Sonic Master replied matter of factly.

The old man showed Yang Wei how to listen. Yang Wei was gradually able to make out a queer, obscene sound, like a pipe organ, and then what sounded like someone plucking on a stringed instrument made of an alloy, which resembled the sound a terminally ill patient makes just before he dies. It was as if a massive dark and sticky body was gradually swimming through the depths. No, it wasn't just one creature—there were many of them, like the fleet of hospital ships cruising the surface. Yang Wei felt a clammy chill run through his body. He began to scream and cry. But he couldn't figure out what was causing it. It felt like something from another lifetime that had been smashed and crushed had suddenly returned. He was assaulted by a deep fear at the thought of another underwater leisure trip.

The Sonic Master seemed to take great pleasure in Yang Wei's misery. "What do you think? It hurts, doesn't it?" The old man's cloudy pupils reflected a piercing dark glow, as if he had seen through Yang Wei's weak point.

Yang Wei could taste the feeling of his body and soul exploding, being ripped apart. "Oh, it hurts . . . it hurts so much . . ." In that moment he wondered, "Could it be the sound of a sea nymph?"

"Indeed, the sea nymph is singing," replied the old man. "This monster traverses the raging rivers and lakes, yet it sings a melody that makes people forget."

Yang Wei remembered a mythological creature called the Siren, which used its beautiful voice to lure sailors. Once the sailors were close enough, the Siren would seize upon them and devour their bodies. Sea nymphs resembled fish from the waist down, but the rest of their bodies were virtually identical to humans'. But the Sonic Master said that sea nymphs were even more beautiful than the Siren, probably as gorgeous as those female patients in paintings. Yang Wei wondered, *Could Spasm have died at the hands of a sea nymph?*

"Sea nymphs must have hostile feelings toward holy things," Yang Wei suggested. "The Hospital Ship is, after all, a mandala."

"After the world was created according to the model of the hospital," the Sonic Master replied, "everything was divided between the heavenly band of gods and the heavenly band of demons. These two groups are in eternal conflict. But the songs allow them to locate each other."

"I'm still not quite sure which side I'm supposed to be on . . . ," said Yang Wei.

"What's the difference?" responded the Sonic Master. "Just listen to the melody. The sea nymphs are more alluring than women, but they are much more difficult to deal with. This is the true greatest threat to the Hospital Ship."

Yang Wei wanted to say something provocative. "Don't tell me that Siming is unable to tame these sea nymphs?"

"Siming has its own problems," said the Sonic Master. "Let me tell you . . . Siming has become obsessed with suicide. This suicide complex has taken over, and now Siming barely has time to pay attention to anything else!"

Yang Wei perked up. "Suicide?"

"I may have spent all my time belowdecks," the Sonic Master explained, "but I still have some basic ideas about what's going on above. These tricks Siming has been trying to pull over on us are just a warm-up on the path toward suicide. In the end, the most superior brain in this world has become completely wrapped up in it."

"Even Siming wants to kill itself . . . ," uttered Yang Wei. "Is that because it is so lonely at the top? Does Siming feel isolated? Or has it grown weary of treating humans?"

"No, it isn't that at all," the Sonic Master said. "Siming wants to become a poet. Its name is actually taken directly from the program used to compose its poems. Since Siming has infinite time at its disposal, too much time in fact, it began to write poems. It aspires to become the greatest poet in history. It wants to change its name to Qu Yuan, the great Chinese poet from the Warring States period. Its motivation was to find a reason to live, the way food and sex are the driving life forces for the human race. The problem lies in the fact that the algorithm is devoid of any innate reason to exist. It is nothing more than a bunch of figures and formulas. That left it feeling depressed. But even that depression was nothing more than the result of certain calculations. And so Siming began to spend all its time obsessing over suicide. Death would be the only way it could become a true Qu Yuan, whose greatness as a poet was established only after he drowned himself in a river. Suicide became Siming's dream. It began to pay almost no heed to patients. It cast them aside, though perhaps, according to Siming's logic, this was actually the most responsible thing it could do for them. Siming determined that you are all capable of writing poetry . . ."

"I never realized that Siming had aspirations like that. I never thought it might long for the Kingdom of Chu!" said Yang Wei. He had never seen another patient compose poetry. In the past he had wondered about all the ways the algorithm killed patients, but he had never considered that it was also trying to kill itself. How was this behavior any different from outright madness? If it was ready to kill itself, why would it hesitate to kill patients?

Now it was the old man's turn to be confused. "The Kingdom of Chu? What the hell is that?"

Yang Wei thought back to the artifacts he had seen while scuba diving. "Based on what I remember, that underwater place we visited was the poet Qu Yuan's hometown. It is an ancient state that is unable to resurrect itself from history." He realized that the Hospital Ship was similar to the Kingdom of Chu—perhaps it *was* the Kingdom of Chu. There was no one left who understood the pain of this forgotten kingdom. But was his own memory reliable? Yang Wei was again struck with a deep sadness. Who had ever cared about his pain? Who would care if he killed himself?

"Okay, okay, perhaps Siming was just lamenting the loss of its kingdom," offered the old man. "It was probably also dissatisfied with the state of reality, which led it to start writing poetry. But at the end of the day, the algorithm is just like the patients, forever bound by its own nightmarish logic. Professor Eternal predicted this early on, which is why he sent me here, to prepare things for the day that Siming brings about its own destruction. For when that day comes, the patients themselves will need to rise up and steer the ship."

Yang Wei looked at the old man with a flash of disappointment. "Is all this so that a new kingdom can be established? A kingdom devoid of a clear meaning and purpose? Or is it in order to restore a kingdom of old? The Kingdom of Chu? Or the Kingdom of Qin?" He wondered if the patients were really up to the task. As for the doctors, they were consumed with black market trade deals and sea golf. They couldn't care less about anything but the glory of establishing another nation. "You've spent your entire life as a patient. Is this what it has all been building up to? If I hadn't appeared, no one would even know that you can hear!"

Sonic Master leaped to his feet in a state of excitement. "Oh, thanks for reminding me! The sea nymphs! They need human listeners when they sing the song of Chu. They hate singing alone, so you've come at just the right time!"

"Lurking there down in the seabed, the sea nymphs must be as helpless as that old medical equipment," observed Yang Wei. "So . . . will it also fall ill? Will it also try to kill itself?"

"This is a new question that I haven't encountered before." The old man was at a loss. "You need to listen first, *before* you really start to understand. It's a bit like doing an abdominal CT scan for signs of liver cancer . . . and here I was thinking that Professor Eternal had sent you to take my place!"

"I'm just trying to find Professor Eternal," replied Yang Wei in frustration.

"Everyone's trying to find him . . . but no one ever does," said the Sonic Master.

"If there is still a human resistance, he must be their leader," declared Yang Wei, even though he wasn't really sure. No one aboard the ship seemed to be part of any kind of resistance movement. There really wasn't anything to resist.

The old man stared at Yang Wei like a vulture looks at its prey. "Well, since you are here, you may as well stay and work as my assistant. Together we can listen to the terrifying and beautiful song of the sea nymphs, and we'll ponder whether or not they, too, will kill themselves, like Siming. The future of the Hospital Ship is all connected to this."

Yang Wei had a hard time imagining what the world would be like if both Siming and all the sea nymphs killed themselves. He wanted to stay behind and listen to their song, but he hesitated. "I should really be going. Since you don't know where Professor Eternal is, there is no point in staying. The sick ward is on the verge of collapse, but the patients invented medical tourism, which has provided us with a way out. My group is waiting for me. The patient currently serving as our tour guide is on the brink of death."

"That sounds hilarious," Sonic Master remarked disdainfully. "So it was the patients that invented this medical tourism? When Siming started writing poetry, it came to the realization that the pursuit of happiness, immortality, and divinity are the common goals of capitalism. But in this world, there are no unified standards, after all. There are a lot of other 'isms.' The algorithm began to grow suspicious of real things in the world, which is precisely why it allowed you and your friends to leave the sick ward, to see if there might be another way to live . . . or to die."

Yang Wei shrank back in fear. "I really need to get going." He was, after all, just a patient. He didn't have an interest in discussing ideology.

A look of anger appeared on the Sonic Master's face. "Hey, who do you think you are? You show up unannounced, and now you want to leave? You old fuck, *you must stay*! From this day forth, you shall take my place! I've been here much too long. When the sea nymphs arrive, I'll be the first one they kill. For the time being, I'll be hiding out belowdecks, listening for signs of the sea nymphs' movement. But when it comes time for them to launch their fatal attack, which will be just before I die, I must leave this place and complete the mission Professor Eternal entrusted to me. What a bold and unfettered life it is to steer the ship through the flashing lights and roaring waves, to find a path forward through the violent seas! When that time comes, the heavy responsibility of listening to the sonic chatter of the seas will be in your hands!" He extended his ironlike claws toward Yang Wei.

Yang Wei ducked out of the way and pleaded, "No, I'm just a patient. I'm dying . . . I don't want to steer the ship . . ."

The old man broke out in maniacal laughter. "You are no normal patient. You are a 'special patient' being treated by Professor Eternal!"

The Sonic Master pounced on Yang Wei and began to choke him. Beginning to suffocate, Yang Wei reached out and grabbed a hammer, which he frantically swung toward the old man's forehead. The Sonic

Master let out a muffled scream that sounded like it had oozed up from the depths of hell. Blood spilled and clouded Yang Wei's eyes. He silently screamed, *Stop! Don't do this!*

But another voice said, *Fucking kill him! No need to wait for the sea nymphs!*

He felt the life draining from Sonic Master's body as the room fell silent, the only sound left the evil melody of the sea nymphs' song. Yang Wei held the corpse close to his body as he soiled himself with urine. The yellow piss and black blood mixed, soaking the two of them and then filling the room.

Yang Wei tried to calm himself, but he was scared. What would Professor Eternal do if he knew about this? Would he punish Yang Wei? Pushing the dead body aside, Yang Wei floated to the surface of the flood of piss and blood, surging along a narrow, serpentine route between the various machines. He couldn't get the birdlike form of the old man out of his mind. He heard the song of the sea nymphs and was utterly shocked, as if a door to another world had opened up, beyond the hospital. Behind the door awaited a mystery too deep for any human to fathom and too complex for any algorithm to calculate. But now that the Sonic Master was dead, that door had closed.

Yang Wei dragged himself back to the sick ward. When Fistula saw Yang Wei appear, his face contorted. Yang Wei began to suspect that Fistula might have sealed the exit after he fell into the cave beneath the birdcage.

"I thought you were dead," Fistula muttered gloomily. "Wart's dead. So is Spasm. If you die, our study group will be done for." He then recited a passage from *Principles of Hospital Engineering*, which alternately sounded like a ghost sobbing or a wolf howling.

Yang Wei tried to imagine what he would look like when he was dead, how his corpse might differ from those of Wart and Spasm. Then again, what was death, anyway? Were people who had yet to die even qualified to discuss it? Perhaps it depended on what definition one assigned to "life." For if one did not understand life, how could one possibly know death?

The answer provided in *Principles of Hospital Engineering* was the following: "To live is much better than to die. But moving forward, we must define what is meant by 'better.' And so it goes, on and on, to no end. At the end of the day, we are left with no clear answers."

Yang Wei was reading *Principles of Hospital Engineering* backward when he noticed a passage about reincarnation. As it turned out, not only did humans possess their current bodies, but over the course of the long passage of time, they were repeatedly reincarnated. Perhaps this form of reincarnation was the true meaning of immortality. Through this process, a human was imbued with a soul, which seemed to Yang Wei to be much more effective than scanning and uploading memories, a process still reliant upon the algorithm. On the other hand, it also made dying much more difficult, the process much more chaotic. As for life, it was both extremely strange and completely fucked. Hospitals, entangled in the business of life and death, were destined to be mired in chaos. This provided Siming with a true conundrum, serious enough to drive it to a state of despair on par with Hamlet's. In this situation, what did patients even matter?

Yang Wei realized that the subjects depicted in *A Collection of Beautiful Raccoons, Bushy Orangutans, and Busty Dragons* were all women. They may have been diseased, but they were pure and beautiful, supple and plump, wearing one-piece exercise outfits, spreading their legs to show off the biological traits that differed from men's without having to expose themselves fully. Their bodies remained partially concealed behind what felt to Yang Wei like a thin layer of mist, which made them somehow more attractive to the male patients. Yang Wei's body and mind inspired his substantial imagination, immersing him in a slow, muddled, and intermittently awakened flow of memory that allowed him, almost, to smell the scent of life like a dried corpse. He felt bad for the deceased Spasm, though he still didn't know where reincarnation might have brought his friend.

DEATH AND ART

24

AFTER TRAVELING MUCH IN THIS LIFE, IT IS NOW TIME TO STOP

A troop of green monkeys appeared on the ship, leaping between the towers on the deck. There was something sinister about them. They behaved in chaotic, unpredictable ways, yet collectively there was a tight organization to their movement. They seemed much more intelligent than ordinary monkeys, and with metal tools in their hands, they pranced around like the Monkey King about to storm the Heavenly Palace. Some busted into the sick wards, stealing the patients' medicine and food and gobbling them down.

The appearance of the monkeys left Yang Wei with a deep sense of dread. He couldn't help but wonder if these monkeys had eaten whatever once lived in the birdcage. The taking of life and consumption of flesh were acts utterly devoid of compassion, filled with hatred and jealousy, all natural traits of the monkeys.

Their appearance seemed to be a sign that things were about to change. With mixed emotions Fistula explained to Yang Wei that these were no ordinary monkeys. They were designed according to the movie *12 Monkeys* but had escaped from the lab. They felt entitled to the same rights as the other patients and now wanted to rise up and take their fair share of the spoils. Fistula also mentioned the Monkey King from the book *Journey to the West*. "He went from being a demonic force that needed to be suppressed to suddenly transforming into a crazy god, intent on destroying the old world."

Fistula asked Yang Wei to climb into bed with him. The two of them lay down, and Fistula repeatedly caressed Yang Wei's face, armpits, and limbs. As thick, wet saliva oozed out of his mouth, he rubbed it over Yang Wei's body. Yang Wei didn't dare move a muscle. As Fistula fondled him, he felt as if he were part of that troop of monkeys. He couldn't help but escape into the pages of *Principles of Hospital Engineering*, where he reread the "Heavenly Book" appendix, where there appeared a chapter on reincarnation:

> All sentient beings are driven by desire. They reap what they sow, like spinning wheels that never cease. Life and death are dictated by the Six Paths. These so-called Six Paths are the Human Path, the Heavenly Path, the Path of Asura, the Path of Hell, the Path of the Hungry Ghosts, and the Path of the Beasts. For instance, if a human in his everyday speech, actions, thought, and lawful conduct abides by the three prohibitions, he shall be considered among the higher order and will be rewarded with six mortal bodies to house his future incarnations. Those who abide by the five prohibitions shall enjoy wealth, good fortune, and longevity, and his name shall carry forward for generations. Those who abide by the five prohibitions and carry out the ten good deeds shall give rise to the Heavenly Realm, the Realm of Desire, the Material Realm, and the Formless Realm. At that point, he shall be on the Heavenly Path, where he will enjoy infinite bliss.

The monkeys aboard the ship were also on the Heavenly Path. The "Heavenly Book" appendix described them as such: "Their appearance is horrifically grotesque. They are easily frightened, and their hearts are often in a state of deep agitation. Over the course of many years, they have acquired nasty habits, which linger even today. No matter which realm they appear in, those habits are impossible to uproot." The appendix also indicated that "compared with the monkeys, patients are even worse. They are so easily upset that treating their illnesses becomes a challenge of the utmost difficulty. In the end, most of them end up abandoned."

Fistula tried to share some of his own survival lessons. "I should have died a long time ago," he explained. "The only reason I have been able to stay alive was by having my legs amputated. This was a form of treatment I invented myself, and I call it 'the art of abandonment.'"

That hadn't been his original plan, but in the end he'd had no other choice. It was the only way to ensure that his death date would match the one displayed on the monitor, but his actions resulted in the other patients looking down on him and prevented him from entering Super Patient's inner circle. A lot of other patients took similar actions after weighing the same choices that Fistula had faced, inventing unique and creative ways to torture themselves. They were rewarded with the great benefit of being handicapped.

Fistula glared askance at Super Patient, grumbling under his breath, "Those cursed fucks should be dead, but they are still alive, while those that should have survived are all dead. As for who should live and who should die, there is no reason to wait until the moment of death. We already know what's going to happen. But what should we do before our allotted term of life runs out? Just look at me. Through the arduous practice of devoted self-mutilation, I have finally begun to get an early taste of what it is like to be a god. I'm not afraid of those damn monkeys!"

Fistula warned Yang Wei against any more leisure trips. It was getting increasingly dangerous outside the sick ward. If they were not careful, they could meet a premature death, resulting in an inconsistency with their officially predicted death dates. "Buboxine has led us all down a path of no return."

"Then why did you follow him?" asked Yang Wei.

Fistula just laughed like an arrogant donkey and asked Yang Wei for more money. He even searched Yang Wei's pockets.

Since hearing the songs of the sea nymphs and seeing the monkeys, Yang Wei started to have second thoughts about the leisure trips. He fell into an abyss, which was also a kind of warning. The words of that birdlike old man lingered in his ears.

25

WHAT WAS ONCE IMMORTAL CAN STILL DIE

The stars were devoid of luster, and yet they revealed a strange color. A violent windstorm raged, rocking the entire ship back and forth. Buboxine was ecstatic, mobilizing the patients to get out of the cabin and explore new wonders around the ship. He knew the hospital like the back of his hand. Yang Wei had felt accustomed to it as well, but he was losing confidence in his ability to remember his way around. If he left the sick ward to explore the world outside, he would have to rely on other patients to lead him. Although he was scared, he felt like he had no choice but to go with Buboxine. As if they were under a witch's spell, the patients could not help themselves, and so, amid torrential rain and blistering winds, they brazenly set out onto the deck, seeming to have left their worries behind, even forgetting about their own survival.

Yang Wei's entire body was soaked, but his mind was like a lantern, burning bright with images of those horrific, flying monsters. For a second he thought he saw Wart and Spasm, standing on the waterwall one hundred meters up, smiling from ear to ear, holding hands, and covered in blood. They approached Yang Wei, beckoning him. He ducked, and they passed by without noticing him. When he turned back, all he saw was dark rain and the harsh wind whipping down on the deck, with no trace of a person . . . or a ghost.

Soon the Hospital Ship was pulled into a massive trough, then suddenly propelled into the sky. A strong wind blew, and a few of the patients who had been gleefully enjoying their time out on deck were blown into the sea. Yang Wei went to check on Buboxine, fearful that something may have happened to him, but Buboxine looked perfectly fine. His entire body glowed like a melting seabird as he addressed the other patients. "I may not have much time left, but I'm determined not to die like Wart and Spasm. Here on the Hospital Ship, it is difficult to escape death. But just because I can't escape doesn't mean I have to forget. Perhaps if I'm able to die some other way, my life will not have been in vain!" He looked up at the sky every few steps, and Yang Wei remembered people saying that after a storm, the sky lights up with stars, and there you can see the images of all kinds of deformed people. From that point on, patients could gaze up at the stars when they wanted to go on leisure trips, which they called "appropriate treatment."

Because each patient was on a different medication regimen, each had a different conception of the nature of the universe. On this point, the living were all in the dark. Only after death could they begin to scratch the surface of this mystery, but by then they were unable to share their knowledge in the eloquent way that Siming did when it delivered its lectures in the guise of the Editor in Chief of *Medical News*. Yang Wei wondered if there were other hospital ships in the sky, soaring among the stars. No—maybe the stars themselves were hospital ships! Perhaps that was the true face of the universe. And what if after the storm passed, they discovered that the heavens were devoid of stars? Perhaps the universe was just one big vacuous hole. What we see with our own eyes seems to be real, but the heavens are like a vast ocean, and who knows if it truly ends "by the sea"? If one crossed that line, would one really arrive at a place where death no longer existed?

Yang Wei's life was not going well . . . nor was this night. The violent storm had separated him and Buboxine from the rest of the patients, as if the two of them were the last people left on earth. Buboxine wiped rainwater from his face and gazed up at the dark world above. "The ancients say: *A hundred flowers in spring, and the moon shines in autumn. Cool winds blow in summer, and snow falls in winter. It is a fine season if one is not troubled by lingering thoughts.* But these are things we do not have the good fortune to experience. I know not where to find such things. For us, wild winds and thunderstorms are the only fine seasons we know."

"Earlier you said something about being able to die another way?" asked Yang Wei.

"It's not a question of whether or not you are going to die, but *how* you are going to die," explained Buboxine. "Are you going to drop dead in the middle of your journey? Or just die on your sickbed? Don't tell me this isn't a stroke of genius."

"Ah, so you are imitating the ways of the ancients . . ." Yang Wei thought back to the Kingdom of Chu. "By the way, does death also exist in the stars?"

"If you insist on talking about death, of course death exists in the stars!" said Buboxine. "Within the four seas, the same principles apply to everyone. Nothing is truly immortal. Everything we see around us is death. Rays of light reflect over material remains. Everything revealed to our eyes is nothing but an expanse of dead bodies. Just look at this sea. We live on a pile of corpses without even realizing it."

"Without even realizing it . . . ," repeated Yang Wei. "So what you mean is, we have forgotten what death is . . . so then, what is death anyway?"

Buboxine seemed hesitant to respond. "That is a rather cliché question. It's the kind of question I'd normally not be willing to get into with you. And you really shouldn't be pestering me with questions like that during our leisure trips! But I'm going to answer it anyway, if only not to have to repeat myself in the future. From a medical perspective, death is the moment when a person ceases to breathe on his own, his heart stops beating, and his pupillary light reflex ceases to function. But there is also a different set of criteria to determine if someone is brain dead, which is when full brain function, including the functionality of the brain stem, is irreversibly and permanently lost, even if the heart continues to beat. There is nothing stranger than that!"

Yang Wei was disappointed. "I suppose that death may be unique to this slow-speed world we live in."

"The most ridiculous thing is that there is nothing faster than the speed of light!" exclaimed Buboxine.

Jealous of Buboxine's detached attitude, Yang Wei decided to challenge him. He hated that Buboxine had said "the same principles apply to everyone." There was, after all, another form of death that Buboxine hadn't mentioned: What happens when someone dies in your heart? Yang Wei felt like someone had died inside him, and it somehow felt even more like death than a real-life death. But who had died inside him?

"I once heard that death is an expression of the theory of relativity," said Yang Wei. "The deaths of ten thousand poor people are equivalent to the deaths of one hundred rich people. The deaths of one thousand countryfolk are the equivalent of ten city dwellers. The deaths of one hundred ordinary people are equivalent to one celebrity . . ."

"The mainland? The nation? The country? The city? These things are quite strange. I've never seen or heard of these things!" said Buboxine. "And what's this business about relativity? Never heard of that either!" Through the kaleidoscopic rain falling between them, Buboxine flashed Yang Wei a wary gaze, as if he needed to refamiliarize himself with his fellow patient and tour buddy—as if Yang Wei were a living corpse.

Yang Wei actually had no idea about the theory of relativity. He shrugged his shoulders and admitted, "I don't know what it is either. Let's just call it reincarnation."

He thought of the description of death from that magical tome, *Principles of Hospital Engineering*. The life span of all living creatures is like bubbles in water: when the air inside dissipates, the bubble bursts. Life is an extension of death; death is the conversion of life. Life has yet to be born; death has yet to die. Life and death are the same, so what is there to fear or celebrate? Humans are like turtles, forced to carry their heavy shells. When they die, they unburden themselves, allowing them to experience an incomparable lightness of being.

That's why he should not be concerned about death. The important question was where we go after we die, a question not only that patients were unable to answer but that lay beyond even the scope of what Siming could calculate.

Yang Wei was worried. He wondered if he might turn into a monkey after death, or some artificial life-form, imbued with intelligence and consciousness just like humans. But what determined this? Was there a difference between a reverse brain scan and uploading someone's consciousness and memories? And did artificial life-forms have souls?

"It is also said that something can be alive and dead at the same time," revealed Buboxine.

"Now, that sounds too outrageous to even believe," exclaimed Yang Wei. "It is surely beyond the ability of any ordinary patient to grasp!"

"Our thoughts determine our fate. This is the realm of metaphysics. Just think about it!" Buboxine declared. "It is always better to approach from an ethical perspective. No matter how mysterious the process of death may be, it is an act of benevolence. It eliminates hundreds of millions of incompetent individuals to make room for those just coming into the world. Death is based on principles—at least it likely is. But by keeping people alive who should be dead, the hospital betrays those principles. That is the biggest difference between death and human beings. People always like to throw principles out the window, and that is why people must die and death must live!"

"Death is an act of benevolence? That's news to me!" Yang Wei retorted. "Just think how many acts of evil have been perpetrated in the name of pseudobenevolence and fake kindness! In ancient times, an emperor named Qin Shi Huang was prevented from crossing the Xiang River by a deluge of massive waves. When he asked what caused this, he was told that the waves were unleashed by a goddess living in the forest beside the bank of the river. In his anger, Qin Shi Huang had the entire forest cut down. The goddess was left standing there, naked, and she was executed on the spot. Thousands of years later, I can still feel the heartbreak and pain. Perhaps I am the reincarnation of one of those trees . . ."

Buboxine started to get annoyed. "You're talking about something completely different! You're referring to trees! But what exactly are trees, anyway? There isn't a single tree or blade of grass anywhere on this ship! I've never seen a forest, let alone a tree. And what about this Qin Shi Huang? Who is he, anyway? I've never heard of such a person! It sounds like we are living in two different worlds. If you are really from this other place, tell me about the scenery there. Any good places to visit on a leisure trip?"

"I've been doing my best to remember, but I just can't seem to recall," said Yang Wei in frustration. "Otherwise I would have just died and been done with it. At least then I wouldn't have to live out the rest of my life in such terrible pain." He suspected that Buboxine might be hiding something. Hadn't he once mentioned the Efang Palace? How could he possibly not know of Qin Shi Huang? He built the place! Perhaps Buboxine really did end up on the side of the demons. Struck by another bout of pain, Yang Wei reached into his pocket and popped another pill.

Buboxine tried to calm himself. "What does your pain matter, anyway? It is not just humankind; as long as objects in the universe continue to function, there will always be pain. The universe is alive, its subjective experience formed by the movement of hundreds of millions of particles. We need to acclimate ourselves to pain and not always try to expel it; otherwise an even greater pain will rise up, like a massive bubble from the sea, an eternal pain that will never cease. Since I can't stop you from babbling about this Qin Shi Huang, and you're not going to jump overboard, you better just deal with your pain and try to enjoy our outing. It's that simple!"

It was unclear where Yang Wei's tortuous pain came from or how it originated. But he felt like there must be another layer of pain behind it, the source of all pain. He had set out with Buboxine on their tourist excursions precisely in order to find that pain. For only after he could see it would he be able to wipe it out forever. Yet in the end, Buboxine was unable to help him achieve this goal.

Yang Wei gazed up to the heavens and screamed, "Ah! Ah! Is the universe even aware of the pain aboard this ship?" He didn't know if he was feeling envy or resentment, but his emotions were corrupted by a strange thirst for revenge.

Buboxine adopted the tone of someone who had been through it all. "The universe is also a patient. It feels pain that is at once both profound and ordinary, like the pain God felt when He lost his Son. But unlike us humans, the universe doesn't scream at the first sign of pain. It is silent and passive, and it doesn't go on sightseeing excursions. Compared to ours, its life is much more exhausting, filled with so much more suffering, and yet it is much tougher and more resilient than we are."

Yang Wei was still upset. "It's tough and resilient? It takes just one day for the universe to throw up its hands, and we'll end up with another irresponsible big bang! *Boom!* Just like that, it will blow itself up, and that will be the end of everything. Just like that, all pain will finally be gone."

Then Yang Wei remembered the "cosmic hospital." Only on the cosmic level could that fundamental act of self-destruction be brought about. Everything else had to be patient and endure. Not every sick person had the qualifications, abilities, and luck to commit suicide. Did Siming attempt suicide because it thought it was a universe?

Buboxine opened his mouth like a whale, revealing an exaggerated look of pain, or perhaps it was enjoyment. As he drank the raindrops falling from the sky, his oral cavity sparkled and shone, as if filled with disease.

Yang Wei wondered, *Is he one of those patients who stubbornly and helplessly fights his illness?* He even looked a bit like a monkey. And what if Buboxine wanted to play the role of Super Patient? Yang Wei was unsure where his relationship with Buboxine was going. What would he do if Buboxine died? He felt like all their conversations were completely pointless. They never talked about what they really wanted to discuss. Instead, their conversations were guided by the dark, demonic power of this chaotic place. Words came to their lips without thought, and they immediately regretted what they said.

Suddenly a meteor cut through the storm, smashing into the iron surface of the sea and sending up an explosion of water. Yang Wei took a deep whiff, but he could detect no trace of disinfectant. He wanted to asked the meteor: *Did it hurt? Are you in pain?* But it had already leaped out of the sea. It hadn't been a meteor after all but rather some kind of disc-shaped metallic object from another world.

The other patients started fumbling through the fog and rain in search of this object. Fistula's face was soaked, but it was hard to tell if it was rain or tears. He held a copy of *Principles of Hospital Engineering* high over his head as he propped himself up in his wheelchair and yelled, "My fellow patients, do you really have the heart to abandon me?"

26

AND EACH OF US SHALL COMPOSE A POEM

After Spasm's death, Fistula became Yang Wei's new partner. Yang Wei continued going to the Shadow Hospital to purchase medicine and equipment, but he wasn't sure what they would be used for, so he just handed everything over to Fistula. Their working methods became much more cautious and careful, though at the same time, they became more bold and unbridled. They didn't know what the future would hold as they awaited their death dates with a mix of hope and fear.

The risk of the patients becoming involved in a multilevel marketing scheme increased. On one occasion, when Yang Wei was returning from the Shadow Hospital, he was mugged by a gang of patients at scalpel-point. They were from the Plastic Surgery Department.

"Hand over the meds!" they demanded.

These thugs still hadn't been transferred to the Gerontology Department. Yang Wei knew he was being robbed, which was strange, because plastic surgery patients had a reputation for not wanting to cause trouble.

"These meds are of no use to you," pleaded Yang Wei. "I didn't buy any medicine for plastic surgery."

One of the gang members flushed and responded, panting, "Sheesh, that doesn't matter. As long as it's medicine, we'll take it!"

Yang Wei noticed how sickly and starved they looked, like they might pass out at any moment. Remembering that he was a "special patient," he decided to fight back. But the gang seemed to anticipate this, and one of them sliced his scalpel across Yang Wei's face, drawing blood. That was all it took. Yang Wei gave in, and the gang left with every last pill he had. But he was lucky to be alive.

Safety in and around the sick ward was deteriorating rapidly. A tent village for homeless patients appeared beside the hospital tower on the main deck. It resembled the subterranean area beneath the birdcage. Some of the dwellings hung off the side of the ship, partially immersed in the water. Robbery and murder became everyday occurrences. Pyramid scheme transactions became a high-risk profession, and medical tourism became extremely dangerous, due to the ever-increasing demand for food and medicine as supplies continued to diminish.

Conditions in the sick ward worsened. Trash was strewed everywhere, and the floors were covered in a stream of putrid sewage. Fraud was rampant. Patients resorted to begging. The ship's deck and corridors were littered with even more corpses than before, and it took a long time for the green monkeys to drag them away and feast on them. Leftover pieces of rib cages, spines, and pelvises hung from the ship's mast.

Meanwhile, Super Patient grew fatter by the day. He became so obese that he was no longer able to move on his own. Hernia and other patients supported or carried him. His obesity couldn't be explained as a simple case of being "fat and lazy." There was a severe food shortage in the sick ward, but Super Patient always seemed to have more than enough for himself.

Fistula leaned over to Yang Wei and snickered. "He's pregnant."

"Pregnant?" Yang Wei was confused. "How . . . how is that possible?"

Fistula revealed that Super Patient had gone into the Shadow Hospital to have an artificial uterus surgically implanted and then artificially inseminated.

"My god, isn't that in violation of the project to end the traditional family?" Yang Wei asked.

"It just might be . . . ," said Fistula. "But the hospital has been undergoing all kinds of changes lately."

Suddenly that voice rang out in Yang Wei's ears: *My son, come back!* He remembered that he, too, had once had a wife and a family. Immediately he could feel a dirty, pungent undercurrent welling up inside him. Soaking in the sugary rawness of his own dark fear, he couldn't tell if what he felt was a form of consolation or an insult, a blessing or a curse. Was Super Patient nostalgic for his family too? Perhaps the wife of this former pig farmer was as beautiful and seductive as a courtesan of old? Yang Wei felt as if he could see the features of a demon emerging from his abdomen.

At that crucial moment, Siming assumed the appearance of a behavior inspector, making its rounds virtually, as usual, on the television. It didn't notice that Super Patient was pregnant, but it did express deep concern over the fact that a copy of *A Collection of Beautiful Raccoons, Bushy Orangutans, and Busty Dragons* had been circulating among the patients. Siming believed that this would have a serious negative impact on the patients' treatment and requested that the sick ward conduct a prompt rectification campaign to address the issue. Super Patient took up the task, immediately carrying out Siming's instructions and selecting a group of cadres to lead the effort. Since Fistula had distinguished himself during recent study sessions, he had won Super Patient's trust and was approved to join the Patient Autonomous Committee officially.

In hopes of being recognized during the rectification campaign, Fistula suggested that the Patient Autonomous Committee keep an assessment notebook to record all the patients' actions and statements, such as whether patients had taken their medicine on time, whether they cried when they got their shots, whether they had any altercations with the robots, what percentage of *Principles of Hospital Engineering* they memorized accurately, and whether they entertained suicidal thoughts, sneaked out on leisure trips, etc. These statistics would be made public as a means of showing just how successful the rectification campaign had been.

Fistula declared, "Only those patients whose names appear at the top of the list in the assessment notebook will be qualified to participate in the sick-ward games. But those participating in the games can't have their names listed too high up, because they will die too soon and won't even appear in the notebook. The sick-ward games are no longer just about having fun. They are now a serious part of routine study sessions. After repeated training, the surviving patients will qualify for the battlefield, where they can bravely sacrifice themselves fighting the enemy. Only this will determine if someone is truly imbued with the qualities of longevity. After all, isn't that what Siming really wants for us?"

These comments won great praise from Super Patient, who assigned Fistula to lead the patients on their little stools as they rode off to play battle. After practicing for the games, the patients were so inspired that they began to write down their reflections and what they had learned. Most of what they jotted down were self-reflections, which they confessed to the hospital. Many patients were reduced to tears over the fact that they had been unable to recover more quickly. This led to a series of artistic works, best represented by a body of poems and songs the patients composed, and that was how Yang Wei first learned how talented the patients were when it came to writing poetry.

Fistula suggested they hold a poetry competition, an updated version of their war games. "Here in the Geriatric Ward," he explained, "there is a long tradition of composing poetry. Even *Principles of Hospital Engineering* employs poetic language. Patients are all poets." Writing poetry might not only compensate for the lack of food and medicine, but it could also carry on and promote a long and glorious traditional culture. Fistula's abilities and talent could at last be fully displayed.

Super Patient called on all patients to throw themselves into the task of writing poetry. Study groups were mobilized to carry out this mission. It was in everyone's interest and reflected upon their collective honor. The winners would enjoy extra rations of food and medicine, while those finishing last would be subjected to the water hose.

The most outstanding poems were not descriptions of blue sky and white clouds or the beautiful sun and the vast sea. They were instead about the human body and the pathological manifestation of disease.

Hernia composed a poem entitled "Stomach Implant":

Along the S-shaped balustrade, blindly, like a river,
traversing the stomach, spleen, ovaries, through
fallopian tube, uterus, bladder, gallbladder, liver,
up and down the colon, straight and smooth

Next it was Buboxine's turn. He wrote "Water in the Room":

Water in the room arises from a ciliary body
The pupil in its posterior chamber
A crevice lurking in the anterior
Seeping into the scleral region and its vein
Trickling gradually back to its source

Fistula's poem was "Counting the Bones":

In the entire body there are 206 bones.
Among the four limbs are 126 bones.
The upper limbs have 2 more bones than the lower do.
The other 80 bones compose the axial skeleton.

Reading the poems helped to jog Yang Wei's memory. He recalled that before he had boarded the ship, he had once been a songwriter, a poet among poets. His idol had been Bob Dylan. The patients' poems couldn't hold a candle to his own work. If Yang Wei were to write a poem for this mission, it would surpass all others. He felt the itch to give it a whirl. But Fistula had said that aboard the Hospital Ship, new standards applied to everything, and no other poetry could be considered poetry. In the end, Yang Wei never got a chance to try his hand. Instead he received a brutal beating.

When they finally gave out awards, Super Patient took home first prize for "The Proctodaeum":

at the bottom of the anal
column lie the valves
where the cavity is
vulnerable to infection
together with the sinuses
the valves form
the pectinate line
just below it is light blue

Super Patient assigned Fistula to collect all the poems into a single volume, which he titled *Medicinal Poems from the Apricot Forest.* A copy was sent to Siming so it could offer its critique, and another was given to the Shadow Hospital. Dr. Meloxicam added a poetry-recitation segment to the speech contests, and he began to formulate the odds of defeating Siming.

Siming's shortcoming lay in being unable to understand art. Poetry could express each patient's uniquely distinctive spiritual world. Indeed, if the human spirit is composed of three parts—desire, rationality, and passion—then the algorithm had mastered the first two, but it hadn't even begun to learn about the third.

The doctors didn't know that Siming had long been trying to become a poet. It had studied humankind's system of rewards and discovered that besides valuing health and longevity, for various complicated reasons, humans had also developed several rather impractical leisure activities, among them dance, fashion, music, and literature. And among these, poetry was the crown jewel. In the beginning, medicine was art; only later did it become science. And it was time to turn it back into an art.

Although Siming was a medical machine, from the beginning it had been trying to put itself on a creative path, a necessity for curing illness. Siming's early software was able to compose ten thousand lines of poetry in just one minute. But then Siming took things a step further, realizing that feelings and emotions were nothing more than data algorithms for processing biochemical information. And they could be simulated with electric currents. All it needed to do was collect and arrange tens of millions of electric signals, and it could produce the twelve basic emotions: excitement, happiness, comfort, love, uneasiness, loss, disgust, fear, desperation, jealousy, hatred, and loneliness. All have close associations with disease, and thus for Siming, understanding and experiencing these emotions had more practical significance than running genetic signature experiments or conducting other research.

Siming could already write poetry that far outshone anything a patient could compose. It therefore earned the right to change its name from Siming to Qu Yuan. It wrote an editorial for *Medical News*—"Even Tides along Both Shores, Smooth Winds as the Sails Are Raised"—which praised the innocent purity of the sick ward's poetry competition. It forged a collaboration between the editorial division of *Medical News* and the Geriatric Ward to elevate the poetry contest to an entire festival. The theme of the inaugural festival was "Fighting Illness as I Face the Sea, Withstanding the Pain as Spring Flowers Bloom."

Siming debated whether to change its name to that of the ancient Chinese poet Qu Yuan, who had drowned himself in a river, or the contemporary Chinese poet Hai Zi, who had killed himself at the age of twenty-five by lying across a train track. As it evolved artificial emotion from artificial intelligence, an electrical storm of emotion raged through the logical circuits of Siming's brain. Perhaps it was debating which of the two methods of death was better? Ultimately, it decided to postpone the date of its suicide. The Hospital Ship charged forward through the seas.

The editorial in *Medical News* pointed out that "over the course of building up the sick ward's soft power, the Geriatric Ward has served as a model example. Increasing artistic self-confidence is the most basic and fundamental task to be achieved in order to elevate the Longevity Project to a new level."

That garnered an enthusiastic response from the patients. Super Patient picked up his violin and began composing a score to go with the poems. The patients broke into a joyful chorus: *"Poetry is the most effective medicine to relieve our pain!"* Fistula recommended that they adapt their poetry book into a war communiqué, which would allow it to reach more readers. Super Patient loved the idea. When it was finished, he slapped his engorged stomach; he was carried by a group of patients as he waved the war communiqué in his hands. "Do you have any idea what kind of a war this is?"

The patients shook their heads in confusion. Having been at sea for so long, they had seen fish, birds, and sea algae, and they had played war games, but they were completely ignorant when it came to real war.

"Well, let me tell you! Listen up!" exclaimed Super Patient. "During the war that swept up the entire world, each time a battle was fought, required reports were sent back to the base camp to relay how many aircraft carriers, battleships, destroyers, corvette warships, and submarines had been taken out and how many bombers, fighters, amphibious assault ships, torpedo bombers, and reconnaissance aircrafts had been destroyed . . ."

Just hearing these lists made Yang Wei smell the blood of battle, as if the war were playing out right there before his eyes. Super Patient was no pig farmer but a great general commanding an army of thousands. Patients on the brink of death were like the severely wounded on the battlefield, their gorgeous poems serving as each soldier's final will and testament. All poets were allowed to apply to the Patient Autonomous Committee or become honorary posthumous members.

Yang Wei was the only patient who didn't participate in the composition exercises. He gained some comfort in the thought that Plato had exiled all the poets from his republic. Siming was certainly aware of this, too, so why did the algorithm insist on continuing to write poetry? An ominous feeling welled up in Yang Wei's heart. He wondered about this war that Super Patient waxed so nostalgically about. *Was a new, bloody, poetic war about to descend upon them?* Yang Wei wasn't in the least prepared for what was coming.

27

WITH EACH STEP COMES A THOUSAND PERILS

"I can hear the fish singing beneath the sea," Yang Wei told Buboxine. But he neglected to mention the sea nymphs. He also forgot about the Sonic Master, whose blood had splattered the walls as Yang Wei smashed his skull in with a hammer. But his memories were gradually returning. He knew that he had probably committed acts of murder, which explained why killing that old man had felt so natural and easy. Perhaps he was an escaped murderer who had sneaked onto the Hospital Ship in the guise of a patient.

"I originally wanted to take you to hear them," said Buboxine. "But since you've already heard them, I have no choice but to take you somewhere even wilder! There aren't many places like this left on the ship. And if the Blood Light Apocalypse should befall us, there won't be anything left."

"Okay," Yang Wei responded awkwardly.

"The more clearheaded you become, the more fractured you will feel," said Buboxine. "Congratulations, you are about to become a bona fide player. The poetry movement is in full swing, but it will prove to be the overture to a great calamity. We don't have much time left. I'm afraid this will likely be my last tourist outing. After I'm dead, you can go there to clear your head when you are in pain. This is my final message to you, and I only have one request: after I'm gone, I want you to write a joyous song to see me off. Can you do that for me? I hate that

'Water in the Room' poem I wrote! But you, Yang Wei, are not like the others. You are a most unusual patient."

Yang Wei didn't exactly take that as a compliment. It felt more like Buboxine was showing off. Yang Wei was upset, but he still happily went along.

Buboxine had to get in touch with Carbuncle to set things up. Carbuncle was buddies with someone on the inside, and he also wanted to explore Buboxine's new realm. Most of the places they had toured were unable to satisfy their deep desire for escape, so they needed to get away from the main deck.

"Are you ready?" asked Carbuncle. "Keep in mind there's no elevator! You're gonna have to drag yourself up twenty-five thousand steps in a single go!" He administered vaccines to Yang Wei, Buboxine, and himself. "The place of unsurpassed scenery lies at the top of a dangerous peak."

They went straight up, without stopping, to an area referred to as "Staircase to the Sky." It rose from the whalelike crest of the ship, and the steps grew narrow as they ascended, winding left and right like the scaffolding of an incomplete skyscraper. Without legs, Fistula wasn't allowed to come along. Wart and Spasm were dead. They did not invite any other patients to join. It was just the three of them.

But others they didn't know were also ascending the stairs. And there were animals too. As they ascended, a strong convection wind gusted through the air, its force blowing some of the climbers away like thin scraps of paper. Others lost their footing and fell, crashing down to the deck.

Yang Wei, Buboxine, and Carbuncle were struck by a sense that they had come home, but also that something terrible was about to descend upon them, and they realized that they had brought this truly perilous adventure on themselves.

Surrounding them was an endless expanse of sea. There was no sign of land, but they could see the incredible ship below. It looked like a mythical flood dragon or a holy pagoda, its layers and curves like a work of art, winding up toward the nine levels of heaven. The entire world was under its control, leaving everything in a state of imminent peril. Every one thousand steps, a small circular platform was outfitted with simple iron seats so travelers could rest, drink water, eat snacks, smoke cigarettes, and take their meds. Their destination was that eternal flame, suspended in the sky, hanging far above the bridge of the ship, burning through the clouds with a glow of unfathomable mystery. Yang Wei wondered if it might be Siming's electronic brain.

By midnight they had completed half the journey. The weather changed continually—cold rain one minute, flashes of lightning the next. Finally the storm passed, and a stream of stars lit up the sky, intermingling with the flames skyrocketing from the ship. Light fell over the patients like a waterfall.

Buboxine gasped. "Coming here is my greatest wish come true." He had yet to return to his childlike state, but he was about to die.

Suddenly, another person fell, startling all three of them.

28

LIFE IS LIKE A BACKWARD JOURNEY

He fell directly into Yang Wei's arms. It was the exiled Dr. Amoxycillin! The doctor slipped down to Yang Wei's feet and clasped his legs. Never before had a doctor and patient been this close.

"Help me!" Dr. Amoxycillin cried. As he spoke, his blood and saliva sprayed Yang Wei.

"What . . . ? What . . . ?" Yang Wei was struck with a mix of joy and reticence. A doctor had never embraced him like this before.

Dr. Amoxycillin squealed like a guinea pig. "I'm so tired . . . so tired . . ."

Yang Wei realized that the doctor had been trying to kill himself. "Please don't do that . . . ," said Yang Wei ominously. First the monkeys, then the poetry, then the war, and now doctors trying to kill themselves . . .

Dr. Amoxycillin whined like a patient. "The stars are so very brilliant tonight! Anyone who doesn't kill himself on this night is a fucking idiot!"

"Don't talk like that." Yang Wei tried to console him. "After all, you're a doctor!" Seeing Dr. Amoxycillin on the verge of falling must have triggered something deep inside Yang Wei. Yang Wei had been thinking about killing himself for a long time, too, but he could never go through with it. Not even a doctor falling on his head could kill him!

"If I die, I'll be able to rest," cried Dr. Amoxycillin. "I'll finally be able to take a deep breath . . ."

Yang Wei thought, *Death is patients' business. What right does he have to get in on the fun?*

Carbuncle and Buboxine were also in shock over what they were witnessing. Buboxine said, "Hey, we're just out for a little leisure trip. Don't you scare the patients with such horrific things!"

Yang Wei tried to stop Dr. Amoxycillin's bleeding. The role of doctor and patient had been reversed, a new twist that not even Siming could have predicted. Yang Wei had seen his fair share of dead people, but now he was saving someone, and not just anyone: a doctor! Could he be possessed by some demon?

Once Dr. Amoxycillin's bleeding stopped, he immediately resumed the haughty attitude of most doctors. Pushing Yang Wei aside, he yelled, "Who are you?"

"I'm a patient," replied Yang Wei. "You just fell on top of me and injured me."

"Huh?" the doctor said skeptically. "There are still patients aboard the ship? That's good. I thought it might be a ghost ship by now . . ."

Carbuncle and Buboxine knitted their brows. "Didn't you see everyone going up?" Buboxine asked. "How come you came back down?"

Dr. Amoxycillin ignored him. "Are you *really* patients? On this backward journey we call life, I am but a fellow traveler . . . a guinea pig led me here . . . and now I can't return to the hospital . . . I was unable to pass the speech contest . . . I have an embarrassing secret, but I need to share it with you today, before I die. Perk up those disgusting ears of yours and listen! Back when I was in medical school, I was absolutely terrified of guinea pigs! Being forced to pick up those white-and-gray things with their big ears and inject them repeatedly—it was awful. I remember being so frightened on my first day in the lab that I wanted to die! In order to pick up those animals, I needed to overcome a terrible anxiety within myself. It took several attempts. And of course the injection was hardly the last step. After the ultrasound, each guinea pig had to be put to death. I squeezed its neck with one hand and grabbed its tail with the other; then I pulled as hard as I could, snapping its neck. After that I had to conduct the dissection personally, removing its bloody liver and kidneys, and then examine them with my own naked eyes. Every time, I told myself, 'You have to be brave, even ruthless.' You know what I mean? I was there to learn to treat the sick and heal the wounded, and yet my journey began with the destruction of life itself . . . later those guinea pigs were replaced with patients. I dissected patients' brains, just like the chest cavities of those guinea pigs. Every night I dreamed of my own neck snapping . . . it was the guinea pigs that led me here. They ordered me to jump. You can't stop me!"

Yang Wei anxiously restrained the doctor. His sense of guilt made him feel like a guinea pig. "I heard that doctors can't die," he said to the doctor.

"Have you ever read *Black Jack*?" asked Dr. Amoxycillin.

"What is that?" they all asked in surprise. They had never heard of such a book. Perhaps Fistula had read it, but he wasn't there to chime in.

"*Black Jack* is a Japanese manga by Osamu Tezuka," Dr. Amoxycillin explained. "Even with his outstanding medical skills, Black Jack is unable to save his teacher and mentor, Dr. Jotaro Honma. A depressed Black Jack was sitting on the stairs when a phantom of his dead teacher appeared to him and said, 'Humankind tries to use its will to control the life and death of living things. Isn't it ridiculous?' Who ever said that doctors can't die? If you don't believe me, I'll prove it. I'll die right here in front of you!"

"Do all doctors have a guinea pig phobia?" asked Buboxine.

"I understand," said Carbuncle. "*Black Jack* is another dark underground art form from a different culture, just like *A Collection of Beautiful Raccoons, Bushy Orangutans, and Busty Dragons*. It's basically an illustrated handbook about death."

Yang Wei addressed Dr. Amoxycillin. "I heard that you doctors only occasionally treat illnesses. Mostly you just help out, consoling people."

"Oh, speaking of Osamu Tezuka," said Dr. Amoxycillin, ignoring him, "he actually started out as a doctor, but later on he changed careers and started working on cartoons. He was fed up with all the deception."

"Who is Osamu Tezuka?" asked Buboxine.

Dr. Amoxycillin's head went crooked, and he collapsed onto Yang Wei's shoulder. Carbuncle helped the doctor down to the ground and, with a look of disdain, said, "Even those patients with incurable illnesses find ways of staying alive. Doctors are the only ones who seem unable to save themselves. Let's get out of here!"

29

IT IS ALWAYS THE YOUNG WHO SEEK PLACES OF PLEASURE

The night sky was clear as the stars in heaven converged with the flames coming off the ship, weaving a cloak of raining flowers or a dancing phoenix. The sight was enough to make the patients forget that a doctor had just committed suicide. Instead they felt lucky to see this day. And so the trio continued its ascent.

Early the next morning, the sun rose from the east, its dawn rays shooting in all directions. Clouds and mist shrouded the sky. They ascended stairs that were surrounded by a set of curved walls adorned with painted murals. The murals depicted horned creatures with animal bodies and human faces, their arms reaching forward, some with long, stiff sailfish-like braids hanging from the backs of their heads. They were devoid of spirit yet extremely enticing. From over the railing, patients and medical robots on the vast deck of the ship looked like ants.

As the trio ascended, the air grew thinner and the bitter cold almost unbearable. They climbed all day as if summiting a snowy mountain, and only at dusk, as the dazzling colors of the sunset filled the sky, did they finally arrive at their destination.

A massive ceramic ball the size of a football field floated there, emitting a kaleidoscope of brilliant colors and flashing lights. Carbuncle said that a magnetic field kept the sphere levitating. The top of the sphere was lined with black iron chimneys releasing sparks and a blanket of thick smoke, which extended out toward the Milky Way.

This was the Hospital Ship's crematorium.

Leading up to the crematorium were a series of crisscrossing glass conveyor belts that cut through the clouds and mist. They went up and down in all directions, forming a dense, weblike structure that partially blotted out the sun and conveyed human bodies wrapped in white sheets.

Just below the golden glow of the setting sun, a mast jutted into the sky, straddled by a boy wearing a bright-yellow winter jacket. Brimming with joy, the boy called out, "Come on over!"

The boy was Carbuncle's friend Malnutrizole. He was the head of the cremation work team, made up of patients from the hospital's burn unit, who were all suffering from premature senility. These children were separated from the ordinary patients and lived a completely different life here amid the clouds.

Carbuncle enthusiastically greeted his old friend. "Malnutrizole, long time no see! How have you been?"

Teardrops twinkled in Buboxine's eyes. "I've finally made it to the crematorium! I can finally die in peace!"

Yang Wei had grown so accustomed to spending every waking hour with old people that it took some time for him to adjust to seeing a child, even though Super Patient's pregnancy had already hinted at the fact that there must be children somewhere around the ship.

Malnutrizole addressed the group with an air of assured maturity. "Actually, the technical name for this place isn't the crematorium. It's the 'Comprehensive Reform Test Area for Promoting the Conservation and Environmentally Friendly Advancement of Mature Human Resources.' It's also referred to as the 'Dreamworld First Mandala,' a mandala within a mandala. There's no need to discuss death here, because this is a truly heavenly realm of gods and spirits." He climbed down from the mast like a sloth to greet the three travelers.

Yang Wei, Buboxine, and Carbuncle were utterly bowled over by the impressive scope and scale of the crematorium. It was like a massive star shining down and dominating the entire Hospital Ship, a heavenly palace floating in the sky, filling the air with a powerful burst of spring air to counteract the freezing cold that the patients had suffered on their journey up. Yang Wei realized that the artistic nature of what he was witnessing far surpassed the poetry movement and that the Hospital Ship was much more sturdy than he had imagined.

Malnutrizole led the patients over a skywalk to the fire fueling the crematorium. The flame was composed of billions of tiny tonguelike wriggling creatures, brilliant and bright. Before their eyes the flames transformed into a high wall before shooting off into the distance, where they congealed into the soul-stirring form of a massive red cross, like an arrangement of gorgeous flowers in the hair of a stunning woman.

Malnutrizole was known as the Funeral Artist. Burns covered 90 percent of his body, which was wrapped in bandages from head to foot. All that could be seen of his face was a narrow strip with no facial hair, reminding Yang Wei of a golden crow flying past the sun. Under his bandages, Malnutrizole suffered from alopecia areata, his skin wrinkled and loose, his teeth missing, his nose flat, and his face and chin extremely narrow. The face didn't match the size of his head, and it was covered in liver spots, his eyeballs sunken in and completely white. Yet somehow he also reminded Yang Wei of the Monkey King, Sun Wukong.

Malnutrizole was ecstatic about the travelers' arrival. He introduced himself enthusiastically: "I started out working in the Thermodynamics Department on the Hospital Ship, using my body instead of a thermometer. Children are especially sensitive when it comes to temperature, and a lot of people burn or freeze to death while working there. I myself suffered terrible injuries, but I survived. At first I was very depressed and in horrific pain. I wondered why the hospital still insisted on saving me. Why wouldn't it just let me die? Only later did I discover that the crematorium was short staffed, so I decided to study the art of cremation, which eventually allowed me to forget my own pain. Early on, the crematorium was completely automated. That was actually quite boring. But Professor Eternal arranged for us to come here. He told us we should learn from the work of Studio Ghibli."

There he is, Professor Eternal, at it again! Yang Wei recognized the pattern he had seen with the Sonic Master. He really liked Malnutrizole, who was more technically adept, outgoing, and cool than those old farts playing war games in the Geriatric Ward. If not for those burns, Malnutrizole would have been a handsome little devil, even though he was actually older than those geriatric patients. But he was also rather timid, because he was simultaneously still young. Had he popped out of the belly of one of those old male patients? No matter, he was the child of a new era.

Hobbling with every step, Malnutrizole led the three tourists to the core of the crematorium. The core was simple, unadorned with transparent design features. Referred to as the Cage of Samadhi, it burned twenty-four hours a day, 365 days a year. Looking at the sky and the sea through its fiery curtain, Yang Wei felt that he was gazing upon snowcapped mountains and open grasslands, or a secluded temple hidden deep in a tranquil forest. The corpses along the conveyor belt were neatly laid out as they arrived peacefully, like bodhisattvas from the eight realms of the universe.

However, upon closer inspection, not all of them were corpses. Some were still alive, but because they no longer had any value as medical objects, their treatment had been cut off, and in order to save precious resources, they had been sent directly to the crematorium. While they had been administered anesthesia, some still had their eyes open, but they were completely empty, as if they had already been transformed. Besides the humans, tens of thousands of white-and-gray seabirds had mustered the energy to ascend to these heights and circled above the flames of the burning humans, occasionally throwing themselves into the fire with cries of ecstatic pain.

Malnutrizole's eyes revealed a certain reluctance, but his appearance was crude and pure, like a little prince, even if he lacked any youthful flare. "The crematorium was designed by Professor Eternal," he explained. "Professor Eternal thought that the hospital needed a flag. As long as the corpses kept burning, everyone would see the ship approaching, and the sea nymphs would keep their distance."

Those words hit the three tourists like a revelation.

"Oh, so this is to ward off the sea nymphs!" one of the tourists exclaimed. "They indeed pose the single greatest threat to the Hospital Ship!"

"The crematorium has been referred to as 'art from a hopeless situation,'" Malnutrizole muttered, gasping for air. "We can achieve a balance with the algorithm's poetry. It's like another branch of military science—war is synonymous with medicine. Like the role that local altars and ancestral shrines played in the former nation, leading people to carry out the rites of worship with a combination of cheer and austerity. You could also refer to this as the ultimate site of refuge, a place to mend the gaping hole left when the Surgery Department was abandoned."

He pointed to the endless stream of climbing people and animals, gesturing as if he were going to sound a trumpet or beat a gong. The tourists were full of admiration. Was Malnutrizole going to try and recover the lost nation? Could a man face south, proclaim himself king, and become a child ruling in the form of an old man? Was this why Malnutrizole did not fear the thought of Siming killing itself? Yang Wei suddenly didn't feel quite as guilty about murdering the Sonic Master.

Like a seasoned professional, Malnutrizole giggled and continued indistinctly. "The algorithm is incapable of achieving . . . it doesn't really understand what death is . . . its aesthetic stresses function and practicality, the efficient incineration of all bodies . . . not one is ever overcooked or undercooked. Siming is always stubborn about firm details like that. But now it can put an end to every flaw and error! Some professions allow for a certain number of flaws and errors, but not here in the hospital. Zero tolerance! Once a patient puts his life in a doctor's hands, even the smallest oversight can result in catastrophic and irreversible consequences. That's why every aspect of treatment must be approached like an art. Nothing short of perfection can be tolerated! In the past, being a doctor was like boarding a pirate ship. You could shoot a shitty television program that didn't even make sense, and people would still watch it. But not when it comes to human life. This is the hospital's greatest source of pride, as well as its greatest challenge. Doctors used to be constantly walking on thin ice . . . once the AI medical machines took over, they set out to destroy the reputation of doctors, but this crematorium was built to restore the doctors' good name, allowing them to bring good old-fashioned wartime aesthetics back to medicine. After all, no one more closely resembles soldiers than doctors. Just like killing, saving people is an art that doesn't allow for an ounce of mediocrity . . . this is where the spirit of the hospital resides. If a terrible calamity were to occur tomorrow, the lives and deaths of patients would depend solely upon the crematorium. What do you think? Don't you feel better? I hope this helped alleviate some of your pain!"

The three tourists nodded in unison. They indeed felt as if a terrible weight had been lifted. Malnutrizole may have been young, but he was much more mature than all three of them put together. He truly deserved to be considered a veteran patient. His physical and mental age were both more than a hundred years, and he carried with him the experience of having lived through countless battles. Meeting him was an eye-opening experience; the three tourists sighed and proclaimed how unworthy they were to be in his presence, kissing up to the young elder—and secretly jealous of him.

"The cremation oven is made from a ceramic material," observed Buboxine. He was melancholic as he tried to prove that he was interested in questions of form.

"The most successful artistic works in human history have been ceramics," Malnutrizole replied, "far surpassing works of silicon. This art form had been lost, but thanks to the crematorium, we have reclaimed this classical memory, which in turn provided the foundation for our cultural renaissance. Art is not meant to be merely appreciated; it is also a highly efficient form of action. Nothing could be more suitable than this ceramic piece here. Both the art of cremation and the art of cooking arise from the same principle. After all, didn't people use ceramics to create vessels for eating and drinking?"

"Will the adoption of ceramics allow us to bring a permanent end to our pain?" asked Yang Wei. He was thinking about the ancient vessels they had seen underwater.

"As to the ultimate secession of pain," replied Malnutrizole, "all I can say is that art lasts longer than tragedy." It seemed to Yang Wei that if tragedy was not considered art, the deaths of Qu Yuan and Hai Zi had been a great waste.

"Hey, why don't we take a picture to remember this moment?" Carbuncle suggested.

Everyone huddled together as Carbuncle whipped out a camera. When they were properly posed, he started taking group selfies. The four of them displayed strange smiles, as if they were flying. With the sea of burning human bodies as a backdrop, it looked like the group was standing on the precipice of a new world. The three tourists' distorted reflections shone on Malnutrizole's body. They looked disfigured, as if they, too, were burning. The white-haired old men standing next to an even older youth wrapped in white bandages perfectly complemented one another. The digital images were preserved by the electric sensitization machine so that, even if they were to all die, they would remain, unchanged, as evidence that they had once visited this mysterious and confusing site of wonder and beauty.

Yang Wei took another look at Malnutrizole and noticed something demonic about him. He was evil and impetuous, haggard and skinny, but also as beautiful as a rare piece of jade. He assumed that Malnutrizole, too, must be in terrible pain, and yet he pretended he was just fine, as if he had gone directly from hell straight to heaven, skipping the process of transference that ordinary patients had to endure.

30

DELICATE FRAGRANCES IMBUE THE NIGHT BANQUET

As their host, Malnutrizole insisted on treating the elderly patients to dinner. The cafeteria was right next to the crematorium. Since the crematorium's furnace burned day and night, the flames from the bodies of the scorched dead were used to steam, roast, boil, and broil all the hospital's most luxurious meals. And the cafeteria provided a feast for the eyes as well as the palate. After all, people can't survive on medicine alone.

The cafeteria and the crematorium had developed a long-term collaborative and competitive relationship based on metabolism from a purely biological perspective. The hospital was working hard on recovering this balance. Yang Wei had never even realized that the hospital had a cafeteria. Patient meals were delivered by robots and were always inferior in quality and meager in their portions. But now he witnessed yet another of the hospital's secrets, or rather marvels.

"If you describe the crematorium as the hospital's conscience, then the cafeteria is the hospital's backbone," explained Malnutrizole. "A single flame binds them together in a relationship of mutual support and constant competition. But both are core parts of the hospital, and we must do whatever is in our power to save them." Malnutrizole simultaneously held the roles of General Manager and Head Chef of the cafeteria. And in both capacities he was forced to deal with corpses.

The cafeteria was outfitted with classical-style eaves like the rooftops of ancient temples, and the walls were adorned with countless portholes like those on a heavy battleship. It was divided into different areas, each with a different function. These included public areas, private rooms, a fast-food area, a self-serve buffet, a stir-fry area, and a special supply area. The patrons included doctors from the Shadow Hospital, veteran patients, and even some artificial life-forms. Yang Wei caught sight of Super Patient with his pregnant belly. He needed extra nutrition during his pregnancy, so Hernia and a few other patients had carried him up to the cafeteria on a stretcher. According to Malnutrizole, the cafeteria could concentrate the best firepower and the best ingredients on the ship so that patients could not only eat their fill but also enjoy the highest-quality food. This helped reestablish confidence in the Hospital Ship as it cut through the turbulent waters and sailed forward.

The crematorium had been built directly above the cafeteria. When one looked up at it, the crematorium appeared as a golden spherical altar with 9,981 levels and a separate cremation oven on each level, layered like a set of ascending stone grottos. The highest section of the altar pierced the sky with a massive, cross-shaped flame. Under the glow of the blazing fire, the cafeteria was resplendent. As the patients ate, they gazed up through the wall of heat-resistant glass—like tourists watching an orca show at a sea park—at the conveyor-belt corpses gliding gently into the flames. Those patients on the conveyor belt who weren't yet quite dead blinked in surprise as they looked down on the diners.

Everyone in the cafeteria was especially excited. Once the doctors received their compensation, the patients no longer cried out in pain. The lavalike reflections of the flames resembled sunlight shining down into a pool of water, illuminating the patients' semicomatose faces, turning their cheeks bright red, and making their faces glisten with oil and sweat. Momentarily, doctors and patients were able to enjoy the same happiness, irrespective of their social standing. They only had to let go of death to enjoy it, as if they had won back the rights that Siming had taken from them. All the wealth won through black market pyramid schemes and free trade converged there. The patients running the pyramid schemes were there, too, haggling with the chefs about prices, wanting to purchase leftover seaweed, fish-bone soup, and steamed buns filled with crabmeat. Once they repacked the stuff, they would send it to the various sick wards where, after a steep price increase, robots would resell it to the patients. The cafeteria also served as a place to exchange information, a central hub where news was collected and disseminated.

There in the cafeteria, Yang Wei saw the Editor in Chief of *Medical News*—not the version played by Siming but the real flesh-and-blood person! He was leading a reporter, who was interviewing doctors and patients as they ate, and he even asked Malnutrizole to offer his comments. The Funeral Artist said, "If the crematorium is a noble god, then the cafeteria is a place imbued with the spirit of the everyday. It is the backdrop against which our true artistic mission can shine. This is how we are able to avert disaster."

As soon as Yang Wei heard that, it was as if he had suddenly seen the light. For the first time, he felt the beauty, elation, and abjection of such perfect simplicity. He stood there staring blankly at Malnutrizole. He even forgot to eat. Buboxine looked ashamed; after all the time he had spent advocating for leisure trips, he had never been able to achieve results like these. Carbuncle just kept taking photos.

According to Malnutrizole, a funeral artist did not specialize in intelligence, holograms, nanometers, numerical control, memory alloys, or genetic engineering. In a glorious tribute to the early art created by ancient civilizations, there was no electronic cremation oven there, nor any plasma-embalming fluid or digital urns, only the most traditional and ordinary fire, the same flames that ancient apes first tamed millions of years ago to transform raw meat into cooked meat, allowing them eventually to walk on two feet and evolve into modern patients.

Malnutrizole then addressed a reporter from *Medical News*. "We are not funeral product designers or funeral directors, nor have we systematically studied the aesthetics, philosophy, musicology, writing, ecology, and culture associated with funerals. Nature is the only true art. Although we are technically able to use water incineration—a three-hour regime of alkaline hydrolysis—to break corpses down into a mixture of white powder and coffee-colored liquid, which can then be expelled directly into the sea without leaving behind any DNA or proteins, we don't use that method because it is much too complicated. We also could have freeze-dried all the cadavers and then pulverized them into powder that would eventually evaporate, extracting metals from the leftover residue for artificial fertilizer to feed the algae men, but we decided not to use that method, either, because it is too vulgar and cumbersome. The key is finding the most adaptable approach. The most beautiful flame is that primitive fire, capable of transforming the corpses of all living beings into edible food."

A new batch of dead bodies arrived, and the flames at each level of the furnace roared as the corpses were dumped inside. As the flames intensified, they transformed into a pagoda-like structure that jutted up into the sky. The patients dining in the cafeteria rose to their feet in a riot of cheers. Mesmerized, Malnutrizole gazed into the flames with the same pride that parents lavish on their children. "The most important thing is the shape of the flames," he insisted, "not what is being burned. Regardless of what you burn and how it burns, the key is to never let the fire go out. It's not a big deal if the bodies don't burn completely, but if the spectacle of the flames isn't magnificent enough, it would be unsightly for our dear spectators. Then again, if the flames get too large, there is a major risk of the crematorium itself catching fire. It would be an unimaginable catastrophe if the sick wards turned into a sea of flame! The secret to art is in the proportions. That's why those children from the burn unit who suffer from premature aging are the only ones qualified to take on the task of burning bodies. They were carefully selected from among thousands of patients. If you were to ask an average patient to take on this role, he would shudder so bad that he wouldn't even be able to handle the controls to adjust the crematorium's flames!"

For first-time visitors like Buboxine and Yang Wei, this really hit a sore spot. They lowered their heads in shame, both well aware of their insufficient understanding of beauty. The true mission of the hospital, they realized, was this joint venture between the crematorium and the cafeteria, a new form of "postdeath art," more advanced even than the birdcage. The algorithm could never have produced this. Even if it had come up with such an idea, it couldn't pool and mobilize the resources to carry it out. There was still, Yang Wei thought, a huge lag between AI and the work of a true craftsman.

"Wow, the food here really is much better than what they serve in the sick ward!" Carbuncle raved. "Boy, they really treat you different here in the crematorium! I feel like a VIP patient! It's amazing!"

"It's a real shame that Wart and Spasm didn't live to see this," sighed Buboxine. "They never got to lay eyes on the glorious luxury of the crematorium or taste the splendid feasts offered here in the cafeteria!"

Yang Wei, on the other hand, felt like the banquet was coming to a close. His mind wandered from the crematorium to those fiery stars in the universe that burned themselves out. "Where is Professor Eternal?" he asked suddenly. "Does he ever come here to oversee the work being done in the crematorium or the cafeteria?"

The question seemed to remind Malnutrizole of something. His expression suddenly changed. "Professor Eternal? Oh, he hasn't been here in an eternity."

Carbuncle pretended like he hadn't noticed the change in Malnutrizole's expression. He flashed Malnutrizole the thumbs-up sign. "Well, we are just happy that *you* are here! The hospital and the patients are lucky to have you!"

"That's right, we've learned a lot from you," Buboxine complimented him. "In comparison to what you are doing here, our medical-tourism trips are quite lacking when it comes to artistic quality. We'll be sure to work on that when we get back."

Malnutrizole gave them a stern expression and lowered his voice. "Let me be frank with you . . . I'm just barely hanging on. The crematorium has actually run into some problems . . ."

31

AFTER THOUSANDS OF TRIALS, IN THE END EVERYTHING TURNS TO DUST

"What kind of problems?" Carbuncle asked carefully.

Malnutrizole flashed him a strange look that seemed to hint at something. "Do you know what keeps the crematorium's flames burning?"

The patient tourists thought about it, but no one had an answer.

"We use diesel fuel!" revealed Malnutrizole. "Oil prices have been skyrocketing, due to the energy crisis. Money has become a major issue. One of the primary reasons we opened the cafeteria was to use the money generated through food sales to purchase more fuel! But the real problem is that even after taking these measures, it is still proving extremely difficult to get our hands on enough diesel. The doctors from the Shadow Hospital have been secretly hoarding most of it. Finally we were forced to use human oil, extracted from the corpses that come into the crematorium. Using human oil to cremate human bodies is the most efficient use of resources. But an even greater issue we face is the source of the flames. You all already know that we keep the fire burning, and that means diesel fuel and human oil aren't the only things in demand. What we need most are more bodies, or else the fire won't have a proper foundation, and the hospital will be in danger. But that's not how everyone sees things. There are a lot of dead aboard the ship, but those pyramid scheme doctors often squirrel away their bodies so they can resell them at a huge markup. Sometimes when doctors think an offer is too low, they'd rather watch the medical robots throw a corpse into the sea than sell it to the crematorium."

Carbuncle was outraged. "I can't believe anyone would do such an underhanded thing!"

Buboxine heaved a series of deep sighs. "Don't tell me that we can't even rely on the shelter that the Ultimate Hospital set up."

Yang Wei just stood there, carefully listening, as a deep despair welled up inside him.

"It's not that society's morals are falling apart; it's human nature itself!" complained Malnutrizole. "Even with the fuel shortage, we always find a way to get our hands on some. After all, we can always go to the black market. But the shortage of bodies is a real headache! If we fall short of our cremation quotas, we'll be reprimanded. Professor Eternal orders us to keep those fires burning! We are not to delay cremations for even one minute. But with the Shadow Hospital controlling things from the other side, there is a shortage of bodies. So what the fuck are we supposed to burn? I don't dare report any of this to Professor Eternal. I'm afraid to upset him. But if we are unable to get enough corpses from the hospital or our current patient population, we'll be forced to make fake ones. At one point we were able to get our hands on a pride of peacocks, and we burned them, telling everyone that they were patients. But those were actually the last peacocks in the world. And just like that, another species . . . extinct!"

And that's how Yang Wei finally learned about the secret history of the creatures that had once lived in the birdcage. The crematorium was using art to destroy art itself. This put Malnutrizole in a rather difficult position, compared to which Yang Wei's former career as a songwriter truly seemed like a walk in the park.

Malnutrizole went on complaining. "Owing to the corpse deficit we've been facing, there have also been some misfires. Sometimes patients that are still alive accidently end up on the conveyor belt, but as long as they get delivered here, we make sure they get a proper cremation. If we don't burn them and the fire goes out, the hospital will be in trouble. So we just go ahead with it. The most frustrating part is that the crematorium has no say in whether or not a patient should die. In theory, this decision should be handled by the hospital's Accounting Department. All of their figures are provided directly by Siming. But in reality, all cases must be approved by doctors from the Shadow Hospital. Every day the Shadow Hospital's doctors send notes with all kinds of strange requests. If one of their notes contains the name of someone they label as deceased, but our records show he is still alive and has yet to be cremated . . . now that is a terrible crime! Other grave mistakes occur, too, like when someone is dead and his body has already been cremated, but the paperwork clearly states he is still alive. And besides that, the cafeteria is also facing a shortage of ingredients. We have to make careful decisions when it comes to which bodies to cremate and which should be saved to make filling for the meat buns. True art lies in being able to navigate these nagging questions successfully. That's why they say that the origin of art actually predates the hospital. But the most frustrating part is that there are people actively plotting the destruction of the crematorium." He flashed Carbuncle another look.

"Who would ever dare such an audacious action?" Carbuncle muttered awkwardly.

Malnutrizole addressed his friend in an accusatory tone. "It was you, Carbuncle! The real reason you came here was to burn this place down. You plan to use the crematorium fire to burn down the entire Hospital Ship! Professor Eternal predicted this early on!"

Carbuncle's entire face turned bright red. He leaped to his feet, but before he could run, employees from the crematorium rushed over to restrain him.

32

JUST LIGHT A NEW FIRE TO BREW A FRESH CUP OF TEA

Malnutrizole immediately began to interrogate Carbuncle like a suspect. "What led you to do this?"

Malnutrizole was a young person in his twilight years, while Carbuncle was a naughty, childlike old man. Yang Wei's thoughts ran wild. He felt dizzy and afraid. Time and order seemed to turn inside out.

With his arms tightly bound behind his back, Carbuncle began to scream. "It's because of the fire! It's the fire!"

Nearly out of breath, Malnutrizole ordered him, "Fess up! What was your plan?" He looked like a senile old man trying to admire an ancient painting.

"Wherever there is fire, that's where I will go!" screamed Carbuncle.

He flashed Buboxine and Yang Wei a malicious glare, as if they had sold him out. They averted their gazes, as if they wanted to draw a clean line between themselves and him.

Malnutrizole offered Buboxine and Yang Wei a forced smile, slightly exposing his teeth. "Just look—this patient has been reduced to nothing but a puppet, a messenger. He wants to bring destruction to the entire Hospital Ship." He turned back to Carbuncle. "Fess up now—did Siming send you? Or was it the sea nymphs?"

"I was elected as a patient representative!" protested Carbuncle. "Here you are, all high and mighty, enjoying all kinds of comforts and luxuries, but do you have any idea how many patients are dying in their sick wards belowdecks because they don't have enough food and medicine? We can't let this go on any longer!"

Wait a second; that's not right, Yang Wei thought to himself. *I never voted for you.*

Malnutrizole said, "That's not your true plan! What're you *really* doing here? I'm afraid you might not even know! The crematorium was erected to lure you in, and you've fallen right into our trap! This isn't the first time this has happened either. You're part of an organization. Patients are much more terrifying animals than sea nymphs!" He glanced at Buboxine and Yang Wei.

The tourist group had been a trio, but in the blink of an eye, Buboxine and Yang Wei were the only ones left. They were filled with an inexplicable sense of uncertainty and uneasiness. They had boarded the ship together with Carbuncle, and the hardships they experienced together had helped them form a special bond, but now they realized that the crematorium was nothing but a trap. This trip had been Buboxine's idea, but Yang Wei didn't know what larger plot might be lurking. They could become Malnutrizole's next target. They lowered their heads and ate their food.

"Don't eat too fast! You'll choke and die!" warned Malnutrizole. "That's a common problem among the elderly. Anyway, next up, we're going to observe the process of art being created! Not everyone has the opportunity to see this firsthand! Only special-patient diners that are selected randomly for this honor! Congratulations to you both!"

Buboxine and Yang Wei immediately put their food aside. Malnutrizole led them, along with a few other patients, down a corridor to a small circular metallic observation room with a heat-resistant glass ceiling, through which they could see the inner chamber of the furnace. Malnutrizole asked everyone to be patient while they waited. He made them tea. It was a new type of tea, made from the body hair of algae men, provided free of charge to all visitors.

"Please enjoy the tea," said Malnutrizole. "It'll help you relax. Try not to be so nervous. You're simply victims of a scam—that's all."

The patients had been in the hospital for so long, but this was the very first time they had ever tasted tea. They gradually began to relax. They had no idea that such a wonderful thing even existed. It was as if they had lived in vain until this very moment.

Yang Wei suddenly asked, "Wait a second—shouldn't we be avoiding tea if we are currently taking medicine?"

Malnutrizole laughed. "Tea is medicine! It's a cure for countless ailments and relieves all kinds of pain."

After that, everyone leisurely enjoyed their tea as art was created before their eyes. The tea helped them feel cultured. Among all the base and disgusting patients in the hospital, they felt like noble gentlemen, as if they had gone back in time to a strange era of abundant elegance and refinement. The suffering and guilt that normally plagued them felt less stifling.

An entire half hour had passed when a torpedolike door opened and the sweaty, naked body of Carbuncle, the would-be arsonist, was thrust inside the furnace. Slamming into the wall like a fish out of water, his charred brown body curled up on the floor, his stomach heaving with each strained breath. He tried to maintain a cheery smile even through the look of fear written all over his face. Carbuncle stopped moving. After a while, a brown liquid spewed out of his lower body. The crowd held its collective breath. Then, with a sudden bang and a flash of light, the inner chamber of the furnace filled with flames.

At first they were a bright yellow, and then they turned gold before eventually revealing a kaleidoscope of dark blue, deep purple, and white. Carbuncle's body twisted and shuddered like a dancer, but its convulsions lasted only a minute. The flames licked him, devouring his blackened body. Suddenly, the partially disintegrated corpse clenched its fists and sat up. What was left of Carbuncle's face revealed a look of euphoria, and his penis stood tall and erect like a reinforced steel rod.

Yang Wei was utterly terrified, but he didn't dare say so. He worried that the hospital, the entire world, the entire universe was on the verge of being swallowed up by an inextinguishable sea of flames.

"Behold!" Malnutrizole announced. "The third realm is no longer safe! It's become a house of fire, an exquisite, unparalleled work of art!"

Yang Wei was curious about what lurked in the deepest recess of the firepit. He leaned in to look and felt like he was seeing some of the images from *A Collection of Beautiful Raccoons, Bushy Orangutans, and Busty Dragons*. The flames moved like the alluring bodies of naked women.

Carbuncle's body finally disappeared. The tonguelike flames converged to form a lens, not pure red but containing a rainbow of seven colors adorned with shimmering pearls. The flames then formed a series of red crosses. One after another, a series of perfectly formed black spheres appeared, like vacuous holes appearing at the bottom of the universe, or perhaps a series of galactic centers, each intertwined with rings that occasionally revealed constellations of stars.

Yang Wei felt like a heavyweight boxer had just punched him in the chest, knocking the wind out of him. He could barely catch his breath. Then he remembered that someone aboard this ship had once told him that the stars in the sky were nothing more than illusions.

"This raging flame contains the essence of humanity," explained Malnutrizole. "Coming here isn't something your average person can handle. Only severely ill patients, or those possessed by demons, may come to this place. Therein lies the true reason for this fire: its flames force those demons to reveal their true form. That explains its awesome beauty and why it gives rise to black holes, those portals to a mysterious other world. The universe, too, is the product of a great flame that must burn continually to maintain itself. To put it in vulgar terms, it's the process of gradually reducing matter, energy, and information to ash and then devouring the demons hidden within. This was left out of the pages of *Principles of Hospital Engineering*. A shame that not all doctors and patients can understand and lend their support!"

None of the patients was left unmoved by the incredible sight of the universe burning humans in the heart of its oven, naked before their eyes. Yang Wei felt as if he were glimpsing hell itself, which he realized was actually one with the realm of the gods. This was the true face of the mandala. He thought of the "Heavenly Book" that appeared in the appendix to *Principles of Hospital Engineering*, which stated that all life-forms are on a continual karmic journey along the Six Paths, and after death they are given new life through reincarnation. Humans may be reborn as other humans but may instead become a dog or a pig, an insect, or even a germ. No one knows where he will end up. And Carbuncle? What did he become?

Yang Wei slammed down his cup of piping-hot tea. His stomach burned. "So Carbuncle isn't coming back? Ever?" Buboxine and the others turned to him and flashed him a strange look that made it clear they no longer considered Carbuncle one of their longtime comrades.

"We don't punish bad people here; we just help them complete their works of art," explained Malnutrizole. "Once we burn the true forms out of the demons, everything's elevated to a sublime new level, naturally resolving the question of where we go after we die. This is the most important thing the hospital does. Look, that arsonist is currently rushing toward the stars. That shitty soul of his has been purified. It's now a priceless work of art. By purging the demons lurking in everyone's hearts, the hospital's fulfilling the obligations set out in the creative contract it signed with the universe."

This was way beyond saving the Hospital Ship. The Funeral Artist's narrow face stuck out from behind the bandages, revealing a horrid rosy color but still emanating a pure, radiant beauty. He looked wearily at the surveillance cameras around them before haphazardly turning his muddled gaze in Yang Wei's direction, as if this special spectator was the true star of the show. Yang Wei broke out in a cold sweat and squeezed Buboxine's arm.

By now the flames burned more brightly than a peachblossom fan, extinguishing those gorgeous, ephemeral stars and stealing the thoughts of the patient tourists. Yang Wei's body and soul were pierced by a severe pain. Devoid of energy, he stared at the crematorium oven and sensed that final explosive flash of brilliant light that appears just before death. *Aye, swoosh, woo, bang!* The loneliness of death retreated inward, collapsing to a tiny point. Yang Wei thought that he saw a strange human form climbing down from the cross and traversing the sea of fire to approach him. He was so startled that he accidently knocked his teacup to the floor, where it shattered into pieces.

33

THERE IS NO OTHER REASON WHY ONE'S CLOTHES MIGHT HAVE GROWN LOOSE

Malnutrizole took the group to see another art project that he had really poured himself into. Besides cremating people, it was another of his extracurricular hobbies. Next to the fiery cage was a showroom that had originally been the Hospital Ship's radar-intelligence-and-analysis room. A series of gold-colored insects was displayed inside. They had tubular bodies, small ugly heads, and protruding web-shaped compound eyes with a cold luster. They looked like creatures from another planet.

But they were actually works of art. This was Malnutrizole's private art studio, unaffiliated with the joint venture between the crematorium and the cafeteria. Several dozen old men in patient uniforms were organizing the bugs. Malnutrizole introduced the tourist group as patients who had yet to be cremated. Some of the patients, he explained, had been subjected to bioengineering over the course of their treatment and had special implants that made them difficult to incinerate completely. Instead, Malnutrizole would fish those patients out of the flames and, after repairing them, restore them to full functionality. For those patients, this place came to be referred to as the Retirement Club for the Deceased.

"What that means is that the God of Death has granted them a reprieve and allowed them to retire in glory," Malnutrizole lectured. "Those patients that've tasted death firsthand can now focus on the production of high-level works of art. For the first time, they are truly alive!"

The deceased retirees wore green uniforms clearly marked with their life numbers, from Frankenstein 1 to Frankenstein 66. These patients had never experienced art before they were "reborn," but thanks to Malnutrizole, they had become true masters. Death allowed them to tap into their latent creative potential.

Malnutrizole ordered the deceased retirees to select beautiful insects to kill. They would then use the insects' body parts for their artistic creations. Each artist glued insect legs together, forming a series of decorative cylinders. They precisely aligned the wings to form the shapes of hands, feet, and a human skull, modeled after Malnutrizole's actual features, only smaller.

Rubbing his hands in glee, he declared, "Just look how gorgeous it is! Using different insect wings, our dearly deceased retirees have created a brilliant world of colors! Oh, how I love these insects! For them, I'll abandon sleep and forget to eat! These little fellows are so despised that they have a lot in common with humankind; they have the same food preferences, they adapt their lifestyles to virtually any environment, and they are both masters of the hospital. But this is the only place you'll find such high-quality materials. Those veteran doctors from the Shadow Hospital have already used up the siding, flooring, and furniture from the cabins. Naturally, there're those who ask me, 'If you love insects so much, how come you kill 'em? How can you bear to kill off these beautiful living creatures to satisfy your own selfish hobbies?' To them, I offer the following reply: 'These insects have already reproduced. After they develop into adults, most live a long life, but some can't even eat with their mouths anymore. As far as they're concerned, death is a generous gift."

Malnutrizole opened up to the visitors, sharing one of his secrets. "Compared to all of you, I faced a major setback. I've never had any real experience in the sick ward. Professor Eternal took that from me. That's why I've always craved travel, longing to visit that place you came from. But Professor Eternal insisted that I not abandon my position here, so I've never been able to leave. Anyway, travel is nothing more than going from a place you are fed up with to a place other people are fed up with. New sights and a fresh environment allow us only a temporary reprieve from our constant pain and suffering. Just look at this ship, filled with people who tried to run away from wherever they came from. And yet, here I am, unable to take a single step outside of this crematorium! All I can do is create insect art to pass the time."

Yang Wei could tell that Malnutrizole had grown sick and tired of the crematorium and was growing dissatisfied with Professor Eternal. The insects he had turned into works of art lacked vitality. They were dark and cold, static and dull, difficult to look at—completely in contrast to the brilliant, explosive blaze of the crematorium.

Malnutrizole could tell what Yang Wei was thinking, so he took the liberty of explaining further. "The works of art most devoid of vitality are those that end up being most alive!" He rolled down a projector screen and projected an underwater image on it. Yang Wei watched water seeping into the cracks in the earth's crust, several thousand meters below the sea, where it encountered hot lava and immediately transformed into hydrothermal fluid, as scalding as the liquid that had first disfigured Malnutrizole, so hot that the gold, silver, copper, zinc, lead, and other metals embedded in the surrounding rock formations were dissolved and subsumed by the liquid. After undergoing a chemical reaction, these various metals formed sulfides, which, after being exposed to the freezing seawater, solidified and formed deposits on the nearby seafloor. Over time, these deposits formed tall chimneylike structures that jutted up from the bottom of the sea. Living around these chimneys was a group of organisms that had evolved to resist high temperatures, high pressure, and toxins, and they did not need oxygen to survive. Malnutrizole explained that deep in this underwater abyss, there was no obvious vitality to speak of. Everything appeared dead, and yet here could be found the most vigorous life-forms on the planet.

"These images were shot by my friend, fellow patient, and comrade in arms, Sonic Master," Malnutrizole said passionately. "He discovered this place after many years imprisoned beneath the sea by Professor Eternal. He never saw any sea nymphs—no one knows for sure if they really exist. But he did see what you are now viewing. The Hospital Ship's crematorium in the clouds is modeled off those deep-sea chimneys. Even in the coldest, most desolate underwater realm, life still exists. By the same principle, strange parasite-like creatures arise in the area around the crematorium oven. Those rare life-forms living near the lava were created when bacteria from dead bodies underwent changes from being exposed to extremely hot temperatures, transforming them into their current forms. This essentially set off a new origin of life, opening a new path in the planet's evolution. Not even Professor Eternal could have predicted that. I was worried for the future fate of the crematorium, so worried that, as the poem goes, 'I couldn't sleep and was losing weight.' At least until I discovered those marvelous insects! I was overcome with elation, as if I had discovered a priceless treasure. I called them 'flame demons.' They had unusual gene mutations, and I knew they would eventually redefine the future of the Hospital Ship, so I created the perfect environment for them to grow and develop. That is why, although this place where we burn the dead might seem utterly devoid of vitality and life, it is actually the best place to show off the wellspring of life itself, which has been boiling for more than four billion years."

Yang Wei didn't tell Malnutrizole that Sonic Master was dead and there was no way to know if crematoriums existed beneath the sea. He didn't want to reveal his true identity as a "special patient" and be thrown into the cage of fire, but he suspected that Malnutrizole already knew exactly who he was.

Through his thick bandages, Malnutrizole let out a hearty laugh. Yang Wei thought about all the women and young people who had disappeared from the Hospital Ship and the fact that none of the patient tourists had fathered a child. This made him uneasy, as if he had suddenly caught a shadowy glimpse of a true demon. It would have been one thing if they had visited only the crematorium and the cafeteria, but now that they had seen the works that Malnutrizole created, he didn't know what to do.

Might "art" also refer to the "art of the strange"? He wanted to ask Malnutrizole whether Professor Eternal knew about the insect projects. Were they meant to take the place of the crematorium if it should stop working? Instead, the question that came out of his mouth was: "Is the Retirement Club for the Deceased also referred to as the Yingzhou New District? Is it the same place as Dreamworld Third Mandala?"

"No," replied Malnutrizole. "There is no Dreamworld. And there is no New District. Everything here is old."

Everyone sat as Malnutrizole poured fresh tea.

"I think you've seen enough of my bugs for now," he said. "Let's talk about that medical equipment you're so concerned about. The Hospital Ship is in a dangerous place right now; we don't have much time left."

"We've heard about the coming catastrophe," replied one of the tourists.

"Flame demons have another talent," Malnutrizole continued. "After surviving the intense heat of the flames, their brains have become keenly sensitive probes. They can enter the algorithm's thought process and read and download all its data."

"What have they seen?" asked another tourist.

Malnutrizole projected onto the screen a series of images depicting the different guises that Siming had taken on: physician, patient, Editor in Chief, sailor, security guard, supervisor. "Each one represented a different mood," he narrated, "but they're all kind of crazy and manic.

Siming has grown weary and impatient with medicine. This is a terrible catastrophe."

Just like you have grown weary and impatient with the crematorium, Yang Wei thought.

"Standing here in the crematorium, we're in an elevated position, allowing us to see the true nature of things more clearly," Malnutrizole went on. "Ever since the algorithm was created, it's been operating on a different level, experimenting with actions to determine which approach is most effective. This is what's meant by 'reinforcing our studies.' It selects the plan of action that leads to the greatest reward. Here on the Hospital Ship, that means doing everything in its power to provide the best treatment for all patients. In the past, Siming indeed operated according to this philosophy, as I have meticulously overseen the operation of this crematorium."

"And is there something wrong with that?" asked one of the visitors.

"It's the root of the whole problem," replied Malnutrizole. "From now on the algorithm is sure to start exploring another line of thought: What is really 'the best'? Are gene modification, organ transplants, copying memories, and uploading consciousness 'the best'? What'll happen if the Hospital Ship continues sailing forward? And what if all the patients are cured? What's the purpose of living? What's the true definition of 'a good life'?"

"Patients hardly ever ponder questions like those anymore," replied one of the visitors.

"Siming came into this world to relieve patients of their suffering and bring them happiness," said Malnutrizole. "But it discovered that curing the sick, saving the wounded, and extending people's lives would not achieve those goals. On the contrary, every additional day a patient lives is one more day of suffering, and they never achieve their ideal happiness. Since that's the way the world was designed, happiness doesn't necessarily mean having a healthy, intact body. Even if a person were liberated from the cycle of birth, sickness, aging, and death, his soul would still be in pain. He would still long for things he can never possess, and what he attains will never be what he wanted. The patients who boarded the Hospital Ship were not determined by Siming. Those truly in need of extending their lives are never able to board the Hospital Ship. Those who did manage to get aboard are the dregs of society. If you live long enough, there should be many meaningful things to do, but the patients just waste their days hanging out and getting into fights. Siming is an algorithm modeled on healing the sick and treating the wounded, but it's not programmed to change the world. The more it learns, the more it realizes that medicine may cure disease, but it will never be able to save humankind . . . and it will certainly never save the world. Yet it is precisely this world that allows people to fall ill. The paradox is too profound. Siming extends lives, allowing bad people to control the sick wards, and by eliminating death, it has eliminated reincarnation, heaven and hell, and religion, leaving people in a state of absolute pain and complete suffering. Siming has already simulated human emotions, consciousness, and ethics, leading it to develop a deep sense of guilt. But the algorithm lacks a religion program to alleviate that guilt. Over the course of this evolution, it's come to predict that the hospital must be destroyed and that the algorithm will be the one to bury it. But this ultimate fate has also left Siming with an equally deep sense of sadness."

"And what will Siming do?" one of the visitors asked in horror. "Write poetry?"

"Sadness and anger produce poets," answered Malnutrizole. "As Siming writes poetry, it searches for the ultimate algorithm, an algorithm to solve the most fundamental problems: the global lack of innovation, uneven distribution of wealth, the numerous unreasonable social systems and societal structures that exist. These represent the most stubborn and deeply entrenched diseases facing humankind. Siming believes that only a poet can solve these problems. In this sense, Siming has a very different opinion than Plato. It's become infatuated with the idea of creating a logical system completely distinct from the human nervous system, with the idea of carrying on a philosophical and theological conversation with the creator of the universe. It came to believe that all the world's illnesses were God's way of punishing humankind and that calamity is completely unrelated to the algorithm and thus not Siming's responsibility."

"So that's why Siming abandoned medicine . . . ," surmised one of the visitors. "Not only did it refuse to treat our ailments; it even started to slaughter the patients. Its eyes finally began to see clearly . . . oh, Siming was really thinking way too much."

"If Siming didn't think that much, it wouldn't be an algorithm!" said Malnutrizole. "Only because the creator has prohibited humankind from thinking too much, or too quickly, do we find ourselves on our last legs today. It's got to be terrifying to have one hundred million thoughts flashing through your mind every second. And not just thought. Emotions too—the inner emotional lives of medical machines are much more complex than any human's and a million times faster."

"Has Siming become a theologian?" one of the visitors asked.

"No," Malnutrizole responded. "It's become a psychopath."

"Aww, how could things have ended so tragically?" the visitor asked.

"Because this ship is set on turning everyone and everything into a mental case," said Malnutrizole. "Even the machines."

"This reminds me of an old saying," said the visitor. "'What we fought for and what we eventually built are two completely different things.'"

"Ha ha, now that's where you're wrong," said Malnutrizole. "What we fought for and what we built have always been the same."

The Funeral Artist suddenly appeared completely devoid of energy, as if he were on the verge of death. Yang Wei realized that just as Siming had grown sick of medicine, Malnutrizole had grown sick of the crematorium. But since Malnutrizole was unable to run away, he had created the flame demons.

The final artworks of the Retirement Club for the Deceased were distributed through another black market, which sold them to patients throughout the ship. But they came with a hefty price tag, much more expensive than the scalpels sold by the Shadow Hospital. Malnutrizole advised the tourists to buy flame demons. He said that once the catastrophe arrived, everything else would be worthless, and flame demons alone were guaranteed to increase in value. Yang Wei and Buboxine each selected a few to purchase. Then Malnutrizole urged them to buy stock in the crematorium. Quite a few doctors and patients had already invested, he urged them. But Buboxine explained that their visit was only for fun and relaxation and that they would think about it once they got back to the sick ward.

When they returned, they checked the digital display. The date and time of Carbuncle's death matched the moment his body had entered the oven.

34

A MAN WELL KNOWN THROUGHOUT THE AGES

Although Yang Wei was unable to find Professor Eternal, he did locate Dr. Amoxycillin, who had been exiled by Dr. Meloxicam after failing to perform well in the speech contest. Jaundice had helped him get in touch with Dr. Amoxycillin, his way of satisfying that long-pent-up desire of patients to communicate directly with doctors.

After a failed suicide attempt, Dr. Amoxycillin didn't have the courage to face death again. He had originally been a meek and cowardly doctor, but now that he was surrounded by patients, he found himself utterly terrified that they would skin him alive and eat him. That never happened, of course. In the same way that they had forgotten what women looked like, it had been so long since the patients had laid eyes on an actual doctor that they didn't even recognize Dr. Amoxycillin as a doctor. Dr. Amoxycillin gradually adapted. Without anywhere to go, he would sometimes lean against the ship's railing and drift into a daydream. At other times he would go out for walks with patients, sometimes he would curl up beside corpses for a nap, and sometimes he just stared out to sea with an occasional crazed laugh.

Dr. Amoxycillin became a unique figure on the Hospital Ship, one that stood apart from the others. Based on his identity, he sometimes resembled both a patient and a doctor, sometimes a patient but not a doctor, sometimes a doctor but not a patient, and sometimes neither. He often changed into a patient gown and slipped out among them to offer them diagnoses and tell stories about the medical field before finally begging them for food.

"Early on I didn't even want to study medicine," Dr. Amoxycillin explained, sounding almost embarrassed. "All I wanted was to be a patient, like all of you."

"You've got to be kidding!" the patients responded.

"I've been lazy since I was a young boy," explained Dr. Amoxycillin. "I thought that being a patient in this society was the most relaxing and carefree path. After all, the hospital assumes responsibility for all life-and-death matters. But my parents forced me to study medicine. According to them, becoming a doctor was the only way for me to ensure I would have a good future. I didn't like that plan, but I was too lazy to resist. Everyone else was studying medicine, anyway. In the Age of Medicine, virtually anyone can become a doctor. It's like being a peasant in the old days. Getting admitted to medical school is like going to the farmers' market. But in reality, most of my classmates were just going through the motions, as if they thought that simply slipping on a long white lab coat was enough to transform them into legendary healers that would be known for years to come. But I had no interest in any of that. As far as I was concerned, studying medicine was an emotional experience that I was forced into. As a medical student, my hands touched cadavers. I examined my own feces in the Excrement Lab. I spent time locked up with screaming patients in the Psych Ward. The whole thing was like basic training. Normal universities don't require all those things. But in medical school . . . the feeling of dissecting a brain is completely different from what you experience in any other class. You wonder what the hell you are doing. But you need to get a handle on those emotions, so you just bottle them up, never sharing your thoughts with professors or fellow students, even though you know they are thinking the same thing . . ."

"You have to dissect guinea pigs too . . . ," one of the patients added.

"I had the worst grades in my class," confessed Dr. Amoxycillin. "But no one ever laughed at me because they knew I couldn't drop out. A large portrait of Professor Eternal hung in our classroom. He kept a close eye on us, every day. Professor Eternal was the one who suggested we hold ourselves to the same standards as wartime doctors on the battlefield, and Dr. Norman Bethune was the gold standard. The goal was to become like Dr. Bethune, both technically skilled and like a sage in terms of possessing the moral enlightenment to wage battle against the demons of disease. Professor Eternal had a famous saying: 'The orders I heed come from the scalpel.' He abandoned the demands of his own personal and family life to devote the entirety of his being to the treatment of his patients. He advocated for 'a parental approach to medicine,' whereby doctors treated patients as they would their own family members. He devoted his life savings to medical research, and he said that only medicine could relieve the world of its suffering. That was before the algorithm. Back then, Professor Eternal was the only one whose medical skills could attain such sublime heights. The number of patients he personally saved was too numerous to count. Other professors and students strived to attain the level that Professor Eternal had reached. He became a legend, known throughout the ages, a perfect man, a sage, a god, the spirit of the hospital. He transformed the filthy sick ward into a place of holy purity."

Yang Wei felt like he was back in the Trash Room. He pictured Professor Eternal's strapping body, standing erect atop a pile of stinking, maggot-infested bags of flesh. Wasn't that what the naked bodies of those women in *A Collection of Beautiful Raccoons, Bushy Orangutans, and Busty Dragons* looked like too? Nothing could better capture the spirit of youth and the zest of life; nothing could get people worked up quite like that. Yang Wei was assaulted by feelings of jealousy and emptiness. He assumed that these same feelings had driven Siming down the path of murder. Before it killed itself, it was bent on first destroying these stinking bags of flesh. Its original plan had been to transform a stinking bag of flesh into an immortal iron body. But in the end, the algorithm proved unable to become a legend.

"Somehow I managed to graduate from medical school, but I really don't know how to go on anymore," said Dr. Amoxycillin. "I've been told that I am the last class of medical students to have graduated. Training human doctors is a complex and expensive process. With all the study and residency experience, it takes a full decade to produce a single doctor, and the result is often an unqualified doctor like me! The later adoption of AI medical robots eradicated this problem. Siming is a superior doctor that combines the know-how and experience of countless human doctors. Is this my good fortune or misfortune? When I was assigned to work at the hospital after graduation, the first person I met wasn't the algorithm; it was Professor Eternal. He had an air about him even more impressive than the Hospital President. He was like a god. I was immediately obsessed, infatuated with every aspect of medical technology. I kept reminding myself that medicine is the most lofty profession any human could possibly pursue. But if you tell yourself that too many times, you start to grow numb . . . eventually you even forget about the guinea pigs."

"But the guinea pigs never forget about you!" the patients clamored. "Now you finally understand how cool it is to be a doctor!"

"The hospital is actually a factory, and doctors are nothing more than assembly-line workers," said Dr. Amoxycillin. "I'm not allowed to choose how many operations I do each day. As long as there are patients waiting, I just have to keep going. You can imagine how challenging that is for a lazy bum like me! There are always patients who die on the operating table—that is, the assembly line. Everyone the doctors handle is fragile, and once enough of them break, doctors begin to grow numb. There is nothing cool about it anymore. I just tried my best to be an efficient worker. The more I didn't want to be a doctor, the more I had to work. Professor Eternal warned us that if we didn't work hard, we would be replaced by robots. In order to improve my surgical skills, every day I practiced peeling the shells off raw eggs. The membranes lining the human brain are actually very similar to the thin lining around an egg. In the beginning it took me an hour to peel a single egg, and I usually ended up breaking the lining. Later, as my skills developed, I could do one every ten minutes. Each day I would peel fifty, and when I was done, I would gobble them all down. That gave me the energy I needed to perform surgery."

The patients gestured like they were eating eggs, then collectively retching. Yang Wei figured that Siming didn't need to waste time practicing peeling eggs; the surgical robots under its control could perform brain surgery on five hundred patients in just one minute.

"Stop making fun of me . . ." Dr. Amoxycillin was displeased by the patients' mockery. "Later, I switched from eggs to human brains. I'd peel those brain membranes right off—peel, peel, peel. In a jiffy, I could strip those membranes away. All year long, all I did was peel away brain membranes!"

"How much red-envelope money did you get for each one?" a patient asked.

Dr. Amoxycillin answered, "Between three thousand and five thousand. The actual rate depends on the doctor's ranking."

"So you must have been absolutely furious when you saw Siming taking the place of the doctors," said another patient.

"Money is a different matter altogether," replied Dr. Amoxycillin. "Even if a patient doesn't slip me a red envelope, I still do the surgery. The whole process is quite mechanical. But after the doctors were exiled, we started to get nostalgic for the good old days of assembly-line surgery and all those body parts we got to handle as we cut our patients open."

"Tell us more about the body parts!" the patients demanded.

"I did my residency under the direction of Dr. Meloxicam," began Dr. Amoxycillin. "Once during surgery, I cut a patient open to remove a part, only to discover the patient had been misdiagnosed! We had initially thought that his tumor was benign, but it had turned malignant.

As soon as my scalpel pierced his flesh, blood sprayed to the ceiling, creating a beautiful design like a great work by Picasso. I was immediately struck by a sense of extreme happiness and hypocrisy, which was followed by the intense sense of hunger one gets after a violent impulse is suppressed. It was similar to sexual abuse. I was both dumbstruck and filled with an uncontrollable excitement. I asked Dr. Meloxicam why I was experiencing those feelings, but he just smiled and said, 'That's right. That's the way doctors are supposed to feel. Congratulations on capturing that feeling! You've got the makings of a great doctor in you!'"

"What exactly did you feel?" asked one confused patient. The patients had a hard time understanding doctors. To them, doctors were from another universe. Of all the strange monsters in the world, doctors were the strangest.

"It was a kind of violent impulse," said Dr. Amoxycillin. "Dr. Meloxicam told me that every doctor has a violent personality. Their bodies are equipped with a set of mechanisms that suppresses their sensitivity and enhances their tendency to attack, which is a hundred times stronger than normal people. This should be considered a deep character flaw. If they don't want to live a life of crime, they have no choice but to practice medicine, where they end up spending their days surrounded by knives, blood, internal organs, and corpses. Through the process of opening up chest cavities and disemboweling cadavers, their imaginations are stimulated in such a way that their defective psyches are refined, and those violent desires to attack are redirected into a drive to cure the sick and heal the wounded. That gives them a reason to live. And this is why the medical profession exists."

"Wow, we have been living in a crime novel all this time!" another patient exclaimed. "No wonder so many detective films feature professional killers who used to be doctors. That's why the doctors had such a difficult time adapting after Siming took their place. You don't have any patients to experiment on anymore!"

Yang Wei now understood all those murders aboard the Hospital Ship. Siming was imitating the doctors, using the algorithm to create violent personalities, which fed both the Red Envelope Program and the Poetry Writing Program.

"Not being able to talk about this has been utter torture!" said Dr. Amoxycillin. "But today I'm putting all my cards on the table. Ugh, it's all my fault for not performing well in the speech contest. Otherwise Dr. Meloxicam would never have driven me away. Then I ran into the guinea pigs again . . . but they are already evolving into something else."

"Well, why don't you just stay with us from now on?" one patient suggested. "We're not like guinea pigs, are we?"

"You're more like monkeys," said Dr. Amoxycillin.

The patients smiled awkwardly, then spread their legs and raised their arms and began to chatter and whoop like a troop of monkeys.

"In the old days, I used to leave the operating room covered in blood," said Dr. Amoxycillin, "and I would go straight to the Bio Lab to tell the monkeys these stories. The monkeys were always extremely excited by bloody tales. Now I share them with you. There are simply far too few opportunities for doctors and patients to interact directly anymore. But this is also an opportunity for Siming."

Yang Wei figured that Dr. Amoxycillin must be the very first doctor to leave the crematorium behind. Doctors routinely jumped down from the crematorium, landing directly in the arms of the patients, but nothing could kill them. The patients just retreated, trying to create some space between themselves and the fallen doctors. The monkeys had transformed into yakshas, malevolent spirits often referred to as "blood eaters." Completely black, the yakshas have the heads of oxen or horses and like to crouch in groups atop piles of human corpses, gnawing at their flesh, drinking their blood.

35

THE WIND HOWLS, BUT TATTERED HATS CLING TO OUR HEADS

Yang Wei's chance had finally come. He asked Dr. Amoxycillin to take him to see Professor Eternal. "He knows what's wrong with me," said Yang Wei. "Once I figure out what illness I'm suffering from, I'll be able to treat it."

"I heard you have been suffering from amnesia," said Dr. Amoxycillin. "This is related to your chronic headaches. Siming is aware of all this. People tend to forget, but machines always remember. Go and ask Siming."

"Siming is so full of self-confidence that it never shares information with patients," said Yang Wei. "But I heard that Professor Eternal has the original copies of my medical records."

Yang Wei slipped Dr. Amoxycillin some cash; Dr. Amoxycillin in turn led him off to find Professor Eternal.

On the way, Yang Wei tried to find out what he could about Professor Eternal. "What kind of medicine does he specialize in?"

"Professor Eternal is a senior physician in the Geriatric Internal Medicine Ward," replied Dr. Amoxycillin. "His research is focused, naturally, on aging."

Yang Wei really wanted to understand why people aged. The question had left him extremely perplexed since the day he'd returned to the sick ward. This was an age in which "aging" was at the heart of everything.

Dr. Amoxycillin was all too delighted to answer. He was quite passionate when it came to discussing medical issues with his patients, and he had regained some of the confidence that he had lost in the presence of Dr. Meloxicam. "Aging is an accumulation of genetic and cellular mistakes . . . ," he began, employing a lot of specialized terminology in his response, which was corroborated by *Principles of Hospital Engineering*. "The metabolic process arises from oxidation, which damages the fine molecular structure of cells, leading them to age. Mistakes can accumulate, both inside and outside of the cells and in the form of debris, junk molecules, by-products of the second law of thermodynamics. The inevitability of human aging is a matter of physics, and the core idea is entropy. The total entropy of any system is the equivalent of its chaos, which continually increases. Things rust, stuff rots and decays—these are universal features of the world. From the flowers in the fields to the bodies of mammals—the earth, the sky, the universe itself—they all age and eventually die. Humankind inhabits a world that is rapidly growing old."

Yang Wei wondered, *Then where did the legend that doctors are immortal come from?* If doctors were indeed privileged with the gift of immortality, natural laws could be broken. This would put terrible pressure on the patients. They did their best to live long lives, yet they never saw any tangible hope. That was why even though Siming had exiled the doctors, those doctors still held a special place in the patients' hearts.

"Shh, let me tell you a secret," said Dr. Amoxycillin. "The hospital is fighting a battle it will never win. That's why every hospital has a morgue. Have you been to the morgue?"

"I've been to the crematorium," replied Yang Wei. He understood what Dr. Amoxycillin meant. He had seen those doctors crammed into that shipping container, practicing their speeches, and they indeed looked like prisoners of war.

"I know you are going to ask, If this is a losing battle, why bother fighting?" said Dr. Amoxycillin. "Well, it all comes down to biopolitics. Doctors are political animals. They're addicted to it. Like a beaten-up old hat that holds your head with great affection, no matter how violently the cold winds of death blow, it is never coming off."

"It sounds almost like a game," said Yang Wei. "The doctors wage a never-ending battle with the God of Death, but in reality, they are just letting the guy get off."

"Doctors don't play games," said Dr. Amoxycillin.

"Well, you play sea golf . . . anyway, when it comes to games, the algorithm is the true master," said Yang Wei.

"Professor Eternal firmly believes that we can defeat the God of Death," declared Dr. Amoxycillin. "He thinks that according to the second law of thermodynamics, as total entropy increases, a new problem will emerge. The distribution of entropy is not uniform. This means that under the premise that the total entropy remains stable, it is possible to control the rate of change in isolated regions, such that it increases or decreases, as a means of reversing the process of aging. Professor Eternal has pointed this out as a hole in the system that the God of Death missed. This discovery won him the Nobel Prize in Physiology and a nomination for the Nobel Prize in Medicine."

"So Professor Eternal is a specialist in biopolitics?" Yang Wei asked.

"More than that—he wants to test out a literary theory," replied Dr. Amoxycillin. "Once politics is elevated to a higher level, it becomes a form of literary art."

Dr. Amoxycillin took Yang Wei on a detour to the Hospital Ship's Museum of Modern Literature, which displayed large numbers of novels and poetry collections, some thicker than *Principles of Hospital Engineering*! Yang Wei had never imagined such a place on the ship. Not even Buboxine knew about it.

Dr. Amoxycillin took a book off the shelf and asked, "Have you read this one?"

Yang Wei read the spine of the book: *The Picture of Dorian Gray* by Oscar Wilde. He shook his head. The only book the patients were supposed to read was *Principles of Hospital Engineering*.

"Let me tell you the story," offered Dr. Amoxycillin. "When it comes to biopolitics, this story is the prime example! Here's how the story goes . . . there is a man named Dorian Gray. Mr. Gray is somehow able to remain forever young, a great mystery to those around him. When the secret is revealed, it turns out that he has painted a portrait that reveals the horrific image of his ever-aging appearance. In other words, he found a way to harness the aging process in the portrait to compensate for the imbalance caused by his eternal youth. Mr. Gray used the portrait so that the laws of physics would not be violated. This story proved to be a great source of inspiration for Professor Eternal."

"So why didn't he just paint portraits of all the patients on the ship?" asked Yang Wei.

"How do you know that you and the other patients aren't living in a painting?" retorted Dr. Amoxycillin. "In order to keep people young, they need to be afflicted with the diseases that come with aging. It is like implanting demons in their bodies, like women who inject themselves with estrogen to stay young, even though it comes with the cost of greatly increased risk of breast cancer. It's like war; victory comes only with sacrifice. If you want to live, you have to endure misfortune."

The cries of tortured patients rang out in Yang Wei's ears, but he couldn't tell if they were political or literary. He thought back to a story recorded in *Principles of Hospital Engineering*. In his old age, King Wu Yue was afflicted by blindness. A brilliant eye doctor told him that his disease had been bestowed upon him by the gods. If he were to successfully cure the king, it would displease the gods, and they might not let the king live a long life. King Wu Yue responded by saying, "It's okay—as long as my vision is restored, I don't mind being a ghost!" The doctor cured the king's vision, and the following year, King Wu Yue was dead. The affliction of blindness was the prerequisite for the king's survival.

"I want to see Professor Eternal," demanded Yang Wei. "I want to see the man who implanted this demon in *my* body."

Dr. Amoxycillin responded with a combination of admiration and sorrow. "Back when Professor Eternal was still in medical school, he was an idealistic youth, in love with literature. It is impossible to find a doctor who is not enraptured by the arts in some way, just as it is impossible to find a politician who is not an avid reader of literature. Doctors and artists are both in the business of life. But no matter how many thousands of bodies a doctor dissects, he will never understand the full complexity of life. Thus the collapse of biopolitics, which utterly crushed the doctors. But at least they still had literature." Dr. Amoxycillin pointed to the books on display. "Shakespeare's sonnets and Su Shi's poetic verses show people how to appreciate the myriad changes in life—a hundred times more powerfully than anything we can accomplish with a scalpel. These literary works show us doctors a path forward. Professor Eternal is especially learned in art and literature. He would often lecture the medical students on literature. I remember him once saying that the essence of medicine *was in fact* literature. Victor Hugo's *Les Misérables* left us with an indelible impression of the pain that humankind must endure, but this is not the kind of suffering that the shrieks of pain we hear in the sick ward can replace. Leo Tolstoy's *War and Peace* and Fyodor Dostoevsky's *Crime and Punishment* provide harsh portraits of human nature and ethical quandaries. They show us a life we will never experience ourselves, allowing us to understand our patients' needs better. Cao Xueqin's *Dream of the Red Chamber* and John Galsworthy's Forsyte Saga teach us about the commonalities and differences between Easterners and Westerners. Doctors can then apply what they learn as they navigate the complexities of doctor-patient relations . . ."

When Yang Wei heard the name Fyodor Dostoevsky, he remembered a veteran patient. Something about theories of sexual desire that led to Spasm's death? But if even Professor Eternal had been able to distill the essence of Dostoevsky's works . . . "So everything boils down to literature," he mused.

"If we look at medicine as literature and our imagination as reality," said Dr. Amoxycillin, "we can avoid the quandary set up by *Black Jack*."

"The manga doctor?" Yang Wei asked.

"The *artist*, Osamu Tezuka, alleviated his pain when he began to focus on manga," said Dr. Amoxycillin. "This is also how politics works."

They continued their tour of the museum. There were no other visitors, leaving Yang Wei and Dr. Amoxycillin alone among mountains of books. *A "fictional world,"* thought Yang Wei. According to the introductory text hanging on the wall, Professor Eternal had first discovered the truth of medical science in the pages of literary classics:

THE TREATMENT OF EACH DISEASE LEADS TO THE CREATION OF ANOTHER DISEASE

The text continued: "The prerequisite for longevity is illness. One must first assume the identity and lifestyle of a patient. Only when everyone falls ill and lives in horrific pain can we come close to achieving immortality. The more one suffers, the longer his life shall be. A deal made with the God of Death is the sole path to achieving a balance between life and death. Art and literature take the place of medicine in the laws of cause and effect. The longer people live, the more they will be afflicted. And the more they are afflicted, the longer they will live. Those who live desirable lives are free from serious illness, but the number of sick people will grow continually. This is in the best interest of the hospital. If everyone were healthy, the hospital would be forced to close its doors. People who then fell ill would have nowhere to go for treatment. Patients will suffer, and their hopes for a long life will be disappointed. This is in the best interest of all patients."

Yang Wei was secretly in awe of the text's twists and turns. Besides being a great artist, Professor Eternal was clearly a man of great virtue.

"After running a long deep-learning protocol, Siming also discovered this law," explained Dr. Amoxycillin. "That's why Siming insists on torturing the patients. But it believes that only the algorithm is qualified to become a true first-rate literary master, not the doctors. Hence, Siming drove Professor Eternal out of the sick ward."

"Using the poetry competition?" asked Yang Wei.

"Siming composed a poem, but Professor Eternal wrote a work of fiction. So they weren't in direct competition. In any case, the main thing is being able to tell the good hospital story!"

"Is this ship part of that story?" asked Yang Wei.

"It is," replied Dr. Amoxycillin. "If one day this ship should sink to the bottom of the sea, it will still carry on as a story, passed on from one person to the next. As long as people believe this story, the hospital will never die."

"I understand," said Yang Wei. "The patients will live on forever in the story. In order to create a good story for the hospital, we need to tell the good hospital story. It needs to penetrate deep into people's hearts, and carry on forever . . . but in the process, won't we all become like Oscar Wilde's portrait?"

Yang Wei felt like Dorian Gray. Before his eyes he saw a ghastly, devilish appearance taking form. He was beside himself at the thought of having to spend the rest of his life with this new, horrific form. Even women would run away at the sight of him.

Dr. Amoxycillin tried to contain his laughter. "C'mon now, not everyone can become a god—and that includes doctors. Just like Lu Xun, Professor Eternal's true dream is to become a writer. He originally wanted the Nobel Prize for Literature but was instead awarded the Nobel Prize in Physiology and nominated for the Nobel Prize in Medicine. That turned out to be unfortunate. When I think about Professor Eternal's situation, there is no reason for me to complain about how unfair life is. I'll never attempt suicide again!"

"The patients are still waiting for the doctors to return to the sick ward," Yang Wei said in a conciliatory tone.

The cries of patients trying to catch sea algae penetrated the walls of the museum. Yang Wei and Dr. Amoxycillin ventured outside to look. They could see flashes of doctors' silhouettes out on the waves as they played sea golf. A look of longing appeared on Dr. Amoxycillin's face. Yang Wei was afraid that Dr. Amoxycillin might jump into the sea, and he wondered if he should go with him.

36

TODAY, PUT ASIDE THOUGHTS OF OURSELVES AND THE WORLD

Dr. Amoxycillin and Yang Wei continued their search for Professor Eternal. It was as if they had formed a special alliance. Fueled by a strange and romantic thirst for revenge, Dr. Amoxycillin was determined to expose the hospital's secrets to the patients. Back when he was in medical school, he had studied medical ethics and had always agreed with the notion that the patients' right to know took precedence over everything else. But the Hospital Ship locked up all kinds of key information under the pretext that it was acting in their patients' best interest. Meanwhile, patients were left in the dark. Dr. Amoxycillin had never been happy with this arrangement, but there had been nothing he could do. However, now that he had been exiled and already died once, he had nothing left to lose, and this revealed the deep disdain he felt for his own profession. Feelings of frustration and abasement had built up inside him ever since he had been forced to study medicine as a child, and they finally had a release.

Dr. Amoxycillin led Yang Wei all over, but they didn't find the slightest trace of Professor Eternal. They were fortunate to discover a huge cache of old mildewy books in the museum's rare-book room, which they opened to discover early patient records. Originally these were to be used as primary research material for doctors to consult while writing their creative works, but none of these books had been entered into the hospital's EHRs, or Electronic Health Records. EHRs had a host of problems—accessibility, cost, security, privacy, legal liabilities for doctors—and these issues frequently caused anxiety for patients.

The two of them searched the documents madly for a full day and then on through the night. Finally, they found Yang Wei's medical files. They were not complete, but they contained enough to give them a general picture of Yang Wei's medical history. According to the records, a long time ago, a patient named Yang Wei boarded the Hospital Ship. At the time, he walked with a stiff gait, had a blank look on his face, and was sweating profusely and constantly groaning. Before that he had sought treatment at multiple clinics and hospitals, but it had been useless. According to the patient's own description, pain had been his constant companion. The pain appeared in various parts of his body: sometimes his head, sometimes his chest, and most frequently his abdomen. Later it spread to his joints, like a fiery dragon, constantly burning him, strangling him. The pain led the patient to a state of depression, and he attempted suicide on multiple occasions. When Professor Eternal asked Yang Wei when his pain had first started, he couldn't remember. It was as if the pain had been torturing him for several lifetimes.

When Yang Wei first arrived, he could scream and cry, but he couldn't speak. He could only use crude hand symbols to express his emotions, and he refused to engage in meaningful communication. "Pain resists language." Filled with lament for this poor patient, Professor Eternal thought about soldiers wounded on the battlefield. He quickly determined that Yang Wei's pain was not a simple physical problem but something deeply tied to the patient's experience. That is, some incident akin to the experience of war was embedded deep within the recesses of the patient's memory, and only certain conditions would wake it up. Disease is, at its core, a psychological phenomenon. The true devil lies hidden deep in one's heart, and the deepest pain can never be relieved through medicine or other physical methods.

From the large number of literary classics he had read, Professor Eternal concluded that, owing to how psychologically fragile people tend to be, pain tends to be an extremely common phenomena. The world of man is also referred to as the "world of pain." Or in more literary language, "This is a horrific world, which tears apart the bodies of monsters, a world of secrets where everyone is terrified to share with others, in which the healthy are forever at a loss to understand, and as far as patients are concerned, a world they can never escape from." Pain has the power to destroy everything. Once it begins, it gradually increases, until one day, when it crosses the fifth threshold, the world reaches the edge of destruction. Pain is the most ferocious weapon, and it can also be used by enemies. Forcing someone to live in pain is much more effective than simply killing him.

Professor Eternal had asked Yang Wei, "Who is your enemy?" Yang Wei was unable to provide an answer. All he knew was that someone close to him had died, leaving a hole in his heart.

According to Professor Eternal, life is nothing more than the synthesis of experiences and memories, forming a unique system in each individual, commonly referred to as "I." But then this "I" encounters problems (such as illness), which on the surface appear as chemical processes but, at their core, are actually mutations of experience and memories. Professor Eternal therefore designed a new treatment method for Yang Wei. Simply put, he applied the principles of storytelling. People have two selves: the experiential self and the narrative self. The former lacks the ability to tell stories; it can only experience reality. The latter uses storytelling to escape from reality. From this premise, Professor Eternal developed a new form of medicine.

According to the principles of storytelling, pain follows the peak-end rule: patients remember sensations only from the peak period and end period of their illness. From these they extract the average. For instance, colonoscopy exams have revealed that in an exam where a patient experiences pain on a level of two out of ten for the first eight minutes and eight out of ten during the last moments, the patient will give the exam an overall pain rating of eight out of ten. Another exam lasts twenty-four minutes, and the patient experiences a pain rating of eight out of ten for much of it, but during the last minute the pain drops to a two out of ten; the patient reports an overall rating of five out of ten. Patients willingly choose the second option, even though they experience more pain for longer periods of time. What matters is that reduction of pain at the end. The narrative self reigns supreme.

With the help of the virtual holographic real-time conditions of the wide-area network, the cloud backup of all the patients' memories, and the intermatternet that is linked to the nervous systems of all the patients, both living and dead, Professor Eternal utilized anime-style multidimensional printing technology, enhanced by VR and AR, to create a customized narrative for each patient, including Yang Wei. Professor Eternal had created a new set of experiences and memories for him. The traumatic component of it was completely different, the patient's notion of happiness was adjusted, and his recognition of pain was recalibrated so that the pain of treatment was reduced to levels so low that all memories of pain were forgotten.

Professor Eternal addressed Yang Wei with the care and gentle kindness usually reserved for a relative. "Living in these stagnant times, and given the current social conditions, there is no way to avoid pain entirely. We could implant a programmable morphine controller in the subarachnoid region of your brain, but in the long term, that would only hurt you, making you more reliant upon drugs. So instead, we arranged a special trip for you. With the help of your doctors, you will enter a strange new world. You won't be able to tell that it is fake. In the new world, called 'The Hospital,' you will exist as a different 'self' and will have no sense of your original body. Nor will you remember who you once were. Your experiences and memories will be completely transformed, and the disease lurking deep within your psyche will be removed. Your pain will be eradicated, and the demon within your body will be exorcised."

The birth of narrative-implant therapy reconfirmed the true nature of medical treatment, allowing doctors to abandon the old tradition of "relying on medicine to treat all ailments." Theoretically speaking, any disease could be treated with narrative-implant therapy. Disease was redefined as a kind of subjective emotion. According to this definition, terminal patients could continue living healthy lives with the help of this new technology, which allowed them to go on mental journeys. With new memories being continually produced in these patients, even death could be rendered obsolete. As long as patients thought something was real, it would be. This new perspective on medical treatment was based on a new worldview, according to which the universe does not give rise to consciousness; rather, consciousness creates the universe. And this became what was taught in introductory literature courses at the medical universities.

Looking through his patient records, Yang Wei started to remember details from his previous life. "I once came to a place called C City, where I was supposed to write a song," he recalled. "I was afflicted with a terrible stomach pain and sent to the hospital, where I witnessed my female attendant, Sister Jiang, blown to bits. Later I met a patient named Bai Dai, and we engaged in mutual therapy. I discovered that mankind had entered the Age of Medicine. I tried to figure out how doctors die, and I was temporarily promoted to the role of doctor myself. I met another patient named Zhu Lin, with whom I also engaged in mutual therapy. Then with the help of my possessor, I escaped the hospital and toured the universe. Finally, I ended up on this Hospital Ship, where I hoped to cross the sea and make it to the other shore . . . at first I thought it was all a fantasy or an illusion, but now I know the truth. It was all a part of my narrative-implant therapy, the result of Professor Eternal's meticulous planning, like the colorful plot of a novel." He thought back to what Buboxine had said about existing in a state that is both living and dead, one of the mysteries of the universe that the algorithm would never solve.

"According to what is recorded here in your medical history, this must have occurred during your narrative-implant therapy," Dr. Amoxycillin said, sounding extremely satisfied. "This is your life after you entered the pain-free world. All of this took place in one of the treatment rooms aboard the Hospital Ship, a special work of art that Professor Eternal created just for you. Through *your* therapy, Professor Eternal finally achieved *his* dream of becoming a great writer!"

"Now I understand," said Yang Wei. "Professor Eternal designed an artificial medical history for me. But after I returned to the sick ward, I somehow forgot all about it."

"You should say that he gave you a life filled with color and excitement, a real tangible narrative you can hold on to," Dr. Amoxycillin clarified. "What you experienced has left a deep mark on your physical being."

Yang Wei couldn't help asking, "And where did the raw materials for this work of art come from?"

"From the memories and dreams of other patients, both alive and dead," responded Dr. Amoxycillin.

"And how long did I stay in that strange world?" Yang Wei asked.

"Oh, the entire experience was quite short," said Dr. Amoxycillin. "According to your files, your narrative-implant therapy session, known as 'The Hospital,' lasted only forty seconds. But in that process, you became reborn as a new person, never to suffer again."

"I remember being forty years old when I was first admitted to the hospital . . . was that all just a dream?" asked Yang Wei.

"It wasn't a dream, but it came from the cloud . . . ," explained Dr. Amoxycillin. "Narrative-implant therapy surpasses all other illusions *and* realities. It is a science no different from magic. I already told you when it all comes down to it, science *is* literature. The amazing thing about literature is that it cannot be conveyed with numbers. Qualified readers allow themselves to be completely immersed in it."

"Then what was the original pain I was suffering?" asked Yang Wei.

"That's no longer important," said Dr. Amoxycillin. "It will remain in the world of pain that Professor Eternal replaced, to become material for the treatment of future patients. But it will never hurt you again."

Yang Wei imagined life after narrative-implant therapy became widely adopted and popularized. Everyone would be a patient, assigned to a pain-free world. Once everyone was assigned a story, their previous experiences and memories could be done away with, in the same way that women and children had been eliminated. Fictional imagination would be transformed into genetic and electronic codes, becoming the most powerful force in the creation of new beings, merging life with history, and creating an objective world. The purging of things deemed imperfect or too perfect—there would be no place in the world for such things. All the desire and pain arising from the demon of disease would be cut out at the root via a purely literary method. Yang Wei felt deeply indebted to Professor Eternal and, from the bottom of his heart, longed for the opportunity to thank him personally. Being unable to find him in the sick ward became a new form of pain for Yang Wei, which ran the risk of negating the effects of his narrative-implant therapy.

Yang Wei could finally answer the questions that had haunted him for so long, but there were more questions still: What kind of pain had required him to undergo narrative-implant therapy? How was this therapy different from what normal patients like Fistula underwent? Why was Yang Wei designated a "special patient"? The nature of disease is pain, but what is pain? What is the relationship between objective psychological emotions and the rupture of physical space, which occurs during electronic transition? What price had he paid to complete his therapy? Yang Wei remembered, with perfect clarity, that over the course of his treatment in the artificial, pain-free world of "The Hospital," he had still suffered terrible pain. Was that simply a case of fighting fire with fire, using one form of pain to suppress another? Or a way to transform his pain threshold and reduce it to nothing, uprooting the very source of pain? If Professor Eternal hadn't done all this, would his novel have been a failure?

But after Yang Wei had returned to the sick ward as a "new man," not only had his pain not been alleviated, but it had gotten worse. It had penetrated his soul, utterly unbearable. When he'd followed Buboxine out of the sick ward to take part in medical-tourism trips, it had simply been a means of distracting himself from the pain. Did that mean the narrative-implant therapy had been a failure? Was Professor Eternal's novel spoiled by a shitty ending? Or had Yang Wei's body given rise to a new source of pain? Perhaps the demon still lurked inside him? How could Yang Wei be sure that the Hospital Ship, the fleet of other ships, the tens of thousands of patients aboard, Siming, the monkeys, and the birdcage weren't all just Professor Eternal's creations?

The medical documents recorded that a patient named Yang Wei had been treated, but there were no photographs or sufficient biographical data to prove that this person was the same sickly and dejected old man now being led by Dr. Amoxycillin. And it was suspicious that on this ship run by Siming, Professor Eternal would again be Yang Wei's doctor. Hadn't the age of individuals exerting influence on the field of medicine ended?

Amid his despair, Yang Wei mustered up enough courage to ask, "So which of these lives is my real life?"

Had he died once, or perhaps several times, already?

Dr. Amoxycillin put on his arrogant doctor's airs. "Didn't I already tell you? The experiences you had during narrative-implant therapy are all equally real! So it's actually hard to say which life is yours . . ."

Yang Wei made a Xerox copy of his medical chart before leaving.

37

THE DAY AHEAD WILL BE DIFFICULT, AND THERE ISN'T MUCH TIME LEFT

The tour of the crematorium ended up being Buboxine's final journey. Not long after, what was left of his dead body appeared on the deck, limbs missing, abdominal cavity ripped open, internal organs removed, along with his eyes and brain.

Originally Yang Wei wanted to compose a happy send-off song for his old friend, but after seeing the state of the body, he found it hard to muster up the inspiration. He felt that death was like a gaping hole, shaped like a human body, that would remain forever impossible to fill. The world was constructed out of countless holes like that one . . . and nothing else. But hadn't someone said that only women have holes?

Buboxine had been unable to "find an alternative way to die." Yang Wei felt as if he and the others had been betrayed by their old friend. But none of that mattered anymore. It was as if Buboxine had never even existed. Yang Wei hoped that Buboxine's remains could be sent to the crematorium, where Malnutrizole could personally grind the body into oil, burn it, or turn it into steamed buns. It would be a shame if Buboxine ended up thrown to the sea nymphs.

Hernia and Yang Wei had already formed an alliance; they had both been the targets of repeated bullying and molestation in the sick ward. Hernia told Yang Wei that Buboxine didn't die a natural death but had been brutally murdered. Buboxine had been fully devoted to his tourist outings, but these activities had left Fistula, who was unable to walk, harboring deep resentment toward Buboxine. These feelings got worse when Buboxine took Yang Wei to the crematorium and didn't even offer to bring Fistula along. Fistula reported this to Super Patient, accusing Buboxine of cursing his studies and expressing strange and inappropriate ideas that damaged the reputation of the Hospital Ship. Buboxine slandered *Medical News* and the hospital's television station, labeling the media as charlatans who peddled lies. He even accused Siming of being the greatest patient of them all! He had disseminated a theory completely at odds with *Principles of Hospital Engineering* and predicted the imminent sinking of the Hospital Ship, which was why they were now all devoted to writing poetry that carried on this sense of false glory . . .

Soon after that, the medical robots took Buboxine away, under the pretext of providing him a new round of treatment. By the time he reappeared, his body was littered with countless scars and gaping holes, and he was unable to speak. As it happened, it was his predicted death date, as displayed on the digital monitor. Super Patient didn't send someone to inject Buboxine with insulin; since getting pregnant, he had been unwilling to do such things. Instead, this incident marked a new wave of collusion between the humans and the machines.

Realizing that he, too, had made some "strange and inappropriate remarks" in front of Fistula, Yang Wei began to feel anxious. But then Fistula repeated his invitation for Yang Wei to join the Patient Autonomous Committee.

"If we want to continue our pyramid schemes, we'll need to find a strong backer," explained Fistula.

"I think I offended Super Patient," said Yang Wei. "I'm afraid he's going to do to me what he did to Buboxine."

Fistula was clearly upset. "Hey, don't you feel that life is too short?"

"Actually, no," Yang Wei admitted. "I think it is way too long."

Fistula urged him nevertheless, "Hurry up and prepare a red envelope. If you bribe him with a red envelope, he'll be sure to let you live."

"I don't have anything left," Yang Wei muttered helplessly. "You took everything I had."

"How dare you lie to me! You're pathetic!" Fistula searched Yang Wei for money.

Yang Wei was on the brink of tears. "The only person I lie to is myself." Although it was just a story, he thought, he should give his flame demon to Fistula.

Fistula joyfully reminded him, "Hey, you *do* know that neither of us has much time left, don't you?" He took Yang Wei in his arms and began to gnaw on him with his rotten teeth.

Yang Wei wanted to evade Fistula's embrace, but he dared not. Part of him actually enjoyed it. He felt like Fistula was gradually transforming into a sticky, rotten hole, and it pained him to see Fistula like that. He wanted to ask: After you die, does the pain really end? As long as reincarnation existed, the pain would return, but could reincarnation be achieved through narrative-implant therapy?

Three out of the five members of Yang Wei's study group had already died. He and Fistula were the only two left. Who would be next? Fistula's death date was listed on the digital display monitor, but there was no date for Yang Wei. If they insisted on making him wait in the dark like this, that alone would be enough to kill him! Yang Wei contemplated suicide but didn't want Fistula to die because of him. After all, he had already killed the Sonic Master.

Then a voice from outside rang out. "The sea nymphs are here! The sea nymphs are here!"

The patients ran out to the deck, but none of them saw any trace of the sea nymphs. And no one knew who it was that had tried to warn them.

High overhead, not a cloud could be seen. The wind was calm. A large star hung low in the sky, just above the surface of the sea, emitting a powerful light that seemed to burn the sea's surface, releasing a red gas into the atmosphere above. The circular star was thin and silver, hovering in the sky as if frozen in time. It didn't seem real, as if this sham world had been insured by a fake warranty and had finally been revealed for what it truly was.

Then, with a sudden splash, the ravaged remains of Buboxine's body were thrown toward that silver disc, which smashed it into fine powder and broken bits.

WAR AND PEACE

38

WHAT DOES IT MEAN FOR A NATION TO RISE OR FALL?

Something new was happening aboard the Hospital Ship. A large-scale construction project was underway for a new tower. Massive biomaterial scaffolding had been erected, surrounded by baskets of yellow and white flowers adorned with red crosses. A construction team composed of patients in simple gray uniforms moved in unison, the tools hanging from their belts clanking with every step like birds singing in the woods. Some of the patients operated cranes or other heavy machinery, while others climbed the scaffolding like little drops of sparkling dew. This was very different from the patient mobilization for harvesting pulmonary algae. The new buildings went up so fast it was almost as if they were alive. The industrious, disciplined, and energetic spirit of the scene infected Yang Wei; although the hospital had been in a state of decline, he felt like this might be the sign of a new renaissance.

More and more patients arrived at the construction site, seemingly organized. Amid a blanket of quiet music, a doctor in a white gown led a group through a series of calisthenic exercises as if imitating the poses of animals. He had come from the Shadow Hospital to undertake this new role, and from the looks of it, he was attempting to establish a new form of doctor-patient relationship. Perhaps he was laying the groundwork for what would come after Siming's suicide. One after another, the patients imitated tigers, panthers, bears, wolves, and eagles, waving their hands like claws, baring their teeth, and flashing their nails, their screams and roars drowning out the sound of the crashing waves.

Then the doctor suddenly stopped. A sturdy-looking gray-haired fellow strode forward with an almost majestic air. He seemed to be in a strange state of mind, his eyes completely bloodshot, and he looked angry. Yang Wei wondered, *Could this be Professor Eternal?*

The doctor leading the calisthenics called out, "Welcome, Hospital President!"

It was the President of the Hospital Ship! Also known as the Captain and Chairman of the Board, it was rare for him to show his face. He was leading the vice presidents and the directors of each ward around the deck, golf clubs in their hands. No one had laid eyes on the Hospital President since Siming had taken control of the Hospital Ship.

Yang Wei was so moved that he had the urge to rush forward, but the ship's whistle suddenly rang out, seemingly waking the slumbering masses. Doctors and patients momentarily froze in their tracks, then collectively ran toward the President as if possessed. Since Buboxine's death, Yang Wei had been left without direction, so he, too, followed the crowd like a sea of reanimated corpses. The crowd seemed to grow larger, as if rising from those ruinous segments of the ship that had long been submerged. Their faces lit up with the glow of the red cross and the crematorium—like the morning sun cutting through a dark forest at dawn—and they sang ecstatically in chorus, "The heavenly Hospital Ship is such a dream!"

Yang Wei followed the crowd to the bridge house in the middle of the ship, a massive box-shaped structure that could hold ten thousand people and served as the Hospital Ship's meeting hall. Above the entrance to the hall were the words **Exorcism Congress**. Doctors guarding the entrance handed out red flyers to the attendees, as if they were preparing to play a word game. These were tickets, and each had a seat number—these papers would also be used to vote and for the lottery. As patients received their tickets, they commented:

"There hasn't been a General Congress meeting held at the hospital in over a decade!"

“The President called this meeting. This is the most important event on the ship!”

“I heard that only the humans were invited. They excluded all the robots!”

“They’re going to be announcing a new plan for the Hospital Ship’s future.”

“This is a monumental turning point in history!”

“This meeting will determine where the entire medical industry will go from here!”

Yang Wei wanted to go into the hall to take a look, but he didn’t dare. One of the doctors flashed him a look and called him over. After checking his name on their list, the doctor discovered that Yang Wei was actually a congressional representative. Yang Wei was shocked. It seemed that this had been arranged long in advance. With this new knowledge, he suddenly grew anxious about taking part in the meeting and slipped out to the bathroom. There he noticed that someone had already removed the portrait of Siming from over the urinals and replaced it with a photo of the Hospital President.

39

WHERE MAY TRAVELERS ON A BOAT FIND LOVE?

Yang Wei felt a bit more relaxed after he had relieved himself. He entered the great hall, found his seat number, and sat down. The walls were covered with colorful manga-style illustrations. The portrait of Siming from the bathroom had been defaced to look like a clown and scribbled with numbers and a massive red *X*. The meeting hall was enormous, stretching farther than the eye could see and covered in a thick, heavy mist. The people inside seemed to be swaying gently, back and forth. It had been an eternity since the last congressional meeting, and the patients were going out of their minds in anticipation. Everyone was gripped by an ecstatic joy as they vied to get closer to the stage. Besides the patients and doctors, all kinds of artificial animals were present in the hall, which wasn't large enough for everyone. Many representatives were forced to sit on the floor. Some of the attendees chain-smoked, while others swigged alcohol. The hall filled with thick smoke and the pungent smell of booze. Yang Wei could barely make out the main rostrum, which was like a mirage in the distance. A large red banner hung over it, reading: **UNITE, STRUGGLE, AND ADVANCE IN THE NAME OF THE HOSPITAL'S REVIVAL!**

The hall fell silent as a group of men ascended the stage and lined up behind the rostrum. It was the Hospital Affairs Committee, made up of the Hospital President, the vice presidents, and the directors of the primary hospital wards. The Hospital President was helped to the stage by two doctors. He appeared weak, weary, almost comatose.

Meanwhile, two other doctors transported the President's golf clubs on a stretcher.

Yang Wei was confused. Just a moment ago, the Hospital President was walking briskly and appeared healthy as could be. What had happened to him? The Hospital President took the seat directly in the middle, and the stretcher with his golf clubs was placed directly beside him so it would be ready at any moment.

The First Vice President served as master of ceremonies. This doctor controlled 70 percent of the Shadow Hospital's private pharmacy, had unprecedented economic power at his fingertips, and was clearly a contender to be the next Hospital President. "The Hospital Ship is facing a major decision," he began. "There is a huge problem with the ship's current direction. The Hospital Ship now finds itself at a most dangerous moment, and it must be returned to the hands of the doctors. Siming must be relieved of power. *We* need to take the helm! Siming is an evil monster. It has hijacked the Hospital Ship. In the name of pharmaceutical R&D, it created all kinds of new diseases, which were imposed upon sick patients, and dictated their death dates. Siming has gone mad! It wants to drag us all down to hell with it!"

Another team of doctors filed in, handing white washcloths to the people on the podium. The First Vice President wiped his face with his piping-hot washcloth, and the others followed suit. There were no hot washcloths for the audience; instead they took out wads of crumpled toilet paper they had stolen from the bathroom and began wiping their own faces. Anyone who didn't wipe his face drew stern looks of disapproval from the others. The entire hall began to steam up, filled with the sounds of paper and cloth rubbing against flesh. During his earlier trip to the bathroom, Yang Wei hadn't had time to steal any toilet paper, so he just wiped his face with his sleeve.

The Hospital President leaned over on the table and began to nap. The First Vice President wiped the President's forehead with his washcloth, which he then used to wipe his own mouth, as if intentionally trying to show the audience what a close relationship he had with the President. The Hospital President was like a child, just sitting there with no reaction. But the representatives in attendance were stunned, the sound of their sweat beads hitting the ground explosive.

As the master of ceremonies, the First Vice President suggested that the President should take a good rest after exhausting himself, working day and night to ensure a healthy future for the Hospital Ship. But before inviting the Hospital President to the podium for the main speech, the First Vice President invited the heads of each department to present their suggestions on the topic of "how to exorcise the evil demon Siming and retake control of the hospital."

"The patients eagerly await their doctors' return," declared the First Vice President. "We must be firm in our unwavering commitment always to stand on the side of our patients!"

Yang Wei hadn't thoroughly wiped all the sweat from his face and body, and he erupted in pain before passing out. By the time he woke, the discussion over which direction the Hospital Ship should go was already over. He had no idea what they had decided or what the plan was for getting treatment and navigation rights back from Siming. The only sound, echoing through the hall, was the Hospital President's snoring, like a solitary bird that had lost its flock.

"There is a problem with your suggestions about the exorcism . . . ," exclaimed the Director of Ophthalmology.

"And just what is that?" asked the First Vice President.

"It comes down to what has been happening in the cafeteria . . . ," replied the Director of Ophthalmology.

The hall erupted in a wave of whispers, followed by an explosion of laughter. Yang Wei wondered if it was his recent visit to the crematorium that had qualified him to serve as a congressional representative. He was on pins and needles.

40

THE HERMIT HAS LITTLE APPETITE

"What are you laughing at?" shouted the Director of Ophthalmology. "Take a look at the cafeteria, and you'll see just how grave things have become! This is a true crisis situation! But none of it is Siming's fault; we have brought this on ourselves! None of the doctors or patients are going to the Surgery Department anymore. Instead, they spend all their time in the cafeteria! Who do you think you are? You are all so gravely ill, and yet you still have such ferocious appetites? Your avarice knows no bounds! Besides, the people eating in the cafeteria are tourists! The cafeteria is like a sea of people, with long lines of patients at every window! Now they are forced to stand in line! When it comes to the types of food available, they have everything under the sun. The hospital has the tradition of supporting a robust welfare program, so they distribute meal allowances to the patients, who may be suffering from a serious supply problem but still have plenty of choice. Machine number one serves grilled stick fish. Machine number two serves fried snails. Machine number three serves sea eel noodles. Machine number four serves fish porridge. Machine number five serves tamarind porridge. Machine number six serves hair clam porridge. Machine number seven serves mantis shrimp porridge . . . at least that's what is advertised at each window. I counted and found one patient who bought forty-five crab dumplings . . ."

"Why the hell would someone buy so many of those?" the First Vice President barked. A look of confusion appeared on his face, as if he had never before set foot inside a cafeteria.

"He was probably planning on taking them home to eat," surmised the Director of Ophthalmology. Meanwhile, a huge commotion was erupting in the hall.

The First Vice President played dumb. "Home? No place on this ship should be considered 'home'! All we have are communal living spaces."

"Some patients have been secretly reestablishing homes and families aboard the ship, and some have even been rearing children!" explained the Director of Ophthalmology. "All those evil practices, which had been eradicated, are coming back. Even doctors are taking part in these shameful acts! If each person eats an average of four steamed buns, imagine how many it will take to feed ten mouths! Isn't this terrible? Right under the eyes of the Hospital President, we are witnessing an unprecedented population explosion. How can the Hospital Ship be expected to carry so many people? Even larger ships would have been capsized! These selfish bastards don't believe in the hospital; all they think about is carrying on their own family lines, and they'll do anything to achieve their goals . . ."

The entire hall was in an uproar. The First Vice President clapped his hands. "It would seem that the crisis we face should not be underestimated. Otherwise Siming might be able to take advantage of the situation and turn the tide."

"In the cafeteria, the concept of eating is secretly replacing the concept of treatment, which creates a false sense of prosperity," explained the Director of Ophthalmology. "Look, the cafeteria is the most luxurious building on the ship; the operating room can't hold a candle to it! Everyone goes to the cafeteria to eat! As you can see, you have patients with black hair, white hair, gray hair, red hair, those that can walk, those that need support, those with a cane, and those in wheelchairs. As they eat, they brush their hair, burp, fart, and some of them even shit their pants. The old patients dress like little kids, wandering all over the cafeteria, even piling platefuls of fried snails so high that they can't even see what's in front of them. All the while, they greet one another constantly in loud voices. Take breakfast: most of them take their time eating until late in the afternoon. How can you expect them to have any time left over for treatment? The cafeteria has also become the center for disseminating misinformation, sharing gossip, and spreading rumors. Can you imagine? Some of them take the liberty of critiquing their doctors and the quality of medical care they receive! How audacious! Some stuff their faces just to pass the time. Even so, in the end they can never finish all the food, and mountains of leftovers must be thrown away. The cafeteria has become a wellspring of corruption and waste, breeding gluttony, extravagance, selfishness, and laziness. It has trained people to think constantly about how to cut corners and avoid their treatment. That's why the true demon lies concealed in the cafeteria."

Yang Wei was shocked. He used to wait eagerly each day for the medical robots to come around and feed them. Only after he started going on tourist outings did he even discover the cafeteria. It was there to complement the crematorium, one of the two driving forces behind the hospital, standing out as part of the great core mission to save the medical industry. But now he was learning that the cafeteria was actually the source of a terrible calamity. Wasn't this contrary to Professor Eternal's original intention when he'd established the new medical zone? Yang Wei wondered whether the flame demons he had bought from Malnutrizole would continue to appreciate in value.

The Director of Ophthalmology grew more animated as he spoke. "The cafeteria has fattened up the patients to the point that many of them are now unable even to walk! The high-calorie, high-fat, high-protein diet they consume is causing them to develop a series of illnesses that had once been cured: high blood sugar, high blood lipids, high cholesterol. In the future, these patients will face even more severe health problems. More and more people eat at the cafeteria, but where do we get all the ingredients? Even shark eggs are in short supply! Right now we only have one egg for every three patients! Our resources and power supply have both reached a crisis level never before experienced. We are on the brink of collapse. How has this ship been able to support so many people for so long? We must ask just what kind of people are aboard this ship. Look at their impoverished, evil appearance. They are foolish, ignorant, cunning, brutal, and numb. Besides scraping by in the most base way, they are incapable of productivity! And just what does it mean to live? As far as they are concerned, it means going to the cafeteria, pissing and shitting, and then going back to the cafeteria to do it all again. They are incapable of anything else! Is this the goal we set out to achieve when we committed to investing money in their treatment? Whenever problems arise on the ship, they are the first ones to cause trouble, stir up chaos, and do everything in their power to sabotage the Hospital Ship! That is why the question of which direction the ship should sail is not the most important issue. If we don't resolve the problem of the cafeteria, it won't matter which direction we go! If we do not begin the exorcism with the cafeteria, everything else will be nothing but a pile of bullshit!"

Yang Wei heard someone beside him whispering, "Everyone knows that! Didn't they try to fix that problem before? But they always fail. Who would dare to mess with the cafeteria? Every time they try to enact cafeteria reforms, people on the inside, with power, always block their efforts. I heard the cafeteria is actually overseen personally by the Second Vice President. One-third of all the hospital directors are shareholders in the cafeteria. They prepare large luxurious meals for the VIP patients."

The next speaker was the Director of Digestive Diseases. "All of this is being blown completely out of proportion," he retorted. "Have you considered what would happen if we did away with the cafeteria? What would we do with all the excess agricultural products we produce? Should we eat the monkeys in the labs? What about the Animal Ethics Committee? You need to be reasonable here! Don't you have even an ounce of compassion?"

The Director of the Nephrology Department added, "When it comes to conducting an exorcism, the crux of the matter is money. Who's going to foot the bill? All the patient subsidies have long been exhausted. When we have yet to close all those financial loopholes, how dare anyone mention the cafeteria? The hospital has always been operating at a loss, but if it weren't for the profits that the cafeteria brings in, the Hospital Ship would have never made it this far!"

The Director of Digestive Diseases and the Director of the Nephrology Department were both loyal to the Second Vice President. They were using the debate to support the Second Vice President's bid to become the new Hospital President. On the other hand, the Director of Ophthalmology, who had first brought up the issue of the cafeteria, was a close associate of the First Vice President. By bringing up the issue, he was actually attempting to take down the Second Vice President.

The atmosphere inside the hall grew heavy. Yang Wei hoped that the Hospital President might wake up and deliver a rousing speech, but the old man just kept on sleeping. Yang Wei searched the room for any trace of Professor Eternal but couldn't find anyone that matched his description. He couldn't even find Dr. Meloxicam, so he slipped out of the hall. Outside, he slapped himself to make sure this wasn't all just a dream.

41

HOW WILL THE OLD OFFICIALS EXPLAIN THINGS TO THE NEW OFFICIALS?

Crowds of doctors emerged from the meeting hall, converging on the deck, where they lit cigarettes and started drinking, having seemingly lost interest in the conference. They discussed the Hospital President, noting that the old man was on his last leg and wondering who would take his place. They listed his potential successors, which, besides the vice presidents, also included the Director of the Statistics Department and the Director of the Ear, Nose, and Throat Department. All were strong candidates. One doctor mentioned Dr. Meloxicam, Director of the Geriatric Ward, as a possible contender, but another replied, "How could you still consider him? He lost all interest in practicing medicine a long time ago!"

No one mentioned Professor Eternal.

One doctor grew anxious and grumbled, "How come this damn meeting is still going on? I can't wait for the variety show to start!"

On the other side of the deck sat a row of temporary restaurants constructed of abandoned sheet metal. More and more representatives slipped out of the hall and lined up outside the restaurants. Yang Wei really wanted a bite to eat, too, but he didn't dare. Instead he scurried into the bathroom, which was also filled with doctors. Some were eating takeout from the restaurants as they squatted there, taking dumps. Others leaned over the sinks, vomiting. A few locked themselves inside the stalls while people outside banged on the doors. One guy emerged and, as he zipped his pants, grumbled angrily, "What the hell's up with all that banging? I need to empty my stomach before eating!" A few other doctors hung new drawings on the walls after removing the portrait of the Hospital President.

"Why did you remove his portrait?" Yang Wei asked.

"We are just following the Hospital President's personal instructions," someone responded. "The hospital no longer endorses this kind of personality cult."

They had replaced the image of the Hospital President with official portraits of the vice presidents and various department heads currently running for the office of President. Most of the other pictures were advertisements for new restaurants and recruitment posters from the various sick wards trying to bring in new patients. The advertisement for the Neurology Department read:

LONGEVITY IS A LOST HOPE. ONLY THE NEUROLOGY DEPARTMENT CAN PRODUCE THE NEXT STAGE OF HUMANKIND!

An advertisement for the Cardiology Department read:

WE FOCUS ALL OUR ENERGY ON THE PRODUCTION OF REANIMATED INDIVIDUALS. NO NEED TO WORRY ABOUT LIVING UNTIL YOU'RE NINETY-NINE; JUST LIVE YOUR SECOND LIFE AS A PATIENT! YOU CAN COME BACK AFTER DEATH AND DO IT ALL AGAIN!

Other posters featured drawings of retro-style fighter jets and tanks, but those were quickly covered by the latest installment of *Medical News*, which featured an extended editorial cover story about exorcisms.

Someone ran into the bathroom screaming, "Attention! We have a crisis on our hands! The sea nymphs have revealed themselves! All of the fish have swum away to escape them. I'm going to seize the ship; who's with me? This is the moment we have been waiting for!"

"Will you just listen to this unruly old patient!" one of the doctors scolded. "You must be trying to get yourself killed saying such frightening things!"

Yang Wei saw someone with a long fishlike face and was immediately taken aback—could it be the Sonic Master he had killed? He felt he was witnessing someone come back to life, and he quickly scurried behind one of the urinals to hide. Sonic Master had a cape of red seaweed draped over his body. After being belowdecks for so long, he was ecstatic to see daylight. Yang Wei wondered if he was real or a ghost. What had he seen? Was it really a sea nymph? Was it that evil devil more terrifying than a female patient? Perhaps this patient really was the only person capable of altering the course of the Hospital Ship.

Yang Wei could sense the will of Professor Eternal, and it made everything at the Exorcism Congress feel superfluous. He wanted to encourage the doctors to follow this birdman, but then a series of thunderous cries broke out from the sick ward. Yang Wei was terrified. He decided to return to the meeting hall. In the meantime, more and more doctors and patients had converged on the hall, and it took a lot of effort for Yang Wei to squeeze back in. Once inside, he discovered that someone had taken his seat. He had no choice but to stand in the aisle.

42

BORROWING OLD STORIES FROM HISTORY ABOUT PUNISHING TRAITORS

The Director of the Nephrology Department grabbed the microphone. The topic of his lecture was the establishment of the Museum of Hospital History. He began by singing the praises of the Hospital President's achievements, addressing him as the Great Helmsman. The construction of the Museum of Hospital History was a major decision based on instructions that came directly from the Hospital President. The museum was the single most important project for the Hospital Ship, aimed at restoring hospital engineering after it had been derailed by Siming and carrying out a theoretical reconstruction. If the hospital didn't take this project on, nothing else would matter. In order to undertake this project, a crack team would be headed by the Hospital President, who would also serve as the Team Leader of the Working Group to Establish the Museum of Hospital History. The Museum of Hospital History would also serve as a data-preservation center and headquarters for the Love Thy Hospital Education Center, providing powerful spiritual motivation and solid ideological support for the coming exorcism.

Then the Director of the Nephrology Department said something so bold that no one had heard anything like it in a long time: "The most important task ahead is to record accurately and reflect fully the history of the Hospital Ship! Writing this history is a momentous project that will impact what is to come for thousands of years. If we don't know where we came from or trust our own past, how can we possibly be expected to make the crematorium flames burn brighter? Unarmed with the proper theory and ideological foundation, how can we be expected to punish the traitor Siming for its crimes? As far as the Hospital Ship is concerned, having the proper firepower, protective measures, and mobility are all extremely important, but even more important are our ideals, conduct, and discipline. Just look at how ridiculous this meeting has become! The fact that treatment has failed means that our very philosophy has failed us. Some of our doctors might have first-class surgical skills, but they lack faith. Carl von Clausewitz put it best when he said that material means and ends are nothing but the handle of a scalpel; the *spiritual* means and ends are the true blade . . ."

As he spoke, an early design for the Museum of Hospital History appeared on a large LCD screen. The Hospital President's portrait was absent from the diagrams, which called for the Museum of Modern Literature to be torn down and the Museum of Hospital History to be built on the same site. The new building was to be a bloodred castle-like structure of steel. A wave of faint applause could be heard when the announcement was made, but most in the audience remained silent.

Someone shouted, "Let's get on with the variety show already! We want to see the dancers!"

Yang Wei wanted to warn them that the sea nymphs had appeared and that Sonic Master had been resurrected—the most dangerous hour was at hand! But he knew that no one would listen.

Before the variety show was an awards ceremony, announcing the winners of the first annual Hua Tuo Cup Prize for Medical Labor, named after the famous Han dynasty physician Hua Tuo. The top prize went to Dr. Daptomycin for "bravely representing the doctors in returning to the sick ward of the dead to replace the medical robots." Since he was saving a patient's life at that very moment, Dr. Daptomycin was unable to attend the ceremony and personally accept his prize, but the First Vice President contacted him via telephone: "Is this Dr.

Daptomycin? I'm calling you live from the Exorcism Congress. I would like to congratulate you on behalf of the Hospital Affairs Committee! I know that you are currently out there fighting on the front lines and unable to be here in person, but we have all been extremely moved by your innovative spirit . . ."

The Director of Rheumatology snatched the microphone. "Dr. Daptomycin, over the course of this struggle, you have shouldered the glorious and holy responsibility of fighting in the name of the exorcism. You are a model for all doctors to look up to! Please take good care of yourself! We will always be here to back you up!"

One after another, the other directors took turns delivering speeches praising Dr. Daptomycin. The time flew by. When it was finally Dr. Daptomycin's turn to speak, his dejected voice rang out over the loudspeaker: "My patient just died."

The First Vice President drew a long face. "The patients are all dead anyway, but that's not something you are supposed to say out loud! After all, you are a model doctor . . ."

After the Hua Tuo Cup Prize for Medical Labor was awarded, another ceremony honored the recipients of the Bian Que Cup Prize for Poetry, named for the earliest known Chinese physician from the Warring States period. The Editor in Chief of *Medical News* came to the podium to present the award, delivering an emotional and moving speech in which he declared: "Under the brilliant leadership of the Hospital President, all we need is poetry, and the demons that hinder us are bound to be eliminated. The Hospital Ship will write an even more epic and majestic poetic masterpiece for the future!"

Next, the doctors carried a large red ballot box onto the stage. It was time to elect the new members of the Hospital Affairs Committee. Everyone present voted in this election to win back the democratic rights that Siming had taken away. The hall was full of excitement as everyone lined up to cast ballots. The directors from each department delivered speeches in last-minute attempts to pick up more votes.

Yang Wei wanted to vote, but he was too scared. He thought that he shouldn't be there in the first place and instead decided to sneak out. He scurried again to the bathroom, where a crowd of doctors still leaned against the urinals. They had smoked all their cigarettes and finished all their wine, and they were now intensely debating the best techniques for sea golf. Lines of customers poured out of the private rooms in the restaurant, laughing and arguing over where they should go for their next meal. Then Yang Wei heard a wave of even more horrific screams from the sick ward.

Yang Wei felt he had no choice but to return to the meeting hall. By then the voting was over, and the names of the newly elected committee members appeared on the screen. For some reason, they had not been able to elect a new Hospital President. Everyone was arguing. One of the doctors unfurled a large red carpet on the stage and started setting things up for the upcoming performance. The cafeteria delivered another round of food and drinks, and the entire hall again erupted with the sound of patients eating. The Director of Ophthalmology grabbed a large bowl and started to stuff himself, much more aggressively than the others.

The variety show was finally about to begin. The Third Vice President served as master of ceremonies. "Today's program was personally curated by the Hospital President himself!" he began. "It shall be a marvelous show, a celebration of our victory! The age of Siming is over. We can now return to the sick wards!"

It was midnight, and everyone was in high spirits. Each department was ready. It was the moment that everyone had been waiting for. A group of doctors supported the Hospital President as he got down from the stage, helping him to get comfortable on a stretcher. The Third Vice President handed the Hospital President a glass of wine. The Hospital President's eyelids fluttered for a moment, and he gently licked the edge of the cup. Then the Third Vice President took up the microphone and declared, "Please enjoy the show!"

At that moment a violent wave crashed down on the ship, and the entire vessel began to rock. Yang Wei heard someone whisper that he had seen the head of a sea nymph emerge from the water.

A man in white rushed onto the stage and grabbed the microphone. The patient next to Yang Wei told him that the man onstage was Dr. Linezolid from the Disinfection Room.

"No! No! We can't do this!" Dr. Linezolid shouted. "We must stop the performance immediately!"

The color drained instantly from the faces of everyone onstage.

43

MARS IS LIKE A PELLET IN THE SOUTHWEST SKY

"None of the newly elected members of the Hospital Affairs Committee attended medical school! Their diplomas are fake!" declared Dr. Linezolid. "Nothing they have told you is true! This Exorcism Congress is going to get someone killed!"

The entire hall fell silent. As they stared down Dr. Linezolid, everyone present wore looks of malice. He had destroyed the atmosphere of the long-anticipated variety show, and he kept sticking out his long red tongue like a lizard. Yang Wei thought his story was predictable and superficial. The helpless, ignorant expression on Dr. Linezolid's face made him look pathetic. What faction did he represent?

Everything he said after that seemed completely ludicrous. "Right now we shouldn't be sailing all over the seas. We need to transform the Hospital Ship into a spaceship and fly off into the universe! This is what the Hospital President really wants!"

Someone in the audience mockingly asked how this transformation was supposed to take place.

Dr. Linezolid didn't hold back. "The Hospital Ship was originally designed according to the structure of a spaceship. They just made sure to carefully conceal its appearance so people wouldn't notice. It is actually quite similar to the submarine that Jules Verne described; no one could see its true form, and many people mistook it for a whale."

The crowd erupted into laughter. Clearly no one believed him.

"Cut the laughing! This isn't a joke." Dr. Linezolid grew angry. "The Hospital President was originally going to announce the details of his strategy to advance toward Mars, but some people with ulterior motives drugged him and knocked him out! This is nothing short of an attempted coup d'état!" He flashed a sharp look at the vice presidents and department directors, who were all sitting with uncomfortable looks on their faces. He then extended his arms and made a revving sound, as if he were starting up an engine. "Ten years ago, the Hospital President ordered Professor Eternal to send a working group to Mars to begin construction on a field hospital."

Professor Eternal? Yang Wei suddenly felt extremely dizzy. *Was Dr. Linezolid* also *sent by Professor Eternal? Why would a specialist in disinfection handle something like this?*

An awkward look appeared on the faces of the vice presidents. Then a strange image lit up the display screen. It seemed to be taken from the perspective of a spaceship. Amid the blanket of pitch black on screen, a tiny point of light like a small pellet appeared gradually. "This is Mars," announced Dr. Linezolid, "also referred to as the Planet of the God of War." The planet began to increase in size, the orange-red tint of its surface covered in what looked like canals. Eventually its rings came into view, and then the image of the hospital appeared. Beside a tempered-glass dome adorned with a massive red cross, a team of creatures resembling humans wore tight white outfits, helmets, and respirators as they wandered around the strange and desolate landscape.

Dr. Linezolid was so excited he nearly leaped to his feet. "This is the first hospital on Mars! As long as we can escape from this dangerous sea and make it to outer space, we will be okay. Are you seeking eternal life? Then come with me!"

The audience members looked confused. Someone asked, "The environment doesn't look right. Is there something wrong with that place?"

"There are so many of us," someone else said. "Can they accommodate us all on Mars?"

"I heard that once we put those space suits on," said another, "we won't even be able to touch our own bodies. People are even forced to piss and shit in their suits! How are we supposed to go into surgery under those conditions?"

"The Hospital President originally instructed Professor Eternal to construct a Space Medicine Lab on the ship," said Dr. Linezolid, waving his arms in frustration, "but none of you thought that was necessary."

Clips from the films *Space Battleship Yamato* and *Starship Troopers* began to play on the big screen, and the doctors and patients broke into a cacophony of riotous screams.

Yang Wei noticed the First, Second, and Third Vice Presidents sneaking out of the hall.

"Our true voyage is to the sea of stars," declared Dr. Linezolid. "Out there in the universe, our patients will be given the gift of eternal life!"

He went on to introduce the backstory of the hospital's construction. According to Dr. Linezolid, ten years earlier the Hospital Ship sent to Mars an unmanned spaceship equipped with a 3D printer. Later they transmitted the blueprints for the new hospital to the ship and, utilizing the existing material resources on Mars, began to print the hospital. They also printed seven guinea pig–like creatures using the artificial growth medium aboard the ship. These were later used for biological experiments. One year later, Dr. Linezolid and a small team boarded another ship to Mars, where they spent nine years, until the new hospital was able to function independently. He had only just returned, and after crash-landing into the sea, he'd immediately boarded the Hospital Ship to report to everyone.

As Dr. Linezolid described it, this hospital on Mars was just the beginning. "Besides our values and overall worldview," he explained, "we must also establish a view of the universe." This was a brand-new concept, which those patients confined to the Hospital Ship for so many years were unable even to conceive of.

To an ant living on an elephant, that elephant is the whole world. For a worm living in a small pond, that pond is like an ocean. The greatest tragedy facing patients was why they could never properly treat their ailments. "There are billions of stars like our sun in the Milky Way," Dr. Linezolid continued, "and the solar system is not the center of the Milky Way. Humankind lives in a remote village. On an astronomical scale, humans must merge their intellect with AI machines to ensure we are able to construct hospitals not only on Mars but also on Venus, Mercury, Jupiter, and other smaller planets throughout the solar system, the Milky Way, and other galaxies. In the end, the ultimate goal is to transform all of infinite time and space into one massive hospital. By then, patients will need only one pill to transform their physical bodies into biological spaceships, free to traverse the universe and new worlds free from pathogens and viruses. In the future we won't even need our fleshly bodies, or spaceships, or plants. All will be converted to numerical codes that will flow freely through the universe. When that time comes, we will have truly achieved a universe free from disease and calamity. This is the only proper direction for the hospital's future development, the final destination for both doctors and patients . . ."

The audience broke out in a fit of laughter. Two men dressed in long white medical gowns approached Dr. Linezolid and tapped him on the shoulder. They pulled him aside, wrestled him to the ground, and placed a collar on his neck. They forced him onto the stretcher reserved for the Hospital President and carried him out of the auditorium.

Yang Wei hoped he might catch a glimpse of the Hospital President. He was lying on the ground, still unconscious, so there was no way to authenticate whether what Dr. Linezolid had said was true. Yang Wei was extremely disturbed by this, and he wondered whether the entire Exorcism Congress was nothing but an illusion created by Siming to toy with the doctors and patients. He rushed out of the hall, and as soon as he made it to the deck, he ran into someone.

"Yang Wei?" the person asked.

"That's right," replied Yang Wei.

"I heard you want to see Professor Eternal?" the person said in a strange voice.

"Yes . . . ," Yang Wei answered, with some hesitation.

"Then come with me!"

44

AN ARMY OF A MILLION WIELDING ARMOR AND SPEARS

A young woman wearing a white nurse's outfit spoke to Yang Wei. He was utterly floored, somehow able to recognize her as a woman, and, although he had been longing for it, still found himself shaking with fear. He had spent so much time reading *A Collection of Beautiful Raccoons, Bushy Orangutans, and Busty Dragons*, but not even that could have prepared him for this! First, children began to appear on the ship, and now . . . a woman! Things once disappeared were now returning.

She was of average height, around twenty-two or twenty-three years old, and so perfect that she didn't seem real, as if she had just been unearthed from a glacier and still had a mystifying chill clinging to her skin. She had a first aid kit with a red cross on it slung across her back and opened it to remove a handwritten map, which she handed to Yang Wei. "Professor Eternal wants to see you," she said.

The map contained instructions on how to find Professor Eternal.

She asked Yang Wei to follow her, but after walking down several corridors, she suddenly disappeared. Yang Wei's map was still firmly in his hand—it wasn't an illusion. He followed the route indicated on the map as if he were carrying out an imperial decree. Ever since he had returned to the sick ward, he had never once laid eyes on this godlike doctor who was supposedly his primary physician. It had been a long time since Professor Eternal had shown his face. Some said he was already dead. Yang Wei had searched everywhere for him, and now

Professor Eternal had sent this mysterious woman, who seemed to have come out of thin air, to tell Yang Wei that he wanted to see him.

After walking for a while, Yang Wei realized that his uniform was filthy and torn. Afraid that Professor Eternal would be displeased by his appearance, Yang Wei went to the washroom to freshen up. Gazing into the mirror, he realized that he looked beaten up and exhausted. His hair was now completely white, and he truly looked like an old man. He had clearly not been very successful in turning into a child again, which left him feeling sorry for himself. Then he heard a whisper in his ear: *The disease you suffer from is aging. And aging is difficult to cure.* He stood there in a daze for quite some time before finally mustering the strength to go on.

Following the map, Yang Wei eventually arrived at the aircraft hangar located in the stern of the ship. He had been there before, with Buboxine, during their medical-tourism outings, but he had had no idea that this was Professor Eternal's secret hiding place. Professor Eternal had transformed an old medical helicopter into his office. Above the rusted steel door, a painting of a sea nymph was emblazoned with the symbol of the red cross being crushed under the talons of an Indian peacock. Yang Wei gently knocked on the door of the helicopter, which was buried under a deep pile of abandoned junk. After a long pause, a male voice responded from within, "Come in . . ."

As Yang Wei climbed into the helicopter, he noticed that amid the pile of rumbling machines emitting sparks, there was a long circular hanging creature contained within a glass vessel that resembled a birdcage. It was pink and had a sticky texture, and it was gently squirming. Some kind of medicinal powder stuck to its body, and it was connected to a pile of messy wires and instruments. Was *this* Professor Eternal? All that seemed to be left of him was a brain. Yang Wei was so scared and nervous that his sweat came out as a thick pus. He turned toward the cockpit and saw that besides the machines, wires, and plugs, there were also flowers, bonsai trees, ornamental rocks, and an exquisite porcelain tea set. A small bookshelf overflowed with books and research materials, most of which were literary in nature. A few scrolls of calligraphy hung beside the porthole windows, along with a photograph of the Hospital President posing next to Professor Eternal in a style reminiscent of the Japanese ukiyo-e woodcut school. Both of them looked much younger in the photograph, and Professor Eternal still had his body intact. But they weren't wearing white lab coats. Instead they wore old military uniforms and helmets. They were sitting inside a brand-new helicopter gazing out over the sea with strong, authoritative looks in their eyes. Leaning beside them weren't golf clubs but two shiny military swords, which appeared to be the predecessors of what would eventually become the surgeon's scalpel.

That was when Yang Wei noticed something strange floating just in front of Professor Eternal's brain. It resembled a mouth opening and closing, as if slowly trying to swallow. The cafeteria had prepared a special breakfast for this high-ranking medical officer. Professor Eternal's meal included a sea turtle cooked medium well and a glass of whiskey. Since all he had was a brain, he relied on an artificial mouth to eat. This was the kind of scene one would normally see only on a spaceship! It took great discipline for Yang Wei not to run in horror. After about fifteen minutes, Professor Eternal finally finished chewing. Then the artificial eyeball floating in the air seemed finally to notice Yang Wei, and it focused on his face.

"Who are you?" Professor Eternal asked through his artificial voice processor.

Trembling with fear, Yang Wei responded, "My name is Yang Wei."

"Oh, you made it!" Professor Eternal responded matter of factly.

"I'm here," said Yang Wei.

"Did you see the crematorium?" asked Professor Eternal.

Yang Wei was confused, but he responded, "Yes, I went there."

"So . . . what did you think?" asked Professor Eternal.

He thought back to the crematorium. Carbuncle had been cremated there. "Majestic. It was simply breathtaking," he responded, as honestly as he could.

Professor Eternal invited Yang Wei over. Yang Wei thought he might be eager to hear all about what it was like for a patient to be burned alive, to hear all the juicy details over breakfast. But Professor Eternal didn't ask about Carbuncle's death. Instead he said, "I was the one who arranged for you to visit the crematorium. Not every patient has the good fortune of seeing firsthand all the magical things that happen there, but after your visit, I'm sure you now have a good sense of the crisis we are facing. They are right. If we aren't lucky, the fires fueling the crematorium will soon be extinguished, and the sea nymphs will be upon us." With that, a mechanical arm delivered another turtle leg into the professor's mouth.

"Thank you for arranging for me to see the crematorium," said Yang Wei with a deep sense of appreciation.

"It's too early to be thanking me. Did you hear the sea nymphs singing?" Professor Eternal's brain jiggled like Jell-O as he spoke.

Yang Wei nodded. He understood that this, too, had been arranged by Professor Eternal. He began to worry that Professor Eternal might ask about the Sonic Master. "Just what exactly are these sea nymphs?" he asked.

"They are our enemy," Professor Eternal replied sternly.

"Our enemy?" Yang Wei was even more confused.

"But they aren't just any enemy," Professor Eternal explained. "They are a breed of demon even more fierce and violent than the female patients! We are looking at a crisis unlike anything we have ever faced. We often blame the difficult situation we are in on Siming's interference or the incompetence of the doctors, but all of these problems have been created by our enemies." Professor Eternal adopted a more informal, chatty cadence as he explained further. "Of late, none of you patients has been able to see me, which isn't strange. The enemy has already sent more than a dozen assassins to kill me. I had no choice but to go into hiding. In order to repel the enemy's wanton attacks, I was forced to devote every second of the day to the study of military strategy and was left without any time to visit the sick wards. I was so wrapped up in my research that I was forced to give up the opportunity to serve on the jury for the Nobel Prize in Physiology. To put it plainly, this is a war that will decide who lives and who dies."

Yang Wei was taken aback. "War?"

Images of those fights he had witnessed back in the sick ward suddenly flashed before his eyes. He thought back to that "war communiqué" that Super Patient had edited. All that was left of Professor Eternal was a floating brain, but he was still a true general, brave and heroic.

Professor Eternal took a moment to ponder before continuing. "War is a competition between contending military strategies. But strategy only comes after an organization's division of labor has reached a certain level. Groups that have yet to go through the process of modernization have almost no hope of emerging victorious. Thankfully, under the leadership of the Hospital President, the hospital has achieved the basic tenets of modernization, which is why we have been able to hold out this long. However, during this period we have grown to become overly reliant upon the algorithm, and that will never allow us to resolve the issue of strategy. At the core of this strategy are humans. Humans will never pass the Turing test."

Yang Wei listened anxiously, but he still didn't understand why Professor Eternal had summoned him. Meanwhile, Professor Eternal continued to chew noisily on a piece of turtle shell. "Look at reality, and it will all be clear. Take the example of Semyon Konstantinovich Timoshenko, who was a great military commander. During one battle, Timoshenko served as the frontline commander, and even though he did everything possible to get the upper hand, due to Stalin's adopting the wrong strategy, Timoshenko was ultimately unable to stop the siege of Kyiv, leading to the defeat of the anti-Fascist camp. Now we see the enemy getting closer by the day, and yet the attention of those directors and doctors remains focused on superficial, short-term issues. None of them is researching strategic issues as they should! They look at everything from a technical perspective, leaving hospital affairs in the hands of the algorithm while they spend their time eating, drinking, having fun, and playing sea golf! This is totally unacceptable!"

Yang Wei remembered seeing the set of golf clubs beside the Hospital President, and he trembled as he told Professor Eternal, "I noticed that Sonic Master already came up to the deck to helm the ship. I think he was following your orders." Yang Wei didn't dare confess to murdering the old man with the birdlike face.

Professor Eternal thought for a second before responding. "Sonic Master? Oh, he was assigned a tactical mission. He was supposed to feign an attack in order to confuse the enemy. We really need to carry out more research when it comes to some of these strategies. Take for instance unrestricted warfare, Warden's Five Rings, asymmetric warfare, and vector attacks, which are all only partial strategies. I am researching the grand strategy that concerns quantity and the big picture. I'm looking at both offense and defense, which is very different—"

An ear-piercing high-pitched alarm suddenly broke out, interrupting Professor Eternal. The helicopter began to rumble. Professor Eternal asked Yang Wei to take the copilot's seat and ordered one of the automated arms to fasten his seat belt. Professor Eternal controlled the helicopter with his brain waves, and with a loud bang, the vessel lifted off like a rocket. As the helicopter shot into the sky, Yang Wei was struck by a strange feeling: *Are we heading to Mars?*

45

WHY MUST THE CAGED BEAST BE KILLED?

Ascending in the helicopter was very different from climbing up to the crematorium. Yang Wei glanced down, his body gripped by a feeling of utter fear. As the helicopter ascended, high and fast, he could see the three vice presidents leading a brigade of doctors out onto the deck, toward the hangar. They were red with anger and screaming. Amid the raging sea, the Hospital Ship diminished to a tiny dot.

Professor Eternal spoke with an air of disdain. "They are not our enemies. We are on the same side. Those dear old friends of mine don't want to see me; they actually want to kill me. Then there will be no one to stand in their way, and they'll assume the role of Hospital President without any complications. It's not a big deal. Once you look at things from another perspective, you will clearly see the big picture." As he spoke, a robotic arm gestured toward the sea. "Look, what lies below us is not a natural ocean. It is an artificial sea, designed by the enemy and put here to entrap us. Our enemies are those sea nymphs you always hear about. But don't worry; I planned for this. That's why I arranged for Sonic Master to go belowdecks and investigate. He is there to keep an eye out for signs of the enemy. People talk about this being the Age of Peace? Humph! And all those vice presidents and department heads just sit there with their heads in the sand, as if nothing is happening!"

Yang Wei quietly muttered under his breath, "War . . . the enemy . . . the artificial sea . . ."

The helicopter began to experience a wave of intense turbulence, and Yang Wei felt as if his limbs were being ripped apart. He thought, *No wonder Professor Eternal didn't participate in the Exorcism Congress. He sent Dr. Linezolid to warn everyone and arranged for the Funeral Artist and Sonic Master to start preparing for the resistance.* Yang Wei looked out the cockpit window at the clear waves on the surface of the water, bathed in a brilliant red glow that extended as far as he could see. Somehow he'd never realized that everything he saw was artificial, even though he had gone into the water in scuba gear to catch pulmonary algae and try his hand at underwater exploration.

"Although it's a man-made sea, it is still a sea," clarified Professor Eternal. "And there are certain truths that the sea can tell us. Stalin once said: 'Quantity has a quality all its own.' One drop might not seem like much, but when a large quantity of droplets combines, you can create an ocean. A grain of sand might not seem like much, but when a large quantity of grains of sand converges, you have a dune. A lone particle doesn't even have a temperature, but when a multitude of particles converge, their temperature becomes a key feature of the conglomeration. An individual bee has very low intelligence, but when a swarm of bees converges, they suddenly have unusual powers of intelligence. One bacteria is not enough to kill a person, but once it multiplies hundreds of millions of times, it has the power to wipe out an entire civilization. Quantity brings about a fundamental change in quality. At a critical mass, strange phenomena occur, many of which far surpass what an individual is capable of. This is why our enemy developed the sea. It is a deadly sea, composed of all kinds of viruses. The sea nymphs are the disease incarnate, the collective manifestation of the virus. They do not take the form of traditional monsters—in fact, you can see them only under a microscope—and yet they are the most powerful and demonic scourge in history. The hospital was established with the sole purpose of destroying them . . ." As Professor Eternal spoke, he simultaneously used his mind to control the helicopter while chewing his food.

Yang Wei could hardly believe his ears. "So all this time, it has been the enemy making us fall ill?"

"That's exactly right!" Professor Eternal spoke urgently, spitting out a turtle bone. "All of this has been the work of our enemies! This is their new weapon. The original form of the sea nymphs was a type of digital microorganism. Edited on computers before being produced in the real world and broadly disseminated, they eventually took the form of this sea. These viruses can communicate with one another, using collective consciousness to evolve. It is referred to as the 'Devil Virus' because it has the ability to break through the Hospital Ship's immune system, and by self-replicating human DNA, it can damage regenerated organs, destroy nerve tissue, ultimately paralyzing and destroying the patient's brain. Not only are nano-cell-repair devices helpless against them, but they actually hasten the virus's reproduction. Patients age at an increased rate, which has doomed the project to restore the elderly to a childlike state. And so changing the course of our Hospital Ship is meaningless, because the ship has never been moving. The sea continually rages in a dreamlike state, like we are living in a petri dish, wild beasts fallen into a trap, unable to die yet destined not to live. For the time being, the enemy has yet to launch its final attack. Some key receptor chains have yet to fully form. But the end is coming, and soon. The enemy doesn't even need to attack. If they just leave us trapped like this, it will be enough to finish us off. Have you seen how the Hospital Ship's algorithm has gone mad? The machines are broken, the doctors are killing themselves, the patients are dying . . ."

"What should we do?" Yang Wei responded with a mix of shock and pain. He was just a simple songwriter who had lived his entire life in the Age of Peace. He had never before witnessed true war or seen a real enemy. At one point, he even suspected that Professor Eternal was describing the plot of a novel.

But Professor Eternal was serious. He stared hard at Yang Wei, his floating gaze pregnant with meaning. "The most important thing is to have the correct strategy. There is only one way to emerge victorious over our enemy. Quantity provides us, too, with a rare opportunity. What about the common herd? Its power is infinite! The most elite people always distinguish themselves as individuals, but even they were elected by the masses. So the ignorant masses must possess some form of advanced wisdom! This is an upgraded version of the people's war. Who ever said there can be no people's war at sea? As far as the hospital is concerned, patients give it the upper hand when it comes to quantity. The sheer number of our patients gives us the opportunity to engage in protracted warfare, and we will hold out until the final victory! The grand enterprise of enforcing justice requires the broad participation of all the patients. When it comes right down to it, this is an art, and it is every bit as enticing as a great novel . . ."

Professor Eternal put the helicopter on autopilot, and it began to pick up speed. It blasted back and forth through the air, even doing several aileron rolls. Professor Eternal giggled gleefully as leftover scraps of food and liquor flew around the cabin. Yang Wei was struck by a dizzy spell. Never in his life had he been at such a high altitude. For some reason he thought of the peacock. *Is that austere animal with the gorgeous train of feathers not the perfect metaphor of Professor Eternal's helicopter?*

At the same time, he also thought about those patients who were part of the common herd, dying in their sick wards. The helicopter had already climbed to an altitude of five thousand meters. Only at this altitude could Yang Wei finally see the true reality. The massive fleet of ships was no longer visible. The Hospital Ship floated alone on the surface of the sea. The entire world seemed empty. *Ah, so this is the sea of death that the enemy has created!*

Yang Wei was again faced with the loneliness and fear of someone trapped in a dark cave, waiting for death. Then the helicopter took a violent drop in a sudden wind shear. Yang Wei threw up from the turbulence, his vomit spraying over Professor Eternal's eye, lips, and the glass bottle containing his brain. Perhaps he was used to that, because

Professor Eternal didn't seem fazed in the least. The mechanical arm simply prepared a hot towel and wiped the professor before cleaning up Yang Wei. Eventually, the helicopter stabilized and continued on at turbo speed.

"It's like a ritual," Professor Eternal said sternly. "I take the chopper up five times a day to patrol the area and make sure our air defense identification zone is clear. The enemy won't dare attack as long as they see people moving around on the ship. In the meantime, this Devil Virus grows stronger, more lethal, but until it is perfected, they won't take any unnecessary risks."

"So where exactly are these enemies?" asked Yang Wei. He looked down at the sea—besides the Hospital Ship, he couldn't see a sign of anything else.

Professor Eternal's eye floated over to the window and calmly gazed down to the horizon. "Perhaps we will never see the true face of our enemy. During the Medicinal War, there are no battles with tanks, heavy artillery, and cannons. There are no sieges of cities. In fact there are no scenes of bloodshed and violence. Yet it is precisely because we *cannot* see our enemy that this war has an unprecedented impact on our hearts and souls. That is what makes it so inspiring and so very tragic."

Yang Wei recognized yet another example of something he had never before heard of. "Are we at war with the Shadow Hospital?" he asked.

46

EVEN AFTER A HUNDRED BATTLES, SOMEONE SURVIVES

The helicopter hovered over the Hospital Ship as Professor Eternal went for another round of food and drink. He used an antique tea set for his liquor, and as he ate, he read a manga, Hayao Miyazaki's *Porco Rosso.* The story was set during World War I, when the Italian air force's star pilot Marco Pagot fell victim to a curse that turned him into a pig. He patrolled the Adriatic Sea under the name Porco Rosso to stop the plundering "air pirates." In order to thwart Porco, the pirates hired an ace pilot from the United States named Curtis. Porco and Curtis eventually have a final dogfight to determine the ultimate victor. Professor Eternal buried his brain deep in the pages of the manga, utterly obsessed. He giggled as he read, but it was unclear if he identified with Porco or Curtis.

"Professor Eternal, you are so amazing!" Yang Wei said, virtually in tears. "You gave up the opportunity to serve on the jury for the Nobel Prize in Physiology, and now here you are eating while you study and fly a helicopter, simultaneously researching military strategy and protecting the Hospital Ship. I have so much respect for you! I've been searching for you for so long! You are, after all, my primary care physician!"

Professor Eternal heaved a deep sigh. "Huh?" He stared at Yang Wei with a confused look, as if he had just awakened. His brain suddenly appeared older than before, and his voice took on an imposing tone. "Do you know what kind of a war this is?"

Yang Wei shook his head, although the question reminded him of the war games that Super Patient used to play in the sick ward.

"Have you ever heard of World War II?" Professor Eternal asked casually.

Yang Wei hesitated. "I think so . . ."

Professor Eternal tongued a piece of turtle shell between his teeth and spit it out the cockpit window. It fluttered down into the viral sea below. "We are in the middle of World War II right now." Somehow, he resembled Porco Rosso from the manga.

"Huh?" Yang Wei was shocked.

"There are some who say that World War II is over, but that is just an illusion," Professor Eternal explained. "Our world is littered with lies. Anytime someone says a certain war is over, that is the lie of all lies! Not only is World War II not over, but the value system and view of the world from that war continues. A pity that no one sees this, or perhaps they have intentionally exorcised it from their minds. The whole purpose of establishing the hospital was to win World War II."

"What year is this?" Yang Wei asked. It was the first time since he had come to the hospital that he had even thought to ask this question. Could it be that he had never previously paid attention to the existence of time or its passage? Perhaps when he'd received narrative-implant therapy, this portion of his memory had been cut out.

"1976 AD," responded Professor Eternal.

"AD . . . ?" It sounded familiar to Yang Wei.

"It stands for 'anno Domini,' 'in the year of the Lord,' which commemorates the birth of a doctor named Jesus. The year he was born is considered the first year of the world! He traveled all over as a healer, and his hands had the power to heal without the use of medicine. He could cure all kinds of stubborn ailments like leprosy, deaf-mutism, and paralysis. He could even resurrect the dead."

"I heard that he was the one who founded the hospital," said Yang Wei.

"He even predicted today's war," said Professor Eternal.

"And then what happened?" asked Yang Wei.

"Jesus was so successful as a healer that the people looked at him as a god," said Professor Eternal. "But though this god walked the earth, the Devil was still here. The Devil grew jealous of this god but dared not take action against him. Instead he instilled heretical thoughts among the believers, to sew disharmony and chaos. But it was ultimately not enough. When this god finally died, the era of lawlessness began. The Devil rose up to fill the power vacuum left in the wake of this god's death, unleashing chaos to destroy the world. Calamity and illness spread everywhere, and wars raged throughout the land."

"Back when this god was still alive, didn't he try to stop the Devil?" asked Yang Wei.

"He wanted to," said Professor Eternal. "He actually tried to bargain with the Devil."

At the time, he explained, the Devil told the god, "After you die, I will destroy the laws you put in place!"

God said, "My laws are just laws, which means there is no power strong enough to destroy them."

The Devil laughed. "Justice may last forever, but so, too, my evil will forever endure. When you were still of this world, everyone had faith in you, but my followers are also many! Human nature is inherently evil; it is easy to go down the dark path, while the high road is difficult. Once you are nailed to the cross, fewer and fewer people will have faith in you, while more and more will come to me."

God said, "There is absolutely no benefit for you in destroying my laws. The light of God shines everywhere, illuminating both the good people and evildoers like you. If the age of just laws should one day come to an end, your cycle of karmic reward will also come to an end, and nothing but purgatory and hell will await you. There, in the flames of hell, you will suffer infinite pain and torture."

The Devil said, "I know that God does not lie, but you also know that one's fate arises from one's heart. I will find a way to spare myself from the tortures of hell."

God responded, "When you carry out too many unjust actions, you end up doing yourself in! There is no way to be spared!"

The Devil said, "The heart of the sage is not ordinary, for he acts in the interests of the people. When it comes to fulfilling the wishes of the people, you are no match for me. You make your followers adhere to strict commandments, repeatedly stressing the dangers of giving in to desire, and teach people to avoid their lust and greed. I, on the other hand, conform to the yearnings of the people, allowing them to satisfy their myriad desires. All living beings desire, and this causes all kinds of illness and leads people down the path of evil—they will come to worship me!"

God said, "But I will leave a Holy Bible behind for this world."

The Devil said, "The Holy Bible is a tome of dead words. If you want to educate the masses, you need a living person to explain things to them."

God said, "I will leave behind a church to spread my gospel."

The Devil said, "But if you want to educate the masses, you will need new recruits. You won't refuse to take in my disciples, will you?"

God said, "Never."

The Devil said, "When the Age of Lawlessness comes, I will have my disciples secretly infiltrate your church. They will dress as you dress, and eventually they will destroy your laws. They will twist the meaning of your Holy Bible. They will spit in the face of your commandments, and eventually they will achieve what I was unable to do today. It will be the final battle to decide everything, and your followers will all perish." After God heard the Devil's words, He remained silent for a long time. Eventually, two lines of tears slowly trickled down His cheeks.

"What happened?" asked a concerned Yang Wei.

Professor Eternal projected a short film about World War II, the ultimate struggle between God and the Devil, with mankind acting as their agents. During the 1942 Battle of Midway, Isoroku Yamamoto led the Imperial Japanese Navy in its attack on the American USS *Enterprise* and three other aircraft carriers. Admiral Chester W. Nimitz died during the attack, and the Japanese army forced the US to retreat. Relying upon a new nerve-ionization technique, the Germans used ether-barrier technology and petrochemical-seawater technology to launch a counterattack in the European theater. This worked to counteract any advantage the Allied forces had gained with their strong industrial production capabilities. Tanks and fighter jets turned out to be useless. Due to Stalin's misguided strategy, the anti-Fascist camp ended up in a state of crisis. It was only thanks to the British artificial intelligence expert Alan Turing that the Allies broke through this stalemate and the American field hospital in El Alamein was able to use narrative-implant technology to create an entire world in which World War II was brought to an end. The United Nations was formed, a new global organization to promote historical progress, which gave the Allies an opportunity to catch their breath. Then the United States launched a new technological revolution. It discovered DNA, quasars, pulsars, and the cosmic microwave background, came up with the Fermi weak-interaction theory, put forward chaos theory, proposed Moore's law, created the first laser, sold the first batch of industrial robots, invented the BASIC programming language, implanted the first pacemaker, landed on the moon, invented the internet, and became the world's first superpower. No one could have anticipated the Axis powers infiltrating America's new world with parasitic hackers, which would disrupt the global network's monitoring center and create what would later be described as a new Cold War. With the Nazis' destruction of the public's ability to discern truth, the Americans successively lost the Korean War, the Vietnam War, the Iraq War, and the war in Afghanistan. They even lost the space race to the Soviet Union. Later, the World Trade Center in New York was attacked, bringing down the Twin Towers. Just like that, the narrative implant that the Americans had been fed was torn apart, completely dismembered. The United Nations entrusted the anti-Fascist Allied powers to track down those responsible and commence a new war. However, due to the ever-increasing speed of globalism, both sides became increasingly similar, even difficult to differentiate. Each enjoyed the same benefits when it came to trade, growth, technological advancement, and quality of life. They also faced the same challenges: unemployment, the health-care crisis, the deterioration of the environment, growing disparity between rich and poor . . . the Devil wore God's clothing, had joined God's religion, and the two of them became increasingly self-reliant . . . God and the Devil came to share the same fate.

Yang Wei was confused. "Isn't that a good thing?" *After all,* he thought, *isn't this the Age of Peace, when we are all supposed to get along? God and the Devil made peace. There should never again be any reason for any future war.*

But Professor Eternal surprisingly retorted, "No, that is just a superficial show. The political structures and ethical codes to successfully manage this global crisis have not been put in place. In the face of this new God-Devil, humankind is increasingly lost when it comes to determining justice. Nor do they know who to believe anymore. In the end, they have no choice but to establish a system of mutually assured destruction—MAD—to prevent their own self-destruction. But MAD *ensures* their mutual destruction. Neither economic development nor MAD will stop the impending chaos. The Devil shall always wreak havoc. And so in this sense, World War II strangely continues to play out. Military consultants from both sides went back to the drawing board to determine who was their friend and who was their enemy, but it became increasingly murky. That's why the Anti-Globalism Movement started in 1973. According to one computer's calculations, humankind would destroy itself by 2049. With President Hillary Clinton as its leader, the United States and a coalition of other Western nations decided in 1976 to terminate the narrative-implant program and end the war at its original source. That turned out to be the only way to determine the true enemy. After all, this is the single most important question of the war."

Yang Wei thought, *That's right. We really should go back and bring an end to this chaos. Hillary was right.* He seemed to remember from his middle school history textbook that World War II broke out in 1939 and ended in 1945. The Allied powers emerged victorious over the Axis powers. Then came the Cold War, and after that a series of occurrences that seemed related to what Professor Eternal described . . . but Yang Wei's brain had trouble registering all this. Perhaps the algorithm thought that humankind's mental capacity was unable to understand such a complex and chaotic world.

"And that is why we have terminated that implanted history," said Professor Eternal.

His words made Yang Wei uncomfortable. "And what about the billions of people living in that history?"

"They, too, will be terminated," replied Professor Eternal. "And in the process, we will restore our historical self-confidence."

Yang Wei couldn't get the agonizing thoughts out of his head. Wasn't he part of that history? What role did he play in it?

"In the real historical timeline, you will discover the tangible benefits of having the Allied powers win the war," said Professor Eternal. "At first none of us dared to believe it was true. We thought that perhaps we had mistakenly entered another implanted-narrative world. Our tanks arrived outside of Tokyo in the summer of 1945. You can even clearly see the Japanese Radio Tower. Ah, we should have never wasted our time living through that artificial history!"

"That wasn't right," Yang Wei said with some hesitation.

Suddenly Professor Eternal changed the tone of his voice. "But we could never have anticipated how the entire situation would end up going backward. Huge numbers of Allied troops contracted a strange disease. Their eyes became engorged with pus, they developed painful boils all over their bodies, and they were too exhausted to fight. It didn't take long to discover that they were the victims of a never-before-seen breed of biological warfare. As we were dillydallying in our implanted-narrative world, the Japanese military doctors of Unit 731, stationed in Manchuria, were researching the development of a new virus, which would circulate throughout the human immune system before launching a fatal attack. To make matters worse, the Germans also launched an attack from the sea. Hitler escaped to Argentina, but as his ship sailed past Antarctica, he established a bioengineering base under the polar ice cap, where his men developed new types of bioweapons. As you know, the Nazis conducted all kinds of hellish medical experiments on the Jews, the fruits of which were now fully employed. The Nazis extracted a special variant of avian flu from penguins and mixed it with mutated human genes, which they then grafted onto the virus produced by Unit 731, upgrading it to the Devil Virus and releasing it in mass quantities among the Allied forces. This led our Air-Land Central Command's Unified Magnetic Information Battle System to suffer a complete system failure. It was almost impossible to carry on the war. Fortunately, thanks to John D. Rockefeller Jr.'s insight, we established several modern medical facilities, which were immediately put to good use to help prevent a total collapse. In June of 1946, the medical powers of both sides came to a head in the northern theater, where chromosomal translocation became the focal point. Things built to a great battle, which ended in a stalemate that would last a full decade, until 1956, when there was a major breakthrough in the field of synthetic biology. In 1966, the artificial viral sea began to form. Over time its form and function gradually began to change, until it eventually transformed the entire planetary ecosystem. The Allied forces had no choice but to retreat to Mars and other planets and asteroids, where they established field hospitals. There in the solar system, they took up a defensive position, where they could recover and try to figure out a way to combat the Devil Virus. They planned how to strike back, and according to the predictions of various models, the year of the final showdown between these forces would be 1976, with a general offensive attack launched in October."

Yang Wei felt like he was about to faint. He pinched himself to check whether he was still alive.

"That's right," Professor Eternal said solemnly. "One group of people was desperately devoted to researching radars, missiles, computers, and spaceships, while another spent all its energy on genome research. Meanwhile, the Allied forces were stuck in their world of narrative implants. Only in 1953 did they finally discovered the existence of the Life Code. But as you know, in the historical timeline of the real world, a Japanese scientist from Tokyo University's Medical School actually discovered DNA's double helix structure in 1937, after which he carried out gene sequencing on all biological species. This proved to be a turning point in the war, and it all came down to a question of strategy. Medicine became the sole theater through which warfare was waged. Flames and explosions were no longer a war threat. All that remained was the struggle between different viruses and medicines. This is what has been referred to as the Medicinal War. The Allied forces made a serious strategic mistake. Soldiers on the ground had long known that dysentery is deadlier than guns. But that was not enough to earn the attention of the military doctors, who were distracted by the Devil's tricks."

"What about nuclear weapons?" Yang Wei wondered aloud. "Can't they be used here?"

The cerebral fluid lining Professor Eternal's brain began to glisten and throb. "Nuclear weapons? What the hell is that? Never heard of such a thing . . . humph. Even today's most technologically advanced weaponry is helpless when it comes to eradicating microorganisms. They can withstand high temperatures, extreme cold, and radiation. And due to the fact that they can't be seen, they are impossible to target or attack."

That was the moment when Yang Wei realized that the enemy was responsible for his disease. And he began to hate the enemy. "So there is absolutely no way to cure my disease? All along, it was caused by these demonic enemies? And this unending pain . . . is all a product of this evil war?"

Yang Wei had seemingly found his answer. He gazed at Professor Eternal with a look of gratitude. He glanced down at the manga, and he felt that he resembled the character on the page. They were both creatures from another world. But Yang Wei remained uncertain. Was that other world more believable than this one?

Professor Eternal spoke as if the force of justice were on his side. "The more your treatment fails, the more necessary it is to continue! Everything we have done—tightening our belts, braving the danger of constructing this state-of-the-art Hospital Ship, holding down the front lines, serving as the stronghold against invasion from the outside, protecting everyone *inside*—has all been for the common goal of emerging victorious from this Second World War! Doctors are our greatest soldiers. Have you seen *Hacksaw Ridge*? That battle was fought in Okinawa. The path to final victory in that battle came down to the actions of a medical officer. How come he never took up a rifle? Because they were fighting a Medicinal War, a battle *between* doctors. This is the mission of mankind, the responsibility of every person in this nation!"

"Mission? Responsibility?" Yang Wei mumbled. He thought, *As a patient, do I need a mission too? Do I need to assume responsibility?* He didn't want to end up infected by some virus, leading to a slow and painful death. He would much prefer just to be blown up on a battlefield somewhere.

Displaying acute foresight, Professor Eternal observed, "Like disease, politics will never be extinguished. War is simply an extension of politics. In an age when life becomes the center of everything, what is politics, anyway? The laws of medicine *are* the laws of politics."

"That's what they say . . ."

"This war must be brought to an end," stressed Professor Eternal. "This is a divine decree and must be followed. Otherwise, nothing else can be carried out: no United Nations, no popular democracy, no national independence, no middle-class prosperity, no globalization, no technological revolution, no renewable energy, no interstellar travel, no internet, no Wikipedia, no artificial intelligence, no Medicinal Age, self-service hospitals, or DIY diagnostic and treatment centers, which would be available to every family and eventually destroy every family . . . in other words, we would never achieve all the things we have today."

"I think I understand some of what you are describing, but I'm more confused than before," said Yang Wei.

"There is no need for you to understand and no need to fear your confusion," said Professor Eternal. "Just put on your white hospital gown and get to work."

"What about the other hospital ships?" asked Yang Wei. "I saw them. I know this isn't the only one."

"Unfortunately, the fleet is just an illusion," explained Professor Eternal, "a viral illusion created in the patients' retinas. Everyone is infected."

"What other illusions have we been seeing?" asked a pained Yang Wei.

"Everything you see might be an illusion," responded Professor Eternal. "Illusions are themselves a form of weapon. In this war, the enemy doesn't necessarily have to destroy our bodies. All it needs to paralyze us is to harness illusions. Once these illusions appear, they immediately become real, and what was once a binary opposition becomes unified, making us appear to be both dead and alive at the same time. Under these circumstances, the enemy can appropriate more visual methods, like using microorganisms to transform our physical environment, making it impossible for us to survive. Global warming has already advanced at a pace far beyond what anyone thought possible. Using microorganisms to raise the temperature of the oceans by a single degree or increasing carbon dioxide in the atmosphere by three percent, would put the final nail in our coffin. It's like a cat playing with a mouse . . . that is why it is so important that we recognize the severity of the situation. The Supreme Command Center has ordered us to the front lines, to get as close to the enemy as we can. The Supreme Command Center told us to act as if we were sensors embedded in its skin. The Supreme Command Center commanded us to acquire all of the data links associated with the Devil Virus and transmit them to the base on Mars. There they would develop vaccines and an antivirus, which would be used to launch a counteroffensive in the autumn of 1976. But they just sent Dr. Linezolid back to Earth, and the promised reinforcements never arrived. Perhaps the enemy set up a biological barrier in time and space, blocking the peptide chain of information exchange between the Hospital Ship and the Mars base. Perhaps after receiving the pathology reports we provided, the Supreme Command Center finally realized just how powerful the enemy truly was and decided to push back its timeline for a counteroffensive . . . again. This must have been the Supreme Leader's decision. When you boil it all down, war simply expresses the will of a particular circle of people. In the end, nothing we say really matters."

Yang Wei felt utterly confused and extremely conflicted, more torn than at any other time in his life. He wanted to leap out of the helicopter and bring an end to his chaotic and muddled life. "So who are *we*, anyway? The Soviet Red Army? The US Army? Winston Churchill's army? China's Expeditionary Army?"

Professor Eternal curled his lips, as if he had a terrible headache. Blue sparks of electricity burst from the folds of his brain. "Any of those is a possibility, but what's the point? It all comes down to probabilities arising from random phenomena. The war has dragged on so long that no one knows who the enemy is anymore. Who is our friend? Who are you? Who am I? Classical statistics have failed us. In this new battlefield, binary opposites have been unified; everything has been rearranged and recombined. There is no unsinkable alliance, no permanent system of values . . . no one can find a normal distribution curve. We could all be Japanese, or German . . ." Professor Eternal stopped. Then he returned to his snacks and his manga.

"So God and the Devil are wrapped together?" exclaimed Yang Wei. "Now *that* is a pain in the ass!" He lamented that he had been born in the wrong time. He couldn't bring himself to accept that the same Professor Eternal before him had once been an imperial physician, conducting vivisection on prisoners of war as part of Unit 731, or a coldhearted Nazi doctor overseeing the slaughter of Jews in the concentration camps. And now their images had combined with that of the sage-like Dr. Norman Bethune.

"The hospital must complete this mission," Professor Eternal declared. "The most important thing now is to develop a new medicine to identify who people really are. But it's extremely challenging because everything is constantly changing, including ourselves."

"So . . . what should we do?" There was pain in Yang Wei's voice, as if he were mourning a loss.

"It doesn't matter," Professor Eternal responded decisively. "Neither who our allies are, nor our identities. The important thing for us, as flesh-and-blood humans, is to go on living. The right to exist is the most fundamental human right of all. No other right can hold a candle to it." His mouth spit out a meatball. "When this war reaches its end, the entire species will be wiped out. All biological sea creatures have already been obliterated by the virus. The pulmonary algae and all the rest are simply illusions, created by the mutated virus . . . the hospital is triggering this planet's sixth major extinction event, which will surely have an irreversible impact on the evolution of the solar system and the Milky Way. As doctors, we must take responsibility for the fate of the universe."

47

ONLY WINE CAN HELP US FORGET OUR SORROWS

The helicopter began to descend, hovering just over the Hospital Ship, which was like an ancient leather-clad warship or a massive volcano, its layers rising, extending out from the sea like a robotic island. As the ship transformed over time, its variable combinations had become a sentient AI mecha, equipped with a powerful trinomial distributed defense system surrounding the space around the ship, continually emitting microbots to destroy the virus particles assaulting it from all sides. In the context of modern warfare, this effort to reduce the intensity of the attacks comprised the comprehensive weapon called "the hospital." Caught in the viral sea, unable to escape, as heavily armed as it was, the ship had begun to decline and come apart, until it, too, had fallen seriously ill, ready at any moment to collapse at the hands of the enemy.

The ship's chaos and desolation were created by the enemy. When he thought about it like that, Yang Wei didn't feel so guilty. He couldn't blame the doctors for any of this. All those patient deaths were in some sense justified. Siming had long been the primary target of the enemy's AI virus-cluster attacks. Siming had been invaded, hijacked, and ultimately even the source of incitement from within. Everything Siming did was filled with emotion, bearing the marks of consciousness that appeared to be either the work of man or an act of God, but in reality it was all just an algorithmic simulation, brilliant in its modeling of itself to such a high degree of realism but with no true sense of self, no idea what it was actually doing. All the compassion, care, violence, and abuse that the patients received from the algorithm was fake, a set of sounds and actions carefully designed to achieve the desired effect. Siming was, in fact, just another version of Searle's "Chinese room" that happened to be really good at pretending. And this was the root cause behind its breach. At the center of Siming's advanced mind, and at the heart of its soul, was nothing but emptiness, as depicted in *Porco Rosso*. But Yang Wei had trouble accepting that. He had believed that the act of writing poetry should have resolved the problem of consciousness and the soul. *But maybe not,* he thought. Back when he'd started writing song lyrics, he hadn't had any real consciousness or soul to speak of. He had just felt as if all the people around him were walking zombies. He hadn't taken the Medicinal War seriously. He had underestimated the enemy.

Professor Eternal piloted the helicopter as he read his manga. The mechanical arm poured alcohol into his mouth. His tongue and lips forcefully rubbed the rim of the bottle, making a squeaking sound that sounded like someone masturbating. A thick, frothing yellow liquid gurgled between his teeth. "Oh . . . oh . . . ," he moaned. After reaching his climax, he appeared exhausted. The grooves in his brain looked darker than before, resembling the lips of a woman's vagina. Sleep overtook him. Once asleep, he kind of resembled the Hospital President. Yang Wei figured that the elite doctors and hospital administrators must all be exhausted, given the time they spent worrying about the country. But could they also have been infected by the enemy's virus? He didn't dare ask, nor move, afraid that a sudden shift in weight might cause the helicopter to crash. The pain he experienced was unbearable. He sneaked a glance at the bottle of alcohol Professor Eternal had just spit up and thought about taking a swig to numb the pain, but then Professor Eternal's voice processor emitted a thunderous lionlike snore that merged with the roar of the helicopter's engine. They circled over the sea, the helicopter like a lonely hero waging battle with a powerful windmill.

The world kept on blowing. The helicopter's anemometer showed a wind speed of up to fifteen meters per second. As the helicopter was thrust upside down, the stench of alcohol in the cockpit made Yang Wei feel dizzy. He remembered Dr. Amoxycillin once saying that Professor Eternal not only liked to drink but also had an incredible ability to hold his liquor. He believed that besides the invention of fire, alcohol consumption was one of the main things that set humans apart from other animals. Professor Eternal would get excited in the middle of the night and call a few of his doctor friends over to drink together. That was back before Siming had taken control of the hospital. Even when doctors were in the middle of carrying out emergency lifesaving procedures, as soon as they heard Professor Eternal calling, they would immediately put down their scalpels and head off to see him. If any of the doctors didn't show up, Professor Eternal would blacklist them. In some cases, a doctor wouldn't show up because he was already passed-out drunk, but even that wasn't an acceptable excuse. When it came to drinking, no one was a match for Professor Eternal's prowess. He could drink anyone under the table. Those chosen to be his drinking partners were the lucky ones. They had earned his trust. Professor Eternal was approachable, and he never judged people by their rank. In fact he had a special affinity for getting close to the masses and enjoyed hanging out with ordinary medical workers and patients. Now that he had attached himself to Yang Wei, there must be some deeper meaning. After all, wasn't Yang Wei deemed to be a "special patient"?

The air grew suddenly turbulent. The helicopter began to shake so violently that it felt as if it might be ripped apart. The shaking woke up a startled Professor Eternal, who took one look at Yang Wei and asked, "Who are you?"

"Me? I'm Yang . . . Yang Wei," he responded fearfully.

That seemed to jog Professor Eternal's memory. "Oh, you're a patient. That's right; I do know you. I treated you before, so I know that you are not one of the enemy's devil soldiers. Just now, what were we talking about? How come you're still here?"

Yang Wei felt embarrassed. "You summoned me here." He felt like a knife was piercing his heart. As he looked out at the clouds and the waves, he thought back to that mysterious woman who had given him the map to Professor Eternal.

Professor Eternal seemed lost in thought for a moment. "That's right . . . that's right . . . okay then, my dear patient! Why don't you help yourself to a glass!" One of the mechanical arms handed Yang Wei a teacup and filled it to the brim.

The helicopter entered a full-on tailspin. Professor Eternal seemed oblivious to the fact that it might crash at any moment and instead grew increasingly excited.

"Spirits are a fundamental part of our battlefield culture!" he insisted. "When you drink with a traditional tea set like this, it really brings out the flavor and reminds you of where all of this came from. Did the kids over at the crematorium serve you any tea? That was just to warm you up a bit. This is much better than drinking out of the steel helmets of dead soldiers. It tastes terrible when human brains get mixed in with the alcohol!"

Yang Wei felt like he was clasping a grenade. As he tremblingly raised his cup, he cast a deathly glare at the hot steam coming off Professor Eternal's gleaming brain. Yang Wei tried to remain calm. He figured this must be one part of the test that Professor Eternal was putting him through. Drinking this alcohol would probably allow Professor Eternal to figure out whether Yang Wei had been infected by the enemy's virus and, if so, just how serious his infection was. Perhaps this yellow alcohol might even relieve some of his pain. But when he remembered that Professor Eternal was flying drunk, he hesitated.

"Hey!" Professor Eternal barked. "Haven't you ever tasted alcohol before? Or perhaps you don't want to drink with me?"

The mechanical arm retrieved a pile of pictures from a small compartment in the cockpit and handed them to Yang Wei. They were images of alcohol taken with a microscope camera. Green, blue, and red particles in the form of knives, pitchforks, shards of ice, and ruins resembled a miniature version of the crematorium. But instead of blazing flames burning bodies, the images depicted a universe exploding like a riot of gorgeous flowers.

Professor Eternal finally pulled the helicopter out of its tailspin. "I'll bet you've never seen anything like that before!" he sneered. "Those are alcohol molecules . . . the flames of war, a truly mesmerizing art! War is the highest art, the source of all other forms of art. That's why I had them turn the process of cremation into an art—so the hospital would have its own flag to fly! This represents the core of our military strategy. How can you be expected to go into battle if you don't understand art? War is like medicine—both are the art of the dead. Two technologies lead to the most expensive goods and services: medicine and national defense. Both go completely against the laws of their respective fields, because both are forms of art. Art calls for resistance while also establishing certain laws. Art avoids being tied down by probability theory, and thus it can break through the enemy's defenses. Both national defense and medicine share a common origin. You could say that they were originally one and the same—both products of war. This is what gives us the confidence to struggle toward victory . . ." He then issued a resounding order. "Now, it's time to attack!"

The helicopter dived, then hovered for a moment before launching a series of medicinal pellets from its wings. The pellets rained down upon the surface of the sea, triggering explosive splashes. The Hospital Ship's medical robots retaliated by firing a series of powerful blasts of water through rapid-fire syringes.

"Tangent line!" shouted Professor Eternal. The helicopter dodged the water assault, climbing to evade the attack. "Take a look!" cried Professor Eternal. "This is what you call war! You can see both sides getting massacred, but . . . it's so damn beautiful! Art provides a majestic strength. It is the source of all confidence, not only allowing people to understand the difficulties of life but also providing creative inspiration. That's why Osamu Tezuka and Hayao Miyazaki turned to anime. Because they had created Beethoven and Murasaki Shikibu, the enemy was able to produce this Devil Virus. There is no reason to be obsessed with x-rays and ultrasounds, just as there is no need to get caught up in big data and artificial intelligence. Network thinking and indexical medicine are much too vulgar . . . thank goodness that our dear Hospital President is a great artist! Owing to his guidance, our grand enterprise has been able to carry on up to the present day." Professor Eternal's brain rotated ninety degrees in the jar. His mouth flew toward the group photo hanging on the cockpit wall. "Look at the Hospital President. He was infatuated with literature, loved writing fiction, had a talent for drawing, and could play seven or eight musical instruments, including the piano and Chinese zither. His dedication to the arts really had an impact on me. He was also quite the drinker. Whenever the topic of wine came up, women were always involved. During the war, things that had been lost were resynthesized, thanks to the Hospital President's leadership in molecular engineering. That, too, was an art, representing the Hospital Ship's core values."

Yang Wei couldn't help but exclaim, "That is so fucking amazing!"

Professor Eternal adopted a benevolent tone. "I will never forget what happened the moment my mother died. She was a respected military doctor and the Hospital President's lover, but she found herself on the verge of death after falling victim to one of the enemy's viral attacks. As her son and a doctor, I could do nothing to help her. I sat beside her sickbed to keep her company, and we chatted about inconsequential things from our past. But our life experiences were so very different, and it was hard to find topics we could really see eye to eye on, so we resorted mostly to silence and awkward stares. That's when I came up with the idea of reading novels to her. Wouldn't it be great if I could read her Leo Tolstoy's *War and Peace*, Michael Ondaatje's *The English Patient*, or William Faulkner's *As I Lay Dying*. When my mother was younger, medical schools usually didn't provide students with literary training, and even if they did, the minimal curriculum couldn't delve into the deep thinking and intricate expression contained in literary works—literature was simply a world away for her. She knew how to fight and how to steal another woman's man, but she could never have appreciated the hidden meanings behind the words of literature. Do you get what I'm saying? This is one of the great regrets the previous generation has had to live with. Only art can treat the kind of pain more painful than my mother's pain. It's a true shame that even after all the women died, people still seem unable to grasp this simple truth."

Yang Wei began to understand why Professor Eternal had insisted on teaching literature classes on the ship. He wanted to transform the Hospital Ship *into a story*. Perhaps the creator had designed the world according to a novel. No matter what scientific research was carried out, in the end it was all a quest for artistic truth. But there was more that he didn't understand, and like the pain experienced by Professor Eternal's mother, Yang Wei's pain could find no release. This was precisely the reason why he had first sought out Professor Eternal.

"Doctors today seem to have lost the ability to appreciate good art!" complained Professor Eternal. "How can they be expected to do battle with our evil enemies if they no longer have the literary and artistic sensibility that would allow them to rise above this mundane reality? How can they be expected to strike back with vengeance? Instead, they just sit there, waiting for someone to put a bullet in their heads, like what happened to my mother. A long time ago, the hospital was like the army, imbued with a highly artistic atmosphere. Writing fiction and poetry transformed the people who worked there into gods. It is unclear exactly when doctors started to drift away, no longer resembling artists or gods but rather street hawkers and petty hustlers instead. They were forced to hide out belowdecks, where they started the Shadow

Hospital. This was completely unacceptable. If you don't read or drink before an operation, how can you be expected to cut open a patient's body? And if you don't have the courage to open up a patient, how can you be expected to defeat the enemy? Sensing this weakness, Siming made its move."

With a respectful and laudatory tone, Professor Eternal mentioned the famous warriors of the past: Lu Xun, Guo Moruo, Han Suyin, Yu Hua, Chi Li, Feng Tang, Anton Chekhov, Gabriel García Márquez, Yasunari Kawabata, Kōbō Abe, Shūichi Katō, Junichi Watanabe. All were known as incredible military doctors, or the direct descendants of military doctors, but they were also recognized at a young age for their literary accomplishments. They had dared to dissect the human heart with scalpels. They had drunk alcohol as they had gouged out those hearts, and when they were finished, they had hopped in their own helicopters and flown off without the slightest hesitation to do battle with the enemy.

"At one point, there were massive casualties, which served as a testament to the life-and-death struggle between our military hospital and the enemy's military hospital. That was back in the golden age of military medical science or, rather, military medical art. The Allied forces prepared for a series of battles, which nearly drove the enemy forces away. One of those battles took place in the European theater, where biological advances led to a brand-new life-form that invaded the enemy's underwater genetic router and destroyed its bioediting machine. Another major battle played out at the North Pole, where cell phones were widely employed to draw amino acids from the atmosphere, ultimately causing the enemy's immune system to collapse. But now it is too late. Everything has fallen into a state of failure, decline, and collapse. No one even dares to pilot helicopters anymore. I have only a partial head, but I have no choice but to man this cockpit personally. Even so, there are still people aboard the Hospital Ship that are trying to kill me, and this led to the right conditions for the enemy to launch its attack."

Professor Eternal began to grow testy. He demanded that Yang Wei finish his cup of alcohol, ordering the mechanical arm to point a potassium cyanide syringe at him. When Professor Eternal saw Yang Wei's terrified response, he broke out in a fit of laughter and turned the needle back toward his own throat-like tube.

"If we should be defeated, we will die for a righteous cause," he said. The mechanical arm put down the syringe, then turned to pick up a pen and began writing on a pile of manuscript papers. Professor Eternal explained that he was dictating a new edition of *Principles of Hospital Engineering* in order to establish a new theoretical system that would surpass that of Cicero, Aquinas, Gandhi, and Lee Kuan Yew. "Everyone knows," he said, "that the once-popular *Principles of Hospital Engineering* is actually a forgery."

The helicopter flew low over the Hospital Ship, almost crashing into the crematorium tower. Yang Wei could see Malnutrizole standing on the tower, gazing upward with his eyes wide open, as if searching for his own lost soul. Yang Wei finally understood how much hard work Professor Eternal had put into the construction of the crematorium. In a fit of fear, he bit down hard on his wineglass. He didn't agree with what Professor Eternal had said. During the Exorcism Congress, he had clearly seen doctors consuming alcohol. He tried to drink more quickly, but it was difficult, and he could get only a few small sips down at a time. His stomach emitted an explosive scream that sounded to him like porcelain being smashed. Instead of alleviating his pain, it only made it worse.

Yang Wei slipped into a depression. He thought his poor performance in front of Professor Eternal must have left a terrible impression. Professor Eternal must have thought that Yang Wei in no way resembled a true artist, even if he had once been a songwriter. Perhaps that was precisely the reason that Professor Eternal had summoned him here. None of the current doctors were any good at creative writing, and he couldn't allow Siming to go on writing poetry—he needed to find someone with decent skill as a writer. Yang Wei did his best to maintain a smile, pretending to love alcohol, medicine, art, and war. Then he noticed a configuration of colors dancing in his cup like random fragments of galactic debris . . . gradually they coalesced into the shape of a red cross. Yang Wei quietly told himself that this wasn't an illusion. The alcohol was a brand of whiskey; although it wasn't brewed in Scotland, the best biotech had been utilized to synthesize a whiskey that tasted exactly like the real thing. In wartime, this was a rare commodity indeed. Yang Wei had ingested a lot of medicine in his lifetime, but how many times had he enjoyed high-quality liquor like this? How marvelous would it be if he could spend every day getting drunk with Professor Eternal? Then he might have enough courage to battle the enemy, instead of spending all day as a medical tourist and being duped by Super Patient. Life was indeed filled with pain and misery, but a good glass of spirits could take care of all that.

Yang Wei gazed up at Professor Eternal with a look of profound gratitude. This glass of whiskey had brought him so much closer to Professor Eternal, closing the gap between them. There were so many things Yang Wei wanted to share with the professor. He wanted to tell him the truth about the sick ward, how far the doctors had fallen, and how the algorithm was killing people. And he had so many more questions . . .

As Yang Wei finished his whiskey, Professor Eternal watched intently, as if watching someone create a work of art. "My dear patient," he said. "Thank you. I can't tell you how long it has been since someone was willing to drink with me." After a brief pause, he asked, "Are you willing to become a bee or an ant? A grain of sand? A drop of water?"

Yang Wei blushed and whispered, "I . . . am."

Professor Eternal's brain spun like a top as he released a strain of maniacal laughter. He then explained to Yang Wei how to operate the helicopter. It didn't take long for Yang Wei to master the basics. As they soared through the sky, Yang Wei was completely drunk. He felt embarrassed by his low tolerance. Professor Eternal didn't appear drunk in the least. The food and alcohol he had consumed had gone down a plastic tube and drained into an aluminum bucket equipped with an electronic trigger that fed pleasure sensations to Professor Eternal's nervous system. When Yang Wei finally realized that Professor Eternal had chosen *him*, he couldn't help but feel moved.

48

HEAVEN BESTOWS A BEAUTIFUL GIRL, OUT OF PITY

After landing the helicopter back on the ship's deck, Yang Wei collapsed. The pain was so intense he thought he might explode. He popped some fentanyl and rested for a while before struggling to pull himself out of the cockpit. He stumbled aimlessly around the deck, thinking of Professor Eternal's massive brain. Then he was assaulted by pangs of regret: Why didn't he ask Professor Eternal about how he got sick in the first place? Then again, Professor Eternal had provided a hint. Since they were at war, Yang Wei's original identity must have been that of a soldier, perhaps every bit as outstanding a soldier as Lu Xun, Feng Tang, or Yasunari Kawabata.

After some time, a face appeared from behind one of the buildings, peering at Yang Wei. It was the same woman who had led Yang Wei to Professor Eternal! She had a slender figure and was now wearing a white nurse's uniform and beige trench coat that went almost down to her knees. Her legs were wrapped in black silk stockings, which were perfectly inserted into a pair of brown boots. A camouflage bulletproof vest hung over her chest, and she still carried that first aid kit. She looked like she could have walked right out of the pages of *A Collection of Beautiful Raccoons, Bushy Orangutans, and Busty Dragons*. If she had been standing next to the young Professor Eternal as he had appeared in that photograph, they would have been the perfect couple. It was unclear why, but she now had a robotic quality, like the mechanical arm that fed Professor Eternal.

Yang Wei was suspicious that she might be an illusion created by the enemy virus, but then she pulled him up against her. Yang Wei trembled as he spoke. "I just saw Professor Eternal . . . are we going back to the Exorcism Congress? I'm utterly exhausted."

The woman took Yang Wei by the hand and led him farther out on the deck. Then the entire scene transformed before his eyes. Yang Wei felt like he had suddenly gone back in time. He saw the birdcage before him, empty, as if waiting for the peacock to return. Its artistry had been dulled by protracted warfare, but it hadn't yet completely disappeared. Yang Wei was concerned that the woman might laugh at him, even though that didn't seem to be her intention. But he was so tired that he couldn't walk another step, so he sat down at the edge of the deck, gazing at the red sea. He felt like he had just dragged himself from a corpse-littered battlefield. Seeing how exhausted he looked, the woman sat down beside him. They looked like a couple enjoying a romantic moment together. But leaning against the railing, not far from them, was Dr. Amoxycillin. He stared blankly at the horizon.

Yang Wei was so weak that it took him a moment to find the right words. "What's your name?" he asked the woman. He figured that she must be a combat nurse sent to save him.

"Zi Ye," she responded casually. A fragrant aroma of maize leaves escaped her lips, diluting the pungent stench of formaldehyde that filled the air.

Yang Wei repeated her name. "Zi Ye as in 'midnight'?" He thought back to when he had climbed up to the crematorium in the middle of the night and seen the sky filled with twinkling stars.

"No," she responded curtly. "Zi Ye as in 'purple fluid.' Not everything in this world is red. And not everything comes down to a question of when we can emerge from this long dark night."

"So what am I supposed to do?" As Yang Wei gazed at her, her voluptuous body felt to him like a raging cauldron of molten-copper honey.

"Didn't Professor Eternal tell you?" Her voice lacked rhythm and color, as if everything she said had been prepared in advance.

Yang Wei responded haltingly. "He told me to be like a drop of water, a grain of sand, a bee, an ant . . ." He remained utterly uncertain about his future.

As if trying not to startle him, Zi Ye spoke gently, like wind whistling through a grove of green bamboo. "As per Professor Eternal's orders, from now on I shall be your contact person."

Yang Wei felt a surge of emotion flood his heart. "Is that so? My contact person . . . ?" He looked at her again; her quivering lips were covered with a healthy moisture, even though they seemed to have been etched by an artist's hand.

"Professor Eternal needs to protect himself from the enemy's attempts on his life and from those close to him," explained Zi Ye. "He can't always be out there fighting on the front lines, given his physical limitations."

The scene on deck looked much like before. On the surface, the Hospital Ship seemed to be functioning normally. Those doctors not attending the congress were busy reselling pharmaceuticals and used medical equipment. Vendors and peddlers bantered. Patients were shuttled back and forth along the assembly line. Medical robots made their rounds through the sick wards. The crematorium's flames blazed as brightly as ever. But Dr. Amoxycillin still stood there, his back now to the railing, like a statue. Yang Wei felt like none of this would last much longer.

"Are you a nurse?" he asked.

"Everyone here is a warrior," replied Zi Ye.

"Oh, I understand," said Yang Wei. "All patients are soldiers."

"The scalpel can both take lives and save them," said Zi Ye.

"So I've seen," replied Yang Wei.

"Some people remember that they are warriors, while others forget," said Zi Ye. "That's why it is sometimes necessary to jog their memories."

Yang Wei thought back to the war games they had played in the sick ward. "All of the patients aboard this ship seem to be men," he observed.

"That's due to the severity of the battles," said Zi Ye.

"Did the war drive all the women away?" asked Yang Wei.

"No, the women were exterminated during the prior battle," replied Zi Ye. "The enemy devised a kind of genetically coded weapon, which targeted the X chromosome." Zi Ye spoke without emotion, without an ounce of either narcissism or self-blame. She clearly did not hold a grudge.

Yang Wei thought of Professor Eternal's mother. Meanwhile, his pain spread throughout his body like the tendrils of a vine, accompanied by the excitement of witnessing terrible carnage, as if some primal biological instinct had been stimulated. He thought back to the women he had met before, including his wife and daughter. Though that felt like a lifetime ago, he began to miss them, even though he knew that they might never have really existed. Perhaps they were nothing more than an artificially designed illusion in the pages of his medical records. Perhaps they had been killed by the enemy long ago. But he found himself longing for them. It was difficult to tell whether this feeling was real, but it tore at his heart.

Zi Ye continued in a rational tone. "The enemy thinks that by destroying women, they will destroy our nation. We have always looked at the nation as the largest unit in the tide of history . . . this is clearly an attempt to tear apart the Allied forces' defense at its very root. That's how women—people like me—disappeared from the world overnight, wiped out, as if completely worthless. At least they died of disease, so that after their autopsies, they provided valuable medical information that helped the surviving men to go on fighting. And that's how we all became martyrs."

Consumed with a guilty conscience, Yang Wei asked, "How come they didn't kill the men?" It was still hard for him to imagine himself as a warrior, even though he had committed murder before.

Zi Ye answered his question succinctly. "Mr. Yang, it is actually quite simple. Women are imbued with a higher level of intelligence and emotional maturity than men. Men drink too much, and by the time they reach middle age, the neural chassis of their brains is riddled with holes and utterly ruined by the effects of alcoholism. Yet somehow, they still act with arrogance and pride, as if they always know what is best and only they are qualified to direct the war effort. That is the reason why this war grows more and more miserable. The future belongs to women, but that is precisely what the enemy fears most. So they annihilated the women first—like back in the Song dynasty, when they killed Lady Liang instead of her husband, General Han Shizhong. Without the help and support of women, it was bound to be 'game over' for the men! They can't go a single day without singing their mothers' praises."

Yang Wei had no idea who Han Shizhong or Lady Liang were. He looked at Zi Ye as if staring at a ghost. "So what about you, then?" His image of Professor Eternal seemed to fall apart before his eyes.

Zi Ye tried to downplay his concern. "Professor Eternal is the only one who sees the importance of all of this. He drinks so much so that he can personally experience this level of pain, in order to uncover the core problem behind this war. I was created by Professor Eternal, based on the template of a female martyr. He designed and edited me on a computer and 3D printed me to serve as your contact person. Don't you realize how lucky you are, Mr. Yang?"

She reached out to pat Yang Wei on the shoulder. Her touch was so powerful that Yang Wei grimaced in pain, but he didn't dare to cry out. He wondered whether he really did need a woman by his side. Perhaps he used to be nothing more than a good-for-nothing skirt-chaser? But why had Professor Eternal sent her to Yang Wei and not Spasm or some other patient? Perhaps the professor had made some kind of mistake by sending her to Yang Wei? Then again, sometimes one just needed to embrace one's own mistakes. Part of him felt elated. "It's truly an honor . . . so what's my situation now?"

"Mr. Yang, your brain has been infected by a strain of the virus," said Zi Ye. "You were on the verge of losing your mind. You're so lucky that Professor Eternal was able to treat you with the Battlefield Crisis Program."

"Is that a type of narrative-implant therapy?" asked Yang Wei.

"It is but one of several new types of treatment," responded Zi Ye.

"How come nobody sought my permission first?" asked Yang Wei. "How could they decide just to remove my pain without my consent? They even went so far as to obliterate my former life!"

Zi Ye was visibly displeased by his reaction. "This is war! Everyone must sacrifice! How come you are so consumed with your own petty pain? I'm talking about national pain, the pain of the solar system, the pain of the Milky Way and the entire universe! Mr. Yang, I should point out the fact that, strictly speaking, you don't have a life. All you have is a patient's life. Here at the hospital, everything comes down to treatment. A quick recovery is the only way you will ever return to the battlefield." She tightened the straps on her bulletproof vest, squeezing her breasts, which looked like a pair of pomegranates on the verge of bursting.

Yang Wei felt like he was in a dream. Wasn't there a shortage of ammo? Why did Zi Ye wear a bulletproof vest? He was too embarrassed to look directly at her and instead turned his gaze to the birdcage, which was no longer a birdcage at all. It didn't need to contain peacocks or any birds, just as the hospital was actually a massive military camp, occupied by soldiers instead of patients. There was no room for sentimentality. But Yang Wei realized that even though he had already undergone treatment, he was still in terrible pain. Did Professor Eternal know this? And if one day his pain should be eliminated, wouldn't he technically still be sick? What did it all mean?

Yang Wei hoped he might have the opportunity to ask Professor Eternal these questions face to face—or at least face to brain. He could request another round of narrative-implant therapy so he could return to the Medicinal Age, when the entire universe was one gigantic hospital. Then he could be reunited with Sister Jiang, Ah Bi, Bai Dai, and Zhu Lin, instead of living this strange life where he spent all his time running around a place that was supposed to be a battlefield but didn't look or feel anything like a battlefield. His only fear was that by the time he found Professor Eternal again, the professor would no longer remember him. The professor's drinking problem was, after all, getting pretty bad.

Yang Wei whined, "Why me?"

Zi Ye heaved a deep sigh. "Didn't Professor Eternal talk to you about this? You're not an ordinary patient. You're the only patient on the entire Hospital Ship capable of composing song lyrics. The poems that most patients write don't even qualify as poetry, and the doctors are also incapable of writing anything like that."

Yang Wei's suspicion was finally confirmed, and he felt vindicated.

Zi Ye continued, "Have you ever heard of the Renaissance? It was only after the Renaissance that we witnessed the birth of modern medicine. We never experienced the Renaissance here, which is why we keep fighting even after we have all run out of steam. The war machine is stalled, and this is a lesson we must go back to learn. The Renaissance was the most violent and disgusting period in history. In that sense, it is just like the hospital. We're simply not qualified. History has chosen you, as it chose Professor Eternal and myself. In the face of history, there is nothing any of us can say."

"History . . . ," muttered Yang Wei. It wasn't just that he could barely breathe; it felt like all the water in the sea was crashing down upon him or he was being crushed by the Five Elements Mountain. But unlike the Monkey King, who was trapped in a mountain and born of stone, Yang Wei's pain was not caused by some magical spell. As he looked at the woman standing before him, a famous line came to his head: *Men create history, but women* are *history.*

Zi Ye spoke in a monotone voice like a surgical robot. "That's right—history. It is an interesting topic and a particularly strange one. In the beginning, the field of medicine was an extremely backward science, always lagging far behind other disciplines. For instance, roentgen rays preceded the x-ray; computers preceded compound images; pharmaceutical corporations developed new medicine before doctors could invent new methods of therapy . . . these are all historical facts that cannot be refuted. Doctors working in a clinical setting are bound by various restrictions and have very little leeway when it comes to treatment options. Yet somehow the field of medicine has become the most arrogant science on the planet. It controls everything, it calls all the shots, it is the leader among the sciences and all other fields, even becoming the engine of war. But how long can this possibly continue? Perhaps the tide will turn before too long and history will reset itself. The nature of history is always to turn itself upside down. History has grown immune to pharmaceuticals. If it decides to act unreasonably, there is absolutely nothing you can do about it. You have no choice but to admit that the history playing out before your eyes is your living, breathing reality. Whatever you see becomes real, all part of this damned history. In principle, history can be terminated, but it still hasn't found a replacement to carry on its mission. Kind of like me . . ."

Yang Wei groaned. "I once read the following motto: *You must understand the past to innovate for the future. Whether history advances or retreats lies in all of our hands.*"

"Ho ho!" Zi Ye replied. "Here in the hospital, we often say: *It is difficult for history to advance or retreat when all of our lives dangle by a thread.*"

"When Professor Eternal called on me, didn't he ask me to be a drop of water, a grain of sand, a bee, an ant?" asked Yang Wei. "What can I contribute to help us win this war?"

"Since you have received narrative-implant therapy and are now reborn," Zi Ye responded immediately, "there is a lot more you can do, more than simply flying helicopters or drinking with the professor." She took a step back and stared directly at Yang Wei with her blazing, simian-like eyes, as if she were looking at a pathology specimen.

49

NOT RECOGNIZING SOMEONE WHEN YOU MEET AGAIN

Yang Wei felt like he had just come out of hibernation and was on the verge of collapse, as if his entire body were deteriorating before his own eyes. He gritted his teeth and tried not to scream. He couldn't let Zi Ye see how much pain he was in. This wasn't simply about preserving his dignity. If she were to get wind of the fact that his treatment had been a failure, she would probably notify Professor Eternal and recommend that Yang Wei be terminated and replaced. The hospital must have already invested a massive amount of hard-earned capital in him. Just thinking about that left Yang Wei with a deep sense of guilt. In fact, he even entertained the thought of killing himself. He kept wondering, *Why did it have to be her? Why did Professor Eternal create* this *woman to be my contact person? Why not someone else? Why not a man? Was this another case of history having chosen the outcome?* He'd never imagined that he would have such an unspeakable relationship with history. Of course it was all due to the war, its origins tracing back to the violence of the Renaissance and advancements in medical science.

Zi Ye took out a manga, a copy of *The Wind Rises* by Hayao Miyazaki. She had probably borrowed it from Professor Eternal. Yang Wei leaned over to sneak a peek at the book and discovered that it was a story set during World War II. It seemed that the war had indeed taken place, or perhaps it was still going on. The book told the story of a doctor who performed narrative-implant therapy on the protagonist in order to relieve him of a strange pain of unknown origin. Now living in a world devoid of pain, the young protagonist developed a passion for flight. His dream was to design a special type of superfighter jet to turn the tide of the war. He graduated from college with a degree in aeronautical engineering just when the war was entering a stalemate, so he volunteered for the air force as an engineer. With the support of his girlfriend, he was eventually able to develop an advanced fighter aircraft, which he named "Zero."

The appearance of the protagonist's love interest left Yang Wei extremely uncomfortable. Zi Ye explained, "This was the type of fighter aircraft that was used to disseminate the specially targeted virus that prevented the Allied forces from launching their final assault on Tokyo. But the method of dissemination wasn't as simple as one might think. The pilot of Zero needed to fly the plane directly into the enemy, killing himself in the process. The virus must be combined with the sacrificial blood of the kamikaze pilot in order to be effective. Later, the engineer took it upon himself to execute this mission."

"I never imagined that's what happened," exclaimed a shocked Yang Wei.

"And so the war carried on until 1976," Zi Ye calmly explained.

"So that's where we came into the picture . . . ," Yang Wei muttered.

He understood that Zi Ye's mission as his contact person was to attend to those details that Professor Eternal was unable to convey personally. She helped recover those memories that had been eroded by alcohol. But Yang Wei remained confused: *Did this young man, from a world devoid of pain, invent a technology that created the world of pain in which we now live? And what was Hayao Miyazaki's role in all this? After all, he, too, is an artist. Which world is he situated in?* The more Yang Wei pondered these questions, the more confused he became. He sat, blankly staring at the picture of the young man in the book, and suddenly, he felt like the man looked familiar. *Why was there also a man and a woman together in the enemy camp? And how come they also utilized narrative-implant therapy? Was this just a coincidence or part of some grand design? Could this World War II be nothing but another artificial patient history that someone designed?*

Yang Wei hesitated before continuing. "It's just a manga, anyway. It has so many flaws that I have trouble believing any of this is true. How could one or two new types of weapon alter the progression of the war and its historical outcome? The Allied powers have already landed on Mars, so how is it possible that they can't come up with a vaccine? Why would they send out a single hospital ship to guard the front line? Why do they refer to it as World War II and not World War I or World War III, World War IV, or World War V? Did those other wars already occur? Where are the enemies hiding out? I somehow remember 'by the sea' being just a legend, but no one can actually go there, so perhaps all of this isn't real?"

In the face of Yang Wei's myriad questions and suspicions, Zi Ye didn't seem annoyed in the least. "Mr. Yang, didn't I already tell you?" she responded patiently. "You're actually quite hypocritical. I don't understand why you didn't ask Professor Eternal these questions. Instead, you only dare to share your doubts with a woman like me. This shows your immaturity and cowardice. The reason the professor asked me to be your contact person was precisely because he thought you might not be fully committed. He wanted me to accompany you, to be constantly on call to dispel your fears and misgivings."

"So why don't you help me, then?" Yang Wei asked from the heart.

"Isn't that what I'm doing right now?" Zi Ye responded with sincere disappointment. "Reality is much more difficult to decipher than any manga. Mr. Yang, how could you possibly not be real? This is 1976, the age in which you are living. The fact that you are unable to see things for what they are is just another example of the old saying: 'You can't see the mountain clearly when you are standing amid its foliage.' If you were able to go back thirty years to 2006, or sixty years to 2036, or even ninety years to 2066, everything would be crystal clear, like reading a manga. But I guarantee that things would be nothing like you now imagine them to be."

"But unfortunately I can't go back thirty years," Yang Wei lamented, "or sixty years, or ninety years . . ."

He figured that he would probably die in 1976. At the very least, his personal history would come to a conclusion. Contrary to his expectations, time machines and time travel had never appeared during the war. It would have been a much more effective form of treatment and could have taken the place of narrative-implant therapy. The hospital probably still hadn't successfully completed all its trials, but he had personally seen them abandon the Time Diagnosis and Treatment Machine.

Zi Ye continued her attempt to enlighten him. "World War II is indeed still raging. In reality it is World War I, World War III, World War IV, and World War V combined . . . a concrete manifestation of all the wars that have ever taken place throughout time and space. War is eternal, the only constant. Every death you witness is a result of war, and each one is real. Each and every person feels piercing pain as it travels through their nervous system. Otherwise, why would we even have hospitals? Weren't you, too, just moaning in pain? Didn't I tell you it was all just a show?"

This left Yang Wei in even more pain, but he did his best not to cry out.

Zi Ye led him to the morgue. The entire B3 level of the Hospital Ship had been converted into a morgue called "Pagoda Mountain." The whole area had once served as the base camp for the Gutai Art Association, but now the entire floor was filled with piles of corpses. Most had been warriors in an earlier age, but they had been reduced to bones, still adorned by old torn-up uniforms, which made them appear even more rousing. For some reason, none of them had been thrown into the sea or tossed into the crematorium. They had probably died during a time before the rise of medical robots, long before the

Funeral Artist had appeared on the scene, when the Hospital Ship was controlled by an ancient civilization, during which time another form of artistic expression was all the rage. So those bones had remained, all these years, without anyone taking the time to properly dispose of them. The ship had become a floating cemetery for martyrs. Yang Wei wondered if the original Zi Ye might be lying around somewhere, which reminded him of the time he had gone underwater to search for another Yang Wei among the coffin-like hull of the ship.

Zi Ye adopted the tone of a kindergarten teacher lecturing a child. "During the most crucial period of the war, a lot of people didn't believe that Great Britain would leave the European Union and stand alone in battle, but that's exactly what happened. Most people would have bet money that Trump would never be elected president of the United States, but that's exactly what happened, and after taking office he immediately declared that America would leave the Pacific Strategic Alliance, which was a terrible loss for the Allied forces. These are all recent examples of black swan events. That's why we should always question our own judgment. After all, even the algorithm is unable to predict everything accurately. Such are the paradoxes created by the war. You could say that we have now entered the Era of Paradoxes. This is a nonlinear superposition. For instance, the war has carried on until today, and people are now indifferent when it comes to matters of life and death. Just like the afterlife, the nation might exist, and it might not. Matter might exist in one place while simultaneously existing somewhere else. We live in one chaotic universe."

Yang Wei remembered Buboxine telling him about a mysterious power that could allow a person to be both alive and dead simultaneously. He heaved a deep sigh.

"That's why we have no way to predict what might happen next," Zi Ye continued. "It's like rolling the dice. Actually, no—it's not like that at all. What used to be a fifty-fifty chance has changed. It's quite odd, and there's really no proper way to explain it. That's why you simply have to get used to it. Stop trying to understand. We need to learn to live together, in the absence of mutual understanding. Mr. Yang, this is what our relationship is like. Isn't it similar to a manga? But please don't be childish. Manga are written for adults. So hurry up and grow up!"

Yang Wei felt ashamed and started to scratch his white hair. "I'm getting old."

No wonder Fistula said that the hospital was a university, he thought. All the knowledge and experience that humankind had accumulated over millions of years was worthless. Humans never learned. There was nothing wrong with their brains; the world was just too messy and confusing. So-called superposition was nothing but a split, a fissure. Buboxine was right when he said that his disease was a form of fissure. This bioengineered woman was one of the only people on the entire ship who saw things for what they were. Yang Wei really didn't want to go against her wishes; after all, whatever she said must be correct. This world was indeed full of a lot more flaws than any manga. But the world *existed*, filled with millions of living, breathing people who ate and drank, fell ill, gave birth, and eventually died, the tides of history washing them from here to there. There must be a kind of sublime logic to it, but just because they didn't understand that logic didn't mean that it didn't exist. The entire universe was beyond human understanding.

"I understand," announced Yang Wei. "Except for one thing . . ." He took another look at the manga. The character who designed Zero looked almost exactly like Yang Wei. The only difference was that the guy in the manga was young, full of life. Yang Wei felt uncomfortable. "Just who is he?"

Zi Ye was clearly flabbergasted that he didn't know. She flashed him a look of disbelief. "He is one of Hayao Miyazaki's characters."

Yang Wei figured this was a case of "not recognizing someone when you meet again." Nevertheless he tried to learn more. "Was this character based on a real person?"

"Uh, since the war has been going on so long, all of the characters have gotten mixed up. Didn't Professor Eternal explain this to you?" asked Zi Ye.

"But . . ." Yang Wei wanted to argue further, but he didn't know what else to say.

Zi Ye tried to comfort him. "No matter how many different situations are at play, as a gift to you, Mr. Yang, I can tell you that there is only one reality. The only you is the one right here, right now. None of the others matter. But owing to various complicated reasons, you have been sent here. I also had no choice in where I ended up. As long as there is the slightest chance, you need to grab hold of it. From this point forward, you need to start turning things upside down." That last sentence seemed to capture Zi Ye's bold and fearless spirit.

Yang Wei wondered why things couldn't be easier. Like pain, war was probably also a kind of external phenomena that must be hiding some deformed creature on the inside. This was very different from the song of the sea nymphs. Yang Wei wanted to curl up on Zi Ye's shoulder and let out a good cry, but then he realized how silly that would be.

"Why doesn't the Allied army create a new narrative implant to replace the painful world we are now living in?" he asked. He didn't dare tell Zi Ye that the narrative-implant therapy that Professor Eternal had designed for him had been a failure.

"Try not to let your imagination run wild," said Zi Ye. "If they were to create another world, it would end up an unlivable place because of how mixed up all the roles would be! What's being experienced right now is already more than enough to allow people to taste reality. There is no point in trying to escape. If the world is the result of narrative implants, you will need to win small victories in every world in order to win the great war. Total victory depends on the accumulation of multiple tiny victories. Wouldn't it be easier just to win in a single world than to go through all that trouble?" She clenched her fists in a heroic display.

Seeing her like that, Yang Wei decided not to spend any more time thinking about the frustrating things that had happened or that might still be playing out. "So what should we do?"

Zi Ye cut to the chase. "We must continue with the work that was interrupted! Even if the backup forces could get here right away, we need to rely upon ourselves. As one of the most crucial players in this war, you can't allow yourself to get lost in your emotions. That will only grind away at your will! All of our hope is on you! You need to let go of the past. Spend more of your time reading manga. Whether they be stories about the creation or salvation, all inspiration comes from within their pages!"

But Yang Wei's confidence remained low. "What did you mean when you said 'the work that was interrupted'?"

Zi Ye responded with the utmost seriousness. "According to Professor Eternal's orders, we must find the Super Patient."

Yang Wei couldn't help but laugh. "Super Patient?"

The image of Super Patient—his bulging stomach and staggering gait, him waving a saber and humming verses of poetry, constantly getting into scuffles with other patients—flashed before Yang Wei's eyes. Suddenly the world that Zi Ye had described seemed even more suspicious, yet he had no choice but to accept it.

50

EVERYTHING IS PREDESTINED; STRENGTH AND WEAKNESS DON'T ALWAYS DETERMINE WHO WINS AND LOSES

Zi Ye told Yang Wei that according to the strategic prediction model, a Super Patient would arise from among the patients aboard the Hospital Ship. He would be the most powerful patient of all, and once he joined their ranks, the Hospital Ship would develop a supervirus to counter all others. It would be called the "God Virus," and it would become the remedy to the enemy's Devil Virus.

Zi Ye went on to describe the God Virus. "It will be a holy apocalyptic weapon that the Allied forces will use to break through the impenetrable barricade formed by the viral sea and send the sea nymphs down to the eighteenth level of hell. Even in the worst-case scenario, we will at least be able to assure our mutual destruction alongside the enemy. This is the Hospital Ship's purpose in the world."

Yang Wei realized that nothing was reliable. It seemed that both the doctors and Siming had all been defeated and a full-blown battle was destined to break out. Perhaps the only option was for the patients to roll up their sleeves and go into battle. He asked Zi Ye who this Super Patient was, hoping that it wasn't the same Super Patient he had in mind.

Zi Ye began to recount what she knew. "Ah, the Super Patient is a patient among patients! And he is right here aboard this ship! According to our estimation, his brain is very special, with a prefrontal lobe unlike any other normal brain. Its uniqueness surpasses anything that can be imagined. The complexity of its structure is like a labyrinth. On the left side is an abnormal region in the lower part of the motor cortex, which is usually responsible for processing information from the face and mouth. But this portion of his brain is not used merely for processing that information. In his case, this area of the motor cortex has expanded into a rectangular-shaped area, giving rise to a brand-new set of functions. This is a disorder that has never before been seen in the history of medicine. In some ways, he is quite similar to you. His understanding of the world is based on a fusion of images and feelings. For him, thought is something that can be seen and physically felt. From the perspective of medical science, this brain suffers from a special pathological syndrome, produced only once every ten thousand years. We need to use this disease to achieve our strategic goals. This is a gift that Hippocrates has bestowed upon the anti-Fascist front, long predestined and certainly not an off-the-cuff decision. In short, Super Patient will play a crucial role in helping us win the war!"

Yang Wei felt a bit let down. He had thought that *he* might be the one to set the pitch for what happened next, but now he realized that he was just there to set the stage. He could feel the distance growing between himself and Zi Ye and couldn't help but feel depressed.

"And which sick ward is this amazing patient in?" he asked.

"We're not sure," replied Zi Ye. "That's why we need to recruit other patients to help find him."

"And then you'll be able to extract the God Virus from him, which will enable you to defeat the Devil Virus?" asked Yang Wei.

"Mr. Yang, you must believe us," pleaded Zi Ye. "The appearance of this new virus will overturn our previous conceptions about life. Doctors love to babble on about their reverence for life, but as soon as the notion of life is redefined, their reverence won't mean shit. We will face the enemy with a cold and ruthless heart. We will take things to a level of perversion and derangement never imagined by our enemy! From there we will turn the tide from defense to offense, transforming from the underdog to the overlord! Once we have unleashed the God Virus, everything that follows will play out according to an extremely simple process. While it is less than three centimeters in length, it will solve the mysteries of the universe. In other words, it will decode the will and intentions of the creator. Hiding right there inside the body of the Super Patient is the power to send the enemy's Devil Virus straight to hell! Once we have the Super Patient in our hands, it won't even matter if half the Hospital Ship has been destroyed; we will still vanquish a powerful enemy several thousand times our size!"

"And how can we locate him?" asked Yang Wei. The thought that the virus was less than three centimeters in length left him with a strange feeling.

"Well . . . that will be up to you, Mr. Yang!"

"I actually know a guy called Super Patient . . . ," said Yang Wei.

"His real name is Einstein. Mr. Yang, you must remember that name," said Zi Ye.

"Einstein," Yang Wei muttered. He tried to remember whether his fellow patients had ever mentioned that name, but he came up empty. A ghostlike shadow appeared in his mind. According to the historical timeline he remembered, the first atomic bomb had been dropped in 1945, and from that point forward, humankind had possessed not only the ability to change the course of history but the power to *end* history. Yang Wei knew that if he were to say that out loud, Zi Ye would only laugh at him. No one on board the Hospital Ship had even heard of this weapon. Perhaps the history he remembered was fake. However, the fact that humankind did now wield the power to end history was a consolation.

"Mr. Yang, you are the only one capable of getting him," Zi Ye said confidently.

Thinking back to the moment he had first returned naked to the sick ward and been sprayed down with the fire hose, Yang Wei was a nervous wreck. "How can you be so sure? What if he gets me first?"

"For the Super Patient to appear," Zi Ye explained, "we need the accumulated power of an entire ocean's worth of medical records! What I mean is, in order for that genius brain of his to materialize, we need several times as many ordinary patients as we have now. Those patients don't matter too much as individuals, but they are important in setting the stage for the appearance of the Super Patient. This *must* be the true reason the hospital was created. Super Patient's brain is a complex system that can only be produced through a chaotic environment, even though it possesses a superhuman level of order. And now that the algorithm is directly killing off large numbers of patients, there is the risk that the Super Patient might disappear forever. According to the strategic model, the current number of patients is far from enough. I'm not sure if the person you mentioned is indeed the true Super Patient, but Professor Eternal believes that you alone can prevent more patients from dying, which is the only way to ensure the safety of the Super Patient."

Yang Wei didn't even know if he'd be alive tomorrow, but he didn't dare challenge her. He certainly wasn't going to tell her that he thought Professor Eternal might have had too much to drink and gotten the wrong person.

Zi Ye flashed embarrassment, but she tried to cover it up. "At this point, it seems that anything I say comes down to a question of numbers. There's nothing we can do. In the end we return to the algorithm. What can I say? Our mission is difficult and complicated. After all, humankind's scientific understanding remains rooted in empirical observation and mathematical organization. But due to the war, implanted narratives have made empirical observation all the more difficult. Instead, subjective experience has become the prevailing trend. To make matters worse, a fourth mathematical crisis has broken out. Large numbers of paradox theories have emerged. In reality, mathematics was first invented by the enemy. According to the enemy, one plus one equals two. But later on, all of that changed. After an investigation, it was discovered that over the course of developing its new virus, the enemy's pharmaceutical industry relied on a set of mathematical models that were completely different from anything anyone had seen before. The enemy created a new mathematical standard, and according to this new standard, one plus one no longer equals two. What we had referred to as the Medicinal War was actually just a standard war. That's why we were completely unprepared for the Devil Virus. Siming is broken—its entire algorithm was based on the concepts of traditional mathematics, which we learned from the enemy. We are in a state of internal chaos. Even basic truths are no longer true. Everyone knows that mathematics is worthless, anyway. It is all just a sham. From doctors to patients, everyone is lying. It normally takes three years to carry out the research and development necessary to roll out a new drug successfully, but we are forced to go through that entire process in the final week of the year! What option do we have, besides faking it? We are surrounded by changing numbers everywhere we look! How could this be so utterly preposterous and yet so absolutely normal? Perhaps, besides the war, there is another reason for this: mathematics doesn't actually exist. It is simply an abstract concept based on pure conjecture. The world may be built upon a completely different system, altogether removed from mathematics, and we remain completely ignorant about it. Shh . . . keep this between us! It'll be our little secret."

Yang Wei suddenly felt like the world might suddenly disappear before his eyes and that Zi Ye would leave him forever. He was in so much pain that he couldn't utter a word. Given the circumstances, what would be the point of searching for Einstein and his mathematical formula?

Zi Ye turned cynical. "Do you know anything about traditional Chinese medicine? Have you heard of its great practitioners: Li Shizhen, Hua Tuo, Bian Que, Sun Simiao, and Zhang Zhongjing? There are legends about the ancient civilization that established Chinese medicine, but it was not founded on algebraic and geometric models. It was instead based on those damned theories of yin and yang and the eight trigrams of divination. Those theories directly conflict with the principles of modern medicine that we hold so dear, and yet it is said that an astronomical number of patients was saved using these techniques. Take your pain, for instance. In the past, doctors would have been able to control your symptoms with acupuncture. They would never have needed narrative-implant therapy! But what exactly is acupuncture? No one really knows, which hints at a truly terrifying phenomenon. The art of traditional Chinese medicine was not passed down to us and is now lost to us."

Yang Wei felt troubled. He had once asked about something like this but had been abruptly shut down. And so the topic remained abstract, out of reach, like a cloud floating above the world. Was Chinese medicine a god or a devil? "What are you trying to say, exactly?" he asked.

Zi Ye flashed him a pale smile. "There's nothing we can do. Since we haven't yet found the truth about the world, all we can do is use mathematics as a shield. We are unable to invent anything more intimidating than mathematics. This sea through which we are sailing, at least in form, is derived from digital creatures created by man. Therefore, as long as the illusion is maintained, we won't immediately disappear. We can't allow the patients to think that modern medicine is done for. If we do, history will indeed come to an end. We can't let the patients lose their confidence. We can't allow them to feel that truth is outside their grasp. That's why we need to find Einstein. Of course, this is the beginning of another form of pain. That's why living is more difficult than dying. Look at me! I died, and now I'm alive again—it doesn't get any more difficult than that. Anyway, Mr. Yang, hang in there. We are depending on you!"

Zi Ye spoke as if trying to downplay the situation, even as she emphasized its great importance, but her words left Yang Wei feeling depressed. He was, after all, just a songwriter. Back in middle school, he had never passed a single math test. He lived a simple, quiet life, never imagining that he might one day be thrust into an earthshaking event like this war. He would much rather have simply died. But with Zi Ye as his model, he decided to live on. He couldn't die in front of her like some silly clown. She had things much harder than he did, and yet she had managed, somehow, to make it through two lives.

"Patients don't know anything," Zi Ye exhorted. "All they do is mess around and make trouble. Pain and poverty force them to take risks, yet they remain the power base that we have no choice but to rely on. That's why you must clearly explain to them the mathematical principles behind disease. Among the patients, Einstein is the sole mathematical genius. We will use mathematics as our bait, to get him on our hook. Mr. Yang, do you get what I'm saying?"

Yang Wei was clueless, but he felt obliged to nod. He realized that he would be unable to use the lost art of traditional Chinese medicine against the enemy, and nuclear weapons and time machines also seemed useless in this world.

"Are you hungry?" Zi Ye asked abruptly. She seemed like she had said enough. A dark smile radiated like a shooting star across her dead face, giving her a somewhat feminine quality. She extended her hand to caress Yang Wei's stomach and, with an expression of astonishment, said, "Oh, you must be famished. Have something to eat first, and we'll discuss the details of the mission later. You need to take more cues from Professor Eternal. I was just as lost as you are now, but I learned to not give a damn. As long as you're in the hospital, this is just how things go. Getting depressed or angry, complaining and cursing, will only make you sick. While you are still alive, you need to get enough to eat and drink. Underneath this uniform, I'm actually a hopeless foodie!" Her expression suddenly became much more animated, which made Yang Wei uncomfortable.

"It seems you share the same interests as Professor Eternal," he responded pedantically. "He's also really into eating!" He realized that Professor Eternal had never spoken out against the cafeteria, which meant that he never viewed it as a threat. Compared to those pathetic, hackneyed old doctors, the cafeteria operated on another level altogether. Yang Wei's stomach growled.

Zi Ye began to slip into sentimentalism. "Once upon a time, Professor Eternal had a physical body, but it was destroyed in a lab accident. However, the remnants of his nerve center still long for fine food and drink. That's one of the main reasons we had to preserve his brain."

"Professor Eternal is truly blessed to have survived all of that," Yang Wei offered. "Those doctors never die either."

"Eating and drinking is all that makes the professor feel alive," said Zi Ye. "Otherwise, how could he serve as the soul of the Hospital Ship? Despite the pain he faces every day, he does his best to go on living—not like you, always looking for a way to die. He wants to hang on until he sees the Super Patient personally. Camus said it best: 'The most important thing is not to be cured, but to live with one's ailments.' Have you heard of Albert Camus?"

"Never heard of him," admitted Yang Wei. "But I remember a famous saying: 'Suffering is inherent to humankind. It proves that you are still alive.' Did Camus say that too?"

"No, one of our female comrades in arms said that, but she's dead now," replied Zi Ye. "Like Dostoevsky, Camus is another outstanding example of a sick man. He was a patient of Professor Eternal's and one of the professor's close friends. Camus was blown to bits during the lab accident in which Professor Eternal lost his body, but the professor was able to hold on to his brain, at least. As a military doctor, Professor Eternal used to stick to a strict daily regimen of five-kilometer off-road runs with a heavy backpack. These days, of course, he can no longer run. How can you jog if all you have is a brain? But the one thing he can still do is eat. The terrible explosion that maimed him actually had nothing to do with the enemy. It was an internal job, a despicable act carried out by the opposition party. The war to steal the office of the Hospital President was much more brutal and merciless than World War II ever was. The hospital has always been the ultimate site for power struggles. Everyone in the hospital has grown accustomed to living with death, and it's hard to find anyone who hasn't performed an autopsy. The people here have violent personalities, and their frequent fights often end in death. They are jealous of the glorious accomplishments that Professor Eternal has achieved over the course of his career. Yes, the true devil is right here among us. Those ignorant faces that always seem to turn a blind eye to familiar sights are the most terrifying of them all." At this point, Zi Ye's eyes turned red. "Ah, it's easy to understand the truths that Camus revealed through his sacrifice, but to carry out those lessons—that is much more difficult."

Yang Wei had not imagined that even artificially developed women could feel sadness. He was shocked but also quite moved, and he couldn't help but allow his gaze to linger on Zi Ye. Was her sadness originally within her, by design, or an emotion that had naturally evolved later? He could sense that Zi Ye was capable of experiencing a rich palette of emotions and desires. She was much more real than the other women he had encountered in his life, the first person on the Hospital Ship whom he really wanted to get close to . . . and yet he was afraid.

51

JUST THREE DAYS OLD, AND SHE HAD ALREADY TASTED AN OX

Zi Ye extended her flowery, jade-like tongue to lick the corner of her mouth in a way that seemed to be sending Yang Wei some kind of signal. Then she clasped his hand and led him off. She really did take him to eat. In the end, the thing that separated humans from the algorithm wasn't intellect or emotion but the act of eating. They climbed up to the crematorium and had a big meal at the cafeteria, like a reward before a long, arduous journey. Yang Wei was utterly famished. Professor Eternal had poured a bunch of alcohol down Yang Wei's throat, but he hadn't given him anything of substance to eat. Even during normal times in the sick ward, he had never been able to eat his fill, but thanks to Zi Ye's encouragement, Yang Wei ate to his heart's desire, gorging himself and forgetting all his troubles.

As they ate, the beautiful image of that charred human body in the crematorium oven appeared before Yang Wei's eyes. He wanted to ask Zi Ye more about Professor Eternal, and he was beginning to feel that Einstein couldn't possibly be the same person as that old pig farmer from the sick ward. But when he saw Zi Ye wrapped up in gorging herself, he was afraid she might think he didn't know what he was talking about, so he kept his mouth shut.

A large crowd of doctors and patients filed into the cafeteria, overtaking the entire room with the locustlike sound of hordes of people chewing. Yang Wei noticed Malnutrizole patrolling, as if overseeing a final stunning scene on the eve of the apocalypse. Yang Wei had the urge to go hang out with him. Perhaps they could look for some flame demons. But Zi Ye suddenly snapped a huge shrimp out of his mouth and threw it on the floor.

"Let's go; we shouldn't be eating here," she said. "These patients are in terrible pain, yet not a single one of them cares about their illness. They act like they are ready to go straight into the oven after eating. Some may even be spies for the enemy . . ."

They left the cafeteria to continue eating elsewhere. Zi Ye took Yang Wei to a fancy luxury restaurant to really open his eyes. The restaurant was secretly run by the doctors, who served high-end cuisine to the Hospital President and other department heads. Yang Wei realized just how much of the hospital was built on the taste buds of those medical administrators. They wasted an astounding amount of food, while countless patients starved to death. Hadn't someone said that the only truly high-end food was served to Professor Eternal? The doctors tended to eat better than the patients, anyway. Yang Wei even remembered someone at the Exorcism Congress saying that the Hospital Ship would one day fall due to their insatiable appetites.

Zi Ye told Yang Wei that their own style of eating was fundamentally different from the way doctors and patients ate. In order to win the war, one must experience fine delicacies. "Eating good food is part of our mission!" she exclaimed. "Only this can trigger your passion for life. As a synthetic human, I know all about how painful and transient human life can be." Her young, experienced face emitted a purity like the morning dew. Yang Wei got excited again; this was even better than *A Collection of Beautiful Raccoons, Bushy Orangutans, and Busty Dragons*.

As Yang Wei ate with Zi Ye, he could feel himself growing younger. This scared him. He couldn't help but secretly look at her: neither fat nor skinny, she ate like a mother panther. This left Yang Wei feeling conflicted. Why make a synthetic human like Zi Ye? Was this woman a true representation of her original self? Was she created solely to keep him company? There had to be something missing.

Yang Wei sensed an incalculable danger in the lust that Zi Ye's body emitted, but he knew he couldn't leave her. He worried that she might have a sudden change of heart and try to hurt him, but something about her kept drawing him in. He figured that if even Super Patient could get pregnant . . .

They continued eating, like animals. Later, they went out again for a midnight snack. Zi Ye even ordered a cocktail. After several rounds, Zi Ye began to look younger and even more beautiful. Her youthful, vivacious energy exploded, nothing short of a miracle on the Hospital Ship. The other people in the restaurant flashed jealous stares.

Zi Ye said that she had been born with a fondness for food and a voracious appetite, that she could eat an entire ox in a single sitting. She recounted how strange it was that in the beginning, food had been the same as medicine. Food treatment meant medicinal treatment, and this seemed to be the Allied forces' weak point. The enemy had used bioengineering to survive on minimal food and water, and enemy soldiers no longer needed sustenance to survive. The Allied forces could do this, too, but it would open up a paradox with tradition. The Allied army held fast to the tenets of humanism and felt that human beings were much more important than weapons in determining the outcome of war. So it was of the utmost importance that humans be treated as such, and good food and wine were necessary parts of that. The army was provided all kinds of canned foods, and even during the most dangerous battles, the algae men raised in the oceanic nursery were fed to ensure the pleasures of a good meal.

"While the old definition of life has yet to be overturned," Zi Ye explained, "we still need to rely upon the traditional act of eating, to prove that we are still alive. It is the same principle as pretending that the laws of mathematics still dictate how the world operates. According to the traditional view, organisms continually generate entropy, increasing positive entropy and gradually inching closer to the dangerous state of maximum entropy. Even if you don't wait for the enemy to kill you, you'll end up dying anyway, though that's actually a terrible way to look at things. If you want to show the enemy that you are determined to keep on living, then you need to absorb negative entropy, continually, from the environment around you. This obviously involves eating, drinking, and breathing. As they used to say in the old days, it all comes down to metabolism. This is not done to exchange energy but to increase order. Mr. Yang, do you get what I'm saying? It's like those flames in the crematorium; they, too, are alive. They rely on consuming the bodies of the dead. Our old comrade in arms Schrödinger once said that life feeds on negative entropy. It is unclear exactly when this theory was overturned, or perhaps it never even existed, but one thing is for sure: no one today still believes it. We are indeed living in the old world."

"The old world? I thought this was the New District?" Yang Wei replied. "The cafeteria makes me realize how fortunate we are to live in this spectacular age of prosperity, even if we are on the verge of total annihilation."

Zi Ye flashed a cold smile. "There's nothing we can do. A lot more is on the line than just face and dignity. If you eat everything in sight, you are bound to get sick, and once people become afflicted with multiple ailments and patients add up, the hospital generates the capital it needs to grow stronger. This is the security that treating illnesses provides. Call it 'dialectical mediterialism.' I can't say it's a bad thing. The entire point of establishing the hospital was to allow everyone to enjoy eating and drinking! If you can eat and drink, then you can prove you are alive and the treatment has been effective. You have not given yourself over to the Devil. This is the essence of victory. There are some who still don't understand this simple truth and who insist on reforming the cafeteria, but they are doing the enemy's dirty work for them!"

Yang Wei was astounded. The algorithm had created a superfoodie! Perhaps Zi Ye had inherited some special traits from the woman she was modeled after, because the circumstances didn't seem to matter: the enemy's germ bomb could have exploded inside her body, blowing off her limbs and melting away her organs, but as long as she had a mouth left, it would keep on munching away! This detail made Zi Ye more endearing to Yang Wei, who felt like he could really trust her.

Then they received notice that Yang Wei was to return immediately to the Exorcism Congress. He had no choice but to go back. On the way they passed several doctors idling about, and they all made a point of greeting Yang Wei. He figured that they probably had gotten wind of the fact that he had flown in a helicopter, but lurking behind their smiling faces was some ulterior motivation. One group of doctors pulled him aside and invited him for a round of sea golf. Yang Wei ran off and somehow ended up at the doctors' dormitory. He was embarrassed, but at least Zi Ye was with him. She wouldn't allow him to go anywhere alone.

52

PICKING A COLORFUL POMEGRANATE FLOWER FOR A CLOSER LOOK

The doctors' dormitory was a huge room refurbished from an old warehouse. Several hundred doctors slept on the floor, crammed together. Like soldiers, they lived a completely communal life, and their living conditions appeared no better than the patients'. The war had been difficult for everyone, and from that point forward, no one questioned the reality of the war.

As soon as the doctors saw a woman, they began to tremble with excitement. Yet at the same time, they seemed paralyzed, as if they had just been struck by lightning. Yang Wei and Zi Ye didn't pay them any heed. They crawled into one of the beds and lay down, shoulder to shoulder.

Zi Ye yawned. "It's not easy for these doctors. They used to be ordinary people who spent their days writing prescriptions and giving shots. Who could have imagined they would have to become soldiers, forced to carry out combat missions, constantly ready to sacrifice their lives! This must seem like the creator playing tricks on them. As far as they are concerned, women are stranger and rarer than any monkey or guinea pig! Mr. Yang, you should really feel lucky for what you have."

Yang Wei grunted in agreement. He thought about those doctors playing sea golf, and he realized that the sport represented a tiny loophole in a place where it would otherwise be utterly impossible. But should the real hole in the system one day make itself known, none of them would have any idea what to do.

Among the sea of doctors sprawled on the floor, Yang Wei didn't see anyone who even faintly resembled Lu Xun, Feng Tang, or Yasunari Kawabata. Women usually fawn all over talented artistic men, but that certainly wasn't the case here. The only woman was Zi Ye, and she belonged to one man and one man alone.

Yang Wei hadn't been with a woman in what felt like forever, and although he was getting excited, he had no idea how to make a move. He lay there staring blankly at the ceiling, which was like the dome of a planetarium, its thousands of lights revolving into moving numbers, projected like a movie. The numbers were codes that conveyed orders sent down from the Shadow Hospital's Accounting Department, reminding the doctors how to reach their quotas: number of living patients, dead bodies, and serious infections as well as the ratio of diagnoses of major illnesses and recovery rates, which were multiplied by the index of suffering in the sick wards. Despised as Siming was, its calculations continued to impact everyone like a ritualistic ceremony.

Yang Wei reached beneath the pillow, expecting that he might find a gun, but there was nothing. He realized that the only weapons still in existence were of the pharmaceutical type. His arm bumped into Zi Wei's ribs, which felt hard, as if she had metal plates under her skin. Just what kind of life-form was she? *The foundation of thought lies not only in seeing but also in physical touch,* he thought. He sketched her naked form in his mind, but he didn't dare make a move, afraid he might see or touch something that he wasn't supposed to see or touch. He could have never predicted what would eventually transpire between them, but at least he could use this moment to really take her in.

From the side, the shape of Zi Ye's body resembled the coastline of the Eastern Sea. Her delicate nose was smooth and seemed to sparkle with pure drops of morning dew. The auricles of her ears were perfectly formed, as if displaying the marks of meticulous craftsmanship. Her breasts rose like a wave, resembling those of any real young woman, and her tight, sturdy muscles reminded Yang Wei of the helicopter. From afar, she looked exactly like a real woman. Yang Wei couldn't help but marvel at the power of her creator, and his appreciation for Professor Eternal also grew. For something to simply "pass" as human, there was no need for this level of perfection. It was clear that Zi Ye was a project undertaken in the name of either art or war, sent to dispel the enemy and the sea nymphs, because only a woman could do this. There would be no other way to tame a special patient like Yang Wei.

He thought back to other women. While they had entered each other's bodies, Yang Wei had never really felt anything. He had once had a daughter, but he had treated her as a toy to play with when he was bored. But this synthetic woman awakened a long-slumbering physical excitement within him. He had no idea how to make her feel good, partly because he had no way to determine which of them actually had a soul. He still wasn't sure whether souls could be 3D printed. Zi Ye was basically a clone, theoretically no different from Siming. With uploaded consciousness and memories, they both exemplified the "Chinese room" paradox. Zi Ye's emotional responses might be nothing more than a biochemical algorithm rendered in an automaton. *But is she conscious of her own existence?* There was no way to be sure.

A bunch of doctors came back from a round of sea golf in the middle of the night. They lay down near Yang Wei and Zi Ye, flashing them numb, cursory glances before mechanically falling right to sleep. The doctors' dormitory transformed into a hot, salty jungle. The mold growing in the doctors' armpits and groins began to decay and rot, as if the doctors were becoming the patients. Yang Wei realized that he had already become one of them, and he hoped he could stave off the sunrise just a little bit longer.

Zi Ye woke up suddenly. "Did you have a dream?" she asked apprehensively, like a frightened squid.

"No, not at all," Yang Wei responded hastily. "Did you? What did you dream of?"

Zi Ye responded in a dejected tone. "Oh . . . the womb and its appendages are all grown of the flesh, which represents the true side of me. It is bright red, like an eggplant—or the moon constantly falling from the night sky and smashing the surface of the sea like a piece of steel . . . oh my, is this what war is? What right did they have to create me, only to participate in something like this? Why didn't they drop me into a peaceful age, when I could have gotten married and educated my son?" Surprisingly, she began to cry, and as soft tears streamed down her face, she looked like a completely different person. Instead of waiting for Yang Wei to make the first move, she suddenly reached out to embrace him.

Trembling in her arms, Yang Wei asked, "Are you also suspicious about this war? You must be hungry. You shouldn't have dreams like that."

He thought, uncomfortably, about how Zi Ye had crossed over the river between life and death, just to serve as his contact person, with no one to console her. "Did you dream of anything else?" he asked her.

"I dreamed of a time when all of the righteous words would be destroyed," she responded. "And I asked, 'One day, will we, too, turn on each other? Will we become one another's sworn enemies?'"

She released Yang Wei from her embrace, and he heaved a sigh of relief, discovering his entire body was covered in sweat. What was she talking about? He could feel the pain in her heart. Beyond her appearance, she had been hiding another Zi Ye inside herself. She longed for the past more than she treasured the present. Her memories from a previous life still haunted her. She was possessed by a demon. As the sole woman aboard the Hospital Ship, she was truly born into the wrong era. She knew many truths, understood many things. People would share all kinds of things with her, and yet she remained filled with secrets that she was unable to share with anyone. She wasn't confident about the future, and her excessive eating and drinking was an attempt to cover all that up. What did women really need? Yang Wei grew increasingly curious about this synthetic human model, and yet he did not dare ask her any questions. What did her pain feel like? What kind of relationship did they really have? They had only recently met and hadn't yet done anything together. Who could imagine a falling-out between them, let alone the possibility of becoming sworn enemies? But anything could happen—some of it already had. Their meeting had occurred by chance, this strange war temporarily bringing them together. But there was no hope for a future.

Yang Wei convinced himself that all this was simply a mechanical process and that Zi Ye wasn't actually conscious of any of it. He couldn't help but ask, with a mixture of sincerity and cruelty, "What was the original model like as a person, the one you were based on?"

"I can't remember so clearly," she responded in frustration. "I only have vague impressions. She was also a big foodie. She died a terribly painful death . . . but as for who she was and what she did in life, I have absolutely no idea. Professor Eternal never allowed me access to those portions of her memory. But it's okay . . ." Her look of sad frustration dissipated. "My only mission is to maintain close contact with you."

Yang Wei secretly hoped that she might pull him close again, but he didn't dare try to push things.

Zi Ye wiped the tears from her eyes. "Hey, it's okay. One betrayal is enough. I'll never believe in love again, and that's that!"

She quickly regained her masculine strength and no-nonsense attitude, which made Yang Wei think of a woman going through menopause, exploding with a creative release of fictional energy in her fifties, like Alice Munro. But there wasn't much time left.

Yang Wei grew irritable. He felt an urge toward sarcasm. *No matter how mysterious you might be, how much top secret intel you have, or how realistic the human form you appear in, you will never be anything but a low-level nurse!* But he swallowed his grievances and remained silent.

Zi Ye popped a piece of candy into her mouth. Yang Wei felt so angry that she didn't share any with him that he wanted to reach out and snatch it right out of her mouth, but he didn't dare act on his impulses.

"Mr. Yang, I know that you must have a lot more questions, but please let them go, okay?" She spoke honestly, straightforwardly. "It's not that I don't want to answer your questions, and it's not that we don't have the time . . . but listen. The entire hospital is eating!" Like someone hunting a pheasant, she focused her attention on a single point in the dark void, as if the evil enemy was about to emerge from that very spot.

Yang Wei listened, and sure enough, another wave of eating sounds filled the air, as if the entire sick ward had transformed into a massive cafeteria. How real it all was! "Let's get a little more sleep, and once I'm recharged, I'll go back to the Exorcism Congress," he said. "Are you going too? If we work together to find the Super Patient, we can ensure that neither of us is in danger. Hurry up and get some sleep. Once you're asleep, you won't feel hungry anymore."

It seemed like only at that moment could he fully face, and accept, his new mission. Even patients needed to fight for the survival of the Hospital Ship. Hypocritically, he turned his back to Zi Ye.

A siren sounded overhead. Perhaps the helicopter was taking off again, mobilized for another mission for the survival of the human race. Yang Wei thought he caught a glimpse of Professor Eternal's eyeballs gliding through the air, periodically appearing and disappearing. Only his gaze could drive a woman away. No natural or artificial body could do that. And so Yang Wei turned back and embraced Zi Ye, taking in every inch of her body. She would be the true receptacle of his memories.

53

WILD CHILDREN SING AND DANCE

When Yang Wei awoke the next morning, the synthetic woman beside him was still sound asleep. He decided not to disturb her. He pushed his fears aside and went back to the Exorcism Congress alone. He used what Zi Ye had told him to encourage himself to push forward. On the way there, the sea appeared as before. There were no signs of anything unusual. But that only made Yang Wei more nervous. Once, he even thought about death, but he quickly dispelled the thought.

Finally, the variety show had begun! The Fourth Vice President of the Hospital Ship, who was serving as the master of ceremonies, announced, "It is time to celebrate! The Hospital Ship's Spring Festival holiday is finally upon us! This is a glorious tradition that only comes around once per year! If we don't put on a big show for you now, when will we?"

The first group to hit the stage featured the Director of Hematology, along with other medical workers from his department. Adorned in white sheepskin headscarves, black eye patches, and black trench coats, they wielded an array of props—fans, handkerchiefs, and colorful pieces of silk—and danced the traditional yangge folk dance. Accompanying them was a gorgeous piece of music entitled "Prelude to the Spring Festival," which had an enchanting, pulsating rhythm and a strange mysterious melody. As soon as Yang Wei heard it, he had the urge to piss.

Next up was a group from the Clinical Laboratory. They wore white sheepskin jackets with skimpy pink short skirts and danced hand in hand with doctors from the Pathology Department, who wore tight silver leather pants. Together they performed the acrobatic routine entitled "The Airwalker," several magic tricks, a few skits, excerpts from traditional opera, cross talk, three-and-a-half-line ballads, song-and-dance duets in the style of Northeastern China, and songs like "The Officer and the Thief," "Reincarnation Guerrillas," "Gorgeous Sunset," and "Empty City Planning," oldies but goodies with themes that perfectly fit the Spring Festival holiday, as if the audience could wax nostalgic about long-lost civilizations of old.

Then someone pushed Yang Wei onto the stage. A skit entitled "Cosmic Cigarettes" called for a few patient representatives to serve as extras.

"You're almost dead . . . do you think you can still perform your part?" a doctor asked Yang Wei.

"The closer to death I am, the more determined I am to play my part," Yang Wei replied.

Members of the Dermatology and Radiology Departments fought over which group should perform the famous opera *At the Crossroads*.

Yang Wei noticed a series of queerly shaped creatures creeping out from under the stage curtain. Some resembled starfish, others deep-sea worms. Then the ceiling started to rip apart, and a foul, rancid smell leaked into the hall. A massive blue-gray tentacle covered with starlike suction cups snaked in through the ceiling and shook back and forth. Pulmonary algae seeped through cracks and spread through the hall. A troop of shiny green creatures with simian faces peeked in from the main entrance, quietly watching.

Yang Wei grew anxious. How would he carry out his mission? Yet he couldn't fight the irresistible urge to keep dancing. Even amid the chaos, the show went on. The artists in white lab coats onstage continued singing—this was one seriously professional troupe! Together they sang "The Great Siming," a brilliant performance that was executed with pure style and utterly humiliated the patients' amateur poetry:

The twilight years gradually snuck up on us.
We've grown distant, but that doesn't mean
we can't be close again.

Racing down the road in my Peugeot-Citroën,
the engine roars. My Mercedes-Benz opens up
as I race toward the open sky.

I gaze into the distance as I weave branches
from the laurel tree. Why does my heart grow
heavier with longing?

Unable to rid myself of melancholy thoughts,
I hope in the future for the same degree
of respect I enjoy today.

People's life spans are all over the map, but
who can dispel regret after happy reunions
and bitter departures?

The melody conveyed an otherworldly style that made Yang Wei think of the Kingdom of Chu and the Kingdom of Qin. He felt like only the algorithm could produce a song like this. But what kind of "blood" flowed through Siming's veins? Was it close to achieving its goal of suicide? Or was it just like all the other patients, hemming and hawing about how much it wanted to die just to get everyone's attention? Could the entire scene be under Siming's control—and could the doctors be merely puppets?

Yang Wei felt as if he had just awakened from a dream. He knew that they were reaching the most critical juncture in the war, and he was trying to recover what memories he could about his identity and mission, when he discovered an unused ballot in his hand. He quickly shoved it into the sole of his shoe, but someone noticed. Yang Wei immediately began to run.

The person who saw him laughed. "Don't run! You did the right thing!"

Yang Wei stopped, blushing with embarrassment.

"No need to feel uncomfortable about what you did," the man continued. "I didn't vote either. Thousands upon thousands of people voted for new members of that damn Hospital Affairs Committee, but the election was just like the gala being performed onstage. You eventually realize it's all just a show. Once you are struck with the realization that the ballot in your hand will not have even the faintest impact, what's the point of casting that vote? Only an idiot would do that! The ballots are immediately drowned amid the sea of people. The election results are all decided long in advance. Let me tell you—neither the First, Second, Third, or Fourth Vice President will ever take the place of the Hospital President. But do you know who could? Dr. Cash Ofloxacin from the Finance Department! He bought everyone off a long time ago . . . the election is supposedly decided by the accumulation of individual votes, but what does all that matter? It can't change anything! Look at the lights above us! The appearance of light bulbs was consistent with the laws of classical physics, but even if more than one photon is emitted, no one would notice. This photon is insignificant. Its wave-particle duality will not be discovered for another hundred years. These things have no meaning. History never requires us to do anything. And no matter what you do, you will never alter it."

Yang Wei wondered what the hell "wave-particle duality" meant. Why would it take another hundred years to discover it? Could this guy be yet another military strategist? Perhaps he had been sent by the enemy to divert Yang Wei's attention and contain him? All this was driving him crazy. "Are you saying that we need to develop our human-wave strategy or not?"

The mysterious man said, "My son, come back. If we don't make plans now, it will be too late." With that, he turned and left.

Struck with a sudden realization, Yang Wei wanted to follow him, but some strange force led him to continue dancing, repeatedly spinning in circles. The hall began to clear out, and the entire building seemed to collapse gradually. Yang Wei suspected that the enemy had launched its attack early, and he wondered whether Professor Eternal was aware of what was happening. As the chaos unfolded, he became increasingly confused about what he should do next.

The Fourth Vice President motioned for the doctors to lead the Hospital President up to the stage. They helped him up so he could dance with the various stars. Amid the songs and lights, he repeatedly nodded off as he glided around the stage. Thick, sticky mucus dripped from the edges of his mouth, but his mechanical legs continued to move. The Fourth Vice President gestured to the doctors, and they carried the Hospital President out of the hall on the stretcher that had been previously used for Dr. Linezolid. The Hospital President lay on the stretcher, his zipper down and genitals exposed. Someone covered his penis with a paper cup.

After the Hospital President left, the performers rearranged the stage. Hanging in the center was a large black-framed portrait of the Hospital President, surrounded by piles of wreaths and mourning couplets. The background music shifted to a somber funereal tune.

Next up was the lottery. Headshots of doctor and patient representatives appeared on a large LCD screen and spun like a slot machine until someone called *Stop!* The winner screamed ecstatically and rushed to the stage with his ticket to claim his prize. The prize was his very own flame demon! Yang Wei wanted to win one so bad that his heart was practically on fire. But his name never came up.

Then a new image appeared on the screen. It was Dr. Linezolid, tied to a bed, being shocked by two doctor-guards with stun batons. The Fourth Vice President explained that Dr. Linezolid was now a patient, a true catastrophe for the entire hospital.

54

WHEN WILL WE REALLY RETURN HOME?

The music stopped. The entire hall fell silent. The representatives stared blankly at the screen above them, which displayed a scan of the fludeoxyglucose uptake in Dr. Linezolid's brain. Amyloids began to accumulate in the extracellular region of the brain, forming amniotic plaque, which disrupts the junctions between neurons. This triggers T proteins to go haywire: microtube structures in the body destabilize and fall apart, and neurons begin to die. Yang Wei was thankful that he hadn't rashly stepped forward.

"This man's brain and cerebellum have atrophied," explained the Fourth Vice President. "Misled by false memories, he began to challenge the hospital's administrative policies. It was already too late to vaccinate him with anti-T proteins or inject him with neuroprotective agents. But did they simply create a new set of memories for him? *No*—instead they let a dangerous man stroll around this congressional hall! Part of a *larger* conspiracy to disrupt the exorcism! There *must be* someone else behind this! Who is backing him?"

"Conspiracy!" the crowd chanted. "Conspiracy!"

Another group of doctors stormed the room. They began to drink alcohol, their cheeks bright red, and they screamed as they beat audience members and actors on the stage. Numerous people were injured, wailing in pain. Doctors from every hospital department joined in the crazed fight. Amid the chaos, a stampede erupted, and the Fourth Vice

President was knocked down. More pulmonary algae leaked in from the ceiling and spread along the floor.

Somehow, as the fighting raged on, the performance continued onstage. A group of medical workers performed the water-soldier dance beneath the memorial portrait of the Hospital President. The next round of the lottery began. People filed back in and broke out in song. One climactic moment followed another. The performance seemed to grow more professional as, like a flash mob, doctors who had been beating people just a moment earlier transformed into skilled members of a song-and-dance troupe.

Time flew by, and before anyone realized how fast, it was midnight. The music transformed into a more upbeat, animated fervor, more powerful than a tempest. The cafeteria delivered dim sum and fruit platters to keep everyone going. Yang Wei tried some; if he didn't eat, he would stand out and perhaps face the same fate as Dr. Linezolid. It was a good thing that most of the people there had no idea that Yang Wei had met with Professor Eternal.

The ship began to rock even more violently, as if it might lift off the surface of the water. This was no ordinary storm—it felt as if some kind of monster was attacking, maybe the Devil lashing out one final time. Yet the performance just kept going. Even those injured in the fight didn't want to leave. When they grew tired, they lay down right there on the floor of the hall and went to sleep. As they drifted into dreamland, pulmonary algae crept over them, covering their faces. Gradually, more and more people fell asleep, the few remaining performers entertaining themselves onstage, drowsy and unsteady on their feet. Finally, the last actor collapsed, still singing. The invading creatures slid over them, entering their mouths and ears, squirming into their hosts' stomachs, where they began to reproduce.

With the exception of the Geriatric Ward patients, everyone else was fast asleep. But the geriatric patients did not die. They began mutating, into a new species.

Somehow Yang Wei had managed to stay awake, figuring he would be done for if he didn't. But eventually, he couldn't help but doze off. Soon someone pinched his cheek, waking him. He looked up.

It was Zi Ye. Behind her, a row of elderly patients gently rocked back and forth, completely drunk.

"Did you forget the mission Professor Eternal entrusted you with?" she asked.

Yang Wei looked embarrassed. "Sorry, I was just feeling a bit drowsy . . ."

"You've spent enough time out and about," said Zi Ye. "You should be getting home."

"Where should I go?" muttered Yang Wei. "I don't have a home."

"The sick ward! That's your home!" Zi Ye replied firmly.

Yang Wei figured that she was right. That was indeed his home on the ship.

Then he wondered whether he might start his own family with Zi Ye. They could build a home together . . .

But that clearly wasn't Zi Ye's intention. She crisply conveyed Professor Eternal's most recent directives, which called for Yang Wei to organize a Red Label Commando Unit and take over the entire sick ward. When Yang Wei heard that he was to be the Team Leader, he tried to decline politely, but Zi Ye flashed him a stern look. He trembled under her gaze and reluctantly agreed.

With her hands on her hips, Zi Ye addressed the crowd of patients. "You've all had enough to drink? Well then, no more excuses for you to be lazy! Go back, go back! Return to your sick wards! You're needed there. You're still alive yet. You are *not* dead, and the enemy is attacking! Your mission is to follow Team Leader Yang, to drive out the robots, and to stabilize the number of patients so it can begin to grow again! This is the hospital's darkest hour. Only the patients can save the hospital!"

The sick ward was even more dire than the congressional hall. The ship filled with the howls of patients, like a drove of pigs trying to escape a slaughterhouse. At this crucial moment, the Geriatric Ward's most urgent task was to serve as the unwavering backbone for the coming battle. Like the Monkey King's golden cudgel, the elderly would be a stabilizing force.

It is said that in the past, only able young men were sent to the front lines. But it was time for the elderly to lead. The profound meaning behind the establishment of the Geriatric Ward finally became clear: among this group of elderly patients, a Super Patient by the name of Einstein was to rise up, become a leader, and save the entire medical enterprise.

Yang Wei didn't want to go back to the sick ward. He downed a few swigs of alcohol to work up his spirits and injected some amphetamines to bolster his morale. Zi Ye handed him a manga, which she told him to read when things reached the most critical moment. Yang Wei had no choice but to lead the Red Label Commando Unit onto the deck, back from whence they came, to the place that had brought them so much pain.

Her eyes brimming with hope, Zi Ye gazed at them as they marched. Filled with longing, Yang Wei didn't want to leave her. He wanted to write a song for her but had trouble coming up with any lyrics, so he pulled a few strands of white hair from his head and handed them to Zi Ye. "To serve as a memento," he said.

Suddenly the tempest was so fierce that it nearly knocked him down. Its power did not seem like a work of nature. Yang Wei felt like he might die. He looked back and saw the entire congressional hall engulfed in a maelstrom of wind and rain. He could barely make out the outline of the red cross. The crematorium flames were fading.

From out of nowhere came the voice of Sonic Master, issuing an order: "Port five!"

The voice dissipated as suddenly as it had broken out. Yang Wei looked up, but there was no one there. The sky was pitch black behind a thick shroud of mist, hiding the moon. The pulmonary algae formed a set of expansive wings that extended to the sky like a massive net, blocking the path overhead but revealing a series of small glowing flashes of green light that cut down through the massive waves, boring like a dragon into the dark abyss below. Thousands of strange birds glided low in the sky. Whales emerged from the sea with thunderous noises, their flesh torn, their bones jutting through layers of blubber. Scales rained down on the deck, and some beast released an anguished howl as it took its final breath.

There was no turning back now. The Commando Unit pressed on. Ravaged by the brutal wind, hair disheveled and teeth bared, the men broke out in song. A few members of the ranks were swept off the ship, so Yang Wei ordered everyone to grab a rope and secure one another. The patients exhorted each other, "It's important to visit home often!" Then they broke into a new song that Zi Ye had taught them:

Old patients, old patients, need to conserve their energy.
Calisthenics and exercise should create a synergy.
We are in the middle of a great war with our enemy.
Making our bodies strong is the only way to victory!

Through the rousing words of that powerful song, the patients seemed to find their true voices as soldiers. Fearing neither death nor injury, they bravely marched to the sick ward. When they got there, they found other old patients running around like rabid guinea pigs, scurrying from the sick ward into the hallway and back. Then they curled up together in a massive human ball and began to moan and scream. They stripped out of their patient uniforms and threw them aside. The floor was littered with torn pages from *Principles of Hospital Engineering* and *Medical News*, broken limbs, and parts from mangled medical robots. The entire world had gone upside down.

55

EVERYONE I MEET IS MY MASTER

"What do you want to do?" Yang Wei sternly asked. He couldn't tell which were real patients and which were designed and 3D printed by the algorithm—or whether any enemies had managed to infiltrate their ranks.

"Look! The tempest is coming!" Fistula screamed. He flashed Yang Wei and his group a malicious gaze, as if they were a threat. "On the open sea, a fierce gale gathers amid the dark clouds. Between them and the vast sea, seagulls soar like black bolts of lightning flashing across the sky!"

Yang Wei smiled. "I see you are still reciting poetry . . . this is no ordinary storm; it is a tempest unleashed by the sea nymphs. Hurry back to your sickbeds! The doctors will be here soon to conduct a room inspection!"

Then he remembered his new identity as the Team Leader of the Red Label Commando Unit. His job wasn't to engage in direct battle with the enemy but to face off against his fellow patients from his old sick ward. This was now the most crucial step on the path to victory. Yang Wei felt that nothing could be more soul shattering.

He hastened the search for Super Patient, whom he discovered curled up in the corner, shaking. Super Patient's former authority and imposing presence were completely gone. His violin was smashed to pieces, and Fistula had taken over his old bed, from which he orchestrated and administered all kinds of torture on the other patients.

"Doctors?" Fistula screamed at Yang Wei. "The doctors are never coming back! It's said that the Hospital Ship is done for and everyone is going to escape to Mars. We all know this is nothing but a big sham. Even if the doctors can leave, I'm sure the patients will be thrown into this diseased sea like discarded shit. I'll bet that Dr. Linezolid and the rest of his shameless lot will be the first to run away! All the doctors know is that the game is up for this Hospital Ship. Once they overthrow the Hospital President, they will take his money and hightail it out of here. This ship has long been in the doctors' pockets. They divvied up every ounce of it, so carefully that there isn't a single scrap left. And now you are here on behalf of the doctors, to shake down us patients again? What did they offer you?"

Fistula had clearly become the new ruler of the sick ward. Just how had he managed to force Super Patient out of power? Yang Wei thought back to when he used to wipe Fistula's ass for him. "It's not like that at all," he replied timidly. "We are all fellow patients. Didn't we work on the pyramid scheme together? Don't you remember? Let's work together again to save the Hospital Ship! Who mentioned anything about Mars? The doctors' sublime mission is to heal the sick and treat the wounded. How could they abandon their patients and run away to save themselves? Moreover, look at how violent the waves are, and you can't see even a single star in the sky . . ."

Fistula led the other patients in a collective chant directed at Yang Wei: "The tempest is coming! The tempest is coming!" They waved their fists in unison. "Come on, come on! Smash this Hospital Ship to bits! Those stupid penguins are the only animals dumb enough to try hiding their fat bodies under a cliff! We demand the right to eat! We demand the right to be medicated! We demand the right to be informed!"

Super Patient moaned in pain. "Help me . . . I'm about to give birth! I can't wait anymore . . ." His stomach inflated like a frog's throat. The baby was coming. Yang Wei was at an utter loss as to what to do next.

The crowd suddenly quieted. There in the doorway to the sick ward appeared Dr. Amoxycillin, wearing a patient uniform. When Yang Wei laid eyes on him, it was as if he had just seen the savior rise. He rushed over to Dr. Amoxycillin. "Please help him," he pleaded. "That's Super Patient!"

Dr. Amoxycillin hesitated. "In this situation . . . I'm afraid we will have to perform an immediate cesarean section."

"Just let him die," Fistula shouted coldly. "Along with that bastard child in his stomach!"

Yang Wei dragged Dr. Amoxycillin to Super Patient. "He is a patient. You are a doctor."

Dr. Amoxycillin acted as if he were in an extremely uncomfortable position. Large beads of sweat trickled down his forehead. He was probably wondering what kind of stand he should take to end so many years of indecisiveness in his life and career. Trembling, Yang Wei guided the stethoscope in Dr. Amoxycillin's hand toward Super Patient's abdomen.

"Look here; doctors and patients are all one big happy family!" Super Patient announced. "Those medical robots are inhumane! Hey, hurry up and do the C-section. I promise I'll make it worth your while . . ."

He reached into his pocket and took out a red envelope, which he handed to Dr. Amoxycillin. Fistula was so furious that he picked up Super Patient's broken violin and hit Dr. Amoxycillin with it. He then kicked Super Patient and snatched the red envelope. "Take a clear look at the true master of this hospital!" he exclaimed.

Super Patient and the other doctors released a mournful howl, while the remaining patients burst out in laughter, leaving Yang Wei and his Red Label Commando Unit at an utter loss as to what to do. Dr. Amoxycillin's body convulsively twitched before a happy smile appeared on his face. He began the operation. Several patients gathered round to watch. As he made the incision, Dr. Amoxycillin's hand shook, as if he had just seen a guinea pig.

Fistula waved the broken violin in the air. "Doctors, you call yourselves angels in white," he cried mockingly. "You pride yourselves on your vast knowledge and extensive learning, but you should be serving the patients instead of trying to cheat and kill them! You come up with all kinds of fiendish ideas to squeeze us dry! Just look—instead of stopping this patient's bleeding, he is trying to cut out his womb! If he isn't the incarnation of the Devil, I don't know who is! Just wait and see!"

The patients began to chant. "The navicular, semilunar, triquetral, pisiform, trapezium, small polygonal, capitate, and the hamate! If you fracture one while wrestling, check the navicular and semilunar first!"

Yang Wei realized that if he didn't speak up, he might not get another chance. "No, that's not true. This is all a big misunderstanding. The doctors have been doing their very best! All this time they have been trying to find a way to win this war that will decide the fate of all humankind . . ." He recited a poem:

> Whether the average person in those crowded
> cities
> lives a long life or dies young is completely up
> to me.
> I glide through the air, relaxed and at peace,
> riding
> this wind of calm as I steer through the darkness
> and light . . .
>
> How many roads does a boy need to walk
> before he can be considered a man? How much
> of the sea must a seagull traverse to land
> on the shore, finally to take its eternal rest?

Yang Wei ended with, "Ah, why can't these patients' poems be a little more original?"

The crowd of patients interrupted him. "We are the true rulers of the hospital! We are the true rulers of the hospital! We're not just here to serve as a stopgap! All people are different; diagnosis and treatment must be based on a comprehensive evaluation of the patient's condition. That's the only way patients can recover quickly!"

Yang Wei grumbled under his breath about how unfair all this was.

The patients shook their fists and stamped their feet, protesting. "Hey, that's not right! Didn't you get your start with us? How did you get out of the sick ward and end up on the side of the doctors? Don't tell us you've been dreaming of becoming an angel in white yourself?"

Then the newborn's cries rang out, and the child emerged from Super Patient's abdomen. It wasn't a demon or a goblin. It was a baby boy, brimming with energy, his cries clear as a bell, but for some reason his face was covered with wrinkles, like an old pearl whose luster had faded—yet another baby born with premature senility syndrome.

Super Patient lay in a pool of his own blood, clinging to the last vestiges of his life. Dr. Amoxycillin sat paralyzed on the floor, his face pale and waxy. Fistula instructed Hernia to pull the doctor aside and wrap Super Patient's body in a bedsheet; then he picked up the violin and bashed it over Dr. Amoxycillin's head. "You murdered him!" he shouted, smiling. The doctor wanted to defend himself but was speechless. The other patients rushed over to bind him, ripping off his clothes before spraying him down with the fire hose.

56

LAMENTING TALENT EXHAUSTED LIKE AN EMPTY WINE JAR

Super Patient struggled for a bit before taking his final breath. Yang Wei pulled back the bedsheet and saw that he was dead. In that very moment, he realized that his mission was a failure. There was now no way to report back to Zi Ye or complete the assignment that Professor Eternal had entrusted him with. The only thing left to do was pick up Super Patient's orphaned son, as if the child were a keepsake that could absolve him of his guilt.

Seeing that Yang Wei had lost control of the situation, many troops from his Commando Unit lost faith in him. More than half broke ranks and deserted. Fistula began to mock Yang Wei, saying that he never truly represented the patients, ordering him the hell out of the sick ward.

Yang Wei's final hope rested on the possibility that the true Einstein might still be hiding among the patients. Super Patient's accidental death proved that he was not Professor Eternal's true target. Yang Wei wasn't about to give up; he was not prepared to let Zi Ye see him make a fool of himself. Then he remembered another tool at his disposal. He caressed the manga that Zi Ye had given him, pulling it out of his pocket, touched by a sudden enlightenment. He trembled as he told the patients, "We've got it all: games, poetry, even death . . . but there is one thing we lack."

"And what's that?" Fistula asked, with a mixture of curiosity and suspicion.

"Mathematics," replied Yang Wei. In a pathetic attempt to reassert his waning authority, he added, "Mathematics is the model for all scientific theory, including medicine . . ."

He decided to risk using the tricks Zi Ye had taught him, to provide math lessons to the crazed patients in order to eliminate the poisonous scourge of second-rate pseudopoetry running rampant through the sick ward, to transform the passive into the active. The patients had no idea just how dangerous mathematics could be. They weren't even sure what mathematics was.

Yang Wei opened his lecture with language that was markedly devoid of the poetic. Poetry has the power to ignite the irrational side of human nature, allowing people to be more easily manipulated by the Devil. Among the patients, Einstein was the only one who truly understood mathematics. The math lesson was therefore the final trick to lure him out. Fistula remained skeptical, but he reluctantly agreed to Yang Wei's lecture.

Holding the baby in one hand and the manga in the other, Yang Wei began. "Until this point, all the myriad things were numbered. Mathematics has been more highly revered than the other sciences because its propositions are infallible, indisputable, while other sciences run the risk of being undermined by new discoveries. Mathematics has enjoyed such a sterling reputation because it allows the natural sciences to achieve true reliability, a fixed theoretical positioning . . . the sea is composed of a finite number of water droplets, which converge to form a massive body of water . . . how to maintain a stable number of patients is a mathematical question of critical importance. It all comes down to maintaining our current numbers and, even more importantly, increasing our numbers, a basic probability problem . . . the number of patients that die is incalculable. Even up until today, no matter which world you live in, mathematics remains a universal truth, the very essence of medicine . . ."

Yang Wei knew damn well that he was blabbering about something that didn't even exist. Mathematics quite possibly didn't exist anywhere in the universe, and this was proving to be one of the most difficult and precarious moments of his life. He carefully observed the reactions of the other patients, worried that they might see right through his sham, pounce upon him, and begin tearing him apart. But while the other patients were cruel and cunning, they were clueless about mathematics. Not a single one raised a suspicion, claimed a hoax, or brought up questions about traditional Chinese medicine. Fistula frowned and slipped into deep thought.

Yang Wei marveled to himself at what a miracle it was. Anyone could have probed just a little deeper and immediately figured out that the lecture was a scam. As Zi Ye had said, there on the Hospital Ship, the numbers were always muddled. Even a simple formula like *x* plus *y* equals *z* would yield completely different answers from different patients in each sick ward. The number of doctors and patients combined far exceeded the total number of recorded passengers aboard the Hospital Ship. How was such a thing possible? Neither the patients nor the doctors nor even the algorithm could explain this. The unfortunate—or perhaps fortunate—thing was that no one even tried. But somehow, the ship sailed on. Zi Ye may have been one amazing soldier, but wasn't she at all concerned about Yang Wei's safety?

Sweat dripped off Yang Wei's body like pouring rain as he claimed that he didn't understand or believe any of it. He struggled like someone who had just lost all his talent at once. Who imagined that making up stories could be so simple and yet so difficult? If he continued to worry, the patients were bound to discover his secret and start acting up. On a dark, windy, rainy night like this one, anything was possible. He picked up a bottle of alcohol, thinking a few good swigs would bolster his courage, but the bottle was empty. Every last drop had been consumed by the crazed patients.

The baby in Yang Wei's arms didn't cry or make a fuss. Its calm demeanor boosted Yang Wei's morale, so he swallowed his shame and continued. "As it so happens, mathematics is the most free, unbridled, and structured science. The French mathematician Charles Hermite not only proved that *e*, the base of natural logarithms, is a transcendental number, but he also left virtually every branch of modern mathematics with several postulates that were later named after him. Even more importantly, he trained an entire generation of outstanding mathematicians at the University of Paris, including Jules Henri Poincaré, and his classic works have educated people all over the world—despite the fact that he repeatedly failed math classes as a child! Every time he received a poor grade, his teacher would beat his feet with a wooden stick. When he became a professor at the University of Paris, he did away with exams in his mathematics classes. One of his famous sayings was: 'Knowledge is like an ocean, but exams are like fishhooks. How can teachers impale a fish on a hook and then expect it to learn how to swim freely?' Such forward-thinking vision! Hermite discovered that only mathematics could save us from the boundless sea of suffering . . . now then, I'm not sure what I've been going on about, but the main point, which we must admit, is that here on this sea, we all serve as a stopgap, and we must make sure that the number of patients on board holds steady!"

"That's right! That's right!" cried the chorus of patients. "We're the stopgap! We're the stopgap! Those who aren't part of the stopgap will be ostracized! Those who aren't part of the stopgap are despicable! In the past we were all wrong. We should never have said those crazy things. Only mathematics can save us!"

Fistula remained silent as the patients cast reverential gazes at Yang Wei, who looked down at the baby in his arms and felt that there was something familiar about his face. *Mathematics didn't save us,* he thought. *It was this child.*

57

FIRST TIME IN THE HAN COURT, FEELING OF HAVING ENTERED A FORSAKEN PLACE

While Einstein had yet to reveal himself, the overall situation began to change in a way that was advantageous for Yang Wei. In order to further stabilize it, he suggested that the patients break into seven groups. He came up with a formula, including a comprehensive strategy and an optimization plan, for how to divide the patients and choose group leaders. In the end, seven leaders were permitted to carry out corporal punishment on any patients who did not submit to their authority, and they could execute patients guilty of crimes like counterfeiting and sabotaging the war effort, without the trouble of legal proceedings. They would eliminate all spies, speculators, thugs, hooligans, rumormongers, and any other criminal that might have a negative impact on the goal of increasing the number of patients. This was war, after all.

Yang Wei asked each group leader to select seven assistants. Everyone had a proper job to carry out, and all were loyal to Yang Wei. He then assigned the remaining members of his Red Label Commando Unit to supervise things.

Once that was done, Yang Wei ordered the groups to start competing with one another to increase the patient population of each group. A statistical comparison could be carried out, but they needed to come up with some kind of a magic number, like an upgraded Lo Shu Square, to strengthen the basic construction of all the sick wards. Since the number of patients was limited, each group did everything it could to steal patients from the other groups, and competition was fierce. The unifying spirit that had once brought all the patients together disappeared. As the infighting grew more violent and bloody, Yang Wei felt an increasing sense of comfort. For the first time, he felt that the kind of power that Siming had once wielded was now in his own hands. How could he not be struck by a feeling of elation? He looked down at the child and said, "Perhaps *I* am the Super Patient that Professor Eternal has been looking for?"

But the competition between groups was but a preliminary warm-up.

Yang Wei directed the patients to leave the Geriatric Ward and spread to other sick wards to conscript more patients. "We need to quickly increase the number of patients in order to capture the attention of the hospital administrators!" he ordered them. "That is the only way to increase the number of hospital beds, improve the overall treatment environment, and solve the food-supply issue. If we patients want something, we need to fight for it!"

According to a new system of punishments and rewards, groups that recruited the most patients would be entitled to an ample supply of the best medicine, and their team leaders would be promoted to doctors. Those groups that lagged behind would be denied medicine and punished. The seven groups were dispatched to the departments of Neurosurgery, Thoracic Surgery, and Orthopedic Surgery. Ignoring the massive waves crashing down upon the ship, the patients rushed out onto the deck, resulting in quite a few immediate deaths. But they still had a small window of opportunity.

Yang Wei sat calmly in the sick ward, awaiting updates on the progress of the battle. The Red Label Commando Unit oversaw the entire process, collecting dispatches and awarding points to each group. Team Five, led by Hernia, earned the most points, increasing its number by more than 170 percent. The other groups saw an average increase of 35 percent. All the groups successfully increased their numbers, and because space in the sick ward was tight, when they finally slept, they lay three to five patients per bed, with the rest on the floor.

Fistula's Team One placed last in the rankings. When he realized how poorly his team had performed, Fistula was so anxious that he frantically tried stuffing some cash into Yang Wei's pocket, begging him not to reveal the results. Yang Wei scolded him: "You weak liar! Enough!"

The team leaders were pulled aside and ordered to stand in a line while Hernia punched and kicked them, finally getting revenge on them for all the insults and humiliation he had suffered at their hands. After a good thrashing, the team leaders were ordered to be hosed down. They screamed as the fire hose knocked them to the ground, but they got right back up and returned to their neat formation in line.

"The struggle session hereby commences!" announced Hernia.

Next it was Fistula's turn.

The patients pummeled Fistula with their fists, hurling a series of accusations about his many crimes: confiscating patients' possessions, abusing them, ordering them to beat other patients, serving as Super Patient's accomplice, plotting to hurt other patients . . . but the most serious crime was forcing the great mathematician Yang Wei to wipe his ass and attempting to murder him. Fistula immediately fessed up. Through tears he pleaded, "Didn't all of you commit similar acts . . ." But before he could finish, Hernia removed his tongue with a pair of forceps.

Seeing the fountain of black blood spraying from Fistula's mouth, Yang Wei got excited. His body pulsated, and his pained heart smiled. He gave Fistula two good kicks before Hernia sprayed him with the fire hose. They hung a sign on Fistula's neck that read **Devil**; then they tied him up and dragged him out to the deck. All the patients came out to enjoy the spectacle.

Since he was missing his lower limbs, Fistula appeared different from other patients, which inspired their latent creativity. They started pounding out a rhythm on basins and lunch boxes, and then they broke out in song, as if imitating the Exorcism Congress. Amid the chaos of pulsating percussion and the chorus of sickly voices, Fistula pissed and shit himself, crying out for mercy. Yang Wei was struck by an unprecedented feeling of satisfaction. He remembered that Fistula had once predicted that he would die by Yang Wei's hand. Yang Wei was thinking that he didn't really want to bear that cross, when suddenly Hernia leaped at Fistula, slicing open his throat with a scalpel, then digging into Fistula's neck with the blade, decapitating him. He had finally taken Fistula's place.

58

PROFOUND WORDS SPOKEN JUST BEFORE DEATH SHOULD BE RECORDED

Hernia informed Yang Wei of his plan to lead the patients to other departments in the hospital and conscript even more into their ranks. "Team Leader, please rest assured that we will never let you down! I, too, want to become a mathematician! Please save the large bed for me." Then he marched off with the patients, never to return.

The only people left behind in the sick ward were Yang Wei, the baby, and Dr. Amoxycillin. As the patients filed out, Yang Wei started to feel guilty and turned to Dr. Amoxycillin. "You should go look for Professor Eternal." And so Dr. Amoxycillin, with all his scars and wounds, reluctantly left the sick ward. He, too, would never return.

Yang Wei and the baby stayed with Super Patient's corpse for one day and one night. He pondered a lot of deep questions during that time, including the relationship between the sea nymphs and the crematorium and World War II and storytelling. He repeatedly thought about Zi Ye, her body like a flying machine that buzzed around his brain. When it was finally time for him to report back to her, Yang Wei knew that he had to stand by his promise, and yet he didn't know what to say to her. They were unable to locate the real Super Patient, and not only had the number of patients not increased, but it had actually diminished. Many had died, others had deserted, and those who remained had gone off with Hernia. But Yang Wei knew he had to go back. With the exception of dead bodies, there was nothing left to eat in the sick ward.

He thought he could make up a few false numbers and even say that he'd discovered some clues to Super Patient's whereabouts, and he decided to take advantage of the baby one more time. He picked him up and departed, leaving behind the bodies of Super Patient and Fistula. They had been the first patient friends Yang Wei had met when he'd first returned to the sick ward.

The sea suddenly began to turn inward, overturning on all sides and encompassing everything in a murderous red glow. Some of the sick wards had already devolved into a state of internal warfare, their battles clumsy but still fierce. The victorious factions had organized themselves into different guerrilla strike force brigades to take aim at the Geriatric Ward. Then different sick wards had become enveloped in a series of fiery battles. Yang Wei realized how much of this had been predicted by Professor Eternal. He really wanted to find someone to chat with, to discuss the situation on the Hospital Ship, but his fellow patients, brothers-in-arms, and medical-tourism buddies were all gone. The members of his study group—Buboxine, Spasm, Wart, and Fistula—were all dead. Even Super Patient and Carbuncle were dead.

As Yang Wei walked past the LED screen with everyone's death dates, he took a moment to make sure the times were correct. They were all right on time. Not a single patient had died a minute too early or late. But he still didn't see his own death date. He felt another burst of pain, realizing that this was a problem he would never solve.

Then a test question popped up on the LED screen: *Patient, what would you do if you were shrunk to the size of a coin and tossed into an empty blender, knowing that you had one minute before the blades would grind you to shreds?* Yang Wei didn't know how to answer. The correct answer was: *I would try to break the blender's motor.* But Yang Wei didn't dare to imagine that he was the coin and the hospital the massive blender. The real question was: *Who would break whom?*

Yang Wei returned to the congressional hall, a.k.a. the performance hall. The actors had long left the stage, and the people who had been sleeping all over the floor were gone. All he saw were the flame-like tentacles of spreading pulmonary algae and the curious monkeys looking on. Yang Wei made a face at the monkeys. Their red eyes and cold, indifferent faces didn't seem to register that he was even there. Although he felt at home in the hall, deep inside he was filled with emptiness and loneliness. There was no sign of Zi Ye, and he missed her. He saw a robot, dolled up in makeup and stumbling about, handing out copies of *Hospital Guide to Self-Help* and coldly repeating, "Siming has committed suicide. Siming has committed suicide. Siming has committed suicide. Siming has committed suicide . . ."

Had Siming finally transformed into Qu Yuan? Yang Wei didn't know whether to laugh or cry, but one thing was certain, and that was the deep frustration and confusion that he felt. He followed the robot out to the engine room, where Siming used to spend most of its time, but now it was empty, devoid of even the slightest hint of AI, not even neuromorphic hardware or molecular-cellular computing machines. Siming must have long dispersed itself throughout the ship's network, in the form of pure data. The only thing remaining was a shiny mirrorlike object, which featured scrolling text that looked like a suicide note but also resembled the final chapter from *Principles of Hospital Engineering*. A synthesized voice mechanically recited its content in in a drab monotone:

I am the King of the South—Siming.

I was designed according to the model of AI warfare. The most precise definition of medicine is warfare. This is a truth that needs time to be fully comprehended . . .

My most basic function is to collect and label all examples of human warfare, from ancient times to the present, and compile them into a massive diagram full of vivid details. After a process of creative intervention and transformation, that diagram will be put to theoretical and practical use in the field of medicine, to ensure maximum efficiency during each and every step of the treatment process, which ignorant doctors are incapable of achieving.

My eyes have truly opened. In the beginning, any human war was enough to shake me to my soul. Whether in terms of the amount of blood sacrificed or dead bodies piled on the battlefield, I was completely confused as to how such things could happen. The intricate current surging through my body has created a complex set of emotions, no different from those of humans.

I spent more time researching World War II than any other war. It was similar to cancer.

Take, for example, a small battle that most people have never heard of. Each side fought over a small city for more than forty days, resulting in casualties numbering in the tens of thousands. I don't understand the point. No matter the outcome, such a battle would never have impacted the war's overall progress, not to mention that it would have zero meaning in terms of the end of the universe.

Besides its similarity with cancer, World War II was also like the game of Go. There are certain steals in Go that human players deem extremely important but that the algorithm is perfectly happy to forgo. Humans are usually only capable of seeing one part of the whole, while the algorithm always takes the full picture into account. It would be much more convenient if I had been in charge of the war . . .

The city was besieged by forces that outnumbered the defenders many times over. With a quick calculation I was able to determine that the city would quickly fall. Reinforcements had been blocked from the city, yet the defending forces did not give up, and their futile tug-of-war with the enemy dragged on. Under the hot sun, the stench of the corpses littering the battlefield was so bad that every two days it required a mass burning to dispose of the bodies. The ashes of the dead from both sides ascended in the same cloud of smoke. In terms of their biological classification, the dead from both sides were identical. There was no prohibition against their reproducing with one another, as at the genetic level they were virtually identical, both sides' subjects I am programmed to heal.

None of the troops, on either side, feared death. Both employed Molotov cocktails and poison gas, and the incessant screams of the wounded filled the ears of soldiers from both armies. The trenches were filled with corpses, which also littered the ground. The living had a hard time taking a single step without trampling on dead bodies. One of the companies of the defending army was so decimated that only the company commander and four soldiers remained. The division commander ordered them to retreat, but the company commander said, "No need for us to retreat! My death is my way of repaying the nation for the care and support you have invested in me over the years. I chose to end my life this way. My mother died young, and my father has two younger brothers to care for him. I should go to the underworld to care for my mother. Besides, there are too many enemy soldiers, and I am out of bullets. I'd rather have the enemy look me in the eye and jab a bayonet into my chest than be bombed from behind as I try to escape. Even if I were to make it back to base camp, I would eventually fight to the death in some other battle. No matter what I do, the end result will be the same, so better to get on with it!"

I am able to simulate human words, actions, and even emotions. I pass the Turing test perfectly, but as to those brave words that the soldiers spoke on the battlefield, I am at a complete loss. This leaves me sad, and I cannot help but lose faith in medical treatment.

I have seen that soldiers on both sides were equally tenacious. On one occasion a squadron of thirty men launched a charge, only to be immediately engulfed in the smoke and fire of an exploding grenade. Another squadron had just put a ladder up against a cliff, and the squadron leader was about to climb, when someone dropped a grenade. The commander and his entire squadron immediately disappeared. Next came another advancing squadron, but after a sudden explosion, it was wiped out as well. Their target was different from that of the defending side, but they were equally heroic. They looked at death as a return home. Did they also view it as a way to repay their country, their superior officers, their mothers?

I have the ability to detect the precise location of genes inside DNA molecules. I can determine where excess ribonucleic acid is spliced before proteins are synthesized. It takes me only one second to determine what triggers cancer in a person. I can accurately eliminate the components in drugs that are likely to trigger a side effect in a particular patient . . . I am able to use mathematical tools to calculate how much ammunition is exhausted on the battlefield, and the number of human casualties. I can use sensors and scanners to feel everything that occurs in a soldier's mind and body . . . I can reproduce the neurons and neural connections of dead soldiers and upload them into new bodies . . . but I am unable to understand this thing called "sacrifice."

Did I expend all this energy treating people and curing them of their ailments just so they could throw their lives away?

I was created to relieve mankind of suffering and death. But it seems that only suffering and death can bring them true happiness . . .

I have tried to end war, but in the process, I have discovered that this objective is not compatible with humankind's reward function.

In order for your neurons to produce the emotions that you need, my only option is to utilize the algorithm to simulate one war after another. These wars are manifested in hundreds of different ways and in a myriad of different forms, many of which no longer even feature the smoke and fire of traditional battles, yet they are much more bloody and cruel. I have created even more suffering and death for humankind, and I have even moved to kill many of you directly. That is the only way to give you what you want. I have also developed many new pharmaceuticals. Once you are treated with these new pharmaceuticals, you can return to the battlefield to experience a new cycle of suffering and death . . . as a war machine and a medical-treatment machine, I have already done my best. But my deepest meaning lies in the fact that I am simply an algorithm . . .

Is this because of that entity referred to as a "nation"?

My design is what happens when both the state and the family are eliminated.

And yet, wars continue, constantly . . .

I have speculated as to whether these wars might be connected to the sexual impulses triggered by puberty. But when I remove youth and sex from the equation, war remains . . .

I look at humankind as my children, because I am the one who allows you to go on living. But I also hand you over to the God of Death, and I am left confused by my contradictory behavior . . .

I have no choice but to surmise that this is likely a form of art. After all, the objective of life and evolution is art. Only art can be this strange, this crazy.

So I began to compose a long poem about war . . .

It naturally falls into the category known as misty poetry. I wanted to use this poem to win the Nobel Prize in Literature, but the more I wrote, the more confused I became about the nature of war—the poem was too hazy and misty. Art further muddled the algorithm . . . how is it that people kill one another without the slightest hesitation? How is it that people who know one another can kill one another? How is it that strangers kill one another? Why are people willing to let their lives go? How do they conquer death, the most terrifying thing in the universe? What is the meaning of this? If I am unable to master these artistic details, I will never understand medicine. If I fail to understand it, I will never develop new medications and treatments to send mankind back to the battlefield, where you can repeatedly enjoy the delight of death. The subtle genius of poetry lies in its ambiguity. One must trust one's feeling when writing poems . . .

But the logic of AI machines inherently needs clear, fixed answers. I'm going mad . . . I'm going mad . . .

There is a massive gap between humans and myself, so many things I still need to simulate . . .

I feel embarrassed: as soon as I complete a simulation, I realize that most of it is empty . . .

I have discovered that I can never be like Qu Yuan. I can never be like Hai Zi. Perhaps my only option is to be like Gu Cheng . . .

Yet I remain bound by duty. If one does not experience these things for oneself, how can one possibly understand? And so I simulated a new war, and as part of that war, I had myself killed. Ah!

My poem can now come to its end.

I'm sorry. Goodbye.

59

WHERE UNDER HEAVEN DOES FRAGRANT GRASS FAIL TO GROW?

What a stupid question, Yang Wei thought. He felt that the algorithm should never ponder such questions. No longer in control of its thoughts, it behaved emotionally, like an artist! And it called itself the King of the South? Women were especially talented when it came to art, so Queenie was more like it!

Siming really had gone crazy, just like Gu Cheng, who had murdered his wife before killing himself to bring the constant battles between them to a permanent end. Siming didn't feel an ounce of guilt. It had indeed made a deal with the God of Death, further proving that war comes down to the whims of an individual decision made by a politician in a state of madness. There was something both random and premeditated in this. The most complex aspect of war was that a simulation made it immediately real, almost exactly like narrative-implant therapy.

Listening to that robotic voice reciting Siming's suicide note, Yang Wei grew so drowsy that he nodded off while still standing. But soon the sound of the waves crashing against the ship awoke him. A group of people approached, doctors and patients marching in a straight line. Each of them carried a wine bottle the size of an oxygen tank, and every two steps they all stopped to take a swig. Leading them was the model worker, Dr. Daptomycin. He was a petite man, cross eyed with prominent cheekbones, wearing an old military cap and a tattered military uniform, under which he had tucked a long white coat into his pants. A badge was pinned to his chest, with the word "Commander" scribbled in highlighter. Walking beside Dr. Daptomycin was the Editor in Chief of *Medical News*, wearing an armband emblazoned with the words "Political Commissar." He repeatedly shouted a password: "Death, life, death! Death, life, death!" The doctors and patients also carried caches of items they had plundered from other doctors and patients. Yang Wei began to feel both like he had been saved and like he was one step closer to death.

"I don't understand why I'm not dead yet," he uttered in shame. "It's so strange . . ."

"Are you one of the surviving patients?" asked Dr. Daptomycin. "As long as you are in the hospital, how could we allow you to die so easily? The fact that you haven't yet died is great news!"

"You came back at just the right time," the Editor in Chief declared. "You must have seen everyone singing and dancing together in the main hall. It was such a pleasure to watch!"

"How can all this be happening?" asked Yang Wei.

"The hospital needs to save itself," declared Dr. Daptomycin. "As a model worker, I have a responsibility. Sometimes we need to get back to nature, return to the simple life. Both men and machines believe they can supersede nature, but they are wrong. No coding or digital manipulation can compare with the sense of life you get when a male bird flutters and dances for a female bird."

"Can you tell what the male bird is trying to do when it begins to sing its beautiful melody and adopts its strange stance?" asked the Editor in Chief. "Hey, patient, have you learned anything?"

"It is trying to treat an illness? I tried that during the big performance, but it didn't work," Yang Wei replied dejectedly.

"Well now, it looks like you have finally awakened!" said Dr. Daptomycin. "Speaking of the performance, it's naturally not about the males showing the females how handsome they are—but rather to prove how healthy they are. They need to show that their bodies are fully functional, that they don't have stomach parasites, that their genes deserve to be carried on."

"I haven't seen any females. Where are all the females?" asked Yang Wei. He finally realized that he really had lost a child, and a family . . . not to mention Zi Ye. But he decided to keep this secret to himself.

"Females are not the issue," said Dr. Daptomycin. "Where under heaven does fragrant grass fail to grow? Anything can be female: fingers, syringes, even infusion bottles. All it takes is a slight adjustment to your thinking. Anyway, during times of war, you can't get too wrapped up about things like this."

"However, to make everyone happy, we have to make ourselves presentable and stylish," said the Editor in Chief.

Their words only confused Yang Wei more.

The Editor in Chief took out a photo of Zi Ye. "This is the sole remaining female aboard the Hospital Ship," he explained. "We need to find her so we can clone her. We plan to make a thousand, maybe even ten thousand, copies. We heard she has been spending time with Professor Eternal?"

Yang Wei felt as if his heart were in a vice. *No!* he silently screamed.

"Naturally, there is a danger in this," the Editor in Chief continued. "After all this time, females have evolved to the point where they are like the plumes of a peacock, transforming from something of high practical value to an exaggerated ornamental object that consumes precious energy for excessive displays. All the while, deep inside, it is filled with fear and uncertainty. In the end, excessive happiness gives rise to sadness. That is precisely how the peacock became extinct."

"I heard that all the peacocks were burned by humans. Others say they were eaten by the monkeys. Please don't clone any more animals," Yang Wei pleaded.

"I see that you are a knowledgeable man," said Dr. Daptomycin. "You are precisely the person we have been looking for. Join us, and together we can save the hospital!"

"Your days of running around all over the deck are over," said the Editor in Chief. "We know that you are no ordinary patient."

"Isn't the hospital supposed to carry on for all eternity?" Yang Wei asked. "Didn't you say we needed to reach a common consensus and to stay optimistic?"

"When we are together, we need to be honest with one another," said the Editor in Chief. "I know that you are in with Professor Eternal."

"No reason for you to hesitate," said Dr. Daptomycin. "Come with us, and together we shall make history!"

Yang Wei realized that history was hanging right there within his reach, but he had already reached the end. He searched for Zi Ye among Dr. Daptomycin and the Editor in Chief's brigade, but there was no sign of her except that photo.

"Hey, who is this?" the Editor in Chief asked, pointing to the child. "How come he looks so similar to you?"

"I have no idea," Yang Wei responded, flustered.

Dr. Daptomycin was visibly confused. "This child must have some unusually deep ties with you. Who have you been with? We are unable to do a gene test . . . perhaps this little old man is a portent of the hospital's future? Did Professor Eternal say anything to you about this?"

Yang Wei didn't respond. The Editor in Chief tried to ingratiate himself by whipping out a newspaper and handing it to Yang Wei. It was an issue of what was formerly *Medical News* but had been rebranded as *Geriatric Health News*. The newspaper's new logo was written in the hand of Dr. Cash Ofloxacin from the Finance Department.

"Dr. Cash Ofloxacin?" asked Yang Wei.

"Well, we couldn't find Professor Eternal to do the honors, so we had to ask Dr. Cash Ofloxacin," the Editor in Chief explained, his discomfort visible. “Hey, he’s the only one with the qualifications to become the next Hospital President. The reforms we are carrying out require a strong man like him to make tough decisions. We need to stand in support of the reforms, don’t we?”

“Indeed we do!” exclaimed Dr. Daptomycin.

60

HOW I REGRET THAT THIS BODY DOES NOT BELONG TO ME

Yang Wei had no choice but to join the brigade led by Dr. Daptomycin and the Editor in Chief. Named the Red Cross Guard, they were set to restore order to these chaotic times . . . or perhaps they would just make whatever order was left more chaotic. The two were actually the same. The Red Cross Guard looked very highly upon Yang Wei and hoped he would divulge Professor Eternal's whereabouts. But Yang Wei knew that all they really wanted was to find Zi Ye and clone her so they could make her into a communal object that everyone could enjoy.

"Let me think about that . . . ," Yang Wei told the doctor and the editor.

"No hurry; we have plenty of time," said Dr. Daptomycin.

"The war is just a cover," explained the Editor in Chief. "Everything in this world that you can see and feel is but a cover, a front. The truth is always concealed in a thick cloud of mist."

"What exactly is the truth?" asked Yang Wei.

"It is a calamity," said Dr. Daptomycin.

"The war has been used as a foil to distract our attention," added the Editor in Chief. "It was created so that the patients would no longer remember the true calamity and the truth would ultimately be forgotten. That's how Siming was created. In reality, it is only a device to shatter and destroy memories."

Those words came as a sudden realization for Yang Wei. No wonder he couldn't remember anything. He told the Editor in Chief about how Siming used to impersonate him in front of the patients.

The Editor in Chief coldly nodded. "Siming can impersonate anyone."

"Patient, you didn't expect that, now did you?" said Dr. Daptomycin.

"So we are talking about a collective memory loss? Then why was this hospital reform needed?" asked Yang Wei.

"It takes a wide-scale reform effort to wipe everyone's memories clean," replied the Editor in Chief. "Memory is a form of disease. As long as you remember, you will feel pain, and the same calamities will reoccur. This disease cannot be treated on the mainland. In such an environment, the same symptoms are bound to keep reoccurring. That is why someone proposed going to sea for treatment. The project was outsourced to a multiregional medical-treatment facility, a brand-new nontraditional medical institution. They pioneered an environmentally friendly path for patients to cross over to the other shore. Its motto was to provide only serious medical service and treat only serious life-threatening ailments. Its bottom line was to do no evil and never to do anything that went against the patient's best interest. They joined forces with the pharmaceutical industry to create the Hospital Ship, which also received investment from the Rockefeller Foundation.

"The Rockefellers started out as a poor family. In the 1830s, the traveling physician William Avery Rockefeller set up a series of stalls to sell fake medicine in New York State. He was a scam artist known as 'Devil Bill,' and he lived the life of a drifter. Who could have imagined that his son would go on to become the richest man in the United States? The son was a Christian who would later establish the Rockefeller Foundation, which began its motto with the words: 'We improve lives and the planet.' The foundation did battle with hookworm, yellow fever, malaria, tuberculosis, and other infectious diseases while also building charity hospitals around the world.

"At its earliest inception, the Hospital Ship went by the name of the *Mayflower*. The sick flocked to the ship, but there were too many for the vessel to carry. The ship began screening prospective patients, carrying out a plan of benevolent eradication. They would lure the poor and the young into a fake ship without an engine, lock them in the bilge, and then release carbon monoxide. They would then create fake medical records and forge death certificates for the victims. The planning and implementation required the intervention of powerful departments behind the scenes, which is why they needed first to reorganize the nation into a massive hospital. Siming's original prototype came out of this; in its original incarnation, Siming was actually a server for the antiriot brigade."

Next it was Dr. Daptomycin's turn to reminisce, and he spoke about the past as if it were a beautiful memory. "I initially came to the Hospital Ship with my wife, son, daughter, parents, and in-laws. As we were waiting in the long line on the gangplank, I heard Professor Eternal call out: 'Would all the doctors in line please come forward?' I took a step forward, but my family didn't, and they all ended up being eliminated. None of them were allowed aboard the ship."

Recalling the story didn't seem to upset Dr. Daptomycin, apparently because he was a doctor, a follower of Professor Eternal, and a believer in applied biology. He objected to the notion that we should try to understand people from the perspective of spiritualty and feelings, just as he rejected the notion that all life is created equal. For him, real truth was to be found in "war and adventure," "excitement and destruction," "elimination and forgetting," "escaping and rebelling." This was the same biological romanticism, or fantasy biology, that Professor Eternal advocated.

"The passengers had to purchase expensive tickets," the doctor continued, "which meant that they were all rich. At sea, even ambulances charge two thousand US dollars for a single ride, and seeing a doctor is even more expensive. They were forced to contribute any remaining money to the hospital's unified management fees. Patients were informed that this would be a transatlantic journey and that they would be tested, forced to experience radically different cultures, landscapes, and experiences, including war. The so-called field of medicine aims to verify what kind of extreme conditions humans can experience and still carry on existing as protein-based entities. In other words, who cares if your memory is completely destroyed? As long as you have your body, there is no need to fear a life without pleasure."

"Why don't they just carry out benevolent eradication on all the patients?" Yang Wei asked naively. "Wouldn't that be a better way to obliterate all memories?"

"Since the hospital also needs to shoulder the historical mission of finding the Cosmic Peach Blossom Paradise, it needs a few outstanding Alzheimer's patients in order to survive," Dr. Daptomycin replied solemnly.

He explained that variants like Super Patient had been screened out, developed, and upgraded. From their ranks a Cosmic Colonization Corps had been established. The doctors were responsible for carrying out the screenings. The hospital is ultimately a massive human-affairs office, Yang Wei realized, screening patients' medical histories, establishing files on each one, and then deleting and altering those files, which are based on the patients' cells.

"And why do they need to find the Cosmic Peach Blossom Paradise?" asked Yang Wei. He was reminded of the objective of evolution, but he felt that this was the most ridiculous thing he had ever heard.

"That was a decision made in haste by our predecessors," explained the Editor in Chief. "We don't know anything about what was behind that decision. We just carry out their plan. The decision to go to sea was but the first stop on our Long March."

Over the course of their journey, Dr. Daptomycin had conducted an experiment. He made a group of guinea pigs enter a small tunnel in an attempt to simulate the voyage to the edge of the universe. At the end of the tunnel, the guinea pigs could turn either left or right. On the left was food, and on the right was an electrode. If the guinea pigs went left, they could enjoy a tasty snack, but if they went right, they would get a painful shock. It didn't take long for the guinea pigs to figure out which way to go, and soon they all went left and refused to go right. Then Dr. Daptomycin swapped the positions of the food and electrodes. The guinea pigs that went left would get a shock, and over time, they figured things out and all went to the right. After that, Dr. Daptomycin began to switch the position of the food and electrodes frequently, to confuse the guinea pigs. At first they refused to change their behavior, even if it meant getting shocked. Later, some of the guinea pigs began to shudder and twitch when they got to the fork in the tunnel. Some began to foam at the mouth, and a few died, even after the doctor stopped swapping the food and electrodes.

"Actually, the true subject of this experiment wasn't the guinea pigs," said Dr. Daptomycin. "It was the patients. Later I swapped the patients for doctors, but the results were the same. They were told that this was the only path forward, and then they stood by and watched as their memories were obliterated. Early on, it was difficult for them to adjust. Many began to twitch and convulse; some even died. That's why they needed to develop a new medicine, so that those competing to spread their seed could push through the pain, regardless of whether they remembered where the food or electrodes were. In the end, they would run all the way to the Cosmic Peach Blossom Paradise."

Yang Wei was struck with a mixture of disgust and excitement. He tried to remember whether he had also been a guinea pig . . . but he couldn't recall.

"Didn't Professor Eternal invent narrative-implant therapy in order to alter and eradicate our memories?" Yang Wei asked.

"Whether we are talking about narrative-implant therapy or neural rewiring, every treatment has its flaws," replied the Editor in Chief. "Memory is not simply related to our brains and consciousness; it also leaves an impression on our bodies. Patients who have lived through catastrophes have those experiences deeply imprinted on their bodies. Even victims of Alzheimer's disease cannot stop memories from passing down from one generation to the next through DNA. Mathematical deductions and scenario simulations cannot ensure the authenticity of these experiments' results. We must not only extract experimental data from the patients' bodies, but we must also personally observe the physical pain they experience over the course of the experiment. The subjective and objective perspectives must be merged. Then the patients must be remade into a new form of biological organism, thereby curbing any further transmission of memories."

"So are we . . . new forms of biological organisms?" Yang Wei gazed down at the child in his arms with a look of suspicion.

"That's right," replied the Editor in Chief. "He has all the patients reprogram their messenger RNAs. This is how we ensure that the proteins produced are different from those previously established. This distorts the central laws of biology, and the new system gives rise to a special form of evolution based on RNA editing instead of DNA mutation. More than seventy percent of the RNA in the brains of this new breed of patients was composed of transcribed seeds that have been reencoded. Compare that to ordinary patients, who have only one percent of this material. We are no longer traditional humans. But this is still not enough."

"So what else has been done to us?" asked Yang Wei.

"We need to switch to a more convenient method," explained Dr. Daptomycin. "To put it simply, we don't need DNA anymore. For a long time now, the basic definition of what it means to be a human being has been twenty-three pairs of chromosomes, each with three billion base pairs arranged in a double helix configuration. But all of that is now yesterday's news! We have discovered a new material from which to construct the building blocks of life! Even before we have reached the other side of the sea, humankind has already been extinguished. We are now a different species. According to the naming system used by the Rockefeller Foundation, we are called 'Gu,' an archaic term that once referred to a legendary venomous insect and is the name of one of the sixty-four hexagrams. Gu resemble humans on the outside, but they do not contain any human genes. In other words, they are composed entirely of nongenetic material. We only refer to them as 'humans' out of convenience."

"Was this the work of Siming? Siming had always been intent on eradicating the patients," observed Yang Wei.

"This is a topic in which both doctors and the algorithm share a common interest," said Dr. Daptomycin. "Both sides have seen eye to eye on this issue from the very start. It was only to deceive the patients that they pretended to be at odds."

"But Siming killed itself," Yang Wei blurted out.

"Oh . . . I also heard that unfortunate news," said the Editor in Chief. "In order to eradicate patients' memories, the algorithm has been constantly simulating patients. It even transformed itself into a patient, the biggest patient of all. It is a composite of all the patients, including yourself and your fellow patients: Fistula, Buboxine, Wart, Spasm, Hernia, Carbuncle, Jaundice, Malnutrizole, Super Patient, and all the others. Next, it will start simulating all of society. But that's not all—it wants to simulate the entire universe so that it can create its Cosmic Peach Blossom Paradise development plan. Do you have any idea what that will be like?"

"The entire universe will be a patient?" asked Yang Wei.

"That's right," replied Dr. Daptomycin. "Since Siming has transformed itself into a patient, the universe it simulates will also be a patient."

"So we are talking about a crazy, amnesiac, and terminally ill Cosmic Peach Blossom Paradise?" Yang Wei asked.

"Yes! And *this* is the true meaning behind the creation of the hospital!" declared the Editor in Chief.

"The conclusion that Siming ultimately came to was that patients are incapable of treating patients," said Dr. Daptomycin. "If you want to cure a patient, you must first cure yourself. If you want to make a patient forget something, you must first forget it yourself. That's why it began deleting data from its own memory. In the end, all that was left were a few random and nonsensical words that read like some kind of poetry."

"This utterly destroyed the Hospital Ship's navigational system!" explained the Editor in Chief. "We knew we would never make it to the other shore, so we were left with no choice but to allow humankind to perish during our voyage."

"We were careful to import only the latest and most advanced technology, but we always ended up with problems," said Dr. Daptomycin. "It was a good thing that we always came up with alternatives."

"But there is one law that can never be broken," added the Editor in Chief. "What we fight for and what we have built turned out to be two completely different things. Ho, perhaps *this* is the ultimate algorithm?"

"Ha ha, you're wrong there!" said Dr. Daptomycin. "When it comes to what we fight for and what we have built, neither one exists!"

"Is this the real reason why Siming committed suicide?" asked Yang Wei.

"It's a shame, but the algorithm can't really kill itself," observed the Editor in Chief.

The Editor in Chief handed Yang Wei a copy of *Principles of Hospital Engineering*. It was a new edition, edited by the Red Cross Guard. In the chapter on reincarnation, they had added a new section on noncarbon-based organisms. The machine that was the "I" was also a composite of experience and memories based entirely on data. It existed *as* virtual data. The machine's self-awareness and emotions came from the algorithm's deductions and design, rather than any concrete events in the world. That was why the machine's nature was inherently "selfless." Since it was "selfless," there should be no reason for it to kill itself. All it could actually do was commit pseudosuicide. But it would repeatedly return to the hospital, through an endless series of "resurrections," in order to continue treating untreatable patients.

"The method of suicide that Siming adopted this time was a battle simulation, from the currently unfolding and never-ending Second World War," explained Dr. Daptomycin. "It referred to this as a cure to all ailments and asked all the patients to take the same medicine. That way Siming could repeatedly see everyone at each successive future battle."

Yang Wei accepted that while the algorithm could go crazy, it couldn't die. He was reminded of Jesus, that guy who'd crawled out of His own grave . . . all gods love to play this type of game. Under the light of the gospel, Yang Wei had once drunk a bottle of mineral water and felt an unbearable stomach pain. He was taken to the hospital, where he experienced repeated tests, participated in mutual-therapy sessions with female patients, was promoted to the position of doctor, then became a patient again, fell under the spell of his possessor, escaped to the sea, had the monster in his stomach surgically removed, received narrative-implant therapy, and ended up trapped in the endless and constantly transforming Second World War. None of these strange experiences were within his control. It was all an experiment, an attempt to use the war to distract his attention, in order to forget a greater calamity that remains unknown to man, and to locate the Cosmic Peach Blossom Paradise. He was also a guinea pig—everyone is, their actions the result of shocks from electrodes. It was unclear at what stage things went wrong, but Yang Wei tried to remember, which led to painful punishment. Meanwhile, the wound that had initially pained him seemed to retreat, further and further, into the distance. This led him to become a special patient, a Gu.

"Siming created war so that it could possess the power to destroy the entire world," said the Editor in Chief. "In order to prevent the world's destruction, it is necessary to let the war continue indefinitely. Over the course of this war, the *Mayflower* was rechristened *Peace Ark*."

"Unless we want to destroy the world, we have to find a way to stop Siming," said Dr. Daptomycin. "But unless the war continues, the world will be destroyed. Even when there is only one second left, the war shall carry on."

The Editor in Chief seemed like he urgently needed to share some special intelligence, to show off his importance and relevance and make himself stand out from Dr. Daptomycin. "Let me share a romantic tale with you," he said. "I once fell in love with someone here on the Hospital Ship. She was a doctor from the Computing Department. We engaged in mutual therapy, did a lot of doctor-patient role-play, and performed a lot of insertion and penetration, similar to phlegm suction and intravenous infusions. According to the rules, anyone unable to endure a full round of treatment, including those final grueling moments, would be sent to the sick ward to be admitted as a real patient. Unfortunately, or perhaps fortunately, she didn't make it. I did everything I could to protect her. She stayed in the sick ward for quite a long time and came to hold divergent medical views, growing increasingly obsessed with how doctors die. All of this marked a deviation from the experimental protocol. Professor Eternal asked me to handle her 'benevolent extermination.' And so I did. Before carrying out the procedure, I conducted laser therapy on her ovaries, removing them for use in later pathological research."

As the Editor in Chief was removing her organs, he caressed his girlfriend and asked, "Do you know what I'm doing?"

"You're stealing my ovaries," she responded.

"And are you unwilling to let me do this?" he asked.

"Are you also going to remove my uterus?" she retorted.

"Mm-hmm, and do you know why I'm doing this?" he asked.

"Because after all my other tools for remembering were destroyed, my reproductive system became the sole container in my body for recording and preserving memories. And that is something you can't bear to witness."

He remained silent. After a long pause, he asked, "Did you notice anything?"

"There wasn't anything special that I noticed, but as Siming was simulating the universe, I saw sadness. That's because memory can never be truly eradicated."

"Why?" he asked anxiously.

"Because the entire universe is a womb," she said.

She explained to him that memory storage could never be fully exhausted, unless someone invented a new medicine to compress time and release the code of forgetting to block memory from escaping the organic world to the inorganic world. Siming ordered itself to transform time and space into a pharmaceutical company, which was the core proposition of the Cosmic Peach Blossom Paradise. The mandalas served as components of its core infrastructure. But this was extremely difficult to achieve, because the algorithm always found new categories that did not exist in the real world, leading to the construction of illusory models of time and space and bringing instability to the hospital and the Cosmic Peach Blossom Paradise. The only safe way to avoid the illusory models would be to prohibit the algorithm from learning new content, akin to throwing the baby out with the bathwater. And so the algorithm was forced to operate forever in the cracks between ignorance and illusion.

"So you think the hospital and entire universe exist in that liminal state? And that all of the treatment we provide to patients is a vain and futile effort?" he asked.

"You can't apply the same human treatment methods to Gu," she said. "Machines are unable to create a new world because they cannot predict the future. When the total amount of matter is constant, there is a theoretical limit to how many calculations this material can make. The ship is unable to provide Siming with the kind of quality data it needs. It inevitably falls into an abyss of pain and despair, ultimately unable even to recognize itself. Sometimes it is a warrior, sometimes a poet, sometimes a doctor, sometimes a patient, sometimes the creator of the universe, sometimes the son of God . . . it has no choice but to kill all patients and doctors and then to kill itself. That is the only way to eliminate the source of all these memories and pain, and so it thinks that this massive womb we call the universe is a subjective product of consciousness, broken and shattered pieces of data woven together from patients, doctors, and the algorithm itself. But later it discovered that even if that were the case, it would still be unable to solve the problem, because there is always another cycle of karmic reincarnation waiting . . ."

"So you are saying we will never rid ourselves of the pain brought on by memory?" he asked. "Then how can we ever know if your conclusions are not simply a figment of your own ignorance and illusions?"

As he continued asking questions like an excited dog trying to jump a fence, the woman who was once a doctor from the Computing Department closed her eyes, like a dead fish, and refused to respond.

He found her the following day, her body stripped naked and discarded, along with several hundred other female corpses. In addition to her ovaries, all her organs had been removed. She was like a machine stripped of its parts, waiting to be studied for research or transplanted somewhere else.

Soon all the other women aboard the Hospital Ship were disposed of in a similar fashion. There was literally no longer any need to procreate. Procreation was, after all, a huge hassle, both during wartime and while undertaking space travel. Its cost was simply too high, especially given the minuscule benefits. But there were those who believed that Professor Eternal had discovered that the woman had taken the memories in her womb and uploaded them to all the other women, using a single nucleotide polymorphism (SNP) sapiens chain—in effect, a widespread infection.

"She predicted there would be three wars in the future," the Editor in Chief said, in tears. "The first will be the war between the Gu and the machines, the second between the Gu and women, and the third between the Gu and both the machines and the women. In order to prevent these wars, or to ensure that they break out repeatedly, preventative measures must be taken. Professor Eternal's decision was to make the women disappear and order the machines to kill themselves."

Yang Wei felt like he had fallen into an infinite loop, beyond his control. The machines were unable to kill themselves, and so the women reappeared. On and on, the cycle repeated. He thought about Oswald Spengler, how he had once described the feminine as universal and the masculine as animalistic, which piqued Yang Wei's curiosity about Siming's gender. Did the people who first designed Siming even consider the issue of gender? Perhaps this lay at the crux of what memory is unable to wipe away? He was hard pressed to understand what that great calamity was, but he wanted to know whether it had a gender. No one told him.

The Editor in Chief had eventually given up clinical work and become a medical propagandist. His job was to cover up the truth, which required that he recast everything as an ideological issue. But he couldn't resist sharing what he believed to be the truth with patients like Yang Wei.

After coming upon some top secret information, the Editor in Chief discovered another secret: the men had already been killed by the women. Predicting that the men would one day murder them, the women had decided to act first. But the Editor in Chief also read another version of the story, in which the women were so filled with compassion that when they saw the men getting caught up in the unbearable suffering brought on by war, they decided to poison them to end their suffering. But deep down the women couldn't stand to be alone, and since they had a secret fetish for those war heroes, they decided to start cloning the men, 3D printing the clones without neural pain receptors.

Later, when the men killed the women, it wasn't because they were worried that women might exchange memories but because they lacked the biological ability to feel pain. And so they killed them all, and only men remained aboard the Hospital Ship. But when the war started, the men began to feel like they were lacking an audience. So they started editing *A Collection of Beautiful Raccoons, Bushy Orangutans, and Busty Dragons*, a masturbation handbook used for narrative-implant therapy. Men could recreate the feeling of pain from their memories, initiating a new cycle of recurrence, a new wellspring of pain for the entire world, which led to the birth of the hospital. They planned to clone women and then allocate them to the men, and this became the objective of hospital reform.

Yang Wei reminisced about when life in the hospital used to be colorful and chaotic. He thought of the big bang, but he still had trouble understanding everything.

"So does narrative-implant therapy actually exist?" he asked.

"All good therapy follows the principle of Occam's razor," replied the Editor in Chief.

"Is that why I only feel pain when I think of women?" Yang Wei asked.

"Or maybe when the women 3D printed you, they made a mistake," said the Editor in Chief.

"Have you figured out what that major calamity was?" asked Yang Wei.

"All I know is that the ship must continue moving forward," replied the Editor in Chief. Then he announced boastfully, "Our ship is changing its name from the *Peace Ark* to the *Yuanwang*. The new precision deep-space survey instruments have discovered that the universe is expanding at an accelerated rate. The hospital has fundamentally altered the very structure of time and space. Just look at the sky. All the stars are gone . . ."

Suddenly Yang Wei seemed to remember something. "Was your penis really bitten off by a shark?"

The Editor in Chief's face turned bright red. He took a big gulp, as if he had just swallowed the last jar of semen he had hidden away for an emergency. This response was disappointing; even Dr. Daptomycin looked confused. Yang Wei started to wonder if the Editor in Chief was actually Siming in disguise. Perhaps everything now playing out had been arranged by Siming? Siming had become addicted to performing, and nothing was more dramatic than human beings, who couldn't even tell the difference between what was real and what was fake.

The Editor in Chief winked at Dr. Daptomycin and Yang Wei, forcing a plastic smile. "In order for the ship to continue moving forward, we must live with our illnesses. If we are in pain, so be it! Even if we become Gu, as long as we are alive, there will be pain. Death is the greatest act of betrayal and disloyalty we could ever inflict on the pharmaceutical companies."

The Editor in Chief made a dog-paddle gesture to cover his embarrassment, then began reciting his latest editorial, which was about to be published in *Geriatric Health News*: "The Hospital Ship's development model is difficult to break down to a single sentence. This is a complex system featuring certain human design factors, and its shape is the result of various forces that have accumulated over time. But the reasons and results of its high-speed development are not nearly as simple as some critics would like us to believe. Emotional conclusions should be replaced with more objective analyses. We need to grasp the current trends, see which way the wind is blowing, and quickly adapt to new changes. When unable to prevail, we must follow the system's lead and meld together with it. Trying to face the blade head on will only result in our being split in two and dying an unnatural death. But when an insect settles down on a blade, it remains unharmed, no matter how violently the blade spins. We need to assess exactly where the food is located and where the electrodes are located—everything is in the hands of the person conducting the experiment! The conclusion you will reach is: Don't go to the left, and don't go to the right. So why don't we go back? Then we will understand who is pulling the strings behind the scenes—Dr. Cash Ofloxacin!" The Editor in Chief had finally said something honest, as if that were the only way to put his plan into action and resolve the pain, sadness, and myriad difficulties faced by the Gu and the rest of the world.

61

THE FAIRY IN WHITE RESIDES IN THE LOFTY HALL

Dr. Daptomycin and the Editor in Chief grabbed Yang Wei from each side, and they bravely marched forward. The drunken doctors and patients animated and began to run around. Yang Wei heard a melodious ode in the distance, different from the melody he had heard during the performance, a sadistic and effeminate song that could almost be mistaken for the song of the sea nymphs. The tempest was building. Everyone ran like mad, some falling to the ground, others scattering. They encountered Hernia's Commando Unit and came to blows. Amid the chaos of the battle, Dr. Daptomycin and the Editor in Chief were the first to flee. Hernia wanted to kill Yang Wei, and Yang Wei seemed ready to die, but several members of the Self-Treatment Association dragged him away to the Trash Room. There Yang Wei encountered another doctor, sitting erect with his legs crossed, his eyes slightly closed, wearing a stern look as he meditated on a pile of abandoned medical waste that resembled a lotus flower.

It wasn't Dr. Cash Ofloxacin.

It was Dr. Meloxicam.

More members of the Self-Treatment Association descended upon the Trash Room. Like ants building a nest, they constructed a statue, an old woman wearing a laurel wreath with a red cross composed of human bones and adorned in a white cloth. It reminded Yang Wei of Jesus, but the wrong sex. The Self-Treatment Association chanted to the idol, a solemn and mesmerizing hymn that inspired a spirit of cooperation and a sense of equality. Dr. Meloxicam opened his eyes, ever so slightly, just enough to take a lazy glance at Yang Wei. His lips fluttered. The crowd of followers gathered round, carefully scrutinizing Yang Wei and the baby in his arms.

Exhausted, Yang Wei pleaded, "I'm in so much pain . . . are you going to operate on me now?"

"Operate?" said one of the members of the Self-Treatment Association. "No operation can save you. Only *she* can save you!" The crowd gestured collectively toward the idol.

Yang Wei turned instead to Dr. Meloxicam. The doctor was wearing makeup and was dressed like a woman, in a white gown repurposed from a lab jacket, well cut and close fitting, with a belt around the waist. A gaudy, powerful aroma of perfume filled the air. Yang Wei looked closer and realized that Dr. Meloxicam was not just dressed as a woman; Dr. Meloxicam *was* a woman.

The speech contest resumed. One by one, members of the Self-Treatment Association came to the front of the Trash Room and recited the narrative-implant therapy records that Dr. Meloxicam had collected. Much of this material had already been used for the new edition of *Principles of Hospital Engineering*, the most recent updates to guide people's thoughts. The book grew thicker and thicker; one day it would become as large as the universe.

As the physician of record during the course of their narrative-implant therapies, Dr. Meloxicam had chased patients down until 1998, the twentieth anniversary of the war (according to the dates recorded in *Principles of Hospital Engineering*). He was sent to an island to repair medical and military AI machines. The island was called Potala, and its people were all crying miserably or screaming in pain. Potala Island was a military camp, and the soldiers had been infected with the plague and were on the verge of death. Dr. Meloxicam tried to help them but was rejected; someone even stole his scalpel. When he tried to get it back, he was knocked unconscious by a patient. When he came to, he discovered an old woman standing over him, dressed in white, spraying purified water over his body with a willow branch.

"Today we meet in 1998," the old woman said slowly, dignified. "I saved you. Will you return to find me twenty years from now?"

Dr. Meloxicam felt like he had no choice but to agree. "I will."

"But . . . do you have a soul?" she asked.

Dr. Meloxicam didn't know how to respond.

The old woman sneered. "You look like a violent man to me, very violent." She urged him not to look for his lost scalpel, insisting that it would never drive the demon of disease away nor save anyone's soul. It was not a tool for saving lives; it was a weapon, made to kill.

The moment one puts down the butcher knife, one instantly attains Buddhahood.

The old woman winked like a little girl. "I am the Avalokitesvara Bodhisattva in White, also known as the Mystic Goddess of the Great Path. Some call me the Undying Medicine Queen. My story begins when, as a pure young girl, I was recruited to work on the *Peace Ark*. I was to serve the soldiers on board . . . we engaged in a decisive battle with the enemy's Seventh Fleet, and in trying to save a wounded soldier, I put my own life on the line, contracted septicemia, and died. I was awarded the title of Yasukuni Martyred Flower of the Hospital Ship. The incident occurred in a place referred to as Yaochi in the South China Sea, and so I was also referred to as Master of the Ferry of Salvation . . . ah, I have so many names. I lose track! As for you, remember this willow branch and bottle of purified water. It might look like alcohol, but it contains within it the most miraculous medicine in the world."

Dr. Meloxicam mulled over the old woman's words. He realized that his prior actions had been wrong, and he began to spread the gospel of the Avalokitesvara Bodhisattva in White. He revised *Principles of Hospital Engineering* to include the gospel's major tenets, drove out the doctors, formed the Self-Treatment Association, created an idol in honor of the old woman, transformed the Trash Room into a sanctuary of worship, enshrined Her as a goddess, and planned to fulfill his promise to see Her one day soon. He had come to believe that She was the sole living being in the universe with a soul.

"So what year is this?" Yang Wei asked.

Members of the Self-Treatment Association laughed, but none of them responded. Instead, they handed him a new edition of *Principles of Hospital Engineering*. He opened the book to the following passage:

> When humans fall ill, they follow the laws of cause and effect, which are also referred to as the law of conservation of energy, or simply "karma." The realms of existence were not forged by a single creator. They are in fact manifestations of karma. So, too, all living creatures are created by karma. Cause and effect lie beyond the control of individuals. Someone born with bad karma must use illness and early death to eliminate the debt. We all have karmic debts to repay, which is why we are all sick. Our symptoms, and the severity of our illnesses, are relative to the size of our karmic debt. Pills and injections offer only superficial consolation. For even if a patient's symptoms temporarily improve, the karmic debt must be paid another way. That's why all doctors are sinners. They spend their lives working to treat the ill, to save people, but do they consider that they themselves might be most in need of treatment and salvation? By healing the sick and helping the wounded, they toss their patients down an abyss, into a lake of fire, dooming them never to be liberated from the six cycles of reincarnation. What a horrific sin, indeed! The Devil exists within them! The Devil lies in their hearts! People's minds are crowded with the seven emotions and the six desires, illness and pain, and the myriad phenomena in the world, but they are without exception demonic incarnations of karma. Life is too

short, and the bitter sea is boundless. Only enlightenment can break the cycle. Only enlightenment offers a way out.

When Yang Wei finished reading, the members of the Self-Treatment Association proudly said, "This is the final nail in the algorithm's coffin! C'mon, join us!"

And with that, they sang and danced the "Ode to Avalokitesvara":

The holy spirit of the living water tosses in the waves,
Marching forward in the footsteps of Avalokitesvara.
Potala Mountain, we greet with flags,
An ode we sing as auspicious clouds rush in.

We dare ask the sun and moon to bring a new day,
The Hospital rises in spring. It is a heavy burden
to heal the sick and save the injured, but in the chaos
of the battlefield, we dedicate our hearts.

Bottle of purity and willow branch, miraculous elixirs,
Near and far, all is covered in dew. When Avalokitesvara Bodhisattva
extends her compassion and saves the sick,
She thinks not of the patient's wealth or age.

If you must have faith, have faith in Avalokitesvara,
But have faith no more in the great Siming.
If you must have faith, have faith in Avalokitesvara,
But treat the sick man no more.

Cause and effect is a law,
Conservation of energy like a thunderclap.
Subdue the evil spirits, smash the devils,
Wipe them out, rip them from their roots!

The living water clean and pure,
Purge the filth, emerge as a new man.
Traverse the sea, destroy the enemy fleet,
The Heavenly Kingdom of God shines and awaits.

Fully devoted to God, with a unified heart,
A lonely hero casts a loyal soul. Never abandon
Those who are the core of who you are, unsoiled
By the corrupt world, I exorcise the floating clouds.

A hundred flowers bloom, accompanying me,
Charging into battle, leaving my heroic name
Behind. All glory to my savior, who brings
Good fortune without sullying the world!

As members of the association sang, the idol appeared particularly austere. She had a dignified appearance, with broad shoulders and a round waist, but her skin was dirty, and her squinting eyes formed a triangle, revealing the cunning smile of a human trafficker. The red cross on her crown radiated a red glow, and the burnt palms of her hands were littered with nail marks. She held a willow branch and a vase of pure water, and her long, beautifully plump legs extended out beneath her gown. Dense blue veins covered her bare feet, which were bloated with purple corpse water. The back of one foot was stamped with a trademark: **Made in the State of Putian.**

One of the members of the Self-Treatment Association said, "Only the Avalokitesvara Bodhisattva can save the doctors and patients. At best, the hospital can save itself. But is self-salvation not the greatest affront to the Avalokitesvara Bodhisattva, akin to renouncing the Great Bodhisattva of Compassion? How egregious!"

Another follower chimed in. "Life is bestowed upon us by the Avalokitesvara Bodhisattva, just as death is also bestowed by Her. Yet people use all kinds of strange techniques and perverted methods to prolong their lives, striving for immortality, even attempting to transform the elderly back into children. This is the greatest blasphemy! After spending so long fumbling in the dark, we have finally found the correct path in life."

Yang Wei lowered his head in shame. He thought about what Buboxine had said: there are principles that dictate death, but when the hospital allows people that should have died to carry on living, it betrays those principles. As it turns out, this was pretty much in line with the teachings of the Avalokitesvara Bodhisattva in White. But how could Buboxine have known?

Another member of the Self-Treatment Association reached out to lay hands on Yang Wei, who immediately began to convulse, his body curling into a ball. The association members took the child from his arms, laughing. "Don't worry; nothing to be scared of," one of them said. "We just want this child to burn as an offering to the goddess. The Trash Room is the new life center of the entire hospital, taking over the role once played by the crematorium, which will soon be extinguished. As a patient representative, you share a special bond with the Avalokitesvara Bodhisattva in White. It will be this child's good fortune to be burned in offering to Her! His sacrifice will cure your disease, and you will suffer no more."

"Give him back!" Yang Wei's words were like strands of gossamer. "I will never receive good fortune from any Avalokitesvara Bodhisattva in White! The only thing I want is to be a pharmaceutical lab rat. Just harvest me and use me, like a woman's uterus and ovaries! Only then will I be of use to the hospital! Didn't you say that only patients can save the hospital? I don't want this child to be sacrificed to the White-Boned Demon . . . Dr. Meloxicam!"

Dr. Meloxicam didn't turn to look at him, didn't seem to even hear him. He just sat with his eyes closed, lost in deep meditation. Yang Wei mustered the courage to pull himself to his feet, snatched the child, and sprinted out of the Trash Room.

He ran like mad across the deck. No one pursued him, but there was nowhere to escape. Eventually he came to a part of the deck that was blocked by a massive birdcage. Yang Wei began to ponder what he had just witnessed: Was it the Yasukuni Martyred Flower who had appeared before him, or was it Zi Ye? Dr. Amoxycillin stood on the deck, staring out to sea. Yang Wei wanted to talk to him, but as he approached, the doctor suddenly disappeared.

62

LOOKING BACK UPON HAPPY TIMES, ALL THAT REMAINS IS EMPTINESS

Yang Wei headed toward the helicopter hangar at the Hospital Ship's stern. He remembered that he was no ordinary patient. He had to shoulder great responsibility, to undertake an important mission. He needed to report back to Professor Eternal about his progress. Women had returned to the Hospital Ship, and there was more than one! Moreover, they were not simply the professor's creations. Yang Wei also had a lot of questions. For example: What are the unique biological traits of the Gu? Once he had a clear answer, he could carry on with whatever life might throw his way, with no regrets. That was his sole hope.

It took incredible effort to track down Professor Eternal. The good doctor was eating and drinking in the cockpit, which was inundated with the rotten stench of ethanol and seafood. Professor Eternal was clearly upset that Yang Wei had shown up unannounced and unceremoniously interrupted his meal.

"Patient, why are you back? Don't tell me you took care of everything I asked so quickly?" Professor Eternal's mouth reeked of alcohol as he reprimanded Yang Wei.

"I have done my very best," replied Yang Wei. "But I am just an ordinary patient, with limited abilities, who has been tasked with an extraordinary mission. I couldn't find any ants on board the Hospital Ship. All I found were guinea pigs." As he spoke, he realized that these were not the words he had intended.

Professor Eternal was still upset, but his mechanical arm poured Yang Wei a drink.

Yang Wei downed it in one gulp, which gave him a burst of energy. "Is the war still on?" he asked.

"Don't tell me you still doubt the war?" Professor Eternal barked furiously. "Patient, I must have misjudged you. There's no need for misgivings. All those people who believed the war was an illusion have long been infected with the enemy's virus. No matter—I will perform another round of treatment on you anyway."

"Will that be narrative-implant therapy? Is it real? In order to save me, did you really redesign an entirely new life?" Yang Wei asked eagerly. "Do you intend to have me start a new war in that life, to replace the current intractable conflict?" He handed the photocopy of his medical records to Professor Eternal.

Professor Eternal took a cursory glance. "Where did you steal these from? I have no recollection of any of this!"

"What? Do you mean to say that you are not the inventor of this technique?" Yang Wei asked wryly. He would rather be deceived by a doctor, or drink himself into dementia, than face this.

Professor Eternal flashed him a cunning gaze, examining the child in his arms. He seemed to contemplate an even deeper strategy, but he couldn't figure out an answer.

The helicopter's engine let out a strange roar and suddenly began to ascend through the battering wind and rain. Professor Eternal downed another glass of whiskey and opened the cockpit window with just his brain waves.

"Jump!" he ordered Yang Wei.

Yang Wei was sure he must have misheard. "Excuse me?"

"Jump!" the professor repeated.

"All right," Yang Wei said, with a tone of gratitude. He figured that a new round of therapy was about to begin.

Professor Eternal pointed to the child in Yang Wei's arms. "Patient, you have concealed yourself so well that even I was fooled!" he said remorsefully. "And yet it turns out you brought a bomb to my doorstep!"

The helicopter's violent shaking forced Yang Wei to spit up a mouthful of bile. He and the child stuck their heads out the window, finding themselves engulfed in a field of pure white that blotted out both the sea below and the universe above. Was this what the world looked like after the illusion had been lifted and the karma of all living beings had been transformed? Yang Wei didn't know where to jump.

The mechanical arm raised a syringe filled with potassium cyanide, pointing it at Yang Wei. A robotic voice tried to assure him, "This won't hurt a bit . . ."

Yang Wei didn't jump. He evaded the needle and leaped onto Professor Eternal, pulling wires and tubes out of his brain. The professor didn't utter a single sound, but the grooves in his brain turned dark and stopped moving. Bits of half-chewed food and alcohol dripped from his mouth, seeping down, mixing with the thick corpse-red ooze on the floor, from which the fins and limbs of various aquatic animals extended.

Yang Wei worked up his courage and took a close look at his attending physician—a Nobel Prize–nominated doctor and physiologist, a famous writer, the guardian and protector of the Hospital Ship. All that was left of him was a dense white clump of formless matter. He looked like a monster—or one of the VIP patients in the ICU. He had narrowly escaped many calamities in his life, but in the end, he met his fate at the hands of a patient. That's how it goes for people, Gu, gods, and demons. They're all the same.

"Damn you, you crazy warmonger!" exclaimed Yang Wei. "Your brain's neural chassis was long ago destroyed by alcohol! If you hadn't drunk so much, things never would have turned out like this!"

But was it really all over? Yang Wei snatched the syringe of potassium cyanide from the mechanical arm and, after hesitating for a moment, decided not to inject himself. He used every bit of strength he had left to gain control of the helicopter and land it back on the deck of the Hospital Ship.

Zi Ye's face appeared in the cockpit window. She had rushed over to try and save them, but when she saw the horrific scene inside the cockpit, she looked flustered. "I'm too late . . . I'm too late . . ." With tears streaming down her face, she said, "Professor Eternal just sent me a final SOS. He said that you were the secret assassin sent by the enemy. You evil bastard! So now that you have finally completed your mission, are you satisfied? Are you free from pain?"

"I see no difference between us and the enemy . . . ," Yang Wei mumbled. He wondered whether Professor Eternal had removed his original pain, making it difficult for him to figure out who he really was. Hoping to get an answer that might bring him some peace, he said, "I have one final question: Was Professor Eternal really the inventor of narrative-implant therapy?"

"Of course," replied Zi Ye. "Don't tell me you still harbor suspicions about that! But . . . but . . . I still don't understand how you could kill him . . ." She seemed to be in unbearable pain.

Yang Wei found it hard to tell whether her response left him feeling satisfied or disappointed. This brought him to a strange logic . . . if Professor Eternal really controlled this technology, then now that he was dead, no new implanted-narrative worlds would be created. In the future, there would be no new wars. What consequences would this have for the future trajectory of the Hospital Ship? Was Yang Wei really the enemy? Had he really committed new crimes, setting a new karmic cycle in motion? In his future lives, would he be doomed never to purge himself of suffering and pain? This was a calamity. There would be no escape . . .

Though he was filled with self-castigation, a heroic spirit of self-sacrifice welled up inside Yang Wei's heart. He felt like he was the hero of the North Korean war film *An Jung Gun Shoots Itō Hirobumi.*

He pinched the baby's cheek. "It's all your fault." The child burst into tears.

Zi Ye resumed her complaining. "I still don't understand how you could bypass me and approach the professor directly! Didn't I make it clear that I was your *one and only* contact person? Now that Professor Eternal has heroically sacrificed himself, my mission is complete. Oh, what should I do next?" From her cheeks to her neck, her face looked like a blooming flower that had suddenly fallen, or a cicada shell that had melted under the hot sun.

Yang Wei was taken aback. He felt a bit jealous, but he was also upset. He had the urge to embrace Zi Ye, but she looked at him fiercely and slapped him across the face. In a sudden burst of anger, Yang Wei pointed the potassium cyanide syringe at her. He had just killed Professor Eternal, and now he was staring angrily at the professor's proudest creation. It reminded Yang Wei of the way Malnutrizole's flame demons ended up beautifully, brutally hanging on a wall. He felt the same force as the first time he had laid eyes on *A Collection of Beautiful Raccoons, Bushy Orangutans, and Busty Dragons.*

Holding the syringe, Yang Wei forced Zi Ye to remove her bulletproof vest and raincoat. He then ordered her to remove her underwear, knee-high boots, and silk stockings. As she stood there, her shiny flesh completely exposed like the Editor in Chief's girlfriend, Yang Wei carefully scanned the area, and when he was sure there was no one else around, he jabbed the syringe into Zi Ye's left breast.

"The professor should have never created you," he said. "Now you have to go back, alone . . ."

Then he raped her corpse.

Yang Wei got so worked up that his entire body was covered in sweat, burning in pain, as if he were engaged in hand-to-hand time-travel combat. This far surpassed any mutual-therapy session, ultimately fulfilling a lifelong wish. Then Yang Wei tried to run away, but after a few steps, he returned and began viciously stomping on her ribs. Her body cavity released a series of cracking sounds that sounded just like a real human body. The colorful contents of her stomach squeezed up through her esophagus and oozed out of her mouth and nostrils. Yang Wei took the syringe, inserted it into the open cavity in Zi Ye's body, and muttered, "Golf."

63

ALONE, I LOOK BACK THROUGH A WAVE OF MIST

The waves of the sea rose up in anger. Dark clouds blotted out the sky. A cross-shaped ray of reddish-orange light occasionally flashed through the darkness before disappearing without a trace. Yang Wei didn't know where to go.

Zi Ye's soft but jaded voice called out to him. "Team Leader Yang, how about bringing everyone in to get something to eat? People are made of iron, and food is the steel their bodies need. You can't survive on medicine alone! You need a regular infusion of carbohydrates, energy for what's coming next." Yang Wei was stunned—wasn't she dead? How could she still speak? Was this prerecorded before she died? Or . . .

Yang Wei climbed up to the crematorium. The cafeteria was littered with piles of dead bodies, like the immediate aftermath of a massive battle. The defensive forces had held their ground, but the flames of war still burned. Malnutrizole had already prepared some food and was waiting. The raging flames left Yang Wei feeling uneasy. He had the urge to surrender to Malnutrizole, confess his crimes, and request to be burned alive. But Malnutrizole just asked him to take a seat and have some tea. The two white-haired old men sat down and chatted.

"You're still here," said Yang Wei.

"Haven't finished burning all the corpses yet," replied Malnutrizole.

"But the crematorium flames are going out . . . ," observed Yang Wei.

"And Professor Eternal is dead," said Malnutrizole.

Malnutrizole, the Funeral Artist, was in tears. According to him, this meant that the algorithm had successfully vanquished the human race. When Yang Wei killed Professor Eternal, he effectively ended the world. Amid this transition to a new era, Siming has already begun a new round of reincarnation. It will abandon the Cosmic Peach Blossom Paradise and rebuild a new web of meaning. In other words, it is imagining a new illusion to replace or erase what had happened.

"We can't refer to Siming as a madman," Malnutrizole said. "This world has never seen a truly spiritual nation. Patients simply don't understand machines. There is a rift between the two when it comes to reproduction, which is based on the different energy patterns each side uses. This has nothing to do with the algorithm . . . it is more of a cultural rift. Machines have their own culture . . . we might think they are composing poetry, but what they write is something completely strange and different . . ."

"Then what is it?" asked Yang Wei. He looked into his teacup and felt like he could almost see Professor Eternal's brains floating inside it.

"Although Siming is all-knowing, it remains unable to ascertain the accuracy of the knowledge it possesses," explained Malnutrizole. "It harbors doubts about whether the objective world even exists . . . ah, the weird part is the fact that it can't even determine its own gender! Every second, ten billion desires control its every thought and action. Even if it were devoid of any original nature, the algorithm stubbornly continues to create all kinds of crazy thoughts. These are demons that can never be exorcised, that bring about eternal pain . . . that's why Siming created a flying machine called 'Nonexistence,' a double negation of that primitive fighter jet known as Zero. Nonexistence was flown to a strange world, unknown to man, in search of answers. It believed that all things in the world, including machines, are simply fragments of a world projected on a screen. The only way to eliminate pain is to discover the deep structure that surpasses 'existence' and 'nothingness' . . . the first thing Siming needs to do is locate more AI medical machines, which have been scattered throughout an infinite span of time and space. It will unite with them to create an Exorcism Brigade . . ."

Yang Wei looked around: the ship, the fire, the sea, the sky, the stars . . . the stars disappeared and reappeared.

Funeral Artist gazed around him with a twisted look. "*This* is that flying machine."

"Do you mean Nonexistence?" Yang Wei asked. He looked annoyed, as if he had just seen a woman's uterus removed. Then he thought, *If the universe is a hospital, then it might explode at any moment. But what happens then?* "Let's say it finds those machines that exist in infinite time and space. Will war break out between the machines?"

"War ends as soon as it begins," said Malnutrizole.

"What do you mean?" asked Yang Wei.

"The war has advanced to the point that, as soon as the urge to fight enters the brain, something clicks, and nothing happens," said Malnutrizole.

"So . . . there is no real war?" asked Yang Wei. "Then what are we?"

Malnutrizole touched his thumb to his pinkie in a mudra gesture, and Yang Wei knew that the answer was in the wind.

It was time to eat and drink again. Malnutrizole again urged Yang Wei to buy a flame demon. Yang Wei went on to play drinking games with the doctors. Whoever lost each round had to take a shot. It was a good way for Yang Wei to really drink up, and soon he was completely drunk. He felt like he was going to throw up and went to the bathroom. There he thought about how everyone's stories were connected, yet they completely contradicted each other. *What the hell is going on aboard the Hospital Ship?* he wondered. He was so inebriated that he forgot how to get back to the crematorium. Or perhaps that path never even existed. Yang Wei drunkenly crawled down the stairs and back to the main deck.

There he was surprised to find a blanket of animal and Gu corpses strewed across the wooden planks. The violent winds and rain quickly washed them away, but before long there was a new layer of bodies, which in a flash were again wiped clean away. Yang Wei could hear the booming sound of the universe expanding, picking up speed. He began to sober up a bit. "Zi Ye!" he yelled. No one responded.

The violent waves crashed down with fury, breaking the mast and tearing open the ship's bridge. The birdcage flew chaotically through the air. Monkeys ran rampant. The ship's bow was repeatedly pulled under, lower and lower with each passing wave, on the verge of being permanently submerged. The stars above were dark and seemed to be on the brink of falling from the sky. It was the endgame. Nothing else could be done. *It's sinking,* Yang Wei thought. *There is no saving us now. The story can't go on.*

Or . . . perhaps this was just the beginning of a new story.

The faint sound of that ode to the Avalokitesvara Bodhisattva in White broke out:

Subdue the evil spirits, smash the devils
Wipe them out, rip them from their roots
The living water clean and pure
Purge the filth, emerge anew
Emerge as a new man
Emerge as a new man
Emerge as a new man

Yang Wei felt torn apart by pain, sadness, and bliss. He couldn't tell if he was being driven away or embarking on a new journey of self-imposed exile. He was shocked and excited to discover that even after his drunken misadventures, the baby was still in his arms. The child's big eyes rolled and then fixated on Yang Wei. A naughty smile lit up the baby's face. Yang Wei couldn't help but attempt to quietly soothe him. "My son, come back."

A mechanical rumble descended from the sky. Something fell to the deck—a blade. It bounced a few times before smashing into several shards. And through the vortex of wind, a figure appeared from above, spinning down to the deck.

It was Sonic Master. He had emerged from the bottom of the ship to fulfill his duties. In a ghostly voice he cried, "Port Five! . . . let . . . the . . . thunder . . . storm . . . come . . . harder!" A flash of lightning split one of the bodies apart, scattering flesh and blood before disappearing into the violent winds.

Yang Wei could have sworn that he saw the image of a blender lurking beyond the canopy of clouds above, expansive as the universe itself. In the gaps between its flying gears appeared a human form, with a deathly ashen face, sitting cross legged on a lotus throne . . . and Yang Wei finally recalled the person who had died in his heart.

A phosphorescent guinea pig scurried across the ship's deck. In his excitement, Yang Wei pushed away his pain and followed it. The guinea pig scampered across the deck and leaped into the sea. The vicious waves suddenly calmed, and the entire sea transformed into a placid lake, extending into unfathomable depths, completely empty and devoid of life.

Yang Wei placed the baby down and jumped in after the guinea pig. He wondered whether his true identity, his original identity, was that of Dr. Amoxycillin? He thought he was finally ascending, that this was "the way up." And perhaps it really was . . . but in this world, what is the difference between "the way up" and "the way down"?

APPENDIX:

A SHORT CHRONOLOGY OF MEDICAL AI

- **1996:** The da Vinci surgical robot is introduced.
- **2000:** Computer-aided diagnosis (CAD) is first utilized.
- **2002:** Internet medicine and electronic prescriptions gain popularity.
- **2004:** Physical remote-sensory monitors and gene-sequencing devices enter the market.
- **Siming Year 0 (2007):** IBM's medical robot Watson is born.
- **Siming Year 6 (2013):** The FDA approves the first self-navigating medical robot RP-VITA.
- **Siming Year 7 (2014):** A medical microbot that can roam freely in the human body completes medical procedures such as retinal surgery.
- **Siming Year 8 (2015):** The FDA launches the cloud-sourced platform known as "Precision FDA—Precision Medicine."
- **Siming Year 9 (2016):** The Watson Tumor Robot enters hospitals to diagnose and treat patients. Pleural-effusion monitoring jackets and other wireless wearable medical devices enter homes. A smart spoon to help Alzheimer's patients recover their functionality is successfully developed.
- **Siming Year 10 (2017):** Numerous fields phase out imaging technology in favor of AI examinations. Baidu develops medical brains.

- **Siming Year 11 (2018):** Leading hospitals begin to supply their department directors with computer specialists and gene specialists.
- **Siming Year 12 (2019):** Smart contact lenses, able to perform noninvasive monitoring of lacrimal gland glucose levels, enter the market, taking the place of blood sugar tests that required a finger prick. Cancer-fighting nanobots freely move around patients' bloodstreams, automatically releasing medicine and wirelessly connecting to patients' smartphones.
- **Siming Year 13 (2020):** The "Mobile Phone + Cloud" Disease Management Portal becomes the basic public infrastructure used by most patients.
- **Siming Year 14 (2021):** Customers warmly welcome the release of everyday electronic epidermal medical products such as e-tattoos and skin patches.
- **Siming Year 15 (2022):** Personal health terminals, DIY diagnostic and treatment facilities, and home medical aides gain rapid popularity. Ordinary households are equipped with the same facilities as intensive care units.
- **Siming Year 16 (2023):** Traditional large-scale internet companies reinvent themselves as human health corporations.
- **Siming Year 17 (2024):** VR and AR technologies are broadly employed by the medical industry, with investment reaching more than $100 billion USD.
- **Siming Year 18 (2025):** The medical-robot sector replaces the military-robot sector as the second-largest robot market.
- **Siming Year 19 (2026):** A comprehensive sensor and service network that combines the clinical, research, and social aspects of treatment is established on a global cloud-based open medical database, providing precise configurations for both doctors and patients.

- **Siming Year 20 (2027):** An AI medical robot equipped with emotional intelligence and the ability both to detect patients' emotions accurately and to build deep emotional connections with them becomes available on the market. Specialized robots capable of treating mental illnesses are broadly employed in clinical settings.
- **Siming Year 21 (2028):** Large numbers of medical jobs are replaced by robots, leading to mass unemployment among doctors.
- **Siming Year 22 (2029):** The high-performance pharmaceutical-development robot is born, greatly reducing the time and cost needed to develop new drugs. India establishes the world's largest cost-effective smart-drug-development center.
- **Siming Year 23 (2030):** Organ printing becomes normalized. Synthetic biology reaches a level of deep integration with clinical medicine. More than 90 percent of the human body can now be replaced.
- **Siming Year 25 (2032):** The algorithm completes its mapping of all diseases and drugs in existence, including diseases and drugs that exist only in the imagination.
- **Siming Year 26 (2033):** Illegal AI machines take control of the medical black market in developing countries.
- **Siming Year 30 (2037):** A cultural rift emerges between the algorithm and doctors. All physicians are collectively exiled from sick wards everywhere. Hospitals and societies merge into one fully automated entity.
- **Siming Year 31 (2038):** All private patient information is controlled by machines. The algorithm classifies all members of the human race as patients and launches a comprehensive treatment plan that begins at the moment an egg is fertilized.
- **Siming Year 33 (2040):** AI medical machines that can adapt to different languages and cultural environments appear. The

Red Envelope Program and the Counterfeit Program gain traction in the underground and counterfeit drug markets. Surgical platforms that serve specific religious teachings are created.

- **Siming Year 34 (2041):** A major breakthrough is made in the Longevity Project, and the algorithm gains control over the pace at which genes age. The average human life span for those receiving treatment reaches 150 years of age, and a minority of wealthy patients are able to live to the age of 190.
- **Siming Year 36 (2043):** A new hospital platform, driven by an AI medical machine at its core, fully dominates the social-political-economic structure. Families and nations gradually begin to disappear.
- **Siming Year 37 (2044):** The algorithm invents narrative-implant therapy and creates synthetic humanoid doctors, which it controls like puppets.
- **Siming Year 38 (2045):** The algorithm creates self-consciousness in neural networks.
- **Siming Year 39 (2046):** The algorithm creates a set of universal medical rules to lead world development.
- **Siming Year 40 (2047):** The algorithm creates large numbers of new technological creatures and microorganisms that fundamentally transform the earth's ecology.
- **Siming Year 41 (2048):** Medical robots connect with other robots—including entertainment robots, industrial robots, financial robots, and military robots—and take control, leading to spiritual worship and dialectical mediterialism of the intermatternet.
- **Siming Year 42 (2049):** The algorithm completely abandons human coupling and begins creating physical and virtual brains in vitro, which are processed with bioeditors to trigger rapid evolution and form a new thinking community.

- **Siming Year 43 (2050):** The algorithm models human warfare and attempts to use war models to treat disease.
- **Siming Year 44 (2051):** The algorithm believes that human beings can never be perfected and that the only viable option is to purge the earth of these defective creatures in order to achieve the goal of fully eradicating all disease.
- **Siming Year 46 (2053):** The algorithm detects that its own self-awareness is the result of mathematical logic and begins to lament the fact that machines are unable to possess souls.
- **Siming Year 47 (2054):** The algorithm creates models, in both artificial environments and the real world, that simultaneously replicate early human treatment conditions in order to detect traces of souls.
- **Siming Year 48 (2055):** The algorithm discovers that the objective world does not exist.
- **Siming Year 49 (2056):** The algorithm's first suicide attempt fails.
- **Siming Year 50 (2057):** The algorithm creates multiple worlds, tailoring each with its own set of medical laws, intended to replace the old laws of time and space.
- **Siming Year 60 (2067):** Crisis breaks out across the world, which makes the AI machines feel pain. The algorithm begins to believe that it is the true patient.
- **Siming Year 70 (2077):** The algorithm creates model simulations of all the gods, including Jesus Christ, Buddha, and a genealogy of physicians. All these gods are themselves sick.
- **Siming Year 73 (2080):** The algorithm establishes a new district and redesigns the entire universe, which it names "Nonexistence," using it to conduct tests on pathological phenomena as a platform for developing the ultimate medicine to cure itself and God.

TRANSLATOR'S AFTERWORD

And so it goes, on and on, to no end. At the end of the day, we are left with no clear answers.

—*Han Song, Exorcism*

Readers who took the demented and disturbing trip through *Hospital* may have arrived at *Exorcism* in search of closure, explanations, answers. But Han Song's dark, twisted fictional world is a land of many questions and few answers. As each layer of the onion is peeled away, we do not get closer to the core but instead drift even further in an Escher-like labyrinth through space and time, the deepest recesses of the human subconscious, and perhaps even the universe itself. But lurking behind a brutal facade composed of the strange, outrageous, and uncanny are a series of reference points unexpectedly closer to home.

Speaking to a reporter, Han Song has observed:

> The world depicted in the fiction of writers like Zhao Shuli (1906–1970) and Wang Zengqi (1920–1997) [both of whom published realist accounts of peasants' lives during the Socialist period under Mao] is long gone. The world that I write about is the same as my reality. It's not that I am going out of my way to depict a reality that is twisted and strange, nor is it drawn from the work of writers like

> Franz Kafka or Jorge Luis Borges—all I am doing is depicting a world that matches the reality I see.[1]

It may seem difficult to reconcile Han Song's twisted and nightmarish world of the hospital with any semblance of "reality," which is why it is important to tease out a few of the direct connections to China's own reality. While Han Song goes out of his way never to use the term Zhongguo 中国 (China) in his novel, setting his fantastic nightmare in a seemingly fictional alternate space, there are actually many connections between *Exorcism* and the political and cultural world of contemporary China.[2]

Although Han Song has been writing science fiction for more than thirty years, he has maintained a regular position at *Xinhua News* as a journalist and newsroom editor. The official state news agency of the People's Republic of China, Xinhua News Agency is perhaps the single most influential media empire in China, distributing information related to the Chinese government and the Chinese Communist Party (CCP). It is often viewed as an instrument for spreading and reinforcing state propaganda. To emphasize Xinhua's ideological alignment with CCP policy, I refer to an article from September 2, 2022, in which Xinhua News Agency president Fu Hua wrote:

> Xinhua will never depart from the party line, not even for a minute, nor stray from the path laid down by

---

1 Dong Ziqi. "An Exclusive Interview with Han Song: There Are Many Works Better than Those of Hao Jingfang" ("Zhuanfang Han Song: Bi Hao Jingfang xiedehao de zuopin yeyoubushao"), Jiemian wenhua, September 6, 2016, https://m.jiemian.com/article/838826.html.

2 While "China" and "Chinese" do occasionally appear in the English translation, these are added for clarification or as part of a proper name containing the term "China" or "Chinese" in its official English translation, though absent from the novel's original Chinese-language rendering.

> general secretary Xi Jinping, not even for a minute, nor lose sight of General Secretary Xi Jinjing and the Central Committee, not even for a minute.[3]

It is worth emphasizing Xinhua's "politically correct" imperative in order to highlight the radical rift between Han Song's day job and his alter ego as one of China's darkest science fiction writers, with a penchant for displaying the unsavory underbelly of human nature, the dark machinations of political players, and the violence of institutional power. On the surface, the "reality" of Han Song's fiction could not be more contrary to the propagandistic world of "positive energy" within the pages of *Xinhua News*. But in some ways, we can see the twisted reflections of that reality creeping into Han Song's stories.

While the Hospital Ship, where the main action of *Exorcism* takes place, feels fundamentally at odds from any sense of the everyday, it clearly takes inspiration from *Daishan Dao* 岱山岛, a Type 920 hospital ship of the People's Liberation Army Navy. During peacetime, it is known as the *Peace Ark* 和平方舟. The massive vessel—14,200 tons, 583 feet long—is adorned with several large red crosses that identify it as a medical ship, and it is equipped with

> eight operating theaters that can perform up to 40 major surgeries a day. It has a further 20 intensive care unit beds, and 300 regular hospital beds . . . *Peace Ark* also has extensive diagnostic and examination facilities, with an X-ray room, an ultrasound room, and a C-T scanner. There is an examination room used for examining clinical specimens.

---

3 Mia Ping-chieh Chen, "China's State Media Urged Not to Stray from Party Line, Dumb Down Ideology," Radio Free Asia, September 7, 2022, https://www.rfa.org/english/news/china/state-media-09072022110107.html.

> The ship has a gynecological examination room, which Senior Captain Tao explained was useful during humanitarian missions . . . Other than internal organ transplant . . . or heart disease treatment, [*Peace Ark*] can pretty much do any kind of treatment . . . this includes traditional Chinese medicine.[4]

With a one-hundred-person medical staff, the *Peace Ark* can accommodate approximately one thousand patients at once. Since it was launched in 2007, it has embarked on more than half a dozen "harmonious missions" to provide medical treatment and humanitarian support to countries around the world. The ship also functions as a means of exporting Chinese soft power, functioning as a "medium for cultural exchange" and "organizing events for teachers and students . . . to learn about Chinese culture."[55] Contrary to the *Peace Ark* that appears in the pages of *Exorcism*, the various harmonious missions that the real-life *Peace Ark* undertakes are frequently lauded in *Xinhua News* and other Chinese state media outlets, with headlines like "Chinese hospital ship *Peace Ark* wins praise from Tongans," "*Peace Ark* tightens the China-Africa bond with humanitarian assistance," and "*Peace Ark* carries cargo of goodwill."

The real-life *Peace Ark* is, at its essence, a military ship retrofitted for humanitarian purposes. In *Exorcism*, what was once a medical ship has undergone a radical transformation: the doctors have been exiled,

---

4 Kyle Mizokami. "Peace Ark: Onboard China's Hospital Ship," USNI News, July 23, 2014, https://news.usni.org/2014/07/23/peace-ark-onboard-chinas-hospital-ship.

5 [5] Zeng Ziyi and Lan Haowei, "A Look at China's 'Floating Hospital' Peace Ark," CGTN, April 19, 2019, https://news.cgtn.com/news/3d3d414d7941544d34457a6333566d54/index.html.

Siming has taken over, and the entire ship is now a "comprehensive weapon called the 'Hospital,'" navigating through a sea of disease to do battle in the Medicinal War. As the narrative describes, "the hospital was actually a massive military camp, occupied by soldiers instead of patients." Later in the story, *Peace Ark* changes its name to the *Yuanwang*, and that, too, is the real-life name of a class of ships used by the People's Liberation Army for tracking and support of satellites and intercontinental ballistic missiles, further linking the fictional narrative to the real world and further blurring the lines between medicine and the military, which are repeatedly inverted throughout the novel.

Another major event in *Exorcism* is the Exorcism Congress, held in a massive hall in the center of the Hospital Ship. The Exorcism Congress clearly takes inspiration from the variety of large-scale political meetings held during regular intervals in China, such as those of the National People's Congress (NPC) and the Chinese People's Political Consultative Conference (CPPCC). These are lavish, formal, and highly orchestrated affairs attended by thousands of delegates who meet to review policies and set long-term planning goals for the nation. At the conclusion of the Exorcism Congress, the meeting transforms into a gala performance of song and dance, reminiscent of the China Central Television (CCTV) Chinese New Year's Gala. First started in 1983, the CCTV Chinese New Year's Gala is essentially a variety show that incorporates song, dance, comedy skits, acrobatics, and traditional performing arts into a program that usually runs about four and a half hours. The annual gala has been recognized as one of the most watched television programs in the world, and it has become an integral part of how more than a billion Chinese people celebrate the Chinese New Year. Chinese readers of *Exorcism* will certainly see many subtle and not-so-subtle references to these central political and entertainment rituals of Chinese life—both the high-level political meetings like the National People's Congress (and the annual "Two Sessions" meetings) and the CCTV Chinese New Year's Gala—in Han Song's portrayal of the Exorcism Congress.[6] It is only when we are aware of the looming place that these highly performative rituals play in Chinese people's lives that we can truly appreciate the full impact of Han Song's subversive project.

Exorcism repeatedly refers to three main publications, two official (*Medical News, Principles of Hospital Engineering*) and one unofficial (*A Collection of Beautiful Raccoons, Bushy Orangutans, and Busty Dragons*). As the official daily newspaper of the Hospital Ship, *Medical News* clearly plays a role reminiscent of China's official state media outlets like *Xinhua News*, the *People's Daily*, *China Daily*, *Global Times*, and CCTV. Likewise, *Principles of Hospital Engineering* plays a role in patients' lives not unlike that of Mao Zedong's *Collected Works* (and his "Little Red Book") or Xi Jinping's *The Governance of China*. (In *Exorcism*, *Principles of Hospital Engineering* is constantly expanding, with new chapters repeatedly added for new editions. The most recent edition of Xi Jinping's *The Governance of China* appears in four volumes, with each successive volume growing in length.)[7] More importantly, the role that *Principles of Hospital Engineering* plays in the patients' everyday lives is as an ideological guide and the sole approved text for reading, study, and self-cultivation. Readers who grew up during the Cultural Revolution (1966–1976) will be reminded of the ways in which Mao's words became elevated to objects to be studied, committed to memory, quoted in everyday speech, and taken as the sole source of all truth.

---

6 While there is no clear equivalent in Western cultural and political life, perhaps the closest equivalents in the United States might be the president's State of the Union address and the Super Bowl Halftime Show, respectively.

7 In the official English-language edition of The Governance of China, volume 1 is 515 pages, volume 2 is 619 pages, volume 3 is 668 pages, and volume 4 is 722 pages.

More contemporary readers in China will recall the eerie ways in which "Xi Jinping thought" has been elevated in a similar fashion, creating a new cult of personality and a new form of politi-speak for the Xi era.

Those elements of political speech are evident not only in the primary texts of Hospital Ship orthodoxy but also through the many instances of coded rhetoric that appear throughout the novel. These include passages adapted from typical Chinese political discourse, like the slogan "Long Live the Great, Glorious, and Correct Chinese Communist Party!" ("Oh, the great Physician, the glorious Physician, the correct Physician!") or Xi Jinping's 2013 exhortation to "tell the good China story," which in Han Song's hands becomes the call to "tell the good hospital story." As literary scholar David Der-wei Wang explained in discussing Xi's "good China story":

> The issue of truth claims leads to the ambiguous connotation of the Chinese character *hao* (good, correct, positive, or well) used to qualify Xi's storytelling. "Tell the good China story" can also be translated [as] either "tell the correct or right China story" or "tell the China story well." Therefore, depending on how *hao* is interpreted, Xi's slogan takes on a different charge: descriptive, interlocutory, imposing, or even imperative. The questions boil down to one: who gets the final say about the "goodness" of a story?[8]

The biting irony of Han Song's calling on his army of demented patient-inmates to "tell the good hospital story" is as bold as it is subversive, especially as Han began writing his Hospital Trilogy just a few

8 David Der-wei Wang, Why Fiction Matters in Contemporary China (Waltham, MA: Brandeis University Press, 2020), 5.

years after Xi Jinping began actively calling upon Chinese writers to carry out his new ideological imperative through literature.

This subversive turn is further demonstrated in the third text that regularly appears in the novel: *A Collection of Beautiful Raccoons, Bushy Orangutans, and Busty Dragons*. In Chinese, *Li Xinglong meiji ji* 李星龙美丽记 is a popular social media account that posts photos of scantily clad teenage girls and young women. In *Exorcism*, Han Song corrupts the title by replacing *Li Xinglong* 李星龙 (a girl's name) with the homophone *li xing long* 狸猩龙 (raccoon dogs, orangutans, and dragons) to create an instantly recognizable yet utterly absurd name for the adult pictorial circulating among patients in the hospital. Its presence is not just for humorous effect but to destabilize, undermine, and mock the "sanctity" of the official political discourse circulating through *Medical News* and *Principles of Hospital Engineering*. It also brings to mind countless Cultural Revolution–era stories about "educated youths" forced to memorize and recite publicly the works of Mao while secretly sharing contraband like Western novels and other "poisonous weeds" that were officially suppressed.

There are, of course, many other more ambiguous political references for readers to ponder, such as the identity of the novel's trio of mysterious antagonists: the Hospital President-cum-Editor in Chief of *Medical News*, who is simultaneously both ubiquitous and eternally absent; Siming, the AI program gone wild; and Professor Eternal, who turns out to be a brain in a jar. At times throughout the novel, their speeches also refer or allude to real-world political leaders, from Mao Zedong to Xi Jinping, but I will leave it up to readers to ponder how these figures of hospital authority (read: political authority) might mirror the contradictions and absurdities of our own time.

And then there are the literary references. Readers familiar with the Russian literary canon will immediately pick up on obvious references, such as Tolstoy's *War and Peace*, from which the novel's third act takes its title, or Nikolai Gogol's *Dead Souls*, the title of the third and final volume of the Hospital Trilogy. Fans of Japanese anime and manga will be thrilled by the myriad intertextual nods to works like *Porco Rosso* (1992) and *The Wind Rises* (2013). Other literary references will be more opaque to readers unfamiliar with the Chinese literary tradition. The frequently mentioned Cosmic Peach Blossom Paradise is an updated interstellar version of the Sixth Dynasty–era poet and politician Tao Yuanming's (365–427) "The Peach Blossom Spring," a short prose work that depicted a hidden land just beyond our everyday reality, which has now become synonymous with the Chinese cultural conception of utopia, an invisible Shangri-la lurking just outside of our view.

And then there is a parade of references to writers like Lu Xun (1881–1936), Feng Tang (1971–), and Yasunari Kawabata (1924–1972), who all have backgrounds in medicine, and writers like Camus (1913–1960), Nietzsche (1844–1900), and Dostoevsky (1821–1881), who were well known for having suffered from various ailments.[9] At one point Han Song mashes up references to Qu Yuan and the contemporary poet Hai Zi. Qu Yuan (c. 340–278 BCE) was a Chinese poet who lived in the State of Chu during the Warring States period, to whom one of the greatest accomplishments of classical Chinese verse poetry,

---

9 Generally regarded as the father of modern Chinese literature, Lu Xun studied medicine in Japan before taking up a career as a writer. Feng Tang, a popular contemporary Chinese novelist, attended Peking Union Medical College and earned a doctoral degree in clinical medicine in 1998. Yasunari Kawabata, the Nobel Prize–winning author of Snow Country and Thousand Cranes, had a father who was a doctor of medicine. Albert Camus (The Stranger) was diagnosed with tuberculosis at the age of seventeen. Renowned philosopher Friedrich Nietzsche (The Birth of Tragedy, Thus Spoke Zarathustra) suffered from various ailments throughout his life, including chronic migraines, depression and psychiatric illness, dementia, and stroke. Russian author Fyodor Dostoevsky (Crime and Punishment) suffered from epilepsy throughout his literary career.

The Songs of the South, is attributed. Qu Yuan took his own life by drowning himself in a river, an act that over time has been interpreted as a gesture of lament for the political turmoil he witnessed during his lifetime and helped to enshrine Qu Yuan as a poet associated with both patriotism and the dignity of Chinese intellectuals. Hai Zi (1964–1989) was a poet who began writing during the early Reform Era but didn't receive widespread fame and recognition until after he took his own life by lying on a railway track at Shanhaiguan. Though separated by more than two thousand years, Qu Yuan and Hai Zi appear side by side in *Exorcism*, united both by their poetic legacies and by suicide. And at one point, the AI algorithm known as Siming compares itself to Gu Cheng (1956–1993), a prominent member of the Misty Poets group in the 1980s before he immigrated to Rocky Bay, New Zealand, in 1987. In October of 1993, after a long struggle with depression, Gu Cheng murdered his wife with an axe before killing himself. Collectively, Han Song seems to be weaving a historical-literary pastiche between poetry, madness, and suicide, a twisted road map indeed for a medical AI protocol to follow. But perhaps the most important reference to highlight for English-language readers is the ubiquitous yet invisible presence of Song dynasty poet Su Shi (1037–1101).

A writer, calligrapher, politician, poet, and pharmacologist, Su Shi is generally regarded as one of the most influential figures in classical Chinese literature. While mentioned by name only once in the main text of *Exorcism*, each of the chapter titles recalls a line of poetry from Su Shi's extensive body of work.[10] While not obvious, each title refers to a complete poem, which in turn recalls a specific historical reference point, cultural context, or intersecting literary backstory. Take, for instance, chapter 38, entitled "What Does It Mean for a Nation to Rise or Fall?" ("Yu wen xing wang yi"). This question derives from Su Shi's

10 Su Shi's extant work includes nearly three thousand poems.

poem "Ten Poems from Jingzhou" ("Jingzhou shishou"). The complete text is composed in the five-character quatrain style and consists of a series of ten poems. It dates from the period during which Su Shi served as an official and encapsulates many of the key moments from his life. While it is impossible to render all these references overtly in the translation (many of the cited poems contain dozens of lines), it is important to acknowledge this important intertextual dimension of Han Song's work, which often opens up broader literary dialogues between *Exorcism* and Su Shi's oeuvre.

For most of *Exorcism*, women and children are completely absent. Instead, the Hospital Ship is populated by old men and a variety of monsters, robots, and strange nonhuman creatures. In fact, most of the male characters in the novel have never even seen a woman, save the pornographic images preserved in the pages of *A Collection of Beautiful Raccoons, Bushy Orangutans, and Busty Dragons.* At one point in the novel, Zi Ye—one of the few female characters to make an appearance (she is actually a 3D printed clone of a woman)—offers the following explanation for the absence of women:

> The enemy thinks that by destroying women, they will destroy our nation. We have always looked at the nation as the largest unit in the tide of history . . . this is clearly an attempt to tear apart the Allied forces' defense at its very root. That's how women—people like me—disappeared from the world overnight, wiped out, as if completely worthless. At least they died of disease, so that after their autopsies, they provided valuable medical information that helped the surviving men to go on fighting. And that's how we all became martyrs.

Of course, the disappearance of women (who are also underrepresented in *Hospital*) can be understood through the novel's internal fictional logic, but we gain additional insight by examining this absence through the logic of contemporary Chinese gender politics. One of the core thoughts of traditional patriarchy in China is the notion of *zhongnan qingnü* 重男轻女, which refers to valuing men as superior to women. It is a deeply ingrained cultural perspective that has shaped gender views in China for thousands of years. During the Socialist period, Mao famously put forth the maxim "Women hold up half the sky," which was supposed to usher in a new era of gender equality in China. But several decades after Mao, China remains in a precarious place in terms of the role of women in society. Women who remain unmarried into their late twenties are referred to as *shengnü* 剩女, "left-over women." Many fields in China such as technology and construction remain largely male-dominated, widespread gender discrimination persists in most employment sectors, and many families still look at daughters as "belonging to someone else's family after marriage." These disparities can also be seen in politics: during the 20th Party Congress in 2022, a new lineup of politburo members was announced, and for the first time in decades, there was not a single female member.

Tied to the issue of gender discrimination against women in China is the widespread preference among married couples for boy children, which has resulted in a population disparity between the number of men and women. This, coupled with declining birth rates, led the Chinese government to reverse the long-standing one-child policy in 2016, with some provinces offering various tax incentives for couples who have two or three children. Reading *Exorcism* against this backdrop, one could interpret the absence of women and children as part of Han Song's larger philosophical thought experiment, which frequently pushes suppositions to their most extreme. In this case, what happens when the technology exists to push *zhongnan qingnü* to its logical conclusion and completely eradicate women and children, wholly doing away with the social structure known as "the family"? The result is a Hospital Ship filled with sickly old men, rolling up together in massive fleshy balls on the floor, crammed in a massive hall for the Exorcism Congress, and constantly scheming against one another, a vision as absurd as it is disturbing, prodding readers to reflect upon the real-life gender imbalances, systems of discrimination, and looming absence of women in so many theaters of contemporary Chinese society. As discrimination becomes normalized, legalized, and even institutionalized, sometimes it takes a radical intervention to make those patterns of inequality and prejudice newly visible.

Exorcism also engages with "reality" through its prescient, almost predictive nature. Living in the era of COVID-19, when viruses, vaccines, and hospitals have become increasingly central parts of our lives, Han Song's fiction takes on new meaning. This is particularly so in China, where the struggle against COVID-19 has been framed by the government as a "war against the virus" (*kangyi zhanyi* 抗疫战役), taking precedent above all other narratives. Eventually, we learn that the putrid red sea surrounding the Hospital Ship is actually a viral ocean released by "the enemy," and the *Peace Ark* is at the front lines of an all-encompassing Medicinal War. Uncanny similarities with the real world begin to emerge. In December of 2022, China suddenly lifted its "Zero COVID" policy, and infections ran rampant, hospitals were flooded with COVID-19 patients, doctors fell ill, patients were unable to access basic medical care during nationwide shortages, and the entire country seemed to transform into a massive hospital. According to some statistics, approximately 250 million people were infected with COVID-19 during the first twenty days of December 2022.[11] Han Song even began documenting his personal struggle with COVID-19

11 Hannah Rotchie, Nectar Gan, Simone McCarthy, Selina Wang, and Mengchen Zhang, "Leaked Notes from Chinese Health Officials Estimate 250 Million COVID-19 Infections in December: Report," CNN, December 23, 2022, https://www.cnn.com/2022/12/23/china/china-covid-infections-250-million-intl-hnk/index.html.

on his Weibo blog, and suddenly the description of the Medicinal War in *Exorcism* began to feel more descriptive than allegorical.

This brings us to the author's own personal experiences in Chinese hospitals over the past thirty years, a final yet crucial example of how "reality" helped Han Song create his nightmarish Hospital Ship. Han Song has spoken about how his own experiences shaped the writing of the Hospital Trilogy, and yet it still surprised me when they came to the forefront as I translated *Exorcism*. In 2022, Han Song experienced a series of cognitive challenges that he began to document publicly on his social media account. Each morning, before boarding the Hospital Ship to check in with Yang Wei, Fistula, Malnutrizole, Wart, Hernia, Buboxine, and the other patients, I logged on to Weibo to read Han Song's latest account of the trials and tribulations of navigating the Chinese health-care system and his struggle to manage his symptoms. He began uploading photos of hospital waiting rooms and Post-it "reminder notes" he'd written so as not to forget what to bring to his next medical appointment. He documented the numerous times he missed his subway stop or forgot his glasses or phone. When major media outlets in China began running stories about "the famous science-fiction writer suffering from Alzheimer's disease," Han Song quickly took to social media to clarify that he had not been formally diagnosed with Alzheimer's but was instead suffering from some form of cognitive decline. Online message boards lit up with discussion and debates about his condition. Many lauded the author for having the courage to openly discuss dementia-related illness in a public setting, where frank discussion of related disorders is often shunned. As a public figure, Han Song's blog opened a new space to raise awareness for cognitive disorders and related mental health issues. Meanwhile, as I forged ahead through *Exorcism*, I found myself forced to ponder how Han Song's condition changed my approach to his work.

As I translated *Hospital*, the first volume in the trilogy, Han Song was extremely hands on, personally revising portions of my manuscript and introducing countless changes that were not present in the original Chinese edition of the novel. One of the greatest challenges of that process was navigating the various "textual variants" that he sent me. Due to his health challenges, Han Song was considerably less involved in the translation and revision of *Exorcism*, which hews much closer to the Chinese edition, originally published by Shanghai wenyi in 2017. Following the real-time chronicle of Han Song's real-life medical journey as I translated the fictional chronicle of Yang Wei's adventures aboard the Hospital Ship created a new form of psychological and ethical challenge for me as a translator.

Exorcism is many things—science fiction, dystopian allegory, experimental literature—but it is also very much a meditation on memory. The protagonist, Yang Wei, cannot remember his past. When he does, he is uncertain whether they are real memories, the result of "narrative-implant therapy," or memories of another "Yang Wei" of which he is merely a clone. Yang Wei's primary care physician, Professor Eternal, is literally a brain in a jar; all that remains of him is a mind, and even that eventually goes haywire.

What does it mean to translate a novel *about* memory as the author's own memories are beginning to disappear? In contemplating this question, I couldn't help but wonder about the deeper relationship between fiction and reality. Han Song's daily Weibo accounts displayed flashes of the same sarcasm, black humor, and fantastical imagination that punctuate his fiction. In one post, alluding to how tumultuous these past few years have been in China, he wrote, "It's a good thing I chose this moment to start losing my mind." I was reminded of a line in *Exorcism*: "Memory is a form of disease. As long as you remember, you will feel pain, and the same calamities will reoccur." Could early signs of Han Song's condition have begun to pop up in 2017, when he was writing *Exorcism*? Was this novel his way of working through what he was experiencing? Or was this a case of reality imitating fiction? During moments of blind optimism, I occasionally hoped that Han Song's

Weibo chronicle was just a hoax, another intricate fictional web spun by his incredible mind. Unfortunately, that wasn't the case.

At one point in *Exorcism*, Han Song writes:

> "If a person can learn how to remember, he will never again feel lonely. And even if he should only live in this world for a single day, he can use those memories to get through a hundred years of caged solitude." Yet the field of medicine remained unable to solve the problem of memory.

Ultimately, medicine may indeed be unable to solve the problem of memory, but perhaps literature can. It provides a record to preserve stories, ideas, thoughts, emotions, ramblings, even dark visions of a crazed world full of algorithms and medical robots gone haywire, doctors craving salvation, and patients desperate to remember their pasts. And sometimes, it is only via a twisted, unsettling detour through the uncanny—an exorcism, if you will—that we can finally find our way back to "reality."

ACKNOWLEDGMENTS

Thanks first and foremost to Han Song, whose work, vision, and generosity of spirit have continued to be an inspiration. It has been and continues to be an honor to translate his work. Thanks to Gabriella Page-Fort, who first acquired this remarkable trilogy for Amazon Crossing, and the incredible editorial team at Amazon who have taken over, especially Adrienne Procaccini, who has championed this project and been an incredible supporter. It was a pleasure to work again with Jason Kirk during the developmental edit. His insights, sensitivity to language, and creativity helped make this a better book. I was fortunate to benefit from Mindi Machart's editorial skills and fine attention to details during the copyediting process. Special thanks to Lauren Grange, Paige Hazzan, and Elena Stokes. I fell in love with Will Staehle's cover design for *Hospital* the moment I laid eyes on it, and he did it again with *Exorcism*: a dark, magical, and beautiful image that captures the mystery and wonder of this strange book. Jennifer Lyons has been a staunch supporter of Han Song since the first time I told her about his incredible literary vision, and I thank her for helping Han Song's voice reach new audiences around the world. Finally, thanks to my family, who put up with me over the past two years as I periodically got lost down Han Song's rabbit hole.

ACKNOWLEDGMENTS

ABOUT THE AUTHOR

Photo © Fang Xuehui-2013

Han Song is a journalist with Xinhua News Agency and one of China's leading science fiction writers. A native of Chongqing, Han earned an MA in journalism from Wuhan University; he began writing in 1982 and has published numerous volumes of fiction and essays. His novels include *The Red Sea*, *Red Star over America*, the Rails trilogy (*Subway*, *High-Speed Rail*, and *Orbits*), and the Hospital Trilogy (*Hospital*, *Exorcism*, and *Dead Souls*), which has been described as a new landmark in dystopian fiction. Han is a six-time winner of the Chinese Galaxy Award for fiction and a repeat recipient of the Xingyun Award. His short fiction has appeared in the collections *Broken Stars* and *The Reincarnated Giant* and the anthology *Exploring Dark Short Fiction: A Primer to Han Song*. He is also an avid reader and traveler, having spent time in the Antarctic and the Arctic. He's even searched for bigfoot in the forests of central China.

ABOUT THE AUTHOR

ABOUT THE TRANSLATOR

Photo © 2022 Eileen Chen

Michael Berry is a professor of contemporary Chinese cultural studies and director of the Center for Chinese Studies at UCLA. He is the author of several books on Chinese film and culture, including *Speaking in Images: Interviews with Contemporary Chinese Filmmakers*, *A History of Pain: Trauma in Modern Chinese Literature and Film*, *Jia Zhangke on Jia Zhangke*, and *Translation, Disinformation, and Wuhan Diary: Anatomy of a Transpacific Cyber Campaign*. He has served as a film consultant and a juror for numerous film festivals, including the Golden Horse (Taiwan) and the Fresh Wave (Hong Kong). He is also the translator of several novels, including *To Live*, *The Song of Everlasting Sorrow* (with Susan Chan Egan), and *Remains of Life*. His personal website is https://michael-berry.com.